SARAH ZETTEL

RECLAMATION

ASPECT®

WARNER BOOKS

A Time Warner Company

WARNER BOOKS EDITION

Copyright © 1996 by Sarah Zettle
All rights reserved.

Aspect® is a registered trademark of Warner Books, Inc.

Cover design by Don Puckey
Cover art by Donato

Warner Books, Inc.
1271 Avenue of the Americas
New York, NY 10020

Ⓦ A Time Warner Company

Printed in the United States of America

This book is dedicated to my teacher,
Mr. Thomas B. Deku.

Acknowledgements

I wish to thank Doug Houseman, Leonard Zettel, Karen Fleming, and Timothy B. Smith for their expert technical help, the United Writers Group for thir infinite patience in reviewing so many revisions and Dawn Marie Sampson-Beresford, who always listens.

Prologue

" *W*e're in." Coming through the cargo bay's intercom, Hellea's tenor voice sounded watery.

Burig let out a sigh that deflated his paunch to half its normal size. The arms on his chair tightened around his midriff to compensate. A split second later, the hum filtering through the sterile deck plates from the third level drive fell silent. Now, the *Alliance Runner* drifted on nothing but its own momentum and Hellea's calculations.

A series of sharp clicks sounded from across the bay as Ovin opened all the restraint catches on her own chair and shoved its arms out of the way. Burig smiled. Ovin hated being strapped down. Already she was pulling out drawers and raising wire racks up around the thaw-out table, getting them ready for the equipment she would need to hang there if their find went into shock, or worse.

Burig shifted his weight so that the chair leaned him toward the intercom's control board. He touched the VIEW key beside the flat screen set flush against the undecorated, blue tile wall. The familiar pattern of white spheres and gold lines that represented May 16's system filled the too-small square. The *Runner* showed up as an out-of-proportion red dash floating between them. Burig rapped the image twice with his knuckle for thankfulness.

Ovin glanced curiously at him from between the forest of wires and monitor boxes she was building, but she didn't say anything. The bay's stark, white lights gave her profile a hard edge, despite her snub features. Burig tried to ignore her cool eyes. Instead he touched the CALL key for the bridge.

"Hellea," he said toward the intercom, "how soon can you get me through to Director Dorias?"

"As soon as I set up a priority call for an open line," came the reply. "Want it routed down here?"

"If you would." Burig glanced past Ovin at the capsules. All of them waited dormant and dark in their racks, except the one humming and clicking gently by her elbow. "How far out are we?"

"This rate of drift, and all other things being equal, we'll be putting in at Alliance Station in eight, maybe ten hours."

"Thanks," Burig said without any feeling. He shut the view screen off and swiveled the chair away from the wall. The restraints suddenly felt too tight around his waist. He thumbed the catches so the arms fell open to let him stand up.

"What's the matter?" Ovin bent over the stacks of emergency gear next to the thaw-out table. Everything was switched on now, and at full ready. "Not soon enough for you?"

Burig leaned against the table and watched Ovin run through her checks. She kept her attention focused on the readouts as tightly as if she had a full hold and this was her first run. She had only stowed the loose systems that might be damaged in the event of a rough reentry into the system.

Everything else had stayed up and running for the whole trip. Captain Notch had bawled her out about wasting power at the beginning. Ovin had replied that if Notch wanted to risk the cargo, wanted to risk a life, he could drop the ship into a black hole, but he wouldn't do it by intimidating her.

Burig had hidden his smile. Nobody tried to tell Imeran d'or dyn Ovin anything about her specialty more than once. It wasn't worth it.

"I'm just going to be really glad when we can hand her over to somebody else," Burig said. "This is too close to contraband running for me."

"Got a flash for you, Subdirector." Ovin looked down at her charge. "This *is* contraband running."

Burig sighed again. From here, he could see through the polymer shell of the active capsule to the woman inside. The ragged patchwork she wore as clothing looked incongruous trapped under the network of tubes and wires that fed her drugs and nutrients and monitored her condition. The translucent blue of the tubes reflected against her clear, brown skin, making long pale streaks that ran perpendicular to the scars on the backs of her hands. A respiration mask covered her mouth and nose, but Burig couldn't see her chest move at all.

"Well," said Burig, not taking his gaze off the still figure, "it's not like she's really Family."

Ovin pursed her thin lips and watched the data on the support screens. Her trained eye picked out the details of heart rhythm, eye movement, respiration, and brain activity. "That's not what we're telling the rest of the Quarter Galaxy."

"Until we know what we've got and why the Rhudolant Vitae are so interested in them, we've got to say *something*." Burig stared at the screens. Technically, he knew what most of the symbolism stood for, but the jumble of letters, numbers, and colored lines kept flowing into fresh formations before he could make any real sense out of it. "This is not just another batch of cradlers' descendants who've forgotten how to bang the rocks together. I've got an itch in the back of my head about this. This could be the future of the Human Family we're carrying."

"Or its past." Ovin drew her fingers across the polymer

right above the woman's cheekbone. "That place is crashing *old*."

Burig remembered the ragged canyon wall with the deep grooves wind and rain had gouged into the bare, rust red stone.

"Crashing's the word for it . . ."

The intercom's chime cut off the rest of his sentence. Burig rounded the thaw-out table and perched on the edge of the chair just as the screen lit up again. This time, it showed the image of Director Dorias Waesc. Burig had never met him in the flesh, but whenever he saw the Director on screen he thought of Dorias as "the Medium Man." Dorias had a medium build, medium brown skin and hair, a face suggesting medium age, and a sense of humor that was moderately acute.

"Good to see you, Subdirector Burig," said Dorias. "How'd things work out?"

"Lu and Jay came through for us, Director," Burig said with more enthusiasm than he felt. "We got what we went after."

"How's he doing?" Dorias's image leaned closer to the screen as he tried to see across the room.

"She"—Burig slid the visual unit out of the wall and swiveled it around so Dorias could have a better view—"is knocked out in a life-support capsule."

Dorias frowned. "Was that necessary?"

Burig shrugged. "It was how we got her from Jay. I thought it'd be easier to leave her in there until we got someplace that might require a little less explanation than an intersystem ship."

Dorias did not look convinced. "She is a volunteer, isn't she?"

"That's what Jay says." Burig tried to read what was going on behind the Director's eyes. "Is there a problem?"

"No," said Dorias. Burig was pretty sure he was lying. "You're what, five hours out, six?"

Burig shook his head. "Eight to ten."

Dorias rolled his eyes. "All right. I've had a request from Madame Chairman to keep you on the line until you get in-system, so I hope you and your relief are feeling talkative."

Burig looked across at Ovin. Her mouth tightened until it was nothing but a thin, straight line.

"Expecting something to go wrong?" Ovin called toward the screen.

"Always," said Dorias. "It's part of my job."

Like anybody on May 16 is going to be able to do *anything about it,* thought Burig.

Dorias must have read his mind or the set of his jaw. "And if anything does go wrong, maybe we can't help, but we'll need to know about it as soon as it happens. We don't want to risk losing an emergency burst to interception."

"By the Vitae?" Burig asked.

"Who else?" said Dorias calmly.

Burig mouthed "told you," toward Ovin. The entire project had been padded with excessive caution from the beginning. The *Runner* had been registered as an independent cargo ship. Except for Ovin and Burig, it was crewed with contract fliers from half a dozen disparate systems, none of which called themselves Family. May 16 had been watching Vitae movements nonstop from the moment they left dock. All normal. There hadn't been even a twitch in the *Runner*'s direction. Despite that, Burig couldn't bring himself to believe they were home and clear yet.

"So," said Dorias, settling back, "what did you think of the Realm?"

"The Realm?" Burig's eyebrows rose.

"MG49 sub 1," said Dorias. "Its people call it the Realm of the Nameless Powers. Didn't Jay give you a history lesson?"

"That's Cor's job," Burig reminded him. "She was out playing native. We didn't get to hang about to say hello." He rubbed the back of his neck as he realized how harsh his words sounded. "We didn't stay grounded very long. That place . . . it's not exactly easy to get off of, you know. Especially with the number of eyes and ears the Vitae've got in orbit. Has there been any . . ."

The shrilling of the ship's alarm cut through his sentence. Reflex jerked Burig's head up.

"Blood . . ." he croaked out the syllable just as the world shuddered.

Burig's shoulder slammed painfully into the wall. He gripped the edge of the seat reflexively to keep from being thrown to the floor. Ovin dropped herself into her security seat, fastening the belts down and locking the struts into place so she'd stay within arm's reach of the capsule.

The ship jerked back and forth for a bad moment before the regulators kicked in again. The racks jingled and rattled and three of them collapsed. A dozen different alarms sounded and the ship's voice came from every direction. Hull breach, hold evacuation, engine shutdown. Burig's head spun.

What in the God's name's happened! We hit an asteroid? What . . .

"You're being boarded!" shouted Dorias.

"How'd *you* know?" Burig punched up the view from the hull cameras. Over the back of the ship's pitted hull hung a black, unmarked cylinder with its nose buried in the *Runner*'s side.

Ovin's eyes went round. "Who . . ."

"It's the Vitae." Dorias's voice cut across the visual.

The screen blurred and cut to black.

"Couldn't see where they're coming in . . ." Burig hit the CALL key to the bridge, and hit it again.

"Tai is on her way," reported Dorias's voice from the intercom. "Going to intercept them at the airlock . . . blood, blood, blood . . . They're cutting in through the cooling tanks!"

Burig's gaze jumped to the wall in front of him. *How like the Vitae*, he thought ridiculously. *Go straight in. No fussing around with airlocks where someone might be able to slow you down . . .*

"Suit!" shouted Ovin a split second before the breach alarm blared inside the bay.

Burig made it to his feet. The outside image flickered back into place on the intercom. All he could do was stare at the unmarked ship with its nose stuck into the *Runner*'s flank. A thin, silver ribbon of coolant rippled into the vacuum, dispersing in a flurry of sparkling crystal.

Two points of pressure slammed against his back, knocking

some wind out of his lungs, and sending him stumbling toward the cargo bay door. "Suit, Burig!" bawled Ovin.

Reflexes honed by years of drills let him yank the locker open and start shoving himself into the pressure suit, despite the trembling that threatened to overwhelm him. Ovin twisted her helmet sharply, left then right, to lock it into place. Her fingers, blunted by the white gloves, stabbed Burig in the collarbone and rib cage, closing down his seals for him just as Tai, in her own suit, shoved open the hatch.

"Ditch the find!" Tai yelled into her transmitter loud enough to make Burig wince. "And get outta here!"

"No!" Ovin shouted back.

"We can't let the Vitae have it!"

"No." Ovin's steady voice carried more weight than Tai's shout ever could have. "No one's committing murder in my bay!"

The ship's voice droned on, calmly reporting the hull breach, the tank breach, the coolant drop.

Burig's jaw clenched. The *Runner* was already dead. He was probably already dead in his tracks. The realization broke a fresh sweat on his brow. The only thing left to do was to keep the Vitae from getting their hands on what the Family had found.

She's not really Family, he told himself firmly as he pushed past Ovin. Ovin shouted something, but Tai grabbed her shoulders and dragged her toward the airlock. Burig stretched his hand toward the main power feed for the support capsule.

Behind him, metal screamed and shattered. Burig's feet flew out from under him, propelled by the rush of freed air. The deck smashed against his back, splashing a wave of coolant across his faceplate.

Burig rolled onto his knees and tried to scrabble to his feet. Above him, a human figure in a red pressure suit climbed out of the flood of coolant gushing through the tear in the hull. The alarms shrieked. Ovin and Tai shouted. Burig couldn't even stand. Two more suited humans waded out of the broken tank.

The invader lifted a half-meter-long stick from its belt. A twin bore down on Ovin and Tai. The first bent toward Burig.

Burig swung his arm. The invader blocked it almost casually and knelt on his chest. The stick had a razor-edged blade on the end. Burig could see it clearly as it flashed down toward his throat.

Burig gagged on nothing at all. His lungs burned and his arms flailed randomly, splashing coolant across his faceplate. The invader stood up. Burig clutched at his helmet lock. His hands dropped away and a grey haze swam in front of his eyes. There was nothing to breathe and no strength in his arms and the God knew where Ovin was and all he could do was watch while the invaders typed the release code for the support capsule and waited for the rack to retract its hold on their find.

How did they know about her? Burig thought. *How in the name of the God did they know . . .*

With his eyes wide-open, Burig died.

1—Haron Station, Hour 06:23:48, Station Time

A million years ago, someone, somewhere, looked up at the sky and said "I will go there." With that, they launched a cradle full of their own kind into the sky. Eventually, distance and history claimed them and left us here. We rise. We fall. We bicker and we make peace. We create our own children and our own cradles. We find our own kind and we lose them again.

Of ourselves, this is all we will ever know.

Alda of Jorin Ferra from "Concerning the Search for the Evolution Point."

*E*RIC Born watched Haron Station's hull rise. It filled the bottom half of the view wall with an ungainly conglomeration of gold and steel blobs. The scene jiggled slightly as the docking clamps took hold of his ship and hauled it into place over the airlock. Behind him, the common room's terminal chimed twice to indicate an incoming message. Through the doorway that led to the bridge, he could hear the precise voice of Cam, his android pilot, delivering the ship's maintenance requirements to the station's docking authorities.

Eric ignored both sets of noises and kept his eyes on the view wall. Another ship, a massive smooth-edged thing, drifted up from behind the bumpy horizon that the station created. Even without magnification, Eric could see the scarlet-tailed comet emblazoned on its side.

Well, he thought. *You're here and I'm here. I just wish you'd tell me what's going on.*

The terminal chimed again. Eric sighed and dropped into the overly padded chair in front of the communications board. Impatiently, he skimmed the introductory message displayed on his ship's secondary terminal.

HARON STATION WELCOMES THE *U-KENAI* INTO DOCK AND EXTENDS FULL GREETINGS TO OWNER SAR ERIC BORN. ACCESS TO ALL STATION PUBLIC SYSTEMS AND AREAS APPROVED FOR UP TO ONE HUNDRED HOURS. TWO MESSAGES HAVE BEEN TRANSFERRED INTO YOUR SHIP'S HOLDING MEMORY. APPROPRIATE DEDUCTIONS HAVE BEEN MADE FROM YOUR ACCOUNT.

Eric glanced at the itemized deductions and typed in his approval code. Then he touched the RECEIVE key and the first message took shape on the terminal's screen.

As Eric suspected, it was from his employers, whose ship had just arrived. The recording showed a blurry, grey background and in front of it stood Ambassador Basq of the Rhudolant Vitae. At least, Eric assumed it was Basq. He'd seldom seen more than one Vitae at a time, and although they appeared human enough, they all had been white-skinned, hairless, and wrapped in billowing, red robes. Eric always thought of the Ambassador as male, but the delicate bones and thick draping of cloth made it impossible for him to be sure.

"Sar Born," said the image, "please confirm your arrival time to the Vitae receivers. I will meet you at Data Exchange One to discuss your assignment." The message blanked out as abruptly as it had begun.

Eric gave a small, wordless growl of irritation. He'd spent the past thirty hours scrambling to get four separate projects to the point where they could even be understood by some other Contractor, let alone finished by them. Then he'd had Cam almost burn out the *U-Kenai*'s third level drive to get to Haron Station, and he still didn't know what was so urgent.

What can't you discuss over the lines, Basq? Eric keyed in confirmation of his arrival at Haron and his ability to be present at Data Exchange One in an hour. *Haron Station rebalancing their accounts without the Vitae's permission? Or am I just going to go steal some files?*

Eric's two specialties as a systems handler were being impossible to stop and impossible to trace. The combination guaranteed him some of the more . . . interesting assignments the Vitae had to hand out. He didn't mind the clandestine work, and he was grateful to have employers who didn't ask too many background questions, but he liked to know what was going on so he could get ready for it, whatever it was.

He touched the key to bring up the next message. Plain lines of text printed themselves across the screen. A flood of address information spilled out and Eric raised his eyebrows. This one had come nearly all the way across the Quarter Galaxy.

Finally, the heart of the message came into view.

FROM: SAR DORIAS WAESC OF THE CITY OF ALLI-ANCES, LANDFALL PLAIN, MAY 16

ERIC: AS SOON AS CAN, GET A LINE OPEN TO THE UNIFIERS. CONTACT DR. SEALUCHIE ROSS. THE RE . . .

The message ended abruptly.

Blasted antique station. Eric hit the CONTINUE key. A new text line formed.

TOTAL TRANSFER COMPLETED

Eric glanced at the time display in the lower corner of the screen. The hour he had given himself to get to Data Exchange One didn't leave him much slack time. A message from Dorias, though, was a rare occurrence. What was rarer was the message not getting through in one piece. There was only one systems handler who was better than Dorias, and that was Eric.

He looked at the clock again. *Might be time to at least start to find out what's happened.*

Eric reached for the keys, but before he could issue the first command, the receiving light blinked green.

"Now who?" Eric tapped the light to get an ID for the sender. The screen added the words AMBASSADOR BASQ OF THE RHUDOLANT VITAE to the display.

"Garismit's Eyes." Eric keyed the line open and shifted his features into his professionally cheerful expression.

The screen lit up and it might have been the recording playing over again. Basq held the same stance against the same background.

"Good Morning and also Good Day, Ambassador," said Eric. The greeting was one of the few formalities that he knew was used by his employers. Their culture was one of the many things the Vitae kept to themselves. Eric had never been able to decide if they were full-fledged xenophobes, or merely paranoid. Neither attitude made much sense, since their civilization existed by providing skilled labor to most of the Quarter Galaxy. "I sent my arrival time as soon as I docked. Did you get the message? The station seems to be having trouble on the lines . . ."

"I did receive your arrival time, Sar Born"—Basq's voice was a smooth tenor, undisrupted by emotional inflection—"but the assignment is urgent and we require your presence immediately. A transport track has been cleared for you. Please proceed to the pickup kiosk."

So much for slack time. "I'm on my way, Ambassador."

Basq's silence passed for assent and the screen faded to black.

"Cam!" Eric called as he got to his feet. The *U-Kenai* was a well-made, comfortable ship, but it was so small, Eric had activated its internal intercom only half a dozen times in the five years he had owned it. Shouting down the hall was easier.

"Sar Born?"

"Leave a complaint with Haron's Mail Authorities. I've got a partial message here. I want the rest of it, or a refund."

"Yes, Sar Born."

Eric reached into the drawer below the console and pulled out one of the thumbnail-sized translation disks that he kept there.

No way to know who I might have to talk to for this, he thought as he slid the disk into place in his ear. Eric had only managed to learn one of the languages spoken around the Quarter Galaxy, and he still had trouble with that one sometimes. It was only a minor handicap, however, since most people who worked with offworlders wore their own translators.

His palms itched. He'd worked for the Vitae for six years, and he'd never seen them in a hurry before. They were usually far too organized for that. It was a standing joke that the Vitae did not permit emergencies. They interfered with the schedule. *Seems to be the day for exceptions.* He checked his belt pouch to make sure his identification and account access cards were all there. He had the feeling that this job, whatever it was, was going to take awhile and he didn't want to be caught locked out of any of his accounts.

Eric undid the console's stasis drawer. He eased his tool case out of its holder and checked the contents. The delicate probes, virus cards, and line translators all lay snug in their compartments. After a moment's consideration, he hung the spare diagnostics kit on his belt beside his card pouch. *Better be ready for anything.*

He ordered the terminal to hold Dorias's message in storage and, case in hand, walked out the *U-Kenai*'s arched airlock into Haron Station.

The dock's corridor was empty, except for a pair of dog-sized cleaning drones polishing scuff marks off the metallic deck and walls. Haron reserved frills like carpeting and wall coverings for its residential levels. Eric's reflection in the polished walls showed a spruce, alert man whose permanent slouch had much more to do with low-ceilinged corridors than a lack of self-confidence. His curling, black hair had been combed back ruthlessly. His grey shirt, loose trousers, and soft-soled shoes were all well made, but strictly functional.

Eric stepped around the drones. Over their whirring brushes, he could hear the staccato bursts of voices, the arrhythmic tread of booted feet, and all the other miscellaneous noises created by too many people in an enclosed space.

The safety doors at the end of the corridor pulled aside as he reached them. All at once, the still, station air filled with the smells of sweat, perfume, soap, and disinfectant and the babble of half-translated voices. People from a thousand light-years' worth of climates and cultures crowded the warrenlike hallways, intent on accomplishing the business of their lives.

There was even a gaggle of snake-bodied, long-limbed Shessel in seamless, vermilion atmosphere suits forcing a wriggling path between the humans.

Eric stayed in the threshold to give the Shessel a few extra centimeters to get past him. He folded his arms respectfully as they threaded their way by and received a slow nod in return.

It never ceased to amaze Eric how much easier it had been to make himself learn the Shessel's courtesies than it had been to learn the ways of the other humans around him. The Shessel looked so different, it was easy to accept that their manners would be unlike anything he knew, but the other humans . . . in spite of the spectrum of colors and shapes they wore, they had looked so much like the People, he had expected them to act, in most ways, like the People.

Actually, he had expected them to be a bit more barbaric, having never lived under the laws of the Nameless Powers.

Eric felt his mouth bend into a small smile as he remembered his own naïveté. He'd never even considered they might have separate names for themselves. In the Realm, they had just been "the Skymen."

"Coming through!" Eric called, and the shifting crowd gave ground reluctantly. He shouldered his way between a pair of cold climate women in jumpsuits and a gowned and veiled man who was at least ten centimeters taller than he was. At last, he reached the transport track.

A thick crowd milled around a cylindrical kiosk that supported a screen posting the transport schedule. The snatches of conversation that Eric made out did not sound happy. He soon saw why. One of the four-seater "mini-boxes" waited near the kiosk, blocking the track. The screen on its door read RESERVED. Until the box moved, no public transport could use the track.

Eric ignored the scowls as he pressed forward to type his station account number on the board below the screen. The mini-box's door lifted open. He folded himself into the seat and let the holding arms swing into place. The door closed and beneath his feet, the track cranked into life. The box trundled forward a few yards and, with a sharp lurch, began the long, slow descent into the main body of the station.

Haron was an old facility that had been not so much designed as thrown together over a series of decades, which made for narrow corridors, rich histories, and easily crowded facilities. One of the few things the engineers had done correctly from the start, as far as Eric was concerned, was separate the automated traffic from the foot traffic. The box shafts snaking through Haron's piecemeal construction provided bone-rattling transportation, but it was better than trying to fight the pedestrian crowds in the maze of corridors.

Besides, the transit boxes carried comm terminals. Eric slid the board onto his lap and propped the screen back. He keyed open a line to the mail banks. If Dorias's message was important, he might have left an extra copy in coded storage. No matter how skilled the sender, communications across light-years were tricky and there were lots of opportunities for scrambled data.

Entering his ID produced the heading MESSAGES WAITING with nothing under it. Eric called up the account log. Except for the two messages relayed to the *U-Kenai*, it showed no activity since his last trip in. Eric pursed his lips and requested the original receipt time for the message for Dorias.

NO MESSAGE RECEIVED FROM THE ENTERED ADDRESS

What? The box jostled him as it settled onto the level track and started backing up. Eric keyed the request in again, more slowly this time.

NO MESSAGE RECEIVED FROM THE ENTERED ADDRESS

Eric drummed his fingers on the edge of the board. Only two things could have happened. One, Dorias had erased his own tracks. Dorias had a lot to hide, but he wasn't given to unwarranted panic. If he thought there was a chance that either he or Eric was being watched, he'd bounce the message around the net, drop it in the account, and wipe the trail. But he'd also check to see that it had arrived intact. In fact, he'd take precautions to make sure it had.

The other possibility was that somebody had tapped Eric's account and erased the message.

But if that was what had happened, why had they left anything for him to read at all?

What if they were wiping the file right when it got sent to U-Kenai? The thought left a chill in the back of his mind.

Eric mentally replayed the partial message. *As soon as you can, get a line open to the Unifiers.* "To the Unifiers," not "to me." Which was really strange. The Alliance for the Re-Unification of the Human Family normally did not want anything to do with anyone who worked for the Rhudolant Vitae. They held up the Vitae as the main stumbling block to their ideal of an "indivisible family of all those who trace their lines back to the Evolution Point." Eric had never gotten around to asking why Dorias had taken up with them. Dorias was a lot of things, but he was only human when he chose to project that image from his home behind the terminals.

"Arrival in three minutes," said the comm board. Eric pushed the board back into place. No time to check on any of this. All he could do was get through whatever the Vitae had for him as fast as possible and get back to the *U-Kenai.* From there, he could get a line to the Unifiers, and to Dorias, in relative safety. If necessary, he could crack Haron's system open and find out who was playing games with him.

He had to work to keep that grim thought from showing in his expression as the mini-box opened and let him out in Data Exchange One.

The exchange was a relatively open courtyard. Circular work terminals, each big enough for five or six people to sit around comfortably, sprouted out of the deck plates. Curtains of blurred light shrouded eight of the tables, allowing whoever had rented them to work in privacy.

Eric searched the edges of the court until a flash of scarlet caught his eye. Ambassador Basq of the Rhudolant Vitae sat stiffly at the terminal farthest from all three pedestrian entrances to the exchange.

"Good Morning and also Good Day, Ambassador Basq." Eric gave the full greeting before he moved to sit down at the terminal.

"Good Morning and also Good Day, Sar Eric Born," Basq replied. "I trust you have freed yourself for our project."

Eric studied Basq's smooth face, trying to find something new in it, a hint of anxiety or eagerness. "It took some doing. At least two of our clients are going to be filing complaints about their deadlines."

Basq didn't even blink. "That was expected. Their contracts will be reassigned. All deadlines will be met. Are you ready to come with me?"

"Of course," Eric said. "Which lines should I open?" He touched his fingertips to the power key for the terminal. The closest work pad and screen lit up, ready for his identification. From here, he could reserve intersystem network space for up to twenty-seven hours. It was an expensive maneuver, but it did guarantee his ID instant access to major data cores.

"This assignment will not require the networks." Basq stood. "When you are ready, Sar Born." His robes brushed Eric's shoulder as he strode past.

Rebellion flared briefly inside Eric. Abrupt orders from the Rhudolant Vitae were nothing new, nor were assignments where the information was doled out on a need-to-know basis, but this had already been a long day.

"Ambassador"—Eric snatched up his case and hurried to catch up with Basq—"if this doesn't require the nets, why are you contracting me? I'm a systems handler. It's what you've got me on staff for."

Basq didn't even break stride. The other pedestrians moved in tight knots and bundles, stepping between each other wherever they could find room. Basq ignored them like he ignored Eric. He walked in a straight line as if he expected the crowd to get out of the way for him, and because the crowd recognized him as Rhudolant Vitae, it did. Almost no one liked the Vitae, but even the Unifiers, who vilified them, could not ignore them.

Eric bit back a curse. "Ambassador . . ."

Basq stopped in front of a sealed door set into one of the blocky module junctures. Haron had a number of special sections reserved for the really high-paying customers. More than one of them was cut off from public traffic to accommodate differences in environment or security requirements.

Basq faced Eric, tilting his head back until he looked Eric square in the face with his pale, round eyes.

"Beyond this door, you are in Rhudolant Vitae space, Sar Born. Our laws are operative here. Breaches of confidence, security, or duty will be prosecuted according to our laws. Because you are in ignorance of most of our legal system, you will be warned when and if initial transgression occurs. Before we go any farther, do you understand and accept this?"

Eric imagined he could hear the sound of his temper fraying. "Ambassador, I need to know what my assignment is before I agree to undertake it."

"Do you understand and accept the terms I have given you?" said Basq.

Eric gripped the handle of his tool case. This was just about enough. Someone was playing with his accounts until even Dorias couldn't get a message through. The Vitae wanted him for something possibly extremely illegal, which was all right, and totally unknown, which was not. Part of him said get back to the ship and get out of here.

Calm down, he told himself. *I can at least find out what this is about. If I don't like it, I can still walk.*

I'd like to see even the Vitae keep me in if I want out.

"I understand and accept your conditions," he said out loud.

The door slid silently open.

The corridor on the other side looked no different from the dock corridor, but it felt different. Eric's joints and inner ear picked up subtle shifts in pressure and gravity. Their readjustment registered as a dispersed discomfort.

Once his body finished the transition, Eric found himself savoring the feel of the new atmosphere. The gravity was heavy enough for him in here and the air was a little warmer and a little damper than the usual station atmosphere. In fact, it was almost comfortable.

Their footsteps made no sound on the metal floor. Eric could hear the lights hum overhead. If there was anyone else in this section, they hid behind the featureless doors lining the corridor's walls.

The corridor dead-ended in what looked like a small waiting area with three straight-backed chairs clustered around a square table. One more of the blank doors was set in the farthest wall.

"You can leave your kit here." Basq gestured toward the table. "It will be taken to your quarters for you."

To my what? Eric pulled up in mid-stride.

"Ambassador"—Eric kept the case in his hand—"this is well beyond the limit. I need to know what you want from me. Now."

"You will do as you are instructed for as long as you are instructed," Basq said.

Eric's frayed temper snapped abruptly in two. "Not for this treatment." He turned on his heel and started for the main door.

A wave of pain shot through the soles of his feet. He screamed before he knew what he was doing and crashed to the floor on hands and knees.

"You no longer have the option of leaving our service," said Basq before Eric's stunned senses could recover themselves. "That was your first warning."

Fury and confusion roiled inside him. Eric hauled himself to his feet, panting. The floor, he realized, must be wired somehow, but whatever had hit him had completely missed Basq. A dozen illogical insults and exclamations chased each other through his head.

"Why are you doing this?" he finally managed to croak.

"That is not your concern, Eric Born." Eric did not miss the fact that Basq had dropped the honorific.

Dorias, was this what your message was about? Was Basq the one who tried to erase it?

"You will hear your instructions now." Basq made an imperious come-hither gesture.

Eric took a deep breath and flexed his hands. He took one step toward Basq, then swung his whole body around and bolted for the door.

The pain toppled him before he was even halfway there.

His shoulders hit the floor and the pain seared through them. His teeth and eyes clenched shut and tears streamed down his face as he choked on his own screams.

The release was like a blessing. Eric lay where he was, unable to do anything to silence the sobs spilling out of him. With each degrading sound, his anger built. When he could finally raise his head to look at his impassive captor, he knew it all shone in his eyes.

The expression on Basq's face didn't even flicker. "This treatment will not kill you, Eric Born, but it will seriously traumatize you if you require it to continue."

Shaking, Eric got to his feet. He mopped the sweat and tears off his face. "What could possibly be this important to you?"

Basq moved to the door and traced a pattern at shoulder height on it. A portion of the surface cleared away to reveal a square of clear silicate. He stood aside so Eric could have an unobstructed view.

Easy. Eric made himself breathe deeply. *Need to take this easy. I'll get out of here somehow and then this hairless barbarian better look to his skin. I just need time.*

Eric bent down and peered through the little window, using the wall to hold himself upright. The room beyond was airy by station standards. A long table held a pitcher and an empty plate and a stack of what appeared to be artwork folios. Next to them were scattered the pieces of a partly completed woodblock puzzle. A sunken pool of water big enough for bathing steamed in the far corner of the room across from a thick sleeping mat. The corner to the right of the door was curtained off.

His fresh confusion barely had time to take root before the curtain drew back and a woman in rags and patchwork stepped out of the alcove. A strip of coarsely woven, black cloth hid her hair completely. A poncho made of greased patches covered a shapeless tunic of undyed cloth belted with a strip of worn leather. More leather strips bound her thick leggings and straw-soled sandals.

The woman glanced at the door and Eric got a full look at her face. Dark, calculating eyes slanted above her high cheeks.

The skin on her face and throat had been roughened by exposure to harsh weather. Her jaw had a determined set. She made no gesture toward him, however, and Eric decided this must be a one-way window.

After a moment, the woman shook her head and strode to the pool. She squatted down next to the steaming water and extended her hands. Jagged, white lines crisscrossed her dust-colored skin, making a pattern of uneven squares.

Eric felt as if he'd been struck hard in the chest. He remembered, all too clearly, when his hands had borne their own marks. His were elaborate blue-and-green swirls curling from his fingertips to his wrists. Bright, gold circles shone in the centers of his palms. He remembered how shaky they felt when he stood in the streets of Tiered Side with the night's freezing rain spattering against them and the Skymen with eyes like ice and milk told him he'd be free. . . .

Eric jerked his head back to stare at Basq. "She's from the Realm!"

"We require you to act as translator and cultural liaison for us," Basq said. "Beginning immediately. There has already been too much delay."

He looked back through the window. The woman sat at the table now, fitting pieces into the puzzle. He squinted toward her hands, looking for a trace of gold on the palms. There was nothing, just bare, brown skin.

"But . . ." he began incredulously. "What do you want with a Notouch?"

Basq tapped the translation disk in his ear. "That term is not coming through."

"A nothing. A pariah." Eric searched for an explanation. "There's a caste system in the Realm. A strict one. "That"— he pointed toward the window— "is the bottom of the heap. They aren't even allowed residence in the cities. If you were looking for information or power, Ambassador, your contraband runners cheated you."

"We were not cheated. She is what we require."

For what? Eric tried to collect his thoughts. His head still reeled from the shocks he'd been given.

Basq didn't give him time for another question. "We require

that she be made aware of her situation and the necessity of cooperating with us fully. Coercion is time-consuming, but still a viable option and you will make that clear as well. We require answers to our questions so that we can construct a context for her language usage and communicate with her directly."

Eric felt as if the world about him had begun gently rocking. He was supposed to go in there and threaten a powerless Notouch with coercion? What could she have possibly done to get the Vitae so . . . irrational?

Even if she did turn out to be a power-gifted, like him, but who'd never been picked up by the Temple, what could she possibly have done?

Eric shoved the questions to the back of his mind. "Whatever it is you want from her, but there's no guarantee I can get it for you."

"Why?"

He held up his hand, relieved to see that it had stopped shaking. "No hand marks. I had mine removed. The *ma-aman* tell a person's caste and family identity. They also tell if they're an *ayaraku*, a priest, or . . . teacher, is maybe a better translation." He lowered his hands and studied the backs for a moment. "They also mark you as one of the People. One of those named by the Nameless Powers. Without hand marks, she's got no way to know who she's addressing, so she may decide not to trust . . ."

"You speak her language. We require that you get her to begin talking. That is your assignment. You are already aware of the consequences of refusal."

Who in all the worlds do you think you are? The anger that rose in him was almost enough to temporarily block out the memory of the pain. Almost.

Eric let his head droop. "You can threaten me until the suns burn out, Ambassador. I've still had my hand marks removed. She won't know me from a Shessel's brood and she'll have no reason to trust me, even if she's capable of understanding what I tell her, which she might not be."

"If I am satisfied that you have made the fullest effort on this, you will not be hurt further," said Basq.

Garismit's Eyes! Eric resisted the impulse to run both hands through his hair. This was going from beyond comprehension to beyond belief. What could he do? Even if she was a volunteer, as he had been, and had gotten into this on her own, he couldn't just leave her with these . . . things.

A Teacher is the caretaker of all those spoken of by the Nameless Powers. A Teacher is bound by the gift of power and the . . .

Stop it. That's over with. That's dead and drowned.

He looked at her again, nearly mesmerized by her scarred hands and intense face as she fitted two of the puzzle pieces together. She had left youth behind but hadn't arrived at middle age yet. She was his own age, maybe. The lines around her mouth had been drawn by smiles as well as cares. Eric wouldn't have believed there was room left in him for more confusion, but he felt it all the same. There sat a living, breathing representative of everything he had run away from, and part of his soul reached out to her like a long-lost friend.

"All right," he said. "I'll do what I can."

Eric thought he heard a whisper of a sigh escape from Basq. "Is there any other information I can provide you?"

The question is, is there any information you are going to provide me? Eric set his jaw and, with an effort that almost drained what little strength had returned to him, tried to think productively.

"I assume she has seen you?"

"Yes. Her reaction was . . . unexpected."

Eric felt his forehead wrinkle. "In what way?"

"She attacked her caretakers."

Eric took another look at her. She looked like she weighed a hundred pounds less than he did, but the Notouch spent their time at backbreaking labor and the Realm's gravity was stronger than most. She probably could have laid someone Basq's size out flat if she'd tried.

What made her try, though? Aside from being kidnapped. If she was kidnapped. I can't be the only one who was ready to commit heresy to get off that mud-ball. And a Notouch would have even more reason to run than I did.

"Did you show her anything outside the ship that brought her here?" asked Eric. "The stars or the station or anything?"

"She was kept anesthetized until she reached her quarters, since your culture does not yet support the concept of powered flight."

"That's not the only concept my *former*"—Eric stressed the word—"culture does not support. Have you seen the Realm of the Nameless Powers?"

"I have seen representations of it. It is a network of canyons within a range of mountains."

"Which means all their lives, the people there are surrounded by walls. The language has no word for 'horizon' because no one's ever seen such a thing. It makes for a group of natural agoraphobes, among other things.

"The Words of the Nameless Powers, the basis for the 'local religion,' draw a distinction between walls *terezan* and the sides of the border canyons or those mountains. Those are World's Walls, *monderterezan.*

"It's the ultimate heresy to try to climb a World's Wall, because all evil lives beyond them. We are all taught that the Nameless Powers, the gods, erected the Walls to keep their Realm safe.

"If she knew you'd taken her out of the canyons, she might have been hysterical about committing heresy. The Notouch take the Words very seriously. She might think you're servants of the *Aunorante Sangh* . . ."

"The what?" demanded Basq.

The force of his question jolted Eric. "The *Aunorante Sangh*. It means 'shameful blood.' It's the name for the powers of evil beyond the World's Walls. Even the World's Wall couldn't keep them out, so the Nameless Powers had to send the Servant Garismit to move the Realm."

"I see." Basq's calm returned, after a moment's visible struggle. "Go on."

What is going on in that bald head? Eric thought while he tried to find the thread of his reasoning again.

An idea struck him. "Did you take any jewelry or body decorations away from her?"

Basq considered for a moment. "We took a pair of knives from her, and three small stones."

Oh. Well, that explains that, at least. "You probably took her namestones."

"What are they?" A new and completely unexpected note crept into Basq's voice. Curiosity.

Eric framed his answer slowly. His head was beginning to clear and he wanted all the time he could get to regain his strength. "Most of the Notouch carry carved bits of rock or quartz that represent the *dena*, the first . . . the original name. The Teachers frown on the custom," he added, "but only a few of the Notouch communities have ever dropped the practice." A little extra information might make it look like he was accepting his imprisonment. Which might make Basq get careless sooner. "As I said, they take the Words of the Nameless very literally. Taking her namestones probably did a lot to contribute to the idea that you were the Aunorante Sangh, or their servants."

"I see. Is there anything else?"

Eric suppressed a sigh and straightened his shoulders. "I don't think so. Whenever you're ready, Ambassador."

Eric stood back while Basq used the first two fingers on his right hand to tap an uneven rhythm on the surface of the door. The door slid away, creating a breeze that ruffled Basq's scarlet wrappings.

The Notouch jerked her head up. Her eyes did not go round with shock or fear at the sight of Basq, which Eric would have expected, but narrowed to dark slits. The sight of Eric, though, made her draw back in her chair.

Eric walked into the room, keeping to one side of Basq. The Notouch did not kneel as she should have before another of the People. She just watched him come toward her. The pattern of the formal greeting of a Teacher to a Notouch came to Eric easily, as if he'd spoken it yesterday, not ten years ago.

He raised both hands with the palms turned toward the woman. "I stand in the place of the Nameless Powers and the Servant Garismit and so do I greet you who were named when the Powers walked the world." The words of his native language felt strange, almost unwieldy, against his tongue. "I was named by them Teacher Hand *kenu* Lord Hand on the Seablade *dena* Enemy of the Aunorante Sangh.

"How did they name you, Notouch?"

For a moment she just stared at his unmarked hands. Then, the corner of her mouth twitched.

"So, it's true. You did climb the World's Wall." She used the "level-eye" permutations and, for a minute, Eric wasn't sure if she was insulting him or just talking to herself.

Despite himself, Eric was startled. "Who are 'they,' Notouch?"

"Gossipers, Teacher. Heretics. It's been ten years since you vanished and there were all sorts of stories." She spoke directly to him now and still didn't change her speech patterns. Her mouth spread into a knowing grin. "Tell me, are the birth ranks really observed in this place? His people are all bare as children." She jerked her chin toward Basq. "Come to that, so are you."

"What is she saying?" Basq cut in.

"Nothing you'd be interested in yet, Ambassador." Eric lowered his hands. This was not behavior he'd ever seen from a Notouch. They bowed and groveled. They begged to be of use, any use at all. He understood that law and custom that made them behave that way, not natural inclination. Not really. But it had taken him a decade's absence to work that out, and this woman had apparently just been plucked out of the canyons.

"I will decide what interests me, Eric Born." A warning sounded clearly under the ice in Basq's voice.

"You can talk to them?" The Notouch sounded genuinely impressed. "Tell them to give me my namestones back."

"She's asking about her namestones," Eric told Basq.

Basq's forehead drew together around where his eyebrows should have been. "What about them?"

"She wants them back." Eric raised his own eyebrows and gave a small shrug. "I did tell you, Ambassador."

Basq made no reply and Eric turned his attention back to the woman.

"You haven't told me how to call you yet."

"Nameless Powers preserve me." She slid off the chair onto both knees and held her hands in front of her eyes to display her hand marks. "Teacher Hand *kenu* Lord Hand on the Seablade *dena* Enemy of the Aunorante Sangh, this despised one is Stone in the Wall *dena* Arla Born of the Black Wall. She craves your blessing and asks in what way she may serve?"

Without waiting for an answer, she picked herself up off the floor and folded her arms. The sardonic smile slid back into place.

Eric worked to smooth the grimace out of his own features. "She says that she is Stone in the Wall, born . . . originally . . ." He searched for a way to translate the primary name into something that would fit in Basq's world. "Star in the Night Sky. A bit grandiose for a Notouch, isn't it?" he added to the woman.

"This despised one begs her Teacher's pardon if that name is discordant." The casual shrug she gave him made a mockery of her subservient language. "It is what the Nameless Powers bestowed upon her."

Frustration and bewilderment vied for dominance inside Eric. *Where did they find her?*

Never mind, he told himself. *I need any help I can get.*

"Listen quick, Arla Born of the Black Wall, do you want to stay with these people?"

Her eyes shifted toward Basq. "Not really. But I'm not leaving this place until I've found my stones."

"You idiot Notouch." Eric fought to keep his tone conversational. "We're both pris—"

"Have you explained her status to her?" Basq's shell of patience was clearly beginning to wear thin. "I have an extensive list of questions."

Eric spread his hands. "She's very upset about those stones." He could do a great deal on his own, but another pair of eyes at the right time could make the difference between freedom and recapture. If getting her namestones back would put him on the right side of this superstitious woman, very well then. Besides, the more time he spent on this nonsense, the less time Basq would have to get what he wanted. "I can't swear she'll answer anything until she gets them back. I'll try to make things clearer to her."

Eric faced the Notouch again. "Do you want your namestones back?"

"If it so pleases her Teacher, this despised one does." For a split second, the sarcasm faded.

"All right. For some reason his people"—he swept his hand at Basq in a gesture that was much grander than the language he was using—"want you to answer some questions. No matter what I say after this, you keep your mouth shut until they bring your namestones back, understand?"

The Notouch plunked herself down on the chair. She looked up at him with her lips pressed dramatically together.

Eric spread his hands to Basq again. "She won't talk until she gets her namestones back."

Basq said nothing, but Eric could see anger forming in his normally impassive eyes.

"Listen to me, Ambassador. Try to understand. This Notouch is a believer. What you. . . . we . . . think of as a superstitious and primitive religion is reality to her. She can't disregard it any more than you can disregard the laws of physics, do you understand?" *Never mind that she's already broken a dozen or more tenets just by the way she's been talking to me.* "She'll act according to what she knows as real. Those stones are *onar*, a . . . a . . . bond between her and the Nameless Powers. She'll die before she helps the ones who have them."

Come on, swallow it. Swallow it, you arrogant dandy.

Eric waited while Basq thought. He could almost hear the circuits buzzing in the other man's head. Nothing was plain here. Nothing clear or simple.

What in the Realm of the Nameless do you want with Notouch talismans?

Who in the Realm of the Nameless is this Notouch you've found?

And how do I get myself out of here before you translate

this conversation for yourselves? Eric did not glance at the walls. It would have been pointless. There was no way he was going to be able to see Vitae surveillance equipment.

Two red spots had appeared on Basq's cheeks. "Tell her that she will speak. We will hurt her if we have to."

Eric translated the declaration into the Realm's most formal command grammar. "The Skyman says if *dena* Arla Born of the Black Wall does not speak, they will torture her."

She just looked at him and said nothing.

Eric waited for what seemed a decent interval. "You are either going to have to give her back the namestones, or hurt her," he told Basq. "I've made the situation as plain as I can."

Basq laid his hand on the door and spoke. Eric touched his translator. Whatever language Basq used, the disk in his ear couldn't cope with it.

"The stones are being brought back," Basq announced. "Tell her that and then tell her we will have her cooperation."

This time, Eric relayed the message word for word.

"As soon as the stones are in my hands, I'll answer whatever he asks me." The Notouch kissed her fingertips and held her hand toward the ceiling to send the words from her mouth to the ears of the Nameless.

Eric translated her words faithfully. Basq stayed silent this time and Eric took that to mean "good enough."

For now, anyway.

The cell door swished open and a slender Vitae, as bald as Basq, handed the Ambassador an opaque plastic tray. On its ribbed surface rested a trio of polished spheres, each the size of a baby's fist and the color of winter ice.

Eric sucked in a deep breath.

"Arlas."

The Notouch pushed past Eric and snatched the spheres up. One at a time, she held them toward the ceiling. The light glinted against their curved sides.

"What did you say?" demanded Basq.

"Arlas." Eric repeated as the Notouch turned her treasures over in her hands. "It means star, or eye, or, well, diamond,

I suppose would be close. I've only ever seen one set. In the Temple vaults in First City. No one's found any new arlas in . . . hundreds of years." He stared at the Notouch. "Arla Born of the Black Wall," he murmured her name. "Where did you get those?"

"They're my namestones." Apparently satisfied that the spheres were genuine, she began unwinding her headcloth. "You'd be surprised, Teacher, what you find in the swamps." Ignoring the fall of tangled, black hair that dropped across her cheeks and shoulders, she wrapped a fold of cloth around the stones. With practiced motions, she knotted the material to make a long-handled pouch.

Basq nodded to the messenger. He tucked the tray under his arm and touched the door.

"Now we will begin," said Basq.

Eric opened his mouth. Before he could speak, a blur of motion cut across his peripheral vision.

THUNK!

Basq toppled to the floor. The Notouch whirled her pouch and swung it down. The stones cracked against the messenger's skull and he fell in a heap next to Basq.

The door opened. Eric stared at the fallen bodies.

"Move, you high-house fool!" shouted the Notouch.

Eric's senses and reflexes reasserted themselves. He shoved his foot against the threshold to keep the door in place and scanned the corridor. Empty, but that didn't mean safe. The Vitae had to be watching them. There was nothing he could do about that.

Eric sprinted down the hall, vaguely aware of running footsteps behind him. From here, he could see the door to the main station shut tight. He did not allow himself to think about how the floor of the empty corridor could be brought to life at the touch of a remote key.

Eric skidded to a halt in front of the door. There was no time for finesse or distraction. He laid his palms on the thin line where the door met the wall and reached deep into the back of his mind, down into his soul where his power gift lay. He opened a path for it to stretch down his arms and out through his fingertips. Its tendrils coiled around the slender, metallic bars that held the door shut.

"Break," he ordered.

His gift seized the bars. Eric's heart froze. The lock cracked sharply and his heart beat again, hammering against his ribs. Eric pressed hard against the door and leaned sideways. The door slid back. Pain shot up his legs and Eric doubled over. A hand seized his arm, dragging him into the open station hallway.

"Which way out!" The Notouch stared wildly around her.

For a second, Eric wondered what she was talking about, then he remembered she had no idea where she was. He had no time to explain. There were six stories of station between him and the dock that held the *U-Kenai*. A call had probably already gone down to security.

They'll hold the ship, seal the docks. Watch both. They'll close my access to the networks, and watch the halls. When they see me, they'll come get me. He glanced up at the security cameras. *Hello, there.*

His mind raced down unfamiliar paths. *There'll be two guards, three, maybe. Darts, tasers, and uniforms. Orders to take me quietly. Don't panic the paying customers.* He eyed the passing crowd, each one of them a paying customer. *Don't damage the goods either, I hope.*

Eric ran. He dived into the crowd, shoving aside anyone who didn't get out of the way fast enough. He risked a glance behind him. Arla followed his mad dash, almost overtaking him.

The jumble of faces and colors broke apart to give him a clear path to the farthest corridor entrance and he raced toward it.

Footsteps pounded the floor behind him and he fervently hoped they were Arla's. Eric pushed a man in trader's motley into the wall and hurdled a maintenance drone. The footsteps closed, but no shouts to stop came.

Eric ducked around a left-hand corner and yanked on the emergency override for the security door. Alarms blared and the door came open. Eric swung himself up the maintenance ladder. As he did, he saw Arla duck through the threshold, her poncho flapping around her. She took the time to slam the door shut before she grabbed the ladder rungs to follow him.

Up. All the way up, until the metal rungs bit into his hands and his heart pounded in his throat.

They could shut the hatches, trap us. Send guards in to get us. No. They figure why bother? They know where I'm going. Only one place I could be going from here. They'll already have guards there. Why not wait for me to turn up?

Guards trained to use their weapons. The ones who've been told by the Rhudolant Vitae I'm unarmed and she's primitive and neither of us know what we're doing.

Idiots. You've only seen one part of my life.

Three bulkheads passed by them. Four.

"How big is this place?" gasped the Arla.

Eric didn't have the breath to reply.

Five. Six. He stepped off the ladder and pulled the release for the door. It slid aside. Past it waited the corridor to the airlock that was sealed to his ship. The big hatch to the main station had been closed. A red light shone on the the airlock door. Sealed for security reasons. Two men and a woman in crisp, black coveralls stood between him and the airlock. All three of them were armed with tasers, which were out and ready.

Eric's ears rang from exertion and adrenaline. "Soldiers," he said to Arla between gulps of air. "The things in their hands are distance weapons, like slings."

Do I still remember how to fight? He raised his hands slowly until they were over his head. *Do I still remember anything?*

"That's it," said the broader of the two men. "Easy now. You too, woman. Hands up."

Arla stared at the guard, and then at Eric, her mouth open in disdain and shock.

"Don't do it," he said urgently.

"Then who will?"

Arla ripped her homemade sling off her belt and whirled

it over her head. Before she brought it down, the woman guard took her aim calmly and fired. The taser wires snaked out of the barrel and sank into Arla's chest. The shock ran into her and she screamed. The sling crashed against the floor and Arla dropped next to it, curled up like a fetus. All the guards watched her fall.

Eric lunged. His hands clamped down on the nearest guard's outstretched arm and swung him around. The guard crashed into his comrade and they both reeled against the wall. A taser clattered to the floor. Eric slammed the edge of his hand against the first guard's throat. The man gurgled and collapsed. The second guard reached across the fallen body and grabbed Eric's shoulders, effectively blocking the woman's aim. Eric flung himself sideways. He and the guard both hit the deck. With a wrench, Eric rolled them over until he came out on top. He shoved the heel of his hand against the man's nose. Blood spurted across his palm and the guard went limp.

Eric flung himself across the floor and rolled again. Above him, the woman took fresh aim. Eric kicked both legs out and caught her ankle. She crashed against the floor. He hauled her shoulders up and cracked her skull against the deck plates. She grunted and sagged in his arms. His fingers found the catch on her bracelet terminal and snapped it loose.

Eric scrambled to his feet. He shoved the plug from the stolen bracelet into the socket beneath the warning light and twisted. The light blinked from red to green and both sides of the airlock hatch swished open.

Something sharp slammed between his shoulder blades and Eric sprawled across his own deck, pinned down by a weight that squirmed. Reflexively, he rolled, ready to swing his fist out, but the weight had scrambled out of the way. Arla towered over him for a split second. In the next, she bolted down the short hall toward the common room and the view wall.

"Cam! Get us out!" Eric shouted without even trying to stand up.

The engine's hum became a rumble. Over its noise came a scream of pure terror followed fast by the sound of a body hitting the floor.

The Notouch had looked out at open space, and had passed out, as Eric had known she would.

It was, after all, what had happened to him.

Relief and exhaustion blurred Eric's mind until the world took itself away.

2—Painted Canyon, the Realm of the Nameless Powers, After Dark

The Nameless Powers walked their Realm and spoke among themselves. They named the Walls, and the Walls grew strong. The Nameless spoke of the people then and each life they named became True and took up its place in their Realm.

From "The Words of the Nameless Powers," translated by Hands to the Sky for all who follow.

"*B*ROKEN Trail *dena* Rift in the Clouds, don't do this."

Trail ignored Cups's urgent whisper. She kept on looking toward the darkness that hid the walls of Narroways city. The wind blew hard, brushing her cheeks with warmth from the dying fire at her back. Thankfully, it was a dry night and she could sit outside with nothing worse to worry about than cold. Around her, the tents flapped and creaked in the wind that whistled down Painted Canyon. A baby whimpered from the left and someone, it had to be Yellow Stones, snored loudly enough to call back the Aunorante Sangh. No one had woken up when she crawled outside. No one, of course, except Empty Cups.

"She's been gone too long." Trail pulled her poncho around her. "I am going to find out what happened to her."

Cups sighed and crouched beside her. "She wouldn't thank you for it if you did. I saw her face when she left. No interference, that's what she wants. Let her be, wherever she is, Trail."

"No." A lump of wood broke apart in the fire, setting loose a shower of sparks so, for a moment, Trail could track the wind with her eyes. "I am going to find out what the Skymen have done with my sister. I'd be going even if Mother didn't tell me to, that's the whole of it."

The baby's whimper became a wail and groans arose from all around as tired women tried not to wake up.

"Trail"—Cups laid a hand on her head and shook her gently—"think, would you? We need your hands in the pens tomorrow. I've got a promise of two bolts of whole cloth and three new pots if we get . . ."

Trail jerked her head away. "You've got the brains of an ox, Cups. The Skymen are here. They're trying to win over King Silver. The Nameless know why and we need to find out."

"As if it'll make a difference." Cups gouged a fistful of dirt out of the ground and held it up for Trail. "As long as there's mud we'll be sitting in it"—she threw the lump down again—"be it owned by the Nameless, the Heretics, or the Skymen."

"Haven't you heard the story about how, after the Servant moved the Realm, the power-gifted started taking lives on their own authority, not the Nameless's, so the Nameless Powers allowed the People to raise their hands against the Teachers for a time."

"Trail," said Cups severely, "if you're going to teach the apocrypha, do it elsewhere."

"What are you fools doing out there?" The fire's orange light showed Branch in the River's face poking out of the shadow. "Get back in here!" She brandished a leather tent flap.

Cups groaned. "If your sister had any proper feeling," she whispered, "she never would have left her family where Branch could get her claws on them."

Trail's hand smashed across Cups's cheek before she even

knew what she was doing. "Unsay that, Empty Cups, or I'll have your guts for breakfast!"

"And I'll have yours, Broken Trail, if you don't get back in here and quiet down!" hissed Branch.

Cups, holding her cheek and wrinkling her forehead, slunk back toward the tent. Reluctantly, Trail gathered her poncho hem around her and followed. She could feel Branch's smug satisfaction like she could feel the wind whipping around her head.

Trail bowed her head and ducked back into the tent, shuffling on her hands and knees until she found a blanket corner that wasn't snatched away when she tugged on it.

See what a good obedient girl I am, she thought as she rolled herself up in the threadbare fabric. *I always do as I am told.*

And I have been told to find my sister.

Memories of pain chased each other around Arla's skull. The needles that drew the scars down the backs of her hands burned. Cobblestones dug into her knees as she groveled at the city gates. Her jaw ached from keeping her thoughts silent. Childbirth tore her in half.

Gradually, Arla became aware that the pain was more than memory. It burned in her deflated stomach, pounded in her head, throbbed in every joint. Old bile and metallic heat weighed down her tongue.

Other memories. The woman of the Skyman with her strange green eyes and skin that turned red under the light of day. "I've heard the apocrypha, too, you know. I know your family's story. My people are looking for a way to take the Teachers down where they belong. You can help. For your help, you'll lose those hand marks. All you've got to do is bring your stones over the World's Wall and talk to my people."

She is not Shameful Blood. I would know. I would know. Of all people I would know. . . .

They led her up one of the dark canyons, to the threshold of a white building that looked like a gigantic mushroom squatting in the permanent night. The palest, hairiest man she had ever seen had walked up to her. She forced herself to hold her ground.

Dispassionate eyes looked her over. There had been more words and she had agreed to everything unconditionally. A needle bit into her arm, and there had been blackness, until she woke surrounded by bald, babbling children and realized her namestones were gone.

The fear brought by the memory of that waking kept Arla's eyes shut while she sorted out her physical sensations. She lay on her side. Her arms were behind her. Something soft cushioned her right shoulder and her back. The air was as cool and dry as the inside of a Temple. It smelled of nothing at all. She could hear a whirring noise from somewhere underneath her, soft, but constant.

Gentle pressure rested against her ankles and knees. She tried to separate her wrists and couldn't.

Blast him! He's got me tied! The realization overrode the fear and her eyes opened. First, she saw Teacher Hand sitting in front of her. His square chin stuck out a little too far and his black eyes held the glimmer of anger.

A sensation of absence crept into her consciousness.

"Where are my namestones?" she croaked around the sand that seemed to be clogging her throat.

"I have them." Teacher Hand clipped off each word as he spoke it.

Oh thank you, all the Nameless. Arla craned her neck to try to see her surroundings more clearly. Tan walls and a tan floor enclosed them. The place was furnished with big, rounded lumps of stuff, some white, some clear like glass.

"We're hidden from those Bald Children then?" she asked, twisting her head so she could see him better.

Teacher Hand's mouth twitched. "For the moment."

"Where is this?" Arla rolled her eyes to gesture around the room.

"My ship."

"*Ship?*" She tried to match his accent on the meaningless sound.

"The means by which I went over the World's Wall," he

explained through clenched teeth. "What did the Rhudolant Vitae want with you?"

"Why should you care?"

Teacher Hand leaned over her. "It's not a good idea to be snide with me, Notouch." He clenched his fist so the knuckles pointed at her, the first gesture to call down the curse of the Nameless Powers.

Arla's mouth puckered. "You're too late. I've already been cursed. Twelve times, by the First Teacher himself."

His eyebrows crept together as his face gathered up into a frown. "And what could you have possibly done to merit such attention from the First Teacher?"

"Nothing much." Arla let her gaze travel to the ceiling. It was made up of tan squares broken by patches that glowed with a light clearer than any oil lamps. "This despised one was merely inside Narroways's walls when the curse came down upon the whole of the city."

That plainly puzzled him. "Sit up," he ordered.

"As your Lordship commands, this despised one shall do." She knotted her water-weak stomach muscles. Despite the protest of every inch of her, she rocked into a sitting position. The effort broke a fresh sweat on her brow. Her head spun, but she managed to hold herself upright.

Arla glanced around uneasily. She could see the room better now. The white lumps were obviously for sitting on. The clear lumps with legs that melted into the floor were tables, even if Teacher Hand sat on the long, low one in front of the couch she occupied. The wall to the left had three long niches and an open doorway in it. The wall to the right was smooth and unbroken. The wall behind Teacher Hand had been sectioned off into neat squares and decorated with elaborate mosaics. A fat chair stood in front of it.

But she had seen something else before she had passed out. Something formless and huge and . . .

She shook her head, trying to focus her thoughts on things she could understand.

"Where's the other one?" she asked.

"The other what?" Teacher Hand's frown deepened.

"Person. Your friend or bondsman, or whoever you called before . . ." *Before the blackness and the roar. Before I fainted.*

His frown folded into a wryly amused expression. "Cam, you mean? I don't think I'll let you meet Cam just yet.

"Let's start over." Teacher Hand sounded almost as tired as she felt. "Why'd you attack me?"

Arla shrugged her aching shoulders. "This despised one assumed that as she was of no further use, her Teacher would abandon her."

Against all expectation, his expression looked pained. Arla felt taken aback. Perhaps Teacher Hand was not so much the high-house fool she had taken him for.

Don't relax too far yet, she warned herself. *You still know nothing at all about what's going on, and he still has your stones.*

"How did you end up in the . . . that room?" asked Teacher Hand.

She measured him again. If only she had enough strength to fight. She could kick for his head. She could find the door to the outside. If only she knew something, anything about this place she was in, about this "Cam" who lurked out of sight. If only she wasn't so dizzy and thirsty . . .

Stop whining and think of something you can tell him that he might believe.

"I was following you, Teacher," Arla said.

"You were what?" His voice broke on the last word.

"When your Lordship vanished, a lot of rumors started 'round First City. You'd been caught thieving. Your older brother'd killed you to save the family later embarrassment. Teacher Fire in the Dark had finally caught you sleeping with his wife . . ."

"Where in the Realm of the Nameless did you hear that!" Teacher Hand roared.

"There's very little the Notouch don't hear." Her mouth twitched. "The rumor that stuck was that you'd decided adultery and misusing your power gift were too small a set of heresies and that you'd gone with a gaggle of the Skymen over the World's Wall." That part, at least, was true. "This despised one chose to believe that rumor and wanted to find

out how your Lordship had managed it. She succeeded." Arla
hoped he couldn't tell how much that idea unsettled her.

He looked at his naked hands, then at her, then at his hands
again. His face went sick and angry about something he didn't
voice.

"Would your Lordship be so merciful as to give this
despised one a drink of water?" Arla bowed her head.

"You are free to stop that crap any time." Teacher Hand
stood up. "I do not know where you got the nerve, Notouch.
It doesn't go with your hand marks." He paused. "You never
did tell me your call name."

"Arla," she answered, hoping civility might speed up the
process of getting her water.

He snorted. "It would be. Listen, Arla, Teacher Hand is
dead and washed away. I am called Eric Born."

"Eric Born" crossed the room with a careful sideways step
that never completely turned his back to her. He drummed
his fingers against some mosaic tiles on the far wall. A hole
opened underneath his hand. Out of the hole, he pulled out
a clear cup of water.

Despite her best intentions, Arla felt her jaw flap open.

Eric Born's mouth spread in a sharp grin. He seated himself
back on the table and held out the cup to her.

Waiting to see how I'll react, she told herself. *Keep it reined
in, Arla.*

As smoothly as possible, she swallowed the water. It
swished uncomfortably in her empty stomach, but she drained
the cup anyway. She needed it, badly.

"Thank you." She added neither honorific or insult.

He set the cup down. "What did they, the Rhudolant Vitae,
do after they put you in that room?"

"Kept me there, mainly. Every now and then one of them
would come in with a box of some sort and wave it around
in the air and babble at me. It sounded like they were trying to talk. I thought they were insane. Then I thought I'd
been wrong and they were Aunorante Sangh. Then"—she
shrugged—"I started to wonder if I would be stuck in a
single room for the rest of my life. Then they brought you to
me.

"Is there anything to eat?"

Teacher . . . Eric Born made a gurgling sound as if he was trying to keep down a laugh.

"You do not have any idea what you have gotten yourself into, do you know that?" He looked down into the empty cup. "No matter. I suppose I had better feed you." He rubbed his chin. "But I had better show you something first."

"What?" New fear squeezed against the water in her stomach as she watched Eric approach the room's far wall.

"Where you really are." He laid his long hand against the tan surface.

The wall vanished. Where it used to be hung a formless blackness streaked with minute rainbow lights. It stretched up, down, and on all sides. Her eyes strained to find an end, a boundary, anything to give it shape and sense, but there was nothing. Endless, it yawned at her. An open mouth waiting to engulf her mind and soul.

She screamed. She threw herself backward and curled up into a tight little ball, knees pressed tight against her forehead, her belly muffling her shrieks. A voice gibbered at her, said her name, and finally shouted at her, but she could not look up. The blackness waited to swallow her whole. There was no end. No end.

"Arla Born of the Black Wall!" A hand jerked her collar back. The fabric dug into her neck and hauled her head up. "You blasted Notouch, look up!" The Teacher's open hand crashed against her cheek. "Look up! It's gone! LOOK!"

Through the tears of pain, she saw the solid wall back in place.

"Wha . . . Wha . . ." Her whole body shook like leaves in the wind as he let her sag back against the couch.

Eric folded his arms. "That is the space between the worlds. There is no Black Wall and no arlas in it. It's all emptiness. There are other worlds in it, though. Other places where people, like those in the Realm of the Nameless Powers, live. We are flying between them, like insects flying from grass to flower. Do you understand this?"

Arla did not, but she nodded. She could sort the explanation out later. What was important now was hearing it.

She tried to stop the trembling in her limbs and completely failed.

"Why show me this?" *At least I've quit stammering.*

"So you wouldn't get any ideas about trying to attack me when I let you loose."

She thought about herself left alone in this place with no one but a corpse and an unseen presence, lost in the middle of infinite blackness. She bit her lip and humiliation came on the heels of the fear. This was worse than being tied up.

"Turn around," Eric ordered.

Arla wiggled herself around and held out her wrists. She felt the bindings loosen. She pulled her wrists apart and brought her arms back around to her front in a riot of creaking, popping joints. She yanked off the remains of the sticky, clothlike stuff that still clung to her skin. She stretched her legs toward Eric. He slit the black strips neatly with one blade of an open pair of scissors. Arla kept her eyes on him as she rubbed her wrists and arms to get some feeling back. He did not look up.

Eric stepped back, keeping hold of the scissors. Arla wasn't fool enough to try to stand. Instead, she chafed and flexed ankles and knees. She yanked the sticky strips off her leggings and dropped them on the floor. Eric watched her for a moment before he backed toward the window-wall.

"How do you stand it?" Arla straightened her back. "Wha . . . what's out there."

He shrugged. "I got used to it. The shakes vanish fairly quickly. The rest comes with practice.

"Now, you wanted something to eat."

He drummed the mosaic and another hole opened. Out of this one, he pulled two packets of an unfamiliar shape. He ripped something off them, made yet another hole open in the wall, and dropped both packets inside.

When he came within arm's length again, he was carrying two plates, each topped by a palm-sized slab that might have been made out of the same stuff as the sofa.

"I know it doesn't look like food," he said as she took it from him, "but it will keep you going."

She picked up the slab. Its warmth set her fingers tingling.

She bit one corner. The stuff tasted like bitter nuts and had the consistency of old paste. She made herself finish it off anyway, washed down with more water Eric conjured up from the hole in the wall.

The Nameless Powers know I've eaten worse.

"Tell me, what did Narroways do to finally get itself cursed?" The casual words were strained around the edges, Arla noticed.

She swallowed her mouthful of paste. "Refused to give up during the siege."

"Siege?" he said incredulously.

For a moment, she looked at him like he was insane. "Oh, you had gone before that. It was maybe five years after you left, the Skymen made a full-scale bid for support for . . . For whatever it is the Skymen want from the Realm. King Sun announced he was going to make them ambassadors to his court and hear all their petitions. The Teachers kept on saying the Skymen were Aunorante Sangh. First City followed the First Teacher, of course, and sides got taken up and so did weapons. Narroways was cursed and the fighting's been going on ever since." She spoke the last words to her cup. She'd spent the past days trying not to worry about where Little Eye, or Roof Beam, or skinny Broken Trail were. She wasn't getting any better at it.

She set the cup down. Eric was scowling at the backs of his strangely bare hands.

"Thank you for the food," she said to get his attention back. When he looked up, Arla squared her shoulders. "Hear me, Eric Born *kenu* Teacher Hand *kenu* Lord Hand on the Seablade *dena* Enemy of the Aunorante Sangh. You don't want me with you, and I don't want to stay. Take me to a Skyman city, I'll manage after that. I'll find a way to pay you for passage and the bruised back."

He laughed sharply at that, but then sobered. "Stone in the Wall *dena* Arla Born of the Black Wall," Eric said levelly, "you couldn't find your feet in a Skyman city if someone showed you where to look." He shook his head. "All you have seen and Garismit's Eyes, you still don't understand!"

He looked at the closed window-wall. "Garismit's Eyes," he muttered again, "couldn't even find her feet."

"You're not sure of that."

That startled him. "What makes you think so?"

"You've taken my namestones, and you hid the scissors."

He snickered. "That, Notouch, is because you haven't got the sense to be afraid of what is happening to you. Besides, I saw the knife sheaths." He gestured at her arms.

Arla crossed her arms, gripping her empty sheaths.

"And you wonder why I don't want to leave sharp objects lying around." His mouth quirked up into a tight smile before he lapsed back into high-house tones. "Follow me. I'll show Arla where she can sleep."

"As her Teacher commands."

Eric ran his tongue over his lips thoughtfully as he circled the sofa to the back wall. He touched a hand-sized rectangle that was ivory instead of tan. A door-shaped section of the wall slid away as if pulled on invisible strings.

The space on the other side was so small it barely deserved the name "room." An alcove with a slab of the chair stuff in it took up most of the back wall. "Bed" she labeled it. Lines dissected the rest of the wall space into squares. A stool with a hole in it had been welded to the floor in the far corner. That was the extent of the place.

"Two things." Eric crowded his broad frame inside the tiny chamber. "One, the light. Touch here"—he pointed at another white square in the wall, this one above the bed alcove—"once and it goes away. Touch it again, and it comes back.

"Two"—he waved his hand at the stool—"when you need to say hello to a bush, do it in there. Touch here"—this time the square he pointed at was silver—"when you are finished. Understand that?"

"Bed, lamp, bush." She nodded at the appropriate objects. "Stones."

She whirled around. Eric held out the lumpy black bundle she had made of her headcloth and her treasures.

"Thank you," she said as she took them. This time, she really meant it.

"Sleep until you wake up." Eric walked back out and the door slid shut behind him.

Maybe by then I'll know what to make of you, she could practically hear him thinking. *Maybe by then, Teacher Hand, Eric Born, I'll know what to make of you.*

Arla sat on the edge of the bed, and for a moment did nothing but hold the bundle of stones tightly against her chest.

"Where are you taking them, Mother?" asked Little Eye from memory. She had run one dirty, nail-bitten finger across the smooth surface of the stone.

"Mother is taking them to learn about the Skymen." Arla tucked them into her pouch one at a time. "She and they will be back soon."

Nameless Powers preserve me—Arla bowed her head over the stones—*and do not let me have lied to my daughter.*

The memory of Little Eye gave a fresh edge to Arla's resolve. The Skymen sought power in the Realm. Silver on the Clouds, the Heretic King of Narroways, had linked that quest for power to her own. If Arla could learn what was truly going on behind the Skymen's mysteries, if she could bring some skill or piece of knowledge to the Realm, at the very least it would help her family survive the strangeness sweeping the world. At most . . . Arla let her real hope surface. At most she could bargain with the Narroways lords to raise her family up from the mud and have them declared no longer Notouch. Such things had happened before, maybe only in the apocrypha, but maybe those stories would be enough.

After all, stories have been enough for me most of my life.

Don't lie to yourself. Arla fingered her bundle. *If stories had been enough, you wouldn't be here now. You want to make the stories come true.*

She undid the knotted cloth. The bundle fell open and the stones glimmered in the stark light of the glowing ceiling. They had taken no damage from her treatment of them. She had known they wouldn't. Perfect and beautiful, they waited for her need.

Most Notouch hoped their children would grow to display the power gift. It was the one ability that could raise them out of the mud and all the way up to the rank of Teacher.

According to the Teachers in the Temples, at any rate. Arla brushed her palm across the stones' smooth, cool surfaces. According to them, the Nameless created the Royals to rule, the Nobles to administer, the Bondless to trade and travel, the Bonded to make and mend, and the Notouch to serve all. That the power gift could arise in any child of the People was the sign that all were named by the Nameless and all were under the eyes of the Servant.

They had forgotten, or in their arrogance ignored the fact, that there was at least one other kind of person in the Realm.

She glanced at the door.

No. Not here. Not now. He could come back at any second. Sleep is one thing, but if I try a reading, I'll never wake up in time if he decides I'm too much trouble to cart about. She shook her head. *I'll have to wait. I've managed this much, I can wait.*

Despite her long, unimaginably strange day, she was still able to think clearly. That realization brought her almost as much comfort as the weight of the stones against her lap.

I have Teacher . . . Eric Born shaken. That's good. That'll help. Everything I do successfully, every time I get something right about this place, it's a blow to what he thinks I ought to be. That's important. Keeping him off-balance might be as good a weapon as my knives, if it turns out I need a weapon. She looked down at her bundle and stifled the fervent hope that this one Teacher was what he was supposed to be, a preserver of the lives of the People. Her stomach twisted when she remembered the uncontrolled burst of delight she'd felt when she'd heard him give the Teacher's greeting in the middle of the Skyman's chamber. She tightened her hold on the headcloth and cast around for something else to think about.

The easiest was the ship-place around her. It was a Skyman thing, there was no question about that. The Skymen were not part of the realm of the Nameless, so they could not have power-gifted among them. So this ship was meant for use by ordinary people. If that was true, anybody could learn the workings.

It's going to be awhile before I know enough of the Skymen to find out what they want in the Realm. There's nothing I can do about that now.

I can, however, find this Cam.

Arla slung the pouch of stones from her belt again and faced the door. On the right side, about shoulder height, hung a pale, palm-sized rectangle that matched the one she'd seen in the other room. Arla touched her fingertips to it and the door slid away.

Darkness filled the bigger room. A glimmer of light caught her eye and shifted her gaze to the right.

Her heart froze. The window-wall was open. The emptiness with its countless lights gaped at her. Arla's knees collapsed. She tasted blood as she bit her tongue to block the scream constricting her throat. Her arms threw themselves up to shield her helpless head and eyes.

She screwed her eyelids shut and slammed her hand flat against the wall. She must have hit the right spot, because she felt the breeze as the door swished shut.

Blast him! Blast him headfirst into the Lif marshes and wash him into the Dead Sea! Nameless Powers preserve me! I thought I had him! I thought . . . Arla's arms dropped and her eyelids fluttered. *I thought he was going to make a stupid mistake and leave me free to wander, just because he's a Noble facing a Notouch.*

She began to laugh. The low, hoarse noise spilled out of her until her shoulders shook and tears trickled out of the corners of her eyes.

"Arla Born of the Black Wall, you are an idiot Notouch! Even the stones will not change that. Give yourself this. Whatever you think of the Teacher he was, Eric Born is not stupid!" She wiped the back of her hand across her eyes.

But, what is he?

Arla stood up and staggered, catching herself against the wall.

Go to sleep, Arla.

She dragged her poncho off and laid it on the bed. Not trusting her balance anymore, she sat on the bed to undo the laces around her leggings. The leggings themselves peeled off in long strips of cloth that she folded on top of her sandals.

She unbelted her overtunic and dragged it over her shoulders. The scent of herself came off with it.

I hope he has a bath in this place. I reek. She stripped off the knife sheaths and tossed them on the pile of clothing.

One hand strayed to her waist and pressed against the thick, leather belt beneath her undertunic. It chafed. It had been put on her when she first came to her cycles. As much as the hand marks, it said she was old enough to leave the clan as a woman in need of protection and reminding. For a searing instant her skin felt Nail in the Beam's heavy touch and missed it.

Well, get used to that, she told herself roughly. *He'll surely have divorced you by the time you get back home.*

Arla considered taking the time to remove the belt, but a formless notion told her to leave it be. Part of her had been far too relieved to see Eric Born and that part might need reminding, or protection.

She rolled her clothes into her poncho and dropped the bundle beside the bed. She stretched out beneath the blanket and reached up until her hand found the lamp-light square. The room went black. Her mind quickly followed its example.

Behind his cabin door, Eric shucked his clothing and stepped into the cleaner. The sonics shook the dried sweat off his skin, but did nothing to shake the apprehension inside him.

War. Eric's heart thudded. *Over the Skymen. Has it reached the First City? Who's backing Narroways?*

I don't care, Eric reminded himself fiercely. *I DON'T CARE.*

Clean, but not relaxed, he pulled on his spare tunic and trousers and sat in front of the cabin's auxiliary comm terminal. He switched the input setting from keyboard to audio. The screen lit up to show a blank, grey background.

"Ready for input," said a neuter voice from the speaker.

Eric licked his lips. This was going to be a risk. So far, there hadn't been any sign of Vitae pursuit, but that didn't mean they weren't looking for him. Any transmission was a chance to be spotted and tracked. But running blind, as he was now, was even more dangerous than running scared.

"Wanderer," he said in the language of the Realm. "This is Teacher Hand. Tell Dorias I need him."

He settled back to wait. May 16 was light-years away, and getting farther by the second. Eric folded his arms and drummed his fingers against his forearm, trying not to think too much. Dorias had tried to get a warning to him. That meant he knew at least something about what was going on. Anything was better than operating in total ignorance.

At long last, the terminal let out a single, low chime. "Connection made."

Eric pulled himself up straight. "Dorias?"

The blank screen did not shift, but the terminal's voice deepened into an approximation of a male baritone. "Eric! What took you so long? Are you on your way here?"

"Dorias, wait a minute, will you?" said Eric. "I'm not on my own and the Vitae have all gone insane. I only got part of your message on Haron Station. What's going on?"

There was a long stretch of silence. "Eric, where are you?"

"On the *U-Kenai*," said Eric with more than a touch of exasperation. "In flight."

"I'm glad to hear that," said Dorias seriously. "What contact have you had with the Vitae?"

"They tried to incarcerate me." Memory added heat to his tone.

"Do they still have the woman?"

Eric stared at the terminal for a moment without answering. "How did you know about her?"

Dorias sighed. "It's a very long story, Eric. I need to know, do they still have her?"

"No," said Eric. "She's with me."

"Good," said Dorias in the same serious tone. "We need you both here. She was being taken to May 16 when the Vitae waylaid the ship."

"She was what!" exclaimed Eric. "Are Unifiers in the Realm!"

"Yes, Eric, listen . . ."

"There's a war going on in the Realm!" shouted Eric. "It's being encouraged by a group of Skymen . . ."

"Eric . . ."

"And you're saying it's your employers!"

"And I'm trying to stop it, Eric!"

Eric closed his mouth and clenched his fists. He was shaking.

Dorias took advantage of his silence. "The Rhudolant Vitae have been scouting out the Realm of the Nameless Powers for years now. We couldn't find out why. So the Unifiers sent a team in to try to get the natives, the People, to agree to join the Human Family before the Vitae could get their hands on them. But there're complications. . . ."

"What kind of complications?" Eric demanded.

"Madame Chairman asked for volunteers to be brought to May 16. The Vitae hijacked the ship and took the cargo . . . and we don't know why."

"Dorias," said Eric in a low, level voice, "don't play games with me . . ."

"Eric, listen to me. You're being invited to come here, of your own free will," said Dorias. "The Unifiers want to hire you and offer sanctuary to the woman. . . ."

"Stone in the Wall *dena* Arla Born of the Black Wall."

"Eric, if the Vitae want the Realm, your best bet for keeping it from them is to ally with the Unifiers, and don't try to tell me you don't care," he added. "We both know you've never stopped caring, Teacher Hand."

Eric said nothing.

"I'm asking you to trust me, Eric," said Dorias. "Like I've trusted you."

After a long moment, Eric said, "All right, I'm on my way. I'll be there in about thirty hours."

"Thank you," said Dorias, and Eric broke the connection.

"I trust you, Dorias," said Eric to the blank screen and the universe at large. "But how can I trust those fanatics you've allied yourself with? They want her as badly as the Vitae did, and I'm not going to let any of you have her or me until I know what you want us for."

Eric leaned back in the chair and stared at the deck between his bare feet. With startling clarity, he saw two bodies there, faces contorted with the shock and pain that had killed them. Seven years separated action from memory, but his mind still held every detail.

He'd scrambled onto his knees with his heart pounding and his ears ringing, barely able to understand the voice whispering an unbeliever's prayer to the gods.

He'd helped Yul Gan Perivar hide the bodies while Dorias ransacked the ship's electronic memory for anything useful they could carry with them. Three of them had run away in the *U-Kenai*, which was just a shuttle belonging to the bigger ship whose owners had taken him from the Realm and died when they tried to keep him for their own.

That was their mistake. The laws of the Nameless Powers couldn't keep me enslaved. What made them think a pair of human beings could. He tried to feel some measure of pride, or at least satisfaction at that, but all he felt was tired.

Eric shook himself and switched the terminal back to keyboard input and then into intercom mode. He typed a series of new directions to Cam and then opened up an outside channel to a world called Kethran.

Perivar would be willing to help keep Arla out of the hands of the Vitae. If not out of friendship, then because Eric could do him too much damage if he wanted to.

One of these days, there'll be somebody around who helps because they want to. Not because I owe them, or they owe me. One of these days.

Until then, there was nothing to do but wait, and hope he was faster than even the Vitae could be.

Eric watched the spare cabin's door open. As she stood in the threshold, Arla's expression went from petrified fear, to unparalleled relief, to absolute embarrassment as she saw that the view wall was turned off, and that he was waiting for her.

She did figure out how to open the door last night. Garismit's Eyes! Just as well for the Nobles that all the Notouch aren't her grade of brainless! We'd all be dead in a week!

We? Eric winced inwardly. *Them. They. I left that behind. Years and light-years behind.*

In whose dreams was that, Teacher Hand? Not yours.

When he'd finally fallen asleep last night he had dreamed about the Walls. Broken Canyon, where the Nameless Powers had argued over the name for "stone." Tiered Side, where the Servant Garismit kept watch for the Aunorante Sangh. Red Stone, where the first battle between the Nameless Powers and the Aunorante Sangh took place. Old places, holy places, and he still knew the litany and the celebration that went with each.

Just as he knew the laws for the Royal, the Noble, the Bondless, the Bonded, and the Notouch.

Eric shoved the thoughts well into the back of his mind so he could concentrate on the particular Notouch in front of him. She'd also, obviously, found some of his spare clothes. The azure pullover shirt made her a short dress and a pair of his black socks made thin leggings.

Who'd've thought a Notouch would have such fine legs?
Stop it, Eric.

She still wore her own belt and headcloth. The stones were now hanging from her belt in an emerald-colored pouch made of a sash he'd gotten for some forgotten formal occasion.

Eric beckoned out of the doorway. "I wasn't sure you'd make it out. Good sign. I will be able to do something with you after all."

"Oh?" Amusement glittered behind her eyes as she collected her nerve and wits. "You have something in mind then?"

"Yes, I do." He pushed the plate full of ration squares across the table to her. "Here, breakfast." He slid over a cup full of steaming liquid that approximated the brew they called tea in the Realm.

She sat down. "So Cam doesn't get to eat?" she asked as she picked up a ration square. "This is two meals we've had without him."

Eric found himself strangling on another laugh. "You don't let an idea go, do you? All right. Just remember, you asked." He turned toward the airlock corridor. "Cam! Come here!"

Her eyes tracked around to the open threshold. With a smooth, mechanical pace, Cam walked in. It might have been a moving statue of peach-colored clay dressed in saffron overalls. At least that was what Eric had thought the first time he'd seen one.

Arla jerked backward as far as the chair would let her. Eric turned his face away and fought the urge to smile.

Getting her angry at me won't accomplish anything.

"That is a human-copy. It's another Skyman machine. It flies the ship at my orders and answers to 'Cam.'"

"Ah." She did not relax any.

Eric shook his head. "Return to the bridge, Cam."

As soon as Cam was out of sight, Arla settled herself back into a normal sitting position and reclaimed her breakfast, which had dropped to the floor.

"I've been talking to a friend of mine." Eric eyed her for a moment. She absorbed the statement calmly. *All right.* "He thinks he might be able to find a place for you."

"What kind of place?" She took a long swig of tea.

"Does it matter?"

"Not really. I just like to know what I'm getting into, when I can." She stuffed the last of the square into her mouth and licked her fingers. Eric tried not to watch. Notouch table manners were apparently no better than their hygiene.

Stop that too, Eric. She wasn't brought up to know better. It was amazing how quickly the old arrogance came back. For ten years he'd been a servant of one kind or another, and it still came back.

"I'd tell you if I could, but I've got no idea what will happen. Perivar, my friend, was one of the Skymen who took me over the World's Wall. He was also my first friend once I got out here. On top of that, he owes me for a few years of silence. He'll find some place to put you. It may not be pleasant, but it won't be life-threatening either."

"Did you tell him I'm Notouch?" Arla held up her scarred hand and wiggled her fingers.

Eric shook his head. "Not a soul out here would know a Noble from a Notouch, let alone care. You are beyond the laws of the Nameless Powers."

She nodded, looking down into her tea. Her eyes narrowed

a moment at whatever she saw in there before she drank the last of it down.

"There're a few things we have to take care of first," Eric went on.

She eyed him in silence.

"First, you must understand you can never mention where you came from."

She set the cup down. "Why?"

Eric searched for the words to build an explanation. "Some of the Skymen, in their arrogance, or kindness, I have never really figured out which, have decided there are some worlds, or people, that cannot handle meeting them and their ways without falling apart. So they pass laws that label such places forbidden. No trade, no speech, no exchange of any kind."

Arla snorted. "I'm a Notouch from a Notouch world then. I wish the King in Narroways could know!"

"Yes." Eric snorted. "I've met King Sun. He deserves to know that one."

Arla shook her head. "Sun after the Storm doesn't hold the rule anymore. His granddaughter, Silver on the Clouds, became King, two, no, three years ago." In the language of the Realm, there was only one word for the ruler of a city whether male or female. If a person could hold the throne of one of the twenty-nine city-states, they were called King. "It was during the siege," Arla added.

The mention of the war dropped into Eric's mind like a stone. He swallowed and picked up the broken thread of his thoughts. "Not all the Skymen think the same thing about . . . Notouch worlds. Some of them raid those places on a regular basis for talent or knowledge. There's one group, the Alliance for Reunification, that try to bring isolated worlds into what they call 'the Human Family.' But"—he leaned forward—"what is important to you and me is that there are Skymen who consider being taken from a Notouch world a crime and any people from such a world that they catch"—he caught her gaze and held it—"are sent back."

"I am not ready to go back yet," said Arla flatly.

Eric hung his head. "Arla, try to understand. You are over the World's Wall now, and you may never get back."

Emotions flickered across her face too fast for Eric to identify. "I got over. I'll get back when I'm ready." She gathered herself together and managed a fairly casual shrug. "Until then, I'll say nothing about my birthplace."

Eric rubbed his palms together. *Leave it. Let her believe whatever'll give her comfort. She'll learn otherwise soon enough.* "All right. Now, there's only one thing left to do."

"What?"

"Teach you how to look at someplace without walls without having fits."

Very slowly, her hands knotted into fists. "I see."

"The Realm of the Nameless Powers is the only place I've ever seen with a World's Wall," he told her. "All the others are open. Wide-open. I can't take you to Perivar if you can't walk outside."

She hesitated, staring down at the backs of her fists.

"What do I have to do?"

She's got all the nerve the Nameless had to hand out, Eric thought as he stood up. *I'll give her that for free.*

"Let me tie you up again."

"Why?" Her voice stayed calm.

"So you don't hurt me, or yourself when I turn on," he stopped and retranslated the term, "open up the window-wall again."

"All right," she croaked.

"We'll start now." Action, any action, was better than giving himself time to think about what might or might not be happening in the Realm.

He brought out the repair tape again and, as deftly as possible, tied her legs together and strapped her arms to her sides. Then, he trussed her tightly against the chair. He rummaged through the medical drawer and found a dry cloth. He held it in front of her mouth. "So you won't bite through your tongue."

Her teeth clamped together around the cloth and her eyes followed him as he crossed the room. He held his hand over the reader and braced himself.

The view wall switched on. Infinity peeked in at them and Arla went into spasms. Arms and legs tried to flail out. Teeth ground against the cloth and throat screamed. Her eyes clenched themselves shut. Her head thudded against the sofa back. Eric winced and turned his face away. At the same time, he was glad he hadn't had the nerve to try to hold her himself. She would have gotten away, but not before they both had broken bones.

Eventually, she slumped against the back of the chair, breathing heavily.

"Arla Born of the Black Wall, look up."

She was too worn out not to do as he said. Her eyes drank in the scene on the view wall and the whole thing started again.

It was a long, miserable circuit. She'd scream herself out, then get another look at the vacuum and start again. A couple of times she actually passed out and he had to get stimulants from the medical kit to shock her awake so she could start screaming and struggling again.

She's not going to make it. He leaned against the wall. *She may be the most incredible excuse for a Notouch in the Realm of the Nameless, but she doesn't have the strength to get through this. She's going to go crazy, and then I'm going to have to ... to ....* He couldn't make himself finish the thought.

Somehow, though, by force of nerves or desperation, Eric didn't know, she held on to her sanity. She lifted her head from the lopsided angle where it had fallen and opened wide eyes that matched the blackness of the void. She looked out at the emptiness. She did not scream. Her hands twitched but she stilled them. Her eyes stayed open.

"Thank you, oh all Nameless Powers." Eric rubbed tired eyes and ears.

Without switching the view wall off, he cut her free from the tape. He summoned up the memory of his own breaking in. It lent him the sympathy he needed to extend his hands and help her to her feet. She accepted his support without protest, leaning heavily against him.

"Bed," he said to her, as he opened the spare cabin. "Sleep. Some more food. You've beaten it, Arla. Planetside is going to be nothing next to that."

She toppled onto the mattress and flung her arm over her

eyes. Her wrist was a mass of welts from fighting against her bonds.

Something that wasn't contempt, fear, or caution turned over inside him. Eric opened up the path to his power gift and stretched out his hand.

Her arm flinched when he touched her, but did not drag itself free. The reach of his gift found the damaged flesh in her and took hold of it gently. This was more complicated than breaking locks. Her body had already begun the healing, but he had to encompass that beginning in order to speed the process along. All of it. A missed step would bring infection, or worse. Eric's vision blurred over and his heart began to pound in his chest.

And it was done. He released her.

Arla rubbed her smooth, clean wrist. "Thank you."

"You're welcome." He gulped air like a drowning man. "I'd appreciate it if you didn't tell anyone about that either. The Skymen have very strange notions about healers."

"There will be no word from me."

He smiled. "Sleep," he ordered, and left the çabin.

When the door shut behind him, Eric collapsed onto the sofa. He was shaking, and it was not from the adrenaline shock that normally came after a healing.

What is the matter with me? Garismit's Eyes, I don't have time for this! He pounded his fist against his thigh. *Get her away. Now. May the Powers bless Perivar for taking her. I've got to think. Figure out what to do next.*

His mind was not ready to let go yet. Instead, it gathered up all the memories of Lady Fire it could find and handed them across to him. He saw the quiet beauty in her face the second she had opened the door to her house so he could enter and heal her husband's fever. He felt the touch of her mouth, saw the light in her eyes.

He remembered the sweat and screams and blood that came with the birth of their baby. The baby that was dead and buried by his own power-gifted hands. Because that was the Law. That was what the Nameless demanded. Born of an adulterous union, its blood was untraceable. Such blood could be diverted

by the Aunorante Sangh. It had to die and Eric had done as
the Words instructed and Lady Fire had cursed him for it.

And now there was war. Maybe in the First City. Maybe
not. War over the Skymen's presence, and it was known that
Lady Fire had consorted with him and that he had left with
the Skymen and . . .

Maybe the war was for the best. Maybe the Heretics and
the Skymen would weaken the Words, would destroy the hold
they had on the Realm and on Lady Fire. Then he could go
back, and he could . . .

Eric knew he was deceiving himself. Ten years and ten
times as many light-years of travel hadn't been enough to
wipe the Words out of him. No matter how hard he'd tried.
Part of him would never call anywhere but the Realm home,
and it would not stop resenting the ones who drove him away
from it. It would take the death of every Teacher in the Realm
to silence the Words in the world.

Somehow, he doubted liberation of the People from their
superstitions was what the Skymen were after.

I don't care, I can't care! Eric buried his face in his hands.
*It's the Rhudolant Vitae I've got to worry about, not . . . not
the Realm or their war. It's their war, over their laws. Not
mine. Not anymore. Not again.*

He stayed like that for a long time. When he was finally
able to raise his head again, he stared out at the void, hearing
the screams of women in his mind.

3—The Hundredth Core Encampment, Hour 11:34:25, Core Time

Our world is gone. Gone. They stole the whole world while from on high . . . we watched.

Fragment from "The Beginning of the Flight," from the Rhudolant Vitae private history Archives

*W*HATEVER else, I was honest. I held to the terms of my contract. Whatever judgment they make against me, it will not be for breaking my word.

The thought did nothing to warm Basq. In truth, the chill hadn't left his blood since he'd reported the loss of the artifacts. He sat stiffly in the shuttle's padded seat, hands spread on his knees. The robe that covered him was pure white, a color that allowed no status, no allegiance, and no work.

"You do not have to wear this," said Caril, even though she got it out for him with her own hands instead of leaving it to the automatics.

"I do. Eric Born was my study. The security of him and the other artifacts was my responsibility." Basq could still feel the rough edges of the shattered bolts under his fingertips.

"The Contractors will not say it was a breach. They will see there is no way you could have known. All the evidence indicated that he manipulated datastreams, not hardware."

The memories of Caril's reassurances didn't offer Basq any more warmth than preening himself for his honorable behavior had. His study of Eric Born had contributed directly to the rediscovery of the Home Ground. The promotions that had followed had been exhilarating. He had been able to tell himself that memory of his past shame had been wiped away by this success.

Do I have the strength to defend myself again? Do I have the means?

Basq felt his whole body slump farther down in the seat. *I don't know.*

The view wall in front of him showed the gleaming length of tether stretching out to its anchor on the encampment's core. Outsiders compared Rhudolant Vitae encampments to spiderwebs or jewels on strings, depending on how they felt toward the Vitae at the moment. For this gathering, fifteen white and mirror-skinned ships had been moored to the elongated core. Each ship was tethered to its neighbors as well as to the core with bundles of polycarbon cable. When a current was applied, the strands maintained a crystal-fiber structure that allowed the tether to remain rigid. The core's rotation kept the ships at an even distance from each other and kept all the tethers taut.

If the current was cut, the tethers could fray and tear, sending the ships careening out into space.

Basq realized, with a small jolt, why he was brooding on them. He felt as if his tethers had already been torn.

At this distance, Basq could see the curve of the core's mottled side. As the shuttle slid forward along the tether, it looked to Basq as if the core expanded. The curved side became a gleaming wall that blocked out the vacuum and the starlight. Modules and antennae, some more than a kilometer across, rose from a surface of smooth ceramic, but most of the surface was covered with the hulks of tanks. Tanks for fuel and coolant and hydrogen and nitrogen and all the other essentials that needed to be carried with them between the worlds. Like the home ships, the core was fully mobile, if slow compared to the freighters and runners that clung to its sides between the tanks and the tethers.

Basq glanced toward the rear of the shuttle, in the direction of his ship, the *Grand Errand*. He did not move his hand to switch on the view wall that would let him see it.

They will not let me go home again.

Eric Born and the female were too important for any Contractor to let this matter go. The Home Ground was at stake. His failure might have delayed the Vitae's chance to fully return.

The gravity and inertial regulators adjusted themselves so that Basq could feel the shuttle slowing. The view wall showed the docking corridor extending itself from the core to lock onto the shuttle's hatch. Basq stood and smoothed the fabric of his white robe.

Now the real work begins. The invocation sounded in his mind before he could stop it.

The docking corridor led straight into the Home Hall. Basq stepped through the arch into the domed chamber. All around him, simulated constellations blazed on a black background. A sun the size of his head burned to the left. Directly opposite, the blue-and-white swell of the Home Ground filled the entire wall. Rising behind it, a grey moon caught the sunlight. Farther off, planets shone as coins of light, or thumbnails, or pinpricks.

Terra, Luna, Ares, Jupiter, Saturn, Uranus, Neptune. Beginning with the Home Ground, he recited the names he'd learned as a childhood litany. His eyes picked out each patch of light as he named it. The Home Ground. The Host System. All of it lost to the grip of the Aunorante Sangh, the ones who'd been bred to serve and had betrayed their trust. *Beware your own creations, Vitae. They have already robbed you.*

How many times have I heard that? How many times have I repeated it? And when the time comes . . .

A tiny breeze told him the door had opened. Basq turned to see the two Contractors walk forward. Avir, with her chestnut hair braided so it hung down the back of her midnight-colored tunic, looked Basq over with critical eyes surrounded by star-shaped scars. Black-robed Kelat, who stood beside her, was a member of the Amputants. He had only four fingers on his right hand. He would not have the missing one regrown unless and until he walked on the Home Ground. Basq bent in obeisance until his forehead pressed against the smooth, warm floor. These two held his name.

"Please get up, Ambassador Basq," said Contractor Avir.

Basq's heart skipped a beat. *Used my title. Then they don't consider my contract broken yet.* He lifted his head.

Kelat nodded once. "No code or lock currently in place could have kept the artifact designated Eric Born confined if he wanted to escape. You are not at fault. You fulfilled your contracted duties to the level of the available resources and information. We do not need to continue this audience. You are required at the strategy conference." In unison, the Contractors turned and glided into the corridor.

Basq raised himself to his feet and trailed behind them, half-dazed.

Not at fault. Not at fault. The words sang inside him. For a moment, the idea flashed through him that the singing was loud enough for Caril to hear.

Multiphase frescoes lined the corridor walls. Each depicted a sequence from the Flight, moment blending into moment so that the blur of history surrounded Basq and the Contractors as they passed. At Basq's right side, an Aunorante Sangh bowed to a crowd of people, then leaned over a control bank. The scene twisted and dissolved into a shower of sparks. To his left, a trio of Survivors crowded around a ship's empty data-hold and raised their fists to the sky, then they bent to their work, growing old and older until, at last, fresh generations took their place. Beyond that, a globe of the Home Ground rotated serenely. Clouds shifted across its surface and, in a heartbeat, it vanished.

The only single-phase art was held in the ceiling mosaic that spelled out the names of the Home Ground in the oldest languages the Vitae knew.

At the end of the corridor, the wall parted to let them into the conference room.

The Contractors completed the committee. Two Bio-technicians, two Historians, and two Senior Ambassadors already sat at the round table. Basq recognized Uary, the Bio-tech who had been assigned to study the "stones" carried by the female artifact. Uary raised his sculpted eyebrows briefly as their eyes met.

You didn't expect to see me again, thought Basq. *Well, in truth, I didn't expect you to see me again either.*

The robes of all the people around the table were the solid unbroken colors of their specialties, amethyst, scarlet or mist grey. No bands or sigils indicated subranks or allegiance owed to anyone else. These were all encampment leaders and residents of the core. Two Witnesses in their jade green robes stood at the back of the room and watched the gathering. Each wore a camera set over the right eye, giving their faces a distorted, unnatural appearance.

The doors sealed themselves, but privacy did not thaw the air of formality as Basq had expected. Avir and Kelat bowed briefly to the committee. Basq again made full obeisance at their feet, waiting for his name and work to be made known.

Avir spoke first. "I am named Contractor Avir Ose Cien and let the memory show I have been appointed to speak for Advisory Committee 196. Contractor Kelat is our liaison with Advisory Committee 84. Here we speak of the Reclamation of the Home Ground. All we say here will be known as long as Vitae ask 'in those days, what was done?' 'What course did they take to succeed?' or 'What course did they take to fail?' This committee has been convened to advise the Reclamation Assembly about the action required to secure the populated segment of the Home Ground. To further that end, to this committee I bring the work and name of Ambassador Basq of the *Grand Errand*." Basq stood with his shoulders straight and his face calm, as he had learned to do during his apprenticeship. "His observations gave us a great deal of information about the artifacts that still exist on the Home Ground. It is my intention to contract his services fully to the work of this committee and the Reclamation."

Basq's heart began to pound against his ribs. *To the Reclamation? Directly? Me? My hands? My work?* His mouth felt dry. Fear and elation warred inside him. If this happened, his name would be witnessed and remembered for his success, or his failure.

No, I will rise to this. My work will be my seal. My words, my thoughts will be remembered with pride when we walk on the Home Ground.

One of the Historians, a withered woman with silver droplets dangling from her pierced ears and chin, waved two fingers to indicate she was about to speak. "What would be the requirements of that contract?"

Basq fought to keep his eyes straight ahead. He was not present yet. He had been named but not been accepted. To indicate that he could hear what was said about him would have been to admit he cared more about himself than about the work he would be assigned.

Kelat spoke with measured tones. "He will use the data gathered from his observations of the artifacts designated Eric Born and Stone in the Wall combined with the information gathered by Bio-technician Uary and Ambassador Ivale to assess the level of danger presented by the artifacts that exist on the Home Ground and to determine an effective strategy for combating that danger."

From the corner of his eye, Basq could see Uary's gaze rest on him. The set of the Bio-tech's face spoke of resentment. Anger sparked in Basq, but he did not move his eyes to look directly at Uary. The Witnesses also had their eyes on him. He would not begin his remembered existence with such disregard for proprieties.

Ivale was as bald and slender as Basq, but even seated, he towered over the rest of the committee by fifteen centimeters. "Contractors Avir and Kelat, how long have you held Basq's name?"

"By time measured in the Hundredth Core, five years, ten months, four days, and seven hours. Renewals have been specifically requested four times," said Avir

Ivale nodded and opened his mouth again, but Uary signaled for speaking time.

"I have a security issue," he said as Avir acknowledged him.

"Please outline this issue, Bio-technician Uary." There was

an edge in Avir's words. Basq suppressed a smile. Uary had been the one to discover the genetic evidence in Eric Born's blood that had solidified Basq's claim that Born had come from the Home Ground. As a result, Uary's words carried weight, but evidently, not that much.

"Basq permitted Stone in the Wall to regain the composite globes she carried and use them as weapons. He is thus directly responsible for the loss of the human-derived artifacts as well as the globes. I submit that the Ambassador does not know enough about the artifacts to make real-time predictions of their behavior or provide adequate compensation for such behavior."

So that is why your eyes burn, thought Basq. *I lost you those globes.*

"Further," Uary went on, "it is still unknown why the floor restraints were not activated soon enough to prevent their loss."

"A true statement and a fair issue," said Kelat.

Basq almost broke then, to make obeisance to the Contractors, to shout it had been a mistake and there would be no repetition. *Do not deny me this chance. Do not remove me from this work.* Fear underscored the thoughts, because the issue was real and the criticism too well deserved.

Trust those who hold your name. Trust that they have seen this, too. Trust that they have an answer, Basq told himself firmly, but another, older, ever-present fear began to crawl into his thoughts. *No. Even Uary would not try to hold me accountable for Jahidh.*

Avir nodded in agreement with Kelat. "But let it be remembered alongside the facts regarding Ambassador Basq that you authorized the release of the globes to Ambassador Basq without providing proper security or oversight of their disposition. The video record of the transaction shows that you sent only one Intership Ambassador with the globes and did not give him instructions to remain with them and ensure their safe restoration to your laboratory."

Avir's words hung heavy in the air and all the people at the table turned their attention to Uary.

"I acknowledge my responsibility," said Uary calmly. "My

Contractors have my report and my detailed admissions of the fault in my procedure. But that fault was in trusting the knowledge and experience of Ambassador Basq. I am concerned about trusting him too much when the Reclamation of the Home Ground is at stake."

Basq didn't know whether he wanted to scream or simply fall down and die. *Trust, trust, trust,* he ordered himself. *Avir and Kelat will not let this go unchallenged. They will not. How they are remembered is bound up with how I am remembered. Uary will not mention Jahidh, even if there is no way I can make a good answer about his defection. He was removed from my supervision. He is not my fault. He has nothing to do with this.*

Kelat rested his fingertips against the tabletop. "Bio-technician Uary, can you here before formal Witnesses cite flaws in Ambassador Basq's research?" he asked.

"I cannot," admitted Uary.

"Can you cite errors in the conclusions he has drawn based on that research?"

After a long pause, Uary said, "I cannot."

"Then the issue is not organic to the contract we propose for Ambassador Basq. The issue is procedural. If the Ambassador's contract is approved by this committee, I propose an additional contract will be drawn up with a Formal Witness agreed upon by the committee. Bio-technician Uary will have veto powers of the choice of Witness. The Witness will have final say over any and all security decisions regarding Ambassador Basq's work and will have the authority to subcontract other Witnesses and services as may be required to enforce prudent and reasonable security for that work.

"Will that satisfy your issue, Bio-technician Uary?"

Uary considered the matter.

He's going to do it. He's going to remind them about Jahidh. He will lay the faults of my child, my child I was not allowed to supervise, at my feet. He'll cast doubts upon my memory any way he can to keep me off the committee because I lost him those globes and his chance for promotion.

"Contractor Avir, it will satisfy my current issue," said Uary.

A flood of relief washed through Basq and he had to work to keep it from showing. *Even if I must endure a Witness, it's all right*, Basq told himself. *If the Witness watches me, the Witness also watches Uary, and I believe it is Uary who will provide the more . . . entertaining show.*

"Are there any other issues to be raised regarding the contracting of Ambassador Basq?" inquired Kelat.

The silence stretched out and with each heartbeat Basq felt hope grow stronger.

"Then," said Avir, "I invoke the name I hold. Ambassador Basq Hanr Sone of the *Grand Errand*." Basq turned to face her as she recited the conditions of his contract. At last she said, "Do you understand the responsibilities to be laid beside your name?"

"Contractor Avir, I do." Basq hoped his voice was full of calm assurance. He couldn't tell. His heart was pounding too loud for him to hear anything properly.

"And do you believe you possess the skill necessary to complete this contract?"

"I do."

"And do you agree to the appended contract that will place you under the authority and eye of a Formal Witness for the duration of this contract?"

"I do."

"Then we bind your name to this contract," said Kelat. "Ready your resources for the work you are assigned."

Basq made the half obeisance his invocation required. He let all the pride he felt show in his face. It was appropriate now. He was officially part of the committee, and Uary could dine on his objections in silence.

"This committee shall join the Reclamation Assembly in fifteen days as measured in the Hundredth Core," said Avir. "In six core days, this committee will reconvene to compare information and initiate such procedures as are in its sphere of authority so that we may report to the Assembly that we are moving ahead expeditiously." Avir smiled warmly at her committee. "Now, my friends, the real work begins."

"The real work begins," chorused the committee. When

the sound of their voices died away, the Witnesses closed their eyes and bowed. The meeting was ended.

Still dazzled from the turn of events, Basq forgot to move. Avir reached out and shook his shoulder.

"The time for dreaming is when we walk on the Home Ground, Ambassador," Avir laughed.

Basq felt his cheeks heat up. "I was not dreaming, Contractor, I was . . . readjusting."

Avir nodded. "I can understand the need, but there is not much time for that. Let me give you Ivale's name formally."

Basq followed Avir around the table to where Ivale stood talking with Uary. As they approached, Uary looked up from the conversation. A spasm of distaste crossed his features.

"Ambassador Ivale," said Avir. "With your permission, I shall present your full name to Ambassador Basq of the *Grand Errand*." Ivale nodded his acknowledgment. "Ambassador Basq, I present to you the name of Ambassador Ivale Muirfinn Bren of the Hundredth Core." Basq timed his obeisance to match Ivale's. "I leave you to arrange your work," said Avir, and she left them there to join Kelat, who was speaking with the Historians.

"I've never seen a Contractor show such faith in the work of a Beholden," remarked Uary. Basq could hear the forced casualness in his words. "I must access your files, Ambassador, and look into your previous work."

"Should you choose to do so, you will find that I accept both credit and blame as they are due me," Basq replied smoothly. "I do not shirk one while seeking the other."

"Listen to me, both of you," said Ivale coolly. "Do not permit these differences to grow into a quarrel. We cannot afford to be divided in this committee. The Imperialists are making themselves heard in the Reclamation Assembly. The successes the Unifiers have been enjoying over the past years are making many of the Assembly members uneasy. If the Imperialists appear more united and reasoned than we do, they may just get their way and then the Vitae will become nothing more nor less than a race of warmongers."

Basq instantly bowed his head and pressed his palm against

his mouth to seal in any more foolish words. Uary remained unmoved.

"Ambassador Basq," said Ivale. "In addition to the tasks specifically outlined when your name was invoked, I would ask you to place the cases of the artifacts Eric Born and Stone in the Wall into perspective with the larger group of artifacts. Specifically, you are to determine as far as possible how dangerous they are to us and the Reclamation, under what circumstances they would become most dangerous, and what precautions should be taken to prevent those circumstances. My files from the direct observation of the artifacts on the Home Ground are open for your review. You will add the information gained by Bio-technician Uary to your assessments." Ivale glowered at Uary. "And you will cooperate fully, Uary."

Uary's mouth twitched. "Ambassador Ivale, I wish to walk with my children on the Home Ground. The work is what is important to me, not who does it or who orders it."

"As it should be," said Ivale. "I will expect you to take the relevant conclusions that Ambassador Basq discovers into account with your work. We will convene our subcommittee in seventy-two hours with all available current information correlated and ready for presentation. Do you have any issues or additions to raise against this plan?" Formality flattened out the emotion in Ivale's voice.

"I have none," said Basq immediately.

"I have none at this time," said Uary. "I reserve the right to raise any that occur in the future for your attention, Ambassador Ivale."

"You have that right in perpetuity." Ivale straightened a fold in his sleeve minutely. It was a dismissive gesture and Basq took a small measure of satisfaction from the sour look it brought to Uary's face. "Ambassador Basq, your real work begins now. Technician, you must be present as the Contractors assign a Witness to accompany the Ambassador back to the *Grand Errand*."

Dismissed, Basq bowed and left the room as quickly as dignity would allow. He didn't spare a glance at any of the artworks or core inhabitants as he hurried down the spiraling corridor toward the core's center.

The Hundredth Core followed the layout of all the fourth generation cores. At the end of the spiral spread a public annex. Pillarlike communication booths broke up a domed space that rivaled the Home Hall for size and grandeur. The murals of Vitae ships in flight that covered the walls here had all been painted with hand tools and unaugmented skill.

Basq shut himself into one of the booths and activated the control pad as he sat down. Before the list of his options had a chance to solidify in the display space above the pad, his fingers flashed across the controls, opening the lines to the *Grand Errand* and his quarters, and Caril.

Less than five seconds passed before the full-body image of Caril seated in front of her own terminal appeared above the keypad.

"The formal copies of the contracts just arrived," she said, breathless with pride and triumph. "I knew all would be well, but . . ."

"I know, I know." Basq felt himself smile. "But we must leave our celebration for when the work is done. I will be under the eye of a Witness before I arrive back home. Listen, I have been grouped on a subcommittee with Bio-technician Uary. He is determined to minimize my effectiveness, and maybe to disengage me from the direct Reclamation work. Eventually, I may need a way to combat him publicly."

Caril nodded. "Then you may need information about his activities. I can make that my work and I will. I'll have the quarters ready when the Witness arrives. We will be remembered well, Basq. I swear it."

"I swear it as well, Caril. I will see you with unaided eyes within the hour." She smiled at him and Basq shut the lines down.

Basq realized how lucky he'd been to find Caril. Most contracted support staff would not go beyond official duty and would move on as soon as a better contract came their way, but Caril had abiding ambitions and love as well as duty in her soul. Basq had offered to make her a permanent part of his life gladly. She had accepted at once, even though

permanent subservience to one person meant a relative demo-
tion. She had known Basq would rise, even when he had
doubted it. She would rise with him and she truly deserved
to do so.

Basq did not let himself think about what she would have
done if the contracts had not come and the white robe had
become a reflection of his permanent status. Instead, he opened
the lines to the transport coordination section and requested
a shuttle back to the *Grand Errand*. The display informed him
that the shuttle was available and the Witness was awaiting his
arrival at the Home Hall.

Good to know, Basq thought as he closed the lines and shut
the terminal's power off. *I will be ready to receive them into
my life*. He savored the thought. The Reclamation of the Home
Ground was first and foremost, of course, but it would not
be a bad thing to assure a good place for Caril and himself
when the Rhudolant Vitae walked there. Being favorably
remembered by a Witness was the surest course to such a
place, especially if his Contractors and Ambassador Ivale
could say they shared that memory.

The Home Hall was filled with activity when Basq got
there. Members of the committee were being escorted down
the docking corridors by entourages numbering between six
and ten Beholden. Residents of the core greeted arrivals from
the encampment's ships.

The only still figure in the room was the Witness. A dark-
skinned woman several centimeters taller than Basq and at
least ten kilos heavier, she stood like a single-phase statue.
The movements of the other people in the hall did not so
much as ruffle the hem of her jade robe or the ends of her
black hair. She had a soft-sided case slung over one shoulder.
The lens of her camera's eyepiece glinted with reflected light.

Basq concentrated on keeping his face smooth and devoid
of emotion while he racked his brains trying to remember the
etiquette for greeting the Witness one had been assigned.
Before he had to resign himself to making his first remembered
action a public display of ignorance, the Witness moved. With
more grace than even a Contractor, she glided toward him.
As she neared, Basq realized she was an Amputant, but a

much more devout one than even Contractor Kelat. She raised a flexible, silicate hand toward him in greeting.

Why should I be surprised? Most Witnesses are fanatics. That would be especially true for any Witness Uary agreed to. Basq tried not to frown. *I will have to find a way to remind Caril how careful we must be.*

"Ambassador Basq, with your permission I will present you my name." Her voice was deep and had an oddly musical quality about it. "I am Formal Witness Winema Avin-Dae Uratae. Do you accept that I am the Witness contracted to you by the Reclamation Advisory Committee or do you require verification?"

The words triggered the memory of a lesson from his graded schooling. To ask for proof was to impugn the Witness. Impugning the Witness might skew the observation. So, Basq said, "I accept that you are my contracted Witness."

"Then accept that my memory carries you. On the memory of my own self I swear I will remember accurately." Winema said the words with such fervor it might have been her first time uttering them. Basq doubted that was the case. Uary would not let a novice be assigned to him.

Now came the difficult part. He had acknowledged and accepted the Witness. With the formalities observed, he had to ignore her completely. Supposedly, that would become easier with time, but for now maintaining that attitude was going to be a fight. Basq pivoted and started for the docking corridor that connected the shuttle to the core. Winema fell into step behind him, as silent as his shadow. He climbed aboard the shuttle and took a seat near the front. He heard the slight creak as the Witness sat behind him. He imagined he could feel the point on the back of his head where her camera was directed. His scalp began to itch.

It won't always be like this. I'll be free during my off-shift time. She's just contracted to watch me while I work.

Which means she's contracted to watch the dataflow on my terminal. I will have to keep that always in mind. The itch intensified.

Witnesses are necessary, Basq reminded himself. *Especially now that we are dealing with artifacts again. The artifacts defeated the ancestors because they were able to rob them of the information needed to quell the rebellion. They will not be able to do that to us. They will not be able to win that way even if they retain any knowledge of their rebellion and the Flight.* In each of the three thousand cores there were sequestered twenty-four Witnesses with eidetic memory. They held all the vital knowledge of the Rhudolant Vitae. When her contract was completed, Winema would not only transfer her camera's record into one of the datastores, she would recite her memory of Basq to one of the Witnesses in the Hundredth Core. If the artifacts wanted to wipe out all the history and learning of the Vitae again, they would have to murder all the Eidetic Witnesses.

But ruining the Ancestor's datastores was not all they did to defeat the Ancestors, was it? Under the gaze of the Witness, Basq felt the shackles of responsibility take hold. *They have obviously retained their abilities. If they have retained any portion of their memory, any portion of the Flight, how are we going to find a way to stop them from moving the Home Ground out of reach again?*

With an effort of will, Basq shoved the doubts aside. *We will find the knowledge. I will find the knowledge.*

Basq knew it was an arrogant idea, but he did not hesitate to admit to himself that it was also a pleasant one.

Planning his strategies made the trip back to the *Grand Errand* bearable. The itch on the back of his scalp never quite went away, but he was able to cover his awareness of it with lists of things he needed to accomplish in the next seventy-two hours.

Caril was waiting for him when he and Winema emerged from the shuttle into the *Grand Errand*'s gold-and-mauve receiving area.

"Welcome home, Husband," she said as she made her obeisance, bending over the small stack of holosheets she carried.

"Wherever you stand to welcome me is home, Wife." The cliché was a little informal, considering the circumstances, but well within the bounds of propriety.

"These are the contracts which arrived in your absence."

She handed him the sheets. "I have verified their origins and reviewed them for completeness."

Excellent, thought Basq, as he shuffled through the stack of sheets. *This will demonstrate her efficiency and my trust in her*. The heat from his hands and the patterns of his fingerprints activated the displays on each sheet as he touched it. The stack held the contract from Avir and Kelat, as well as the subcontract labeling him Beholden to Ivale. Basq felt warm breath upon his cheek and almost jumped out of his skin. Winema was reading over his shoulder.

I will get used to this, I will get used to this. He waited until his hands stopped shaking to give the sheets back to Caril. "Thank you. You should record my acknowledgment of receipt as soon as we return to our quarters."

"I will make this my work," she said. Caril took her place beside him and they left the receiving hall for the corridor to the lifts. Winema followed without a sound.

The *Grand Errand* was of much newer construction than the Hundredth Core. The support girders and network fibers were hidden by sheaths of crystalline optical matter rather than panels of plastics or ceramics. Although the optical matter was much more flexible than the traditional solids and it had a certain dignity, being one of the private technologies, Basq thought that the solids had a special grandeur. Nothing could be changed aboard the older ships without planning and cooperation. Here, a single technician tapped a pattern to clear a spot in the wall. Under her hand, a square of grey-white wall turned orange and cleared to reveal a web of yellowish fibers. A few meters away from her, a man wearing the grey-and-tan armbands of the support services section pressed a holosheet and flat keypad in the wall and began tapping whatever information flowed through the fibers in that particular section. Doubtless they all had orders and contracts to fulfill, but it was all so . . . solitary and so easy. Almost improperly so. Even the Imperialists could make changes. The public parks had their treaties written across the walls. A swift gesture with his hand had wiped them clear, but the fact that they had been there at all left a bitter sensation in his mind. Basq wondered if he might apply to move himself and Caril to the Hundredth

Core to be closer to the Advisory Committee. It was worth considering.

The lift to their residence section was nearly full. Like all the ships, the *Grand Errand* kept its living quarters in its heart, where they could best be sheltered from accidents and everyday occurrences, like the hard radiation that never stopped bombarding the ship. The crowd parted respectfully to make room for Basq and his entourage. Caril tapped the code for their home level on the wall. Her fingerprints were her authorization and the lift added their destination to the list displayed about the translucent doors as they closed.

"Ambassador Basq?"

Basq turned and looked up slightly. A thin man with a greying, braided beard and a red-and-gold badge that marked him as administrative support for communications stood beside him.

"The word of your new assignment has been spreading across the decks. May I congratulate you, sir? Your work brings a good memory for the *Grand Errand*."

Basq inclined his head. The man was obviously a status seeker, but there was no reason not to be polite, especially with Winema watching. "Thank you. I only hope my future work will do the same." He glanced over at Caril, who stood a little in front of the man. She nodded. She would note the man's badge code before they reached their home level. He might be willing to do them a favor or two if he thought it would add to his own status to be seen to help an Ambassador assigned to the Reclamation. Such people were worth collecting.

The lift let them out in their home level park. The park was not a crude recreation of a planetside grove. Outsiders might need such areas to overcome psychological difficulties caused by long periods in enclosed habitats, or simply to compensate for things they missed. Without the Home Ground to model from, the Vitae shunned such affectations. The park was a place where individual expression and creativity could be practiced publicly. They passed a trio of young women in purple-and-black student robes intently discussing the positioning of figures in the choreo-poem that filled the main display stage. Basq also noticed that two of the free-access terminals showed new titles on their displays. Maybe he and Caril would have time to attend a discussion. It might give them a chance to talk about their work out from under the gaze of the Witness. Then he winced. The wall behind the choreo-poem had been covered with a carefully printed text lecture. Above the tidy print, the linked circles of the Imperialists had been drawn with equal care.

Basq's jaw tightened. When his promotions had granted him access to greater space for personal work, he had requested a residence adjoining a park. If one knew how to read the events recorded in the parks, one could make advantageous predictions about the ship or encampments. Which was, of course, the best reason of all for their existence. They were forums for legitimate arguments as well as pressure valves. In the parks, dissidents could vent their anger before it built up to truly dangerous levels.

But that reasoning had its drawbacks. It meant the most determined and intelligent dissidents kept their activities far away from the parks. Jahidh's thoughts had never appeared there. Basq had watched for them.

He didn't let the Imperialist text or his thoughts break his stride. At this moment, he could not be seen to care about anything but setting to work.

Caril let Basq open their door, as etiquette dictated. The portal slid aside to reveal a hive of activity. All four of Basq's contracted Intership Ambassadors were seated at their stations. The stations themselves were cubical areas marked by pillars of communication fibers sheathed in optical matter. Holosheets or prerecorded requests could be hung from the pillars so that the machines could tap the datastores on other ships for routine retrieval and sort operations. The ISAs themselves handled the calls where complexity or courtesy required personal contact. Their voices filled the air as they advised, coordinated, recalled, or referenced contacts regarding Basq's new status and potential requirements. His three apprentices, all of them shaved and robed in red, bustled between the stations, carrying drinks or extra holosheets or relaying questions between the ISAs.

Basq felt his chest swell with pride. He had dismissed his Beholden before he donned his white robe to go meet with his Contractors. Caril must have recalled them all the second the contracts for his new assignment arrived. She had meant more than he had expected when she said, "I will have our quarters ready."

"Jene," Basq called above the voices. The supervisor of the team put his station into stasis with two keystrokes and presented himself in front of Basq, a little too quickly. Jene was a student Contractor and the purple bands on his robe were cut with black diamonds. One of the honors conferred on Basq with his promotion was Jene. Under Basq's guidance, Jene was learning to coordinate and supervise a team of Beholden. "Have the team suspend their activities and stand ready for new assignments. Compile a report of the status of our current resources and contracts."

"Yes, Ambassador." Jene's gaze slid over Basq's shoulder to Winema.

"Do you see something I don't, Supervisor?" Basq inquired.

"No, Ambassador," Jene brought his attention back where it belonged. "The report will be prepared and logged in fifteen minutes."

"That will be sufficient." When Jene completed his schooling, he would automatically become Basq's superior, but if he was unable to handle the tasks his station required both in terms of complexity and etiquette, he'd have nothing to thank Basq for.

Basq fixed his gaze on his work alcove and headed straight for it. His apprentices stepped around him without a word. Praise and greetings to his Beholden would be handed out once Jene's report had shown him what they had earned.

Let it be seen I run my team properly. No one in this atmosphere will be led to inappropriate ideas or manners. Let it be seen that if Jahidh had not been removed from our care, he would have never even thought of defecting.

Pointless fear, Basq scolded himself. *Why can I not let it go? If anyone had any thought that his actions reflected on me, on us, I would not have been assigned to the committee.*

Without needing to be asked, Caril retrieved two extra chairs from the main room. Winema did not sit down immediately. While Basq pressed the contract holosheets into the fiber-filled walls, Winema opened her bag. She took out two cubical system taps and typed in their activation codes. Caril stepped around her to raise the privacy walls. Grey-white optical matter spread out from the walls, building on itself until it fenced in the entire work area.

Winema affixed the first tap to the arm of Basq's terminal chair. When her hand released it, the red warning light blinked on. If the tap were moved or if its dataflow was disturbed without the proper signals being given, Winema would see a warning on her camera set. So would all the other active Witnesses. She hung the second tap between the contracts.

Visible taps on his terminal, of course, were no guarantee that Winema had not ordered invisible ones to be placed on his Beholden's terminals. It was well within the bounds of her contract to order the entire area to be placed under a continuous data scan.

Winema took her seat next to Caril, and Basq settled himself in the terminal chair. He swung the keypads into place. Although he had meant what he had said to Caril when he greeted her, part of him knew that home for him was really in front of his terminal. This was where he had made the discoveries about Eric Born that led directly to the location of the Home Ground.

Basq's terminal was not the standard type, like the ones his students and Beholden used. Those were designed with processing layers of generalized organic chains between the silicates. The means for making organic/inorganic chips was another of the private technologies. The integration of organics ensured that no outside machine could tap into the Vitae private network because it would be unable to decode the chemical signals that diffused them. The organics in Basq's terminal took the technology a step further. They had been designed from maps of his cerebral cortex and cloned from his own cell structure. Basq's terminal could be used to assemble information in a way that matched the way Basq thought. It was, in many ways, his learning and skill directly enhanced by the speed and precision of a machine.

Basq settled his hands into position on the slip-keys that covered his control pads. There were those who used vocal interfaces, giving orders to their terminals and receiving answers as if they were dealing with apprentices or Beholden. Basq had never liked that. He liked to shuffle and manipulate tangible results. It gave him a better feel for his work.

It only took a moment to slip the keys into new positions so that the board was reconfigured to lock the posted contracts into the main dataflow. Now, the sheets could be read through the network by anyone who needed to verify Basq's authority, but their contents could not be changed without a direct signal from either Avir or Kelat.

The next thing to be done was to call up Jene's report of the current resources and status of the terminals in the main room. Basq slid his keys into the proper positions. The main display space showed him a tidy series of graphs indicating available storage space as well as a chart of the channels that had been opened or reserved.

As it stood, he could instantly contact the persons of Ivale or Uary, or read through the information in their datastores. He also had an open line to the main datastore of the Hundredth Core and one of the ISAs, Paral, wasn't it? Basq squinted at the ID code under the chart; Paral had thought to draw up contracts for time on the lines between the *Grand Errand* and each of the ships in the encampment, just in case they were required. Basq made a mental note to give the ISA his warmest personal greeting.

All the resources he might need were available and all of them ready for his orders. Basq felt a bit dizzy. He was used to juggling budgets and time and angling for the attention of various Subcontractors and supervisors. Those concerns were wiped away. Now he advised the Reclamation Assembly and the information he required to serve them would be delivered whenever he asked for it.

Basq poised his hands over the keys and considered his assignment. An analysis of the level of danger that the human-derived artifacts presented to the Reclamation efforts. How to even begin to answer such a question? Then he remembered his secondary assignment. Assess the level of danger represented by the missing artifacts. It was dangerous to theorize from a sample of one, but if specifics known about Eric Born could be supplemented by the generalities known about the human-derived artifacts populating the Home Ground, then some useful conclusions might be drawn. The new revelations regarding Eric Born's abilities added an extra dimension to the calculations. If Born could manipulate physical objects more massive than streams of photons or quanta, then he might . . . He might . . . Basq felt his heart contract.

He might even be able to tap into the private network.

Basq's hands leapt into motion and the terminal responded immediately. It snatched up his report on the escape from Haron Station and all the conclusions that had been drawn. Basq barely noticed that most of those conclusions bore Uary's stamp. He slid the keys back and forth with deft, determined strokes. The new findings had to be shuffled into the existing files on Eric Born. All observations had to be reinterpreted and a new pattern established that could provide an answer to the new questions. Could Eric Born tap the Vitae network? And, just as important, if he had that ability, would he realize it?

The implications were vast. Assuming that Eric Born was not the only artifact of his kind and he did have the ability to tap the network, the other artifacts did too. Were there range limitations? What would the duration of the tap be? Was there a significant energy expenditure? Answers to all those questions would be needed to prepare for a direct encounter during the Reclamation. No totally accurate information would be available at this point, since no empirical tests had been carried out, but with the terminal he could at least provide a reasoned estimate. Basq had employed all the usual observation practices from the beginning. He had made sure that Eric Born was, at random intervals, given assignments that could be recorded for analysis. When those observations had yielded evidence that Born had not evolved naturally, Basq had watched him even more closely. The majority of Born's assignments had required him to work on space stations or other networks the Vitae Ambassadors had direct access to.

Basq watched grimly as the results of his work unfolded for him. The display space divided itself into three separate areas. One ran direct recordings of Eric Born's observed activities, one showed stylized representations of the results of those activities, whether or not direct visual data were available, and one showed single-phase graphic enhancement of the multiphase information.

There had been less truly useful information in datastores than Basq had hoped for. Eric Born was cautious. He would only use his abilities after all other avenues had been explored. Of those instances when extramechanical intervention had been required, it appeared he did not use it simply to snatch his prize out of its storage space. Instead, he used it on a secondary or tertiary system where he could acquire the information, like a code sequence or secured ID, that he needed to reach the main objective.

The pattern of his procedure was actually quite simple and sensible. Basq supposed the artifacts were endowed with little or no imagination. Eric Born would get as close as possible to his target, which made the conclusion that he was using a finite physical resource to operate his abilities probable. Basq set a priority marker on that conclusion. If he was within half a kilometer of his target, Born would use only one terminal to achieve his goal. Over greater distances, he would use a leap-frogging approach. He would exert his abilities over a terminal that had the mechanical ability to access the more distant datastore or network that held his goal. His observed range using this method could be measured in thousands of kilometers.

Can he be traced? Basq slipped his keys into new configurations, searching the data for the means to track the artifact's invasions. If he could be traced, Eric Born could be returned to the Vitae. Basq could see that his recovery was set in motion right now.

The terminal dredged up an answer after a search time measured in long, slow seconds. Eric Born's invasions were traceable, not because of what showed up when he manipulated a system, but because of what did not. The system hardware would perform the requested function as if all appropriate codes or signals had been given, but no record would be left of which codes, which signals, or, indeed, which authorized person had initiated the function. Blank spots in the usage records could label a clandestine request made by Eric Born, or any other artifact that shared his abilities. Basq marked that conclusion as well.

The fact the artifacts could be traced damped down some of Basq's apprehensions allowing him to enter the next question.

Can Eric Born tap into the private network?

The displayed data froze while the terminal worked the question over. Seconds ticked by, measured by Basq's shallow breathing. The display space finally cleared the frozen images and in their place left a probability graph based on all the information from six years' worth of observation and speculation. Basq's hands curled into fists. Eric Born could do it. If he could locate a single terminal that had a physical access to the private network, he could do it easily. There were thousands of such terminals on space stations and planets where the Vitae worked. They were guarded and wired and tapped, of course, but those were all measures against ordinary threats. Their ultimate protection had always lain in a technology that was not compatible with any other system in the Quarter Galaxy. Against Eric Born, and by extension the other artifacts, that precaution was less than useless.

Which was unsettling, but not completely disastrous, because their invasions could be traced. Specific protections could be set in place.

Basq's mind raced. Eric Born and Stone in the Wall had to be located immediately. If they returned to the Home Ground to alert the other artifacts, they could become the Aunorante Sangh again and the Reclamation would become a war. Basq gathered his raw conclusions together and opened the line to Ambassador Ivale. This could not wait. The terminal would assemble his conclusions into a report and transmit it to Ivale while Basq continued to work.

Basq sighed inwardly. The easy work was done and the obvious conclusions drawn. Now came the test. Could he, from the available information, infer what patterns of resistance, if any, would be displayed by the artifacts remaining on the Home Ground? There was a wealth of carefully collected satellite data available, but the Historical committees had encountered difficulties interpreting it. There was no guarantee that he could successfully integrate Eric Born's observed behavior into that greater, less well understood picture. . . .

Basq leaned forward and set to work.

Caril watched Basq hunch over the boards again. He was going to need a muscle relaxant before he slept, or his shoulders would be aching in the morning. She filed the thought away in the part of her memory that kept her household lists. She flicked her gaze toward the Witness. Winema had her camera eye trained on Basq, but her unaugmented eye took in the entire room, including Caril.

Keeping her face impassive, Caril rose and stepped through the privacy barrier. She moved carefully between the Beholden's work stations. Since she did not stop to give any of them instructions, none of them gave her a glance. She looked back at the feverish, ordered activity that she had organized and allowed herself an inner smile. There was not one flaw here, not one thing out of place or left undone. It would run smoothly without her supervision for hours.

Caril left her home and crossed the park. The choreographers ignored her as she passed them, preferring to continue their argument about balance and light and shadow than to politely acknowledge another resident of the deck. The Imperialist treatise still glowed in green on the wall. She didn't read it. She knew quite well what it said.

The corner of the park farthest from her door held a single user terminal. She sat in front of it and ran her hands across the board, shuffling the keypads into the position she wanted. According to public law, these terminals were unmonitored and couldn't be traced, so you could say anything here, place any text or recording you wanted to in them. In truth, Caril knew, they were almost as tightly secured as Basq's terminal was.

There were, however, ways to confuse the system. First

she composed a message to the market vendors to order dinner for the Beholden and the family. Her own terminal had been co-opted by Basq's team, so for now all the household work would have to be done from the public lines. Apart from the list, she recorded the other news briefly. Jahidh needed to know what had happened so he could plan his next move.

Then Caril arranged the keys into their new patterns with an ease that came from long practice. She waited a few heartbeats and arranged them again. Her news would flit through every park aboard the *Grand Errand*, bouncing back and forth for hours in the crowded lines before it finally hit a transmission point where it could be released from the internal lines and start on its real journey.

Let Basq strive for the honor of remaining a servant to the Quarter Galaxy. She would not make that her work. Once she had thought he understood the need for the Vitae to cut themselves loose from the overwhelming caution that had been instilled in them when the Ancestors had begun the flight, but he had been blinded by his promotions and paralyzed by responsibilities until there was almost nothing left of the person she had tied her life to.

Let him glory in his service to a Reclamation Assembly that spoke of standing side by side with civilizations of babies and monsters. She would not hear them. The Rhudolant Vitae were the First Born and the First Blood of all the humans, the head of the Family, not just another member to be tricked and controlled by the Unifiers. Jahidh had found the proof and he would soon bring home the power to make the Assembly recant.

But there was not now much time. The artifacts were lost and even the Assembly was taking that loss seriously.

She leaned back in her chair and, using a key-slip she'd learned from Kelat, Caril sent both transmissions simultaneously.

Caril tried to relax the cold, hard knot that was forming inside her. She'd heard one too many stories in Chapel about the duplicity of the Aunorante Sangh. She would have died before she admitted she was afraid of what it meant to have not one, but two of them free in the Quarter Galaxy, but she could not make that fear leave her. Uary's decision to let them get completely away was rash in the extreme, but it might turn out to be the best delaying tactic they had. If their people could move faster than Basq, the artifacts might be recovered and stored for safe study.

It wasn't likely, but she could hope. Caril tried not to listen to Kelat's fretting that the Imperialists did not have the structures they needed to coordinate their activities. Kelat had spent too many years buried in contracts, she told herself.

Caril rose. She had learned to live with so much, she would learn to live with this new anxiety.

After all, now that the Assembly had found the Home Ground for themselves, there could not be that much longer to wait for the Reclamation.

Or, at the very least, the resolution.

4—Amaiar Division, Kethran Colony, Hour 09:20:34, City Time.

The survival of a single being is achieved by balance of forces, the same way a planet achieves a stable orbit around a sun, and although the system may be stable for a million years and more, gravity and motion are constantly tugging, straining, pushing, and pulling. If the balance breaks, one side or the other is in danger.

Sometimes it is the sun, rather than the planet.

Ytay Lyn from "Philosophies"

ϒUL Gan Perivar leaned his chair back too fast. The back whacked against the edge of the work counter, jarring his neck and shoulders painfully.

One more year and I can afford to rent some real space. Perivar twisted the chair and checked behind him to make sure that he would not hit any of the beveled, steel poles that broke up what little open space existed between the map table and the counters. *One more year. Two at the most.*

He leaned back, more carefully this time, and stared at the counter. The silver-and-blue keypads were laced with shadows from the webwork of cables strung across the ceiling. *If nothing else unexpected happens between now and then.*

A rattle sounded over Perivar's head and the shadows shook. A silicate capsule about the size of his torso shot through a portal from the next room. Its hooks swung it from cable to cable toward the post beside his right ear.

Marvelous. When Kiv sent his kids to speak for him, it was always serious.

When the capsule's occupant was stretched out, she was three times as long as the transport she used. She tucked eight pairs of her legs underneath her and used the remaining pair to manipulate the capsule's controls. Her primary hands rested on the bumpy controls for the information terminal, while her secondaries folded in the polite greeting. Two of her eyes extended down toward her primary hands. The other two focused on her goal.

Perivar squinted at the pattern of grey blotches on her smooth golden scales. This was Sha, the third-named of Kiv's litter.

Didn't even send his first-named. Gods, gods, gods, he is mad.

Sha used the post to lower the capsule until she was eye level with him. She extended her snout and pursed her lipless mouth. The protective capsule shut in the actual buzzing sound of her voice, but its intercom carried the signal to activate Perivar's translation disk and transmit her message.

"My parent requests information regarding the progress of the routing for packet 73–1511."

Perivar took a deep breath. "Sha, tell your parent . . ." He let the sentence die. "Tell your parent I'm coming in."

Sha's snout retracted, fast. Perivar had come to equate the action with a human gulp. Without another word, Sha reversed her course, sending the capsule back across the cables and through the portal.

Anticipating trouble, little one? Perivar got to his feet. *Me too.*

The workroom had three doors. One led to the hallway. One hung open to display his comfortably disreputable living rooms. The third was a sliding metal partition in the same wall as the capsule's portal. Next to the partition stood a rack containing an oxygen pack. Perivar checked the tank reading to make sure it was full before he hooked its straps over his shoulders. Fumbling a little with the catches, he fitted the shield over his eyes and mouth.

Shrugging his shoulders to settle the tank more comfortably, Perivar slid back the partition to expose the gelatinous membrane that separated Kiv's half of their quarters from his. The membrane had cost more than all the rest of his equipment combined, but it was worth it. Working with Kiv meant contracts from other Shessel and the Shessel had a lot of work that needed doing.

As usual, Perivar paused before the membrane, hoping that one day he'd get used to going through it.

After four years it was starting to seem unlikely.

Perivar stepped through the membrane. The gooey gel pressed against his skin, clothes, and mask and stuck, sealing him inside a flexible envelope that would screen out the ultraviolet rays Kiv and his children basked under. When Kiv stepped through into Perivar's space, the gel kept in his body heat so he wouldn't drop into a stupor in Perivar's arctic climate, or drown in the flood of his oxygen. It was a good method, but not very sturdy, which was why the children used the unbreakable capsules.

Kiv was a bulky, earth-toned match for his five daughters. Uncoiled and standing straight on all his legs, he was so tall his eyes were level with the crown of Perivar's head. A skintight, vermilion garment encased him from his neck to his last set of toes. He'd started wearing the thing as soon as the last of his children were hatched and he made the shift from female to male. Kiv had never been able to explain properly whether being required to wear clothes indoors was a mark of advancement or decline in the Shessel's social order.

At the moment, Kiv was half-coiled around the base of his map table. Like Perivar's it provided information about the space between the stars, but it did so in a series of lumps and indentations that shifted under Kiv's primary and secondary hands. Only one of the other children was in evidence. Ere draped herself across her parent's shoulders and stretched her arms so that her primary hands covered his and moved with them. Kiv buzzed and whistled at his first-named daughter, teaching her to read and understand the map in front of them.

Perivar glanced at the cables overhead. Sha must have taken the capsule straight into Kiv's living rooms to hide with her other three sisters.

"Sha delivered your insult, Kiv," Perivar said. "I heard it and I understood it. Now you understand this. I owe Eric Born more than one favor."

"He's contraband." Kiv did not point his snout toward Perivar, or stop reading the table. "And he is running yet more contraband."

"He swears she's a volunteer." *Gods, I hope she's a volunteer.*

Kiv's hands froze. "What could you possibly owe . . ."

"A contraband runner for?" Ere finished for her parent. She wasn't being rude, she was showing how well she knew Kiv.

"He's not a runner," Perivar insisted. "And you don't want to know what I owe him for."

Kiv buzzed so softly, Perivar's translator couldn't pick it up. Ere shook herself loose from Kiv's shoulders and scurried down his back. Kiv tilted his head and waited until she'd scrambled through the door to their living area before he turned ears and eyes toward Perivar. All his hands left the map board and pressed themselves tight to his long sides. At the same time, he drew himself out so his eyes were level with Perivar's. The fluid motion took Kiv less time than it would have taken Perivar to bend his knees to sit down.

"I understand what you say. Now you understand, Perivar, this worries me. I cannot become involved in activities the human population of Kethran consider illegal. The Embassy Voice will speak against me. I will lose my license and be sent home."

Perivar sighed and his breath made a white mist on his face mask. "Eric says the circumstances are exceptional and that it will only be this once."

Kiv dipped his snout. "I know you think that I'm better off not knowing this, but what did he do to earn such trust?"

No, Kiv, you really don't want to know that. Really. "Helped me . . . break from my old partners. Then he kept his mouth shut and himself absent for six years." The last, at least, was the whole truth.

The short hum Kiv gave out did not translate. He drew back on himself, shrinking and retracting his whole body. Perivar knew enough about his partner's body language to know Kiv meant to make Perivar uncomfortable so he could understand Kiv's discomfort. It worked amazingly well. Perivar's skin began to curdle under the gel. "If trouble comes from this, Kiv, I swear it won't touch your children."

"And how under any sun do you expect to keep such a promise, Perivar?" Despite his harsh words, Kiv stretched his arms and laid all his hands on the edge of the map table. The coil of his body loosened near the base. In response, the tension in Perivar's skin eased.

"How do you intend to proceed?" Kiv asked.

"I'll give Zur-Iyal a call and see if she's willing to run a gene sample for me without going through channels. I'll see the results of that and then I'll know where it's safe to send this . . . person Eric's bringing in. After that, I'll have to see. Her people are from the same Evolution Point as mine, Eric said, so there should be plenty of places I could send her as long as the sequence is reasonably clean." The tank dragged at his shoulders, but Perivar didn't make a move to sit down. Unless Kiv offered him a chair, which would really be a piece of floor or counter, it was rude. Usually, they skipped formalities like that, but right now, Perivar felt the need to prove he could still observe proprieties.

"And when is . . . Eric arriving?"

"He just called me from the ground port. He should be here in another two and a half hours, if they have to catch the public line, two hours if they can find a chauffeur."

Kiv unwound himself from around the map table and stood on all his legs. "I will have to go explain this to my children. We are here, after all, to learn what your people will or will not do." Although his attention remained fixed on Perivar, his eyes sank deep into their sockets. "It has not been easy, Perivar."

"I know."

"It has been good, though, and I want myself and my own to be able to stay."

"I'll make sure it's over soon."

Kiv inclined his head, a gesture he'd learned from Perivar. He swiveled himself around and flowed through his back door.

Breathing another sigh, this time from relief, Perivar retreated into his own side of the workplace. As he stepped through the membrane, the gel slid off his skin, melding with its own substance again.

"Brain." He said aloud as he lifted his face mask.

"Receiving." He and Kiv had not been able to afford their own artificial intelligence, never mind an android, but they did rent time on the AI that operated their building's facilities.

"Get a real-time line open to Zur-Iyal *ki* Maliad at Amaiar Industrial Gardens, personal code A comma nine comma Yul Gan. Then, cross-load the active routing files on packet 73–1511 over to Kiv's map files and compare with the facilities timings and route the data back." He undid the tank catches and gratefully set it back in its rack. "And call the Roseran's bakery and reactivate my account and tell them to send down half a dozen fresh seed cakes to the kids." Another propriety. Where Kiv came from, you did not thank a father directly, you did a favor for his children.

"I have set your priority coding. Request one will be completed in five minutes. Requests two and three will be completed in three minutes. Request four will be completed in fifteen minutes."

"Nothing further." Perivar dropped into his chair and dug the heels of his hands into his eyes. The face mask was supposed to filter the light down to Perivar's comfort level, but any stay in Kiv's quarters still dried his eyes out painfully.

Eric, don't you try to play any fancy games with me, or I'll broadcast what you did to Kessa and Tasa Ad from one side of the Quarter Galaxy to the other.

Six years of relatively clean living; Perivar stared around his workplace. Thousands of packets of information delivered successfully and this was what he had. One room of hardware and two rooms of furniture. He didn't even own the walls around them. He was alive, which was definitely a plus, and if he hadn't stuck by Eric Born, he would not have been. Perivar knew that. When living on the edge had finally become too much, Eric had taken the ship, the pilot, and the ghosts. Perivar had taken the bank accounts, and that had actually seemed to be the end of it. Most of the time he kept the past in its own place and lived for the next shipment and the next deposit in his account. His open, honest, registered, and almost always empty account.

Brain beeped twice to get his attention.

"Open channel established and connected to Zur-Iyal *ki* Maliad."

Perivar straightened up to face the blank display that Brain angled up from the work surface in front of him. His fingers undid the catch on the bottom edge and he lifted the cover from the keypad. His memory strained to recall the watch command. His lips moved as he typed it in. The signal light on the edge of the pad blinked on. Green. No one was watching the line, at the moment. Perivar kept one eye on the signal light and touched the key to clear the view.

Zur-Iyal *ki* Maliad looked back at him with gold eyes half-hidden under a ragged curtain of straight black hair. The color of both was new.

"I like the look, Iyal." Perivar ran his hand through his own hair to comb it back. "Dyes or upgrades?"

"Upgrade on the hair. Stays dry in the rain. The eyes are overlays. UV screens. I'm seeing if I like them or not."

"Handy when you're out in the field so much, I guess." Iyal spent most of her time with the institute's livestock, and it showed. She was a big, round woman. A casual observer might have mistaken her bulk for fat, but only until she moved. As she leaned across the table and folded her arms, muscles rippled visibly beneath her sun-browned skin.

"What can I do for you, Perivar? Or is this social?" The UV screens did not hide the mischievous glint in her eyes.

Perivar chuckled. "Iyal, Iyal, what would your husband say?"

" 'Is he still any good?' " They shared the long laugh. It was an old joke, but it felt good.

"Actually, I need a favor, Iyal."

"Oh?"

"I need a gene scan run. Nothing fancy. Just make sure the specimen's clean and healthy. You know the kind of thing."

"Oh yes. I do know." She drew back abruptly and Perivar thought of Kiv doing the same thing, not five minutes ago. "I didn't think I was doing that 'kind of thing' for you anymore."

"It's a one-off, Iyal. I'm tying down a loose favor."

Iyal's sigh ruffled her new hair across her forehead. "Once, Perivar. That's all the old times are good for right now. We just got a whole shipment of kids from the Vitae's university. If I don't keep myself clean, one of them's going to be earning my pay."

"Once." Perivar laid two fingers over his heart. "The promise goes from here to the gods."

Iyal just watched him. "The Rhudolant Vitae are making sure everybody comes down real hard on . . . the competition . . . these days. I hope you're still in shape."

"Wouldn't be doing this if I wasn't. Check your hard mail bin tonight, Iyal. I'll have the sample in it."

"Good enough. Take care, Perivar."

"And you, Iyal."

She watched him thoughtfully for a minute longer before her hand reached out to her control panel and his screen went blank. Because he didn't request another line, the display lowered itself until it was flush with the counter again.

So, I lied, he said silently to the space where the display used to be. *I wouldn't be doing this if I was sure Eric would keep his mouth shut about me if I didn't.*

Gods, gods, gods. I'd forgotten about this. Don't trust anybody. Can't trust anybody. Everybody's dangling something over you, unless you've got something to dangle over them, and even then it's who's got more and what's worse. Abruptly, he found himself laughing. *I'm getting old. And cowardly.*

It wasn't a general warning that Iyal had brought up about the Vitae, although they were the main reason her job was in danger. Thanks to the talent-mongering Vitae, Amaiar Gardens was one of the few independent gene-tailoring houses left on Kethran.

Kethran was an artificial ecology. A hundred thousand details of the environmental balance had to be constantly monitored, maintained, and replenished. A population surge coupled with an unexplained drought had the Senate screaming for help. The Vitae had quietly offered to take over the administration of the ecology for a comparatively reasonable trade and land contract. They'd moved the majority of the government employees into labs and farms they themselves subsidized, and in three years they had made themselves indispensable.

With that kind of power, they could make more than a few demands without the official power base getting upset. They could, for example, ask for rigid enforcement of some of the legal codes.

Never mind that the Vitae were the largest purchasers and purveyors of contraband bodies in the Quarter Galaxy. It was only one of the areas where they had a low tolerance for competition.

Perivar had sometimes wondered what the Vitae were looking for. They had the most sophisticated gene-engineering methods in the Quarter Galaxy, and yet they bought body after body. It was a clumsy, risky, expensive way of acquiring new genetic patterns. Tasa Ad and Kessa, the heads of the runner team Perivar had been part of, had survived by selling their . . . acquisitions . . . exclusively to the Vitae, or the Vitae's clients.

Perivar remembered the cargo hold on the runner's ship then. Double racks of anesthetized bodies in support capsules. No sound, except for the weird harmony that came from so many support systems droning on together.

What do you think I am? asked Eric's voice from memory.
I think . . . I think I didn't think.

"Perivar?" Kiv's hail sounded through his translator disk.

"Here." Perivar straightened up. "Open up. It's all right."

The membrane housing slid back. Perivar looked through the threshold to see the slightly wobbly scene of Kiv and his family. All five of the kids were in evidence, swarming up and down the poles, working on the control pads, delving under the map table. Kiv held all his eyes and hands open.

"We need to . . ." began Kiv.

"Go over the . . ." Dene scuttled out from under the map table and vanished under the communications counter.

"Shipment of packet 73–1511." Ere took her place of pride on her parent's shoulders, hands out and ready to work.

"Now!" added Ka, as she slithered halfway up her parent's back. Ka hated to be left out.

Perivar nodded, understanding what he saw as a mark of trust. Kiv had nothing precious hidden. Nothing more needed to be said. Perivar leaned over his map table and touched the slave key to synch the two tables together. Ri slid into the capsule and shot across the cables to dangle above him as his map lit up.

The map showed a representation of one-tenth of the Quarter Galaxy from a communicator's point of view. Suns shone as pinpricks of gold; inhabited stations were green and drone stations were blue. The chaos of the communications networks stretched between them as a series of glowing white line segments. Solid lines showed the beam connections. Dotted lines showed the places only a ship could reach. A red grid overlay the entire arrangement, measuring everything out in hundred-light-year squares.

The network had no organization. It was several million shifting threads, made up of everything from cavernous, public databases, to hard-wired private lines, to rented AIs like Brain.

Perivar accessed packet 73–1511's shipment plan. The map displayed the work in progress by turning a series of the white lines orange.

Calling what they were organizing a "packet" was a convenient shorthand. 73–1511 was actually a data transfer from a research station to a third stage colony. A library's worth of specialized manufacturing information needed to be copied across ten thousand light-years' worth of network. It was a complicated process, especially since "simultaneous transmission" was a meaningless concept across the distances the map represented. Even quantum transfers took time. Without careful planning, the channels, even if they were reserved with solid credit, shifted and blurred. The pathway, and all the information, could be lost in a heartbeat.

That much-disliked fact gave Perivar and Kiv their living. They found clients who needed a specific kind of information, found a source for that information, and then, most importantly, found a way to get the information from the source to the client. Each shipment took hours of planning and sometimes more insurance than their combined accounts could afford.

"The K-12 band is going to be open for a station to groundside datadump. That'll take us from Averand to Cole's Spot." Perivar traced a new path on the map table with his finger. The sensors on the surface responded by marking a new orange line on the display.

"Could we piggyback in on a Vitae download from there to Haron?" Kiv dotted in another segment.

"What're they charging?" Ri whistled from the capsule.

"For pickup and delivery through there?" Ere got in belatedly.

Perivar considered the idea. "We can get the rates off Brain. Save that as plan B, though; I don't want to have to depend on the Vitae right now."

"Whee." Kiv's whistle did not translate so the disk simply transmitted the syllable. "That is a thought."

Brain's chime sounded over their heads. "Sar Eric Born and Sar Arla Stone are waiting in the lobby."

Perivar glanced across at Kiv. "Brain. Open the doors and let them up."

"Do you want us to close the housing?" asked Kiv, his secondary hands reaching toward the membrane.

"Only if you want to."

Kiv's whole body rippled. "I think we would rather see what is coming. Ri, come back here."

Perivar caught the heightened pitch and speed of the whistle under the translator's flat voice. Ri obeyed without comment.

As soon as the capsule was safely on Kiv's side, Perivar got to his feet and swung the door to the outer hallway open. Leaving a door closed when a guest was on the way was an insult where Perivar came from, and Eric knew that. Perivar blinked a bit in the hallway light, which was supposed to simulate a sunny day. The lift door opened. Perivar watched as Eric and his . . . companion stepped off.

She looked a lot like Eric had when Perivar first saw him, handmade clothes, hair hidden under a twist of cloth, and hands covered with tattoos, except that hers were stark white lines, as opposed to Eric's colorful swirls. She shared Eric's warm skin tones and black eyes. For a brief moment, Perivar wondered if they were related.

"Thanks for the open door, Perivar." Eric, Perivar knew, expended his small stock of Eshini words on the greeting.

"Your accent is going." Perivar stood back to let them inside.

The woman, Arla Stone, hesitated, until Eric said something in their own language to her. Perivar tapped his translator reflexively. At one time, he'd had Eric help him set it for the Realm's jaw-breaking language. Since they had parted ways, though, Perivar hadn't needed that particular information and the disk's assembly time was going slow.

The woman walked across the threshold, blinked at the lighting change, got a look at Kiv and the kids, and froze.

The translator finally had the file reconfigured and Perivar heard Eric mutter, "I warned you."

So she's straight out of the woods. Wonderful. Perivar strangled a fresh sigh.

Kiv responded to her stare by uncoiling himself until his scalp brushed the ceiling so she could get a really good look. Sha, Ka, and Dene scrambled up on their parent's back, whistling and draping themselves across his shoulders and his lower arms. They wanted to be looked at, too. The other two kept themselves still. Having been raised with humans, all the kids could read the difference between a stare of wonder and a stare of fear. The motionless two chose to acknowledge that difference.

"I wish well-come to you and yours Eric Born and Arla Stone," announced Kiv politely, although Perivar figured he must have been getting the hint by now. Kiv could be willfully dense some days.

"Thank you," Arla croaked. She stepped back and seemed to try to collect herself.

"She says thanks," Perivar told Kiv as the Shessel touched his translator set in his lowest ear and cocked his head.

"Obscure language." Arla wore a translator disk in her ear, so she could understand Kiv, but since she didn't speak any of the languages Kiv's disk was set for, all he could hear from her was gibberish.

"Ah," Kiv shrank back to his normal stance, depositing children on assorted flat surfaces.

Perivar turned to Eric. "We need to talk for a minute." He jerked his chin toward his living rooms.

"I assumed we would. Arla." The sound of her name finally got the woman to tear her gaze away from Kiv. "I'll be in the next room. If you . . ."

"I'll be all right." Her voice held steady but Perivar caught the slight trembling in her hands before she clenched them into fists and pressed them against her side.

Eric opened his mouth to say something but obviously changed his mind. Jaw firmly shut, he brushed past Arla and headed for Perivar's rooms. Perivar's glance wavered between the pair of them for a moment before he followed Eric.

The living rooms were as crowded as the workroom. The chairs and tables were all padded blocks of no style or period. They were functional and sturdy and that was all. The one luxury was the windows. Two walls worth of transparent polymer let the sunlight in, even if the view of the warehouse cluster was less than inspirational.

Perivar slid the door shut and faced Eric.

Gods, he's changed. Wouldn't know him from anybody on the colony.

"When'd the Vitae get hold of this place?" The worried note in Eric's voice shocked Perivar.

"Three, maybe four local years ago. We're a late acquisition. What's the problem?"

"I wish I'd known," Eric said wearily.

Silence fell, thick and heavy.

"We're not on the network anymore, Eric," Perivar said, at last. "Nobody's listening. I need an explanation for this, now."

Eric's shoulders stooped even farther than usual. "I'm in trouble, Perivar. That's the explanation. The Vitae tried to stash me in Haron Station, which is where they had Arla."

Perivar felt the blood begin to drain from his face. "What in the name of all the gods would they do that for?"

"As soon as I know, you'll know." Eric's fingers hooked around each other. "They're after something in the Realm of the Nameless Powers. I'll be drowned and washed away if I know what it is. I thought it was my"—he stared at his bare palm—"power gift, but she . . . Arla"—his hand swept down toward the door—"isn't gifted. The Vitae picked her up out of the Realm and reeled me in to help deal with her.

"I'm on the run again, Perivar." Eric looked up again and the expression in his eyes made Perivar's throat tighten. "I'm going to try to find out what the Vitae want from the Realm, and from me, and from Arla, for that matter, and then I'm going to try to find a way out of it, whatever it is."

Perivar knew the tone he used. He would do as he said, even if it killed him.

Perivar wanted to shout. *This is not two runners nobody liked and a quick bit of mutiny. This is the Vitae! Remember them? The ones who control half the Quarter Galaxy! The ones we spent two years ducking AFTER we got away from Tasa Ad!* But saying it aloud wouldn't have budged Eric any farther than the silent thought did.

"This is all making my partner very uneasy, Eric," Perivar told him instead. "The Shessel don't really understand the spirit of human legalities, so they follow them by the letter."

"So now I owe you," Eric muttered.

"That's not what I care about." *Although it would've been once*, Perivar realized with a shock. "Just finish it fast. I've gotten used to not having to look over my shoulder all the time. I like it this way."

"Maybe one day I'll get to see if I like it too." Eric kissed the tips of his own fingers and raised his hand to the ceiling.

Perivar laid his fingers over his heart. "I hope we both live that long."

They met each other's eyes for a silent moment, weighing, judging, and hoping, but finding no guarantees. Finally, Perivar knew he had nothing to fall back on but their old, brittle trust. It was no comfort to know Eric was doing the same.

"What are you going to do now?" Perivar asked.

Eric looked over Perivar's left shoulder. "Ultimately, I'm going to try to crack the Vitae private network."

"Are you out of your mind!" Perivar couldn't hold back this time. "You might as well try to crack a mountain with your skull! Even you can't get on a Vitae line!"

"Where else am I going to get what I need?" Eric's calm snapped. "Knowledge is power. Somebody"—he stabbed a finger at Perivar—"told me never to forget that."

"I also said there's always somebody out there who knows more than you do," Perivar reminded him.

Eric's eyes shone coldly. "If that wasn't true, there wouldn't be contraband runners. Are we done quoting your words of wisdom now, Perivar?"

You started it, thought Perivar childishly. He forced his voice into a semi-even tone. "Do you have any kind of plan for this insanity?"

"Not really." He shrugged. "After this, I'm going to talk to Dorias. Between the two of us we should be able to string together something."

"If anyone can," Perivar added for him. Eric wasn't looking at him anymore and Perivar couldn't help wondering why not.

"As you say." Eric shrugged. "What else can I do, Perivar? If I don't put an end to this, then I'm a fugitive until I become a corpse or a slave."

Perivar said nothing for a long moment.

"There's nothing else I can tell you," Eric said.

"What about something about your . . . friend?"

"She's no friend of mine." Eric's eyes seemed to see something other than Perivar's face at that moment. "Although, Notouch or not, I could maybe wish she was . . . she's all right, Perivar. She's stubborn and she's got some secret she's keeping to herself, but she learns fast and she seems as determined to stay out of the Realm as I am."

"I'll have to take your word on that." *As well as on everything else.*

"I'd give you more if I could."

"I know." Perivar pushed the door open. "And I appreciate it."

In the workroom, Ri and Dene had Arla under close scrutiny. The pair of them had crammed themselves into the capsule that now hung from a post maybe six inches from Arla's nose. The wariness was gone from her face. Instead, her expression shifted from bemused to bewildered as she tried to keep pace with the kids' yes-and-no questions.

"Will you be staying . . ." Ri started.

". . . with us?" finished Dene. Arla shook her head.

"You came from a long way . . ." Dene started.

". . . away? How far?"

Arla nodded and spread her hands, unable to answer completely.

Perivar glanced through the membrane to Kiv. He was saying something soft to Ere where she lay on his shoulders. The remainder of his brood was draped across his back, whistling encouragement as their representatives tried to get information from the stranger. Kiv's legs were retracted, but his arms and eyes were extended. He was relaxed and, Perivar was willing to bet, a little amused.

"The lines on . . ." began Dene, but Ri saw Perivar step into the workroom. She squeezed her sister's mouth shut with her secondary hands while she swung her eyes toward Perivar and Eric.

Arla also turned all her attention toward them.

"I've set things in motion." Perivar felt his glance slide past Arla to Kiv, who did nothing more than swivel an extra eye toward his children in the capsule. Perivar faced Eric. "Are you going to stick around and watch?"

"No," Eric said, and Arla's head snapped around. "I've got to keep moving."

The two of them exchanged a long, uninterpretable look.

"You leave me in your debt." Under the translation, her voice sounded stilted to Perivar, as if this was a new phrase for her.

"Pay me by not giving Perivar any extra problems." Eric turned away from her a little too quickly. "I've got to go. I only authorized a day's worth of dock time for my ship."

Perivar nodded. "I'd rather not ever see you again, Sar Born."

"I know." And he walked out. Arla did not turn around to watch him leave.

The door shut and left them all closed in together. Perivar looked at Arla, who looked back at him in silence.

What do you think I am? asked Eric from memory again. It was his old voice, heavily accented and awkward. Nothing like the smoothly educated tone he'd used today.

Cargo, thought Perivar. *Checked over, labeled as clean and delivered, or too dirty to fix and dumped.*

Certainly not a person who would look at him like Arla was, vaguely expectant, waiting for him to do something.

"Want to sit down?" he gestured to a chair.

Her eyes tracked his hand and a puzzled expression wrinkled her brow. "Thank you ... I don't know how to call you." The translation fell a long way out of synch with her real speech.

"Perivar," he told her. "My partner is Kivererishakadene. Kiv's the name you have to remember there. The rest of it belongs to the children." Perivar nodded to the two in the capsule.

Taking that as some kind of cue, Ri raised the capsule back up to the ceiling cables and rattled back toward their own side.

Kiv stretched himself out toward the membrane. "Have you borne your children yet?"

Perivar shot Kiv a look, uncertain whether he was being really absentminded this time, or if he was trying to pay Arla back for her shocked stare by making her uncomfortable.

She sank onto the edge of the chair Perivar had offered her. "Four living," she said quietly, and Perivar translated it for Kiv.

Kiv's subtle ripples told Perivar he was trying to make the mental readjustment. The only thing more alien to Kiv than a male without children, was a parent who lived away from them. Even though the kids theoretically understood humans' strange ways better, Ri and Sha piled on top of their sisters as soon as they got out of the capsule, as if the idea that a brood and parent could be separated would magically tear them away. Kiv automatically coiled himself around them, buzzing softly.

Perivar turned his back on his partner. "We need to get a blood sample," he said to Arla, "so we can find out what we can do with you."

"Eric told me." She held out her arm without changing her expression.

Yeah. Perivar shook himself. *Now where'd I put . . . No, I threw that all away. Let's see . . .* He pulled open a corner drawer and found a utility knife and a piece of plastic wrapper. He tossed them both in the heater and set it on sterilize.

When he turned back around, she was still holding her arm out, waiting patiently for him to draw blood.

He laid the knife against her fingertip and pressed down. The skin broke and the blood welled scarlet around the blade. Arla didn't even flinch.

Perivar, we just got the answer. The sample's clean. Tell the client. Perivar, sample's no good. We're going to have to dump 'em. Perivar, sample says they'll be able to take it for at least a year down there. Let the client know we're bringing them in.

He wiped her cut off with the wrapping and dropped her hand.

Perivar, I don't think you understand what you're doing . . . You'll do what you're told you damned barbarian or you're dead . . . Try me, Skyman, just try me.

Leave me alone! he shouted to the memory voices.

Perivar taped the wrap closed around the bloody smear.

"Brain. Get a courier cart up here, on the double; I've got a package for Zur-Iyal at the Amaiar Gardens." He and Iyal had never stopped sending each other things; souvenirs or jokes or small presents. One more package wasn't going to generate any more attention, even from the watchful Vitae.

"Priority rating assigned. Request one will be completed in five minutes." The voice from the ceiling startled Arla but not badly. Perivar slid the sample into a wrapper and dropped it into the hard mail bin. Reluctantly, he turned back to Arla.

"There's not much for us to do until we get an answer on this. You can wait in here." He led her into his living rooms.

Perivar picked a few old schedule printouts up off the sofa and said, "Make yourself comfortable," before he walked out into the workroom again. He closed the door behind him.

"All right." He strode back to the map table. "Where were we?"

"Perivar . . ."

Perivar touched two keys to clear a space in the corner of the display for schedule data. "I think I remember seeing that Haron Station will be supporting a six-layer open channel between . . ."

"Stop this."

Startled, Perivar looked up. On the other side of the membrane, Kiv and all five of the kids stared at him, eyes and ears focused entirely in his direction. For the first time in years, that attention made his skin crawl.

Kiv glided up to the membrane. The kids slipped sideways to let their parent by.

"What are you doing, Perivar?"

He curled his hands into fists and leaned all his weight on his knuckles. "Trying to finish up the routing for packet 73–1511. What are you doing?"

Kiv closed and retracted all his eyes. "If I live a thousand lives, I will never understand your people."

"You've said that before."

"This time I mean it." Only two of Kiv's eyes opened and extended. "The packet can wait another few hours, Perivar. You have another responsibility that requires immediate attention." All of his hands waved toward Perivar's closed living rooms.

"She's not my responsibility," Perivar told the tabletop through clenched teeth. "I'm just moving her through."

There was a long pause.

"So, how did you deal with . . . the contraband before this? When they were your responsibility?"

Perivar kept his eyes toward the map, but he saw nothing at all.

"We kept them in life-support capsules in the cargo hold. I actually spoke to maybe two others besides Eric. I told myself what we were doing didn't matter. They're not human, not like me, just gods-blasted-and-damned barbarians . . ." A red haze filled his eyes. "Better off where we take them, or better off dead. Too stupid to understand what really matters . . ."

"Per-efar!"

Perivar's head jerked up. Kiv had shouted his name, the actual syllables, not the conglomeration of whistles and buzzes the translator straightened out.

"Perivar." Kiv slapped his silicate mask over his face and glided through the membrane, leaving the kids huddled in a complex knot behind him. He filled the workroom and had to bend his body to fit between the counters and the map table. Despite that, he got close enough that Perivar could see the gel glisten on his skin. Perivar fought the urge to back away.

"What happened to you?"

Perivar felt his mouth move, but no sound was coming out. He forced his voice to speak.

"There was a revolution in Eshina. I was a communications hack and a spy on the losing side. Eshina law deports revolutionaries by selling them as indentured servants. Tasa Ad bought me up cheap. He and his sister Kessa headed up a runner team. I was . . . bought to work the communications transfers for them."

Kiv's body rippled, sending rainbows glistening down his back where the light hit the membrane gel. "And you made a bond of some sort with Eric."

Perivar nodded. "We'd picked up Eric off his homeworld. Weird place. Crashing old world orbiting a binary star. Tasa Ad had seen him in action on the ground and decided this one we'd keep. Eric's not his real name, I just called him that because I couldn't get a handle on the real thing. It goes on even longer than yours does.

"He really is amazingly useful. He can . . . do things to machines . . . make them move. Make a computer run just by touching it. Tasa Ad used him as a kind of super–systems digger and we were able to expand our . . . activities from just contraband running.

"Eric and I got along. At least, I liked him better than I

liked Tasa Ad and a lot better than I liked Kessa even though that didn't take much. I taught him a real language, showed him how to take care of himself on the ship, told him about things outside. Played big brother a little, you understand? We became friends, almost without me noticing it'd happened. I'm not . . . I wasn't used to having friends.

"Then we got a new job, a weird one. A guy named D'Shane wanted us to steal an artificial intelligence called Dorias out of a planetary network. The money was . . . really good, so Tasa Ad took it on. We used Eric for most of the work, of course. He found the thing and got it loaded into the isolation box we'd built for it and we took off to hand it over to our client.

"We were two days in flight and Eric came into my cabin. He looked sick, shattered. He said 'Perivar, is it true that the people we transport are being taken without permission?'

"I hadn't stopped to think about it until then, but I realized Eric had no idea what was really going on. Tasa Ad kept him on a short tether when it came to network information, and I'd never spelled out anything to him. He was a volunteer and his people either have no concept of . . . involuntary servitude, or, it's so different from what we did that it never occurred to him that we were kidnapping and selling unwilling bodies. I mean, yes, when Tasa Ad and Kessa got them to the ship, they were drugged out and in capsules, but that was exactly how we got him on board.

"And I'd never told him about me.

"So I said something particularly insightful, like 'And?' And he looked at me like he didn't know whether to be sorry for me or kill me on the spot. After a long time he said 'Perivar, I don't think you understand what you're doing. Dorias does not want to go to D'Shane.'

"'Dorias is a machine,' I said. 'It does what it's told.'

"He said 'Dorias is a . . . I don't know the word he used, but the translator turned it into 'Well-Made Soul,' and he said 'I won't hand him across to D'Shane without his consent.' He walked out and I stayed stuck to the spot, cursing myself for an idiot.

"Then, I heard Tasa Ad yelling. I ran toward the sound.

He . . . they . . . Eric . . . I mean . . . Eric, Tasa Ad, and Dorias's box were on the bridge. Eric was at the comm board. I read his fingers. He was opening up a channel to somewhere, probably to a station, or maybe back to where we'd come from. I saw the cable on Dorias's box and I knew Eric was getting ready to hardwire the AI into the open channel so it could get itself free.

"Tasa Ad was, of course, yelling at him to stop, and when he paused for breath, Eric simply said 'No.' And Tasa Ad reared up and said 'You'll do what you're told, you damned barbarian, or you're dead!'

"That got him. Eric whirled around and yelled, 'Try me, Skyman, just try me!'

"Kessa came in at that point. Shoved her way past me, just as Tasa Ad lunged for Eric. She was armed. A dart gun. The cartridge was red. Serious poison.

"Tasa Ad grabbed Eric's arm . . . and . . . collapsed. Kessa screamed something and raised the gun. I screamed something else and shoved her sideways and she pointed the gun at me and fired. Caught me in the arm. And I collapsed. And Eric grabbed her and she collapsed and Eric collapsed with her and there we all were on the deck together. The thing was, Eric and I were alive. Tasa Ad and Kessa, weren't."

Perivar looked up. Kiv had shrunk in on himself as far as he could go. Not a single eye showed. His arms were nearly invisible and the length of his torso rested on the floor.

"What did you do?" Kiv asked, without even opening his eyes.

"We scavenged the datastore for enough trace information to build a couple of line ghosts and steal the runner's side ship, the *U-Kenai*. Then the three of us ran for it. Dorias took off on his own. Eric and I wandered around for a couple of years, stealing for people like D'Shane . . . once, when we got desperate, we even stole people for D'Shane. He'd blackmailed us into it. It was after that we both decided this was no way to live." He paused. "I should have at least lost my arm from Kessa's dart, but I didn't. Eric took care of that, too." A giggle escaped him. "Took him awhile, that's for sure. Said lucky for me he'd already had practice on Skymen, so he got it eventually. He really is amazingly useful."

Kiv extended his arms and legs so slowly it was almost painful to watch. One eyelid at a time peeled reluctantly open.

"Perivar." Kiv leaned across and even through the gel Perivar could smell the spicy scent that surrounded the Shessel when he got upset. "I cannot live with you like this."

"What?" Sheer disbelief ran through him.

Kiv drew his head back and up until he towered over Perivar as far as the room would allow. "My siblings and I were the last of a line of slaves in the peninsula of Si-Tuk. After the Union treaties, I came out here so that there was no chance they'd be able to claim my children if things shredded. This is important. I swore they would never, ever be exposed to the flesh trade. I belong to my children, Perivar. I cannot ignore their welfare. Your past is your own, and I will try not to care about it, but your present is very much my concern.

"End this, Perivar, or I am severing our partnership and closing our business down."

"Kiv," Perivar thought about turning away but couldn't seem to manage the movement. "Nothing like this is going to happen again."

"You don't know that! How can you know that!" Kiv's whistle rose so high that Perivar flinched. "You ran for this Tasa Ad, you ran for yourself, and now you're running for Eric Born! Who next, Perivar?"

Perivar ducked his head. "Would you mind if I shut the door for a while?"

"No." Without another word, Kiv doubled back along his own length and flowed back to his children.

Keeping his eyes on the walls, Perivar slid the membrane housing closed. It clanged sharply against the threshold before the catch snapped shut.

Perivar stalked to the other side of the room. It didn't help any that he knew Kiv was right. He raised his hands to run them through his hair and let them fall to his side again. He circled the room aimlessly, trying to think and then trying not to think, until his sight began to fade again. Finally, he threw himself into his chair and clamped his eyes shut. He stayed that way for a long time.

Brain's signal sounded overhead. "Zur-Iyal *ki* Maliad has opened a channel and labeled the contact urgent."

Perivar groaned. "Send her through, Brain." He keyed the watch command in just as the view screen cleared. At the other end of the line, Iyal's face looked unnaturally white.

"Perivar. Where did you get this sample from?"

Now what kind of question . . . Then Perivar remembered they hadn't used Iyal to go over Eric's blood. "Is there something wrong?"

"Wrong, no. I just want to know where you got your hands on a construct."

"A what?"

"A construct. A genetically engineered life-form. I've only seen DNA this abbreviated in theoretical texts. What did this come from? It must be kept in a damn jar!"

"It," Perivar bit the word off, "is a woman, Iyal. Walking, breathing, and in need of a bath, actually."

Iyal leaned forward. "You trying to get rid of her?"

"Iyal . . ."

"Don't look like that. I'm not talking about for dissection. Damn-o, Perivar, she, whatever she is, is a work of art! If we could incorporate half of what's gone into her . . ."

Perivar shook his head, trying to clear enough room to think in a straight line. "Iyal, I've been to where she comes from. It's a degenerated culture. They're real good at breeding sheep, but engineering a person . . ."

Her mouth worked back and forth silently. "That would mean she's a descendant, and just one of a population; otherwise, this level of mutation never would have bred true, but still, you'd think there'd be more work space . . ."

"Work space?" said Perivar.

Iyal nodded absently, as if most of her attention was focused on another conversation. "A large portion of any DNA string is white noise. It's got no direct impact on the organism. What it's there for is to reduce the risk of harmful mutation. It's Nature's margin for error.

"When we're tailoring genes here, we leave all, or at least

most, of that extra space in, so we can make use of that same margin for error. Whoever designed this woman's ancestors, though, didn't feel they needed a safety net. Which means they were either phenomenally stupid, which I doubt, or so good at what they were doing that they could make even the Vitae look like apprentice pig breeders.

"Perivar, if she's up for grabs, we'll take her here."

"What would the gardens' director have to say to that?" When she didn't answer, Perivar felt his heart freeze up. "Oh gods, Iyal, you didn't."

"Perivar, there are maybe fifty completely engineered people alive in the Quarter Galaxy and none of them, I mean none of them, are this fully realized. Additions and enhancements are one thing. Anybody can throw a switch. Some places can even rewire the system. But this one . . . whoever built her started with some proteins in a sterile dish and went from there. If we knew even half of what went into it, we could give the Vitae a run for their market, and not just on Kethran either.

"And by the way"—her voice and face hardened together—"I'm not crazy about the fact you think I'd just get her in here and run her through a processor."

"Iyal, at this point I don't know what you'd do." *Which just adds another name to that list.* "You're not talking like yourself."

That took her back. "All right, all right." She waved her hands aimlessly. "Yes, I showed my results to Director *ki* Shomat. I thought we had a calibration problem. I thought the chain *could not* be this short.

"He went over the whole thing again. We got the same results five times in a row and I told him . . . well, I told him. He told me to try to get . . . her . . . we were saying 'it' because what the hell did we know . . . here. What's she need to be comfortable?"

Perivar felt his fingers curling up again and forced them to straighten out. "The usual things, Iyal. A place to stay, food, something she can do to keep from getting bored . . . Oh yeah, she needs some language lessons and she doesn't know an input terminal from a hunk of brick."

Iyal scratched her chin. "All right. The necessities we can fix her up with, and we could always use another field assistant that doesn't need reprogramming. We could even pay her. What's the going contract length for contraband where it's legal?"

"Six years, supposedly. But I never saw a contraband really finish a contract. Permanent extensions are more the way it works. They can't exactly protest to the labor authority."

"Six years should do it, and then some. Will you release her to us?"

Perivar sat still for a while, listening to the hum of the utilities and the silence that was coming from behind the membrane housing.

"Perivar, what is with you?"

"Nothing. Plenty. Never mind, Iyal. I've just been hanging around Kiv too long, that's all. Can you give me an hour? There are some things I need to clear up."

"An hour I can give you, but not much more. Cousin Director is about ready to start eating the carpet over here."

"All right. I'll get things . . . straightened out on this end as soon as I can, Iyal."

"I'll be waiting. And, Perivar . . ." she hesitated. "I may end up owing you the favor for this. Hope to see you soon."

"Yeah." He shut the channel down.

"All right, Kiv. You win." Perivar hoisted himself to his feet and knocked on his living room door.

No answer came, so Perivar pushed the door aside. Arla sat on the sofa with her face to the door, but she did not look up. Her eyes were closed, and her hands were cupped around a small white sphere that gleamed in the light that shone through the windows.

"Arla Stone?" Perivar approached her carefully. Now he could see two more spheres resting on a bright green swath of fabric next to her.

She didn't move. Perivar laid his hand on her shoulder.

"Arla?"

Arla blinked once and lifted her eyes. She searched his face without any sign of comprehension. Her pupils had dilated until her brown irises were nothing but a narrow band around two black holes.

"Are you all right?" He lifted his hand away.

She licked her lips and slowly, slowly focused on his face. "Yes. I am." She shook her shoulders and dropped the stone onto the fabric on the sofa. It made a sharp click as it hit the others. "I'm sorry, I didn't hear you . . . I . . ." She started wrapping the cloth around her spheres.

"You were meditating?" Perivar suggested uncertainly. Even from where he stood, he could see her hands shaking, and she moved with deliberate overcaution, as if she were exhausted, or drunk.

"I don't understand that word," she said. "I was . . . thinking. Putting all the things I have seen into place." She fumbled with the cloth and, after several tries, managed to knot the ends together. Her eyes, he noticed, had returned to normal, but the expectant trust she had shown before was buried.

"If I interrupted something personal, I'm sorry," said Perivar. "Eric never told me much about the religious customs in the Realm."

"It's all right." Arla leaned her arm against the sofa's back and stared out the window. "I should have waited until I was more settled." She laid one hand on the windowpane and fixed her gaze on the street. Her discarded headcloth still lay on the couch, and an untidy braid of black hair hung down between slumped shoulders.

Perivar looked past her to the scene outside. There wasn't much to see. Because it was a terraformed world, most of Kethran's cities were the result of meticulous planning. The process made for the efficient use of space but did not necessarily produce splendid views. The stone and polymer walls of the warehouses blocked out the horizon in one direction and the park in the other. To Perivar, the view looked more like a canyon than a street. Which was, he realized, why Arla was staring at it so hungrily.

"Just got an answer for you," he said. "Let me know if I say something you don't understand . . ."

"Just tell me," she said wearily. "I will understand." She added something under her breath that he didn't catch.

Perivar felt his eyebrows arch, but he said, "All right."

He told her about Iyal's offer. She let him keep talking until he was done and not once did she take her gaze from his face.

"What do you think?" Perivar asked finally.

"I think"—Arla toyed with the end of her headcloth—"that my decision to go over the World's Wall was beyond reckless. It was, in fact, stupid."

"I can arrange for you to go home easily enough." *With one twenty-word call to the labor authorities, in fact.*

Arla wound the black cloth between her scarred fingers. "If I return now, I, at the very least, am dead. I should not have left, I should have found some way . . ." She looked at the backs of her hands. "But this is less than useless. Do we leave for this 'Amaiar Gardens' place now?"

"Only if you want to go."

She gave him a crooked, half smile. "I want the skills it will buy me. If I have to surrender a few drops of blood every so often for that, then"—she shrugged—"it will be worth it. Tell me, though, are you Skymen all so interested in each others' blood?"

Perivar began to wonder what she was hearing through the translator. "Not usually," he admitted. "Listen, Sar Stone, I want you to be clear on one thing. Once you leave here, you leave here. I don't ever want to have to hear your name again, all right?"

For a moment, he thought she was going to ask him why, but she didn't. She said, "I don't care to risk anyone's skin but my own."

"Glad to hear it," Perivar said. "We should go now." He stood aside to let her pass.

It's a decent beginning, he told himself. *The beginning of an end, Kiv. And this time, I'll make it stick.* Perivar laid two fingers over his heart and watched Arla's straight back as she walked unafraid through his door. *I swear it.*

Kelat was not the first to exit the shuttle, or even the twenty-first. He did not care. The hard-packed dirt that pressed unevenly against the soles of his boots belonged to the Home

Ground. The ruins that stood out knife-edged in the sunlight, despite the filters on his faceplate, had been inhabited by the Ancestors. And if they were broken and sagging, and pitted by thirty centuries of dust and radiation, they still waited for the descendants of their makers. Those descendants who now walked under a black sky and tried to come to grips with the fact that they were home.

The thin wind he couldn't even feel through his suit blew more dust onto the drifts that piled up against what used to be a building's wall. The cement had been sheered off at about the level of Kelat's waist, leaving behind a rectangle that must have been half a kilometer on a side. Inside it, rubble lay in heaps, broken by burn craters, which in turn were being filled with yet more dust. Here and there clusters of girders, blackened by time, pushed their jagged fingers out of the dust, as if to see the outlandishly colored forms of the First Company as the Vitae spread out between them at a steadily increasing pace, like children left alone in a new park.

A dozen voices rang around the inside of Kelat's helmet, and his comparison of his Beholden and the committees to children settled more firmly inside him. All detachment had been suspended for the moment, even though six Witnesses in their green containment suits filtered through the gesticulating teams of techs and Historians, storing everything they saw for the memory.

What they saw were lumps of nameless materials, black, brown, and rust red, and clear silver. They saw dust, everywhere. They saw a world that was scarred, maimed, cratered, ungainly, and old beyond description. But everything they saw was theirs. Their home.

Kelat squinted at the horizon. It was impossible to tell whether the hills in the distance were more ruins or were actual geologic formations. He turned, shuffling around until he saw the black hulk of the mountains that sheltered the artifacts. There was no mistaking them. They stretched farther on each side than his eyes could see. Even though there was not enough air left to support clouds, he could arch his back as far as physically possible and still not see their tops. They pierced the vacuum.

In less than a week, the children of the Lineage would be on both sides of those mountains. Kelat wet his lips. Avir was a confirmed believer in the Assembly's stance, but a capable and dedicated Contractor. She would be going down with the Second Company into the populated regions. What she would find there . . . there was no telling, yet. Jahidh's last message had not been good. But Basq had found a way to trace the loose artifacts. Although Basq would have been horrified to hear it, that meant there was still a chance to bring the situation under control. That they would have to do it under Avir's nose saddened him a bit.

Is now the time for this? Kelat chided himself. *You are walking on the Home Ground! Your job is to help coordinate this great work and you can't even coordinate your own thoughts!*

"Contractor Kelat." Kelat became aware that one of the voices in his helmet was calling his name. "Contractor Kelat?"

"Kelat here." He touched a key on his wrist terminal to lay a display grid over the landscape his eyes saw. Each Vitae became targeted by a pinprick of gold light. He swung his gaze back and forth until one pinprick turned red.

"Historian-Beholden Baiel, Contractor," said the voice. "I think you need to see this." An anonymous figure in a Historian's grey suit stood beside a gleaming pillar that was twice as tall as he was and waved at him.

"I'm coming, Beholden." Minding his footing, Kelat picked his way through the mounds of dust and wreckage to Baiel's side.

The Beholden didn't even see him arrive. His attention was totally fastened on the cylindrical pillar.

Kelat studied it. For a moment, all he saw were its surprisingly smooth sides that glinted in the harsh daylight. The top was ragged, like the wall of the ruined building they had landed beside. Indistinct shadows played across it from . . .

Kelat blinked, and looked again. No. The shadows weren't moving across the surface, they drifted inside the pillar itself. Kelat pressed his faceplate against the pillar's side. The pillar reflected his face back at him and he saw his own wide eyes and undignified, slack-jawed surprise. Beyond that, under whatever silicate, or polymer, or glass this was, something shifted. A blob of shadow the size of Kelat's head flowed slowly toward the pillar's uneven top and hung there for a moment. Then it drew its soft edges in toward its center and began to swim, or fly, or creep back toward the bottom.

"Blood of my ancestors," he whispered. "Blood of my ancestors."

An irrational voice in the back of his head wondered if that might not very well be true.

5—Broken Canyon, The Realm of The Nameless Powers, Early Morning

*Why cannot the Unifiers find the Evolution Point? For the
same reason we cannot find the Home Ground. The two
are the same world and we are not just the children of the
Ancestors, we are the first of the Human Race. Why then
should we, the parents, serve these, our children?*
Fragment from an Imperialist text found on the wall
of the fifth level park aboard the Grand Errand.

*T*HE rain came down like the wrath of some ancient god.
Even with his lantern in his fist, Jay couldn't see more than
a yard past the tip of his boots. A solid wall of water reflected
the light right back at him. It wasn't all water, though. Slivers
of ice smacked against his faceplate like they meant to chip
the silicate.

Behind him, the two Notouch women steadied each other.
As soon as the squall started up, they wrapped their headcloths
around their faces to protect themselves from the ice and to
make sure they had pockets of air to breathe. You could
literally drown in some of these rains. Now they held tight
to each other's arms, walking in a measured, rocking gait that
let them balance against each other as they picked their way
over the slick, bare rock of the canyon floor.

If there'd ever been soil here, years of wind and water had washed it away, leaving nothing but granite and sandstone. Jay's lantern showed up bands of pale pink and flecks of gold underfoot that might have been beautiful had there been daylight to shine on any of them.

Jay glanced up. The bulk of the ragged canyon Wall was indistinguishable from the black sky overhead. The darkness left him no way to pick out the clouds and measure their weight or their movement. If the deluge didn't stop soon, he could be in trouble. A river could start down the walls, and in this thread-thin canyon, they'd all be washed away and buried in the swamps. Already the rain filled the hollows between the stones underfoot until the puddles overflowed into one another. In places he was up to his ankles in ice water. The women must have been just about numb, but, then, they were used to this. After four years of tramping up and down in the Realm's insane weather, Jay still couldn't see how they stood it. He thought about Cor waiting behind with the oxen. At least she could climb under the sledge's canvas cover and stay dry.

Finally, the water and the darkness split far enough to let through the white spark of another light. Jay resisted the impulse to hurry. Slipping on the wet stone would take him down hard even through the layers of wool and leather he wore, and he had nothing to catch himself against but more slick stone.

The puddles were turning into brooks, fast. One of the Notouch, Broken Trail, he thought, pointed toward the white light and shouted something to her cousin. Jay beckoned at them impatiently. Empty Cups glanced backward and then forward, and evidently decided she'd come too far to carry through any thoughts of turning around. She trudged forward with her cousin.

Jay forced himself to concentrate on each step until he could see the curving, white sides of the shelter. The brightly lit entranceway opened like a warm welcome. He ducked down the short corridor made of polymer sheets over a jointed framework and breathed a sigh of relief. Behind him, Empty Cups pulled Broken Trail back. The cousins stood in the downpour, shouting in each other's ears to be heard above the storm.

Jay motioned for them to come inside. They obeyed hesitantly.

Always the same, he thought. *They'll walk up a dark canyon and through a downpour, but as soon as they get to the dry, well-lit place, they get scared.*

He stripped off his glove. Cold sank through his skin straight to his bone. He hammered on the inner door. The door peeled back and let loose a flood of powered light.

"Welcome back, Jay," said Lu as he stepped back to let the three soaking travelers inside.

Jay felt the muscles in his back relax immediately in the warm, still air. The icy rain became nothing but a distant thunder outside the curving walls. He pulled off his faceplate and shucked the dripping cape, hanging both on an empty hook amid the emergency gear and corporate issue outerwear that none of the Unifier Team bothered with. He snatched up one of the extra towels Lu kept piled on a spare crate and wiped the spattering of rain off his round face and bald scalp.

The dome was a long way from luxurious. Most of the gear was stashed in polymer crates. The crates were stacked between equipment that still had half its paneling open, exposing wires and chips in bundles of black and orange, blue and green. Jay had at one point wondered what Lu did with his days when he was supposed to be making the base not just usable, but livable. Then he had learned that, for Lu, this jumble was livable.

"Who've you got for us?" Lu beamed through his scruffy, brown beard at the two women and switched to the language of the Realm. "The Nameless called this day fine, for we have met in it." Lu held up his hands. He'd had the hand marks of one of the Bondless drawn on their backs in indelible ink. The women relaxed visibly. Now they knew where they were in terms of how to act.

They both knelt on the shelter's smooth polymer floor. The older of the pair said, "Know, good sir, that this despised one is Broken Trail *dena* Rift in the Clouds and with her is

Empty Cups *dena* Reed in the Wind, and we beg to know
how we may serve.''

Lu suppressed a grimace and Jay shrugged. When they'd
first started the search, Lu had tried to get the Notouch to
stop groveling, but found it didn't work. The Notouch obeyed
the rules of a lifetime and simply didn't trust anybody who
told them that the rules were unnecessary. They were so
stubborn about it that Jay found himself wondering if some
kind of specific subservience hadn't been bred into them by
the old masters of this place. Their caste system had probably
evolved around whatever categories their makers had originally placed them in. But then there was Stone in the Wall
. . . But she had been an exception and it was beginning to
look like that wasn't the only thing she'd been an exception
to.

''First you can serve by getting yourselves warm and dry,''
said Lu, putting his steady smile back into place. ''Come
here, if you will.''

Trail and Cups followed Jay, walking so close together
their shoulders almost touched. Jay had set up an empty metal
crate near the back wall of the shelter. A coal fire burned in
the middle of it. For the first couple of testees, he had tried
to introduce them to heating elements, but none of them would
come near the glowing coils.

When Jay stood back to make room for them, Trail and
Cups approached the fire without hesitation and held out their
scarred hands over the flames, rubbing and blowing on their
knuckles. They stripped off their headcloths and ponchos,
wringing out the extra water onto the floor. Fortunately, Lu
would be spared from having to mop up the mess. The porous
polymer absorbed it and let it drain into the ground underneath.

''Now then, Trail and Cups, hear this,'' said Lu as the
women dried themselves off. ''I am going to show you a
strange place and ask you some questions you may not see
the reason for. To serve, you must stay calm and use the wits
the Nameless bestowed upon you when they gave you your
lives. You'll be home before night touches your rooftops again.
Can you do this?''

''Good sir, we can,'' said Trail, bowing her head humbly.

Lu rolled his eyes. "Then you have my thanks." He glanced at Jay and switched to Standard. "You coming down?"

"No." Jay dropped into the chair in front of the encampment stove and yanked off his boots. "I've got to make it back before the Seablades show up. King Silver wants her Skyman beside her so she can show how badly she's breaking all the rules."

"Well, you know the real rule."

"If it works, don't argue," Jay chorused with him. He stuffed his boots and socks into the stove and set the controls for clothes drying.

"Good luck," he said as he leaned back.

"Thanks," answered Lu. "I still wish we didn't have to do it this way."

Jay made himself shrug casually again. "Those are the orders. No more volunteers go offworld until we find out what the Vitae have done with or to Stone in the Wall." He frowned toward the stove. *Should have had word about that by now, even if it isn't ever going to come from where Lu thinks it will.*

"Whatever you say. You're the boss of this little expedition." Lu shrugged.

"It's not my idea," Jay reminded him. *Believe me, I'd just as soon be shoveling everyone we can get our hands on into the shuttle hold.* "It's the committee's. It's not so bad, though. We do need to be careful. The Vitae are awfully close to making their move on this place."

"You'd know, wouldn't you."

Yes, I would. "Let me alone, Lu. I exiled myself years ago."

"Sorry," said Lu sheepishly. "It's an old habit."

"I know." The stove chimed and Jay opened the door to retrieve his footgear. "Take care."

"Keep your back to the wall."

Jay refrained from mentioning that here it was impossible to do anything else.

Lu waited for Trail and Cups to rewrap their ponchos and turbans before he led them to the trapdoor he had jury-rigged in the floor. Underneath it lay a second hatchway, flush to a

smooth patch of some silicate-like substance that had been
exposed by years of wind and water rushing across it.

Lu dug his fingers into the crack between the hatch and
the silicate and, with a grunt of effort, raised the lid. Cups
and Trail exchanged apprehensive glances when they saw the
smooth-sided, dark well in front of them. Lu pressed the key
that turned on the lights he had strung on adhesive pads down
the side. The illumination did little more than show the fact
that the tunnel's walls were grey and unmarked, broken only
by the string of lights and the jointed ladder Lu had hung
from the edge of the drop.

Lu had tried to drill holes in the wall to make rungs for a
proper ladder, but the silicate wouldn't yield to anything,
including a welding torch.

Nonchalantly, Lu grabbed the ladder's rungs and started
his descent. Cups swallowed visibly, but followed as soon as
she had room. Trail glanced back at Jay, her eyes narrow and
calculating.

Jay started. Stone in the Wall had given him the same look
before she'd agreed to come with him up the canyon.

Do you suppose we've finally hit diamond?

Trail turned her attention toward the ladder and started
down it. Jay realized he was biting his lower lip and released
it. It was a bad habit he'd picked up from Cor. Telltale signs
of nervousness had been creeping into his features more and
more often.

He stuffed his feet back into his socks and boots, pausing
a minute to let the warmth restore at least some measure of
circulation to his feet. Then Jay retrieved his cloak and face
mask and steeled himself to walk back outside. He really
wanted to wait the rain out in the civilized atmosphere of the
dome.

How far gone am I when a portable shelter is civilized?
he wondered irritably.

He shoved the door aside. Without pausing, he ducked out
into the canyon. The door slapped shut behind him.

The canyon's darkness folded around him like another
cloak. The rain had stopped, leaving nothing but puddles with
crusts of ice forming rapidly. The sun was over the walls of

the main canyon, Jay knew, but the night's unforgiving cold and dark lingered for hours longer in this side crack. Still, Jay felt his breathing ease, not just from the change in the weather, but from getting away from Lu. It was always easier to think on his own.

It's so close to finished, I'm getting nervous. And I should have had word by now. Uary's had plenty of time to find out what that woman is.

Just check the transmitter and get back where you belong, Jahidh, he ordered himself.

All three of the team wore the neckline terminals commonly called "torques" that worked in conjunction with their translator disks to allow them to keep in touch with each other over limited distances. But offworld transmission required more power and a lot more circuitry. When Jay had suggested that the spare transmitter should be set up somewhere away from the shelter, Lu and Cor had both agreed. The reasoning he'd used on them was that if the weather, or a hostile native managed to destroy the shelter, there'd still be a way for the survivors to get word out. His real reasoning had been that the communications system needed a weak link he could exploit.

Jay switched the lantern on and strapped it to his arm. He pointed the beam up the rocky cliff, tracking the handholds Lu had so carefully gouged into the stone. He took a deep breath and flexed his hands before he hoisted himself up the rocky cliff. The rock hadn't had the chance to absorb any heat from the new day. It was like climbing a ragged block of ice. Jay gritted his teeth and kept on climbing.

About ten meters above the canyon floor, the cliff broke away. Jay swung his leg over the lip and dropped down into a pocket-sized valley. Places like this were called "flood cups" by the inhabitants of the Realm because they could sometimes fill up with water and spill out into the canyon. This one, however, had several drainage holes drilled in it. Jay only had to splash through a few shallow puddles to reach the transmitter.

The unit was a stack of squat boxes. Everything they used

on this planet had to be sheltered against the torrential rains and freezing cold that came with night.

Jay undid the straps holding the lantern to his sleeve and hooked it onto the side of the transmitter so he could see what he was doing. Then he lifted back the cover on the main unit. All the keys and displays glowed with a steady amber light and were completely blank.

Jay touched a series of commands he had memorized weeks before they landed here. No response came from the unit. No messages from the Unifiers, then. No change in status to report to their people down here stirring up trouble. Cor and Lu spent a lot of time cursing about the lack of attention their project was receiving from the bureaucracy back on May 16, even with the Vitae so interested in the Realm. Jay suspected both of them were on somebody's mud list by now for failing to make scheduled reports.

Neither side knew how many messages were being "lost" during transmission.

Jay touched the keys again in a sequence that Lu and Cor had no idea was valid. The transmitter responded by scattering what could have been a random series of symbols from a dozen different alphabets across the screen. Jay took his translator disk out of his ear and slipped it into the download slot in the transmitter. The screen cleared instantly. Jay reclaimed the disk.

As soon as he had replaced the translator in his ear, Caril's voice spoke to him. "We have released the artifact Stone in the Wall. She and Eric Born were allowed to escape confinement twenty hours prior to my sending this message . . ."

Jay sat in his tiny pool of light, feeling the cold seep into him as he listened to the details.

Blood, blood, blood! he cursed. *Now we have to hunt down her family.* He thought about Trail and her eyes, but couldn't work the brief glimpse of a resemblance into a full-fledged hope. *How could those idiots have done this! They know I've got nothing to work with down here!* For a brief moment, he knew how Lu and Cor felt, bereft of resources and support.

He tried to tell himself it was only a setback, not a dead end. And it would have been very bad if the Assembly had found out how Stone in the Wall functioned before they did, but it was still bad enough. If the Imperialists didn't have a thorough grasp of how the artifacts functioned by the time the Assembly parties came over the World's Wall, the chance to win the Home Ground would be gone.

Of course, the two Unifiers thought that was the deadline for having the Realm's power base reorganized under a monarch who wanted to join the Human Family.

None of which leaves any more time for sitting around here.

Jay climbed out of the flood cup and down to the canyon floor. The sky above him had turned smoky grey, but its light hadn't yet traveled far enough over the Walls to show him his way, so he kept the lantern on and picked his path between the fallen rocks and frozen puddles as fast as he could.

After about three miles, the darkness ended and Jay stepped out of the canyon's shadow into the filtered, hazy glow that passed for daylight in the Realm.

The Teachers said that Broken Canyon was where the Nameless Powers had argued about the word for "stone." The entire breadth of it was a mass of jagged promontories, caves, cups, and gashes. The Walls didn't even stand up straight. They sloped open like the canyon was yawning.

When the Nameless had finally come to an agreement, went the story, they made up for the botched job by painting the canyon in a spectacular fashion. The rain hadn't made it out here, so the colors were still dry. Veins of silver and quartz shot through bands of crimson, rust, vermilion, violet, and sparkling sandstone. Here and there you could even catch a glimpse of a slick, greyish patch of exposed silicate.

Jay could remember the tremor of excitement in Lu's voice when he'd discovered that the slick, grey "rock" was really a manufactured silicate lying under the dirt and gravel of the Realm. It meant that MG49 sub 1 was not just a failed colony, it was a fallen world, and who knew how much of their technology might have survived under the ground?

Broken Canyon measured three miles wide at its base, but he still felt hemmed in by the walls that were too huge to be taken in with a single glance. It got worse when he remembered that these were the smaller walls, and that the black, ragged stretch where the horizon should have been was a hundred times bigger.

Four years, as Jay and his two companions measured time, had passed and he had never gotten used to the sight. Jay looked at the ground and started down the slope through the screen of scraggly trees and underbrush. The spectacular colors of the walls almost compensated for the tan, grey, and olive green of the stunted trees and spiky reeds that poked out of the skimpy patches of soil. Moss and lichens gave the rocks coats of fuzz.

The sounds of life drifted up to him on the back of the omnipresent wind. Hooves and skids clattered against rock and sank into mud. Voices bounced off the boulders in an incoherent babble that seemed to come from all directions at once, all mixed up with the thousand little noises that came from constant motion. Jay shoved his way through a thicket of thorny trees and finally got a clear view of the muddy, pockmarked road.

King Silver had told him, rather proudly, that forcing the Narroways Approach across the canyon floor had cost a thousand lives. The lichen-covered mounds of boulders heaped alongside the roadbed gave a lot of credence to the body count.

A flood of travelers poured down and around the wide road today. Clear, dry spells were not to be wasted, war or no war. Even in the traffic, though, they clung together in knots of their own kind. Caravans of Bondless shouted over their creaking sleighs and snorting oxen. They gave a grudging berth to a gaggle of Bonded trotting along with their overseer. An enclosed sledge that bore the ribbons of some Noble house rattled along at the center of an entourage which shoved an impartial path through the rest of the traffic.

Along the side of the road, framing the scene, the bundles of Notouch women in their ragged motley picked their own paths between the rocks and the weeds. The girls who could walk struggled to keep up with their mothers, aunts, and older sisters. The babies were carried on the stooped backs of the oldest women.

Jay frowned at them. Those roving bands were what was making it so impossible to track Stone in the Wall. If only the Ancestors had been a little more obvious in designing their servants, but, aside from the trained telekinetics, there were no differences between these walking artifacts that could be seen without a gene scan. Uary had theories. The Notouch might have been the "untouched," blank slates that were the control group for the Ancestors' work, or kept to use for later modification. That the telekinesis could crop up anywhere lent credence to the story from their "apocrypha" about the war against the Teachers that drove the power-gifted into hiding and humiliation until they'd learned their lesson.

Or until the others learned they couldn't live without them, thought Jay, watching the ragged parade of so many men and women and so few children.

But none of these theories explained what Stone in the Wall was, or why her family was relegated to the Notouch caste. The traits that made her what she was were not shared by the caste in general any more than the telekinesis was shared by all the Nobles. Cor had met Stone in the Wall in Narroways. She came from a cluster of huts that had no name, and probably wasn't even there anymore. Like most Notouch women, she spent her time roving between cities and farms as a "hired" hand while the men stayed in the village and kept the place from being washed away. By the time Cor had tried to track her family, Stone in the Wall's band was gone and no one would admit to knowing anything about her. Trail and Cups hadn't even been willing to say they'd come to Narroways with a work band.

Chaos, it was all chaos. This was what happened when there was no vision, no conscious plan. Entropy laid hold of individual minds, and everything that had been built . . . collapsed.

Jay squinted over the Notouch's heads toward the longest of the caravans. Its masters, at least, weren't completely oblivious to the hostile state of affairs between Narroways and the Orthodox world. Men displaying the tin helmets of hired guards balanced on the overfull sledges, clutching their axes and metal-studded clubs so anyone who glanced toward them could see they meant business.

The sight didn't say much positive for what the local feeling was about the Seablades coming across from First City. Jay forced the frown out of his features and scanned the roadside for Cor.

She was easy to pick out because she was almost the only still figure in the canyon. Cor leaned against the driver's perch of her sledge, watching the parade. Her oxen chewed the tree branches nearby and she patted the slablike side of the one closest to her absently.

Jay sidestepped toward her. His boots loosened a small scree of stones and Cor tilted her head up.

"You're looking grim," she said as he picked his way down to her.

"I'm feeling grim. There are no messages from May 16 and it's getting later by the second."

Cor glanced at the sky and at the slant of the shadows. "In more ways than one. I'll cuss the Vitae and bureaucrats out later." She unknotted the oxen's reins from the tree branch. Her hands had been marked with the broken triangles of the Bondless class. Unlike his Noble swirls, her marks were real tattoos. But then, it was her job to immerse herself totally in the local culture. That way, she could bring an intimate picture back to the Family and she could get the locals used to the idea that the odd-looking strangers coming to their world were just like them, really.

Jay clambered into the back of the sledge.

"It'd be easier if you'd just learned to ride," she remarked, watching him with an amused smile playing around her mouth. "The oxen are slow and quiet. It's not that tough."

"I am from an overcivilized and decadent people," said Jay blandly as he settled himself on one of the boxes that served as seats in the awkward construction. "I just can't do it."

Cor shrugged, hollered at the beasts, and they all lurched forward.

The countryside crawled past them behind the jostle of fellow travelers. A path cleared in front of them and closed

up behind as people recognized them as Skymen. Jay tried
not to wince as the unpadded box jounced against his backside.
A river of sweat began to trickle down his cheek. Now that
the sun was full up, the day was turning as hot as the night
had been cold.

After about an hour, the scraggly wilderness began to give
grudging space to tamed patches. The Narroways farmlands
were strange places, more cultivated wetlands than fields.
Yards of seine nets covered the grains to keep the plants from
the worst of slashing sleet and hail that could come at night.
The nets were rolled back in places and the Bonded worked
in teams, chopping weeds and mucking out the trenches so
water could flow between the rice plants and keep them from
shriveling into dormancy. Behind a low wall, Bondless carefully tended their orchard. Each precious tree was carefully
tented and you could only see the shadows of the workers
underneath, pruning and grafting. Fruits and root vegetables
were delicacies in this world of grains, grasses, and fungi.

The war did not touch the farms, or the oxen and pigs in
their pens. Food and animals would be needed by whoever
won. But the houses that could be seen from the road sported
red flags, proclaiming there had been war dead there.

Beyond the farms the canyon walls shrugged and shifted
and so the world bent toward the left and tilted down a sharp
gradient. Cor whistled shrilly to the oxen and hauled back on
the reins to check them to a walk as the road sloped sharply
in front of them. An overturned sledge had spilled its contents
onto the roadbed and the Bondless owners shouted obscenities
at each other in between barked orders to the Notouch women
scrambling to retrieve the canvas-wrapped packages before
they were trampled under foot or hoof. The walls drew closer
here, leaving less room for traffic overflow. Even with the
wind, it felt more like being inside than outside.

The sight of the Narroways city wall stretching across the
breadth of the canyon only reinforced the sensation.

There was, as usual, a line at the city gates. King Silver's
men stopped each sledge, inspected its contents, and leveled
the extortionary duty on it. The Kings of Narroways got away
with their legalized highway robbery because Narroways

stood at the junction of three of the most populated corridors of the Realm. If you didn't go through the city, you added at least two weeks to your travel time. And if the weather turned bad in those two weeks, your cargo and your life could be washed away down into the Lif marshes.

The sun was fully up over the walls now and beating down on the damp, confined air of the canyon, raising clouds of steam from the mud and the smell of sweat from the oxen, and, Jay admitted ruefully, from him. He tossed his cape back over his shoulder to try to let some of the breeze reach him.

A fresh crosswind bore down out of Narroways and Jay had to swallow against his own bile. The wind carried the scent of spices, sure, and cooking food and burning tallow. But it also carried the scent of acrid smoke, rotting garbage, unwashed humans, and overworked animals, all mixed with the reek from unburied shit, both from the animals and their owners. The stench of the cities was yet another item on the long list of things he had never managed to get used to.

Finally, they drew up to the gates and Cor raised up her hands in the universal salute. The soldier looked at her marks, then at her warmth-reddened skin, then at her startling green eyes and yanked himself back.

"And the Nameless hold you dear, too," she said sweetly and drove the sledge on through.

Despite its location, Narroways had not been built for traffic. The houses huddled shoulder to shoulder, eyeing each other across thread-thin, mud-paved streets. When the floods came, the residents simply slung rope-and-chain bridges from one roof to the next and went about their business.

As in most fixed towns, both business and living was done on the second floor. Shutters the size of doorways opened up from verandas to catch any breeze and light the day decided to give out. Merchants posted their children on the steps to sound off about what waited for sale inside and to tend the torches smoking the worst of the insects away from the doors.

Today the whole world seemed determined to cram itself into the streets. A dozen caravan traders had wedged animals and sleighs into cramped alleys while they bartered and traded insults with the fixed merchants. The accompanying mobs of soldiers and families spread through the streets. Their bold robes spilled color through the solid stream of rust and earth dyes worn by even the Noble born of Narroways. The hot wind wrapped itself around the jarring noise of too many people in too little space, picked up the smells of food, spices, perfumes, and sweat and mixed it all into a dense morass and spread it out again.

There was barely enough room for Cor to get the sledge through even the main streets and they raised a cloud of curses from the foot travelers as she tried. The city passed around them in a series of miniature plays. Ahead on the left, a Bonded woman argued spice prices with a peddler. To the right, two Bondless toasted each other with a crock of wine. A troop of soldiers on oxen splashed gutter filth on a cluster of Notouch and tossed loud obscenities at each other. An old man with a Teacher's suns tattooed on his palms laid his hands on a child's burned face while a woman in a saffron-colored cloak looked anxiously on. Jay heard the child's gasp even over the babble of street noises.

Cor eased the sledge around a tight corner, and the High House slid into view.

The High House was an honorary name for the King's dwelling. It squatted level with the other buildings behind its own set of carved walls. Even in broad daylight there were six guards at the gate. Cor shouted to them and they hauled back the iron gates to let the sledge through. The courtyard on the other side was empty. They saw no one until they pulled up to the stable. A couple of Bonded hustled the wagon indoors and Cor with them.

"Good luck." She waved as she left Jay on his own.

"Thanks. I'll need it."

The blood-warm rain started down before he was halfway across the courtyard. Jay ducked his head and hauled on his hood to try to keep himself dry. He peeked under the edge to get his bearings. The door lamp glimmered invitingly four feet above the courtyard.

A wind shear drove straight down out of the sky with such force that Jay staggered. He gripped the stair railings and struggled to climb up to the main doors.

This. This is what we've wandered for centuries to get back to. This is what we're ready to go to war with our own kind over. He stumbled into the doorway. *I swear, if I didn't think they'd just abandon me here, I'd tell them we don't want this place. Tell them it's a dying, corroded heap of rocks. I swear the only reason I keep going is so that someone will get me off this forsaken world.*

"My Lord Messenger," said a man's voice.

Jay straightened up. Your day-use name, the first of whatever series you might be lumbered with, was often not so much a name as a description. Jay's was Messenger for the Skymen and the skinny, wrinkled man in front of him was Holding the Keys, King Silver's chief secretary and step-and-fetch-it man. Next to him stood a Bonded boy carrying a basin of steaming water in one hand and a plate of biscuits in the other. A clean towel was slung over his arm.

Jay read the scene. The King wanted to see him, now. The footbath and food were the polite greeting for an arrival, but he wouldn't be given time to sit down and enjoy them.

"The King wishes you to attend her at once," said Holding, while Jay stripped off his boots and quickly rinsed his feet in the basin as the boy set it down. "She sent me to see that you do not delay."

Jay frowned. King Silver was young, greedy, unreasonable, and hadn't learned not to whine in meetings yet, but she wasn't easily panicked. He donned the pair of slippers that the boy produced from the pouch at his belt and wolfed down a biscuit that tasted like wood chips. Something must be going on. Something unexpected.

Jay followed Holding through the stone halls. The lamps in the great hall were lit. The audience was expected soon, then. The Seablades must have beaten him through the gates.

The corridors Holding led Jay through were stone-cold, despite the heat of the day outside. Coal fires in the hearths took off some of the chill but the clay statues and bas-reliefs set against the walls did nothing to soften appearances.

Holding the Keys marched Jay straight to the King's private study. It was one of the few rooms on the second floor that sported a real door. Holding knocked.

"Whoever it is, you had better have Messenger with you!" shrilled the King from the other side.

"I have, My King." Holding swung the door back and stood aside.

Jay marshaled his wits and walked across the threshold.

The study was a jumble of precious wooden furniture piled with vellum scrolls and clumsily bound books. It had been built around one of the eight "shadow pillars" that helped support the High House. Silver said her great-great-great-grandmother had ordered the House built over them, as a reminder that the Kings of Narroways were supported by the Nameless Powers.

Jay had actually considered saying a grace for Silver's grandmother. The pillar and its weird, blobby shadows had sent the Unifiers looking for the underground chambers that had yielded their only real clues to the workings of the Home Ground.

King Silver stooped over her chart bowl, the Realm's equivalent of a globe. It was literally a deep bowl with a map of the Realm painted on its inside.

"There is word," she said, not giving Jay any chance to observe formalities, "that a contingent of soldiers from First City, maybe as many as one hundred, has vanished. Now, where, Messenger of the Skymen, do you suppose they have gone?"

Even by the standards of the Realm, Silver on the Clouds was a tiny woman, which might account for her perpetual belligerence. The scarlet ribbon tattoo that adorned a King outlined her jaw and brow. It stretched badly whenever she gathered her face up into a frown.

Jay mustered a calm tone. "I expect they have gone to take up a new position in case their delegation fails to make peace with Your Majesty."

"I expect that is the truth. Further, I expect that I would not have to worry about them if you would loan me a few of your Skyman miracles so my generals could fend them off. Or perhaps your masters are not so anxious to see Narroways the sole and whole power of the Realm as you have said."

So we're back to that. "Majesty, I have asked for weapons. I have been refused . . ."

"Then you will ask again!" she shrieked, and Jay took a step back. "I will tell you this, Skyman, this war eats at my city. My commanders grow uneasy. A King with uneasy commanders is not long safe, Skyman, and I treasure my safety. Be assured, if I must hand my name back to the Nameless Powers, I will not be doing so alone."

"You are winning."

"Yes." She rested her hands on the edge of the bowl. "But I am winning slowly. If this war we make is not finished soon, Skyman, I will cease to win at all. I will lose and the walls of Narroways will come crashing down over my funeral pyre."

She pushed past him. "You will stand beside me and hear what the Seablades have to say for themselves."

"As always, Your Majesty." Jay did not shake his head at her back, but he wanted to. There were days he seriously regretted helping Silver depose her grandfather.

Holding the Keys, with his typical efficiency, had assembled King Silver's honor guard outside her door. She had expected them to be there and breezed into the center of the ranks. They snapped to attention and marched forward, leaving Jay and Holding to fall into step behind.

The procession reached the threshold of the audience hall and a dozen Bonded touched tapers to the lamps hanging from its rough walls just as the King stepped in. Light flickered against gold and steel jewelry only to be absorbed again by the dull colors of the clothing of the assembled courtiers.

Like everyone else, the Seablade delegation raised their hands before their faces as the King's procession passed. Jay read the marks from the corners of his eyes. Nobles, all of them. Three family members, one of whom was Heart of the Seablade. Jay suppressed a sigh of relief. He would at least be able to get some accurate information about First City's plans. That might just be enough to placate King Silver.

King Silver mounted her dais and stood there. Kings did not have the luxury of sitting through their audiences. Silver could stand for hours without fidgeting, a skill that amazed Jay in spite of himself.

Silver lifted her chin. "It having reached my ears that my kindred in First City would send me words concerning our war, I have brought myself and my Witness forth to hear them." Her voice was too high and thin for the chamber, even though it was bolstered by the ringing formalities of the high command dialect. "Therefore, choose who among you will speak and let the others bear back witness as to my attentiveness and the full nature of my answer."

Two of the Seablades detached themselves from the delegation. Heart of the Seablade scrupulously avoided looking at Jay. His wife, Mind of the Seablade, the blood daughter of the house, on the other hand, seemed determined to keep her attention riveted on him.

The Seablades raised their hands to King Silver in greeting.

"I am Lady Mind *kenu* Mind of the Seablade *dena* Constant Watcher," said the daughter of the house. "I am chosen to speak for the blood Nobles, the Bondless, and the Bonded who are attached to the House and Lands where the Blade is the symbol and the protection. I have leave and permission to speak also for Wall's Shadow, my King in First City." She lowered her hands. "I say that the blood will spill until the floods are red and still we will not yield to this unprovoked and unnatural war that is fought by the master of Narroways only because her wit and will has been stolen by the Messenger of the Skyman *dena* Aunorante Sangh."

Bad enough.

"I am Teacher Heart *kenu* Heart of the Seablade *kenu* Fortunate Speaker *dena* Shadow of the World's Wall," said her husband. "I speak for the Temple and the Teachers. Because this war is provoked by the Aunorante Sangh we say that the power-gifted are free to act against them. We also say that Narroways no longer hears the Word in the Temple and those attached to her, like all Heretics, must die."

Jay had to give Heart this much credit, he held his voice steady as he delivered his pronouncement. But then, he'd said it before. The First Teacher believed firmly in repetition.

"There is forgiveness yet by the law and the Word if Silver on the Clouds as master of Narroways closes the breach in her own heart that let the Aunorante Sangh into her city."

Oh-ho. This was the first time an offer of compromise had been extended from the Orthodox delegates. *Could it be that King Silver's not the only one nearing the end of her rope?*

King Silver touched the tattooed ribbon that adorned her brow. "By the marks of kingship and family, I declare that I and my company have heard and understood the message that you do bear. Now, I charge you hear my words." She lowered her hand. "Those who call themselves the Teachers in First City are but liars. They are the ones who listen to the Aunorante Sangh, not I. Otherwise, they would speak the truth and say that the Messenger, the Listener, and the Scribe, who are all of the Skymen, do no more than bring us greetings from the brothers who have found us in this place where we were moved by the Servant of the Nameless. The Teachers would kill our brothers. I would defend them. I will not change my mind nor stay the hands of those who take up arms in my cause. If there is to be peace, you must cease this threat against our brethren, or you must take my city from under my rain-polished bones."

Jay's stomach turned over. The fate of the Home Ground hung in the balance and it was being argued over by these . . . things . . . who were so out of control that they didn't remember who they were or know what they were really fighting about.

"King Silver on the Clouds," said Mind. "The dark seasons are coming to the Realm. It can do none of us any good to pursue this war when we should be pursuing a harvest and the stocking of coal and oils."

"Then lay down your arms and welcome your brothers," said Silver. "Harbor no murderous thoughts among you. Accept that I am the one chosen to speak for the Realm to the Skymen. This will end the matter."

"Oh, no, Your Majesty," said Heart. "It will not even come close."

Who is that talking, Heart? Jay wondered. *Is that actually your voice I'm hearing?*

"Is there more to be said?" inquired Silver.

"Not by us and not at present, King Silver," said Mind, giving Heart a hard look.

"We thank Your Majesty for your attention," said Heart.

The Seablades retreated into their cluster of servants. The honor guard held the doors open for them to walk through.

When the doors banged shut again, Jay sighed inwardly and tried not to shift his weight. King Silver, oblivious of his discomfort, called her councilors up to the dais and proceeded to review the interview with them in detail, analyzing the contents of the Seablades' statements, deciding what messages to send, what spies to contact, what orders to issue. Jay eased his weight gingerly from his heels to his toes and back again and tried to pay attention.

At last, the King dismissed them and Jay hurried out of the hall.

Despite Silver's constant public announcements as to their importance, the King had not wanted her Skymen to get above themselves, so she had assigned Jay and Cor quarters outside the main building. To get to his rooms, Jay had to cross a roofed, stone bridge with sides open to the wind and weather. With its usual abruptness, the rain had stopped and the sun had turned the day into a steam bath. By the time he was through the door to the side building, he was drenched with sweat.

Unlike the King's study, Jay's room had nothing but a tapestry hanging in the threshold to keep him screened from the passersby. Jay pushed past it and paused for a moment to savor the night's cool that had been trapped by the room's stone walls.

Chiding himself for forgetting the immediate business, Jay pulled back the burgundy curtains. The window actually had a pane of glass that rattled only a little in the wind. Heart knew which room was Jay's. If he was watching, he would see the opened curtains, and hopefully be able to make his excuses to his wife and get away. Jay didn't want to have to wait until dark for the news. He needed to have plans before then.

"Jay?" called a voice through the door-curtain. "It's Cor."

"Come in, come in." He held the curtain back for her.

Cor brushed by him and he caught a glimpse of the dark

circles under her eyes. She slumped into one of the chairs in front of the fireplace. "How'd it go?"

Jay shook his head. "I could've asked for better." He described the audience to her. Cor grunted.

"Jay," she said to the ashes on the hearth, "remind me why we're doing this."

Oh, no.

"Because we need to accomplish the reunification of the Human Family," he said, sitting across from her. "And because the Vitae really don't want us to."

"Oh, yeah, I'd forgotten about that last bit."

"What's the matter, Cor?"

"Nothing new," she rubbed her forehead. "I've just gone native. It's my job, after all. Someone has to completely understand the new membership so we can make them at ease when they join the Family." She said the words like she was reading them off the flagstone floor.

Don't do this to me, Cor. I can't manage you on top of the King, and Lu, and Heart. "We are doing this because we have to." *Both of us are.*

"Jay?" The door curtain moved and Heart stepped into the room.

Cor raised her hands to the Teacher so smoothly it might have been a reflex. Heart bowed toward her absentmindedly, with his hands held up so the golden suns tattooed on his palms flashed in the watery daylight.

"What's the news, Heart?" asked Jay quickly as Heart moved to stand next to him. *And please, please let it be something I can use.*

Heart shrugged and leaned his elbow on the mantelpiece. "Our city is hard-pressed," he said, running his knuckle along a crack in the stone. "The dissent among our neighbors is strong and we have little help. The Realm waits to see who wins this war, Narroways or First City, and then it shall decide what to do."

Jay knotted his fist. "We need you to help make sure King Silver is victorious, Heart. What can you tell us of First City's state of affairs?"

Heart hesitated, leaning heavily against his arm. Cor stood and offered the Teacher her chair. He took it with thanks.

"I do this because we were lied to in the Temple," he said, raising his eyes as if he were pleading with them, "because we're dying. The Nameless have withdrawn their favor from their people. Our children are born dead or deformed or of the wrong lines. And the Teachers say it is not so. They say we think there's trouble because we do not see with the Servant's eyes. They say that as long as we repeat the Words of the Nameless in the Temple, all will always be well."

Cor gave Jay a sideways glance and then looked quickly out the window. *What're you really seeing out there?* Jay wondered. *Who have you been talking to?*

Heart was shaking his head. "King Wall's troops are going to be pulled from Tiered Side to defend the outer towns of First City. They'll be there in three days. If King Silver meets them before they reach there, First City will lose valuable and timely help. But you should move quickly. There's a delegation from First City in Terminus Height, and they may be wavering in their resolution to stand beside you." His face grew uneasy. "You have worked too few miracles, Skyman. There are those who doubt you can bring us any good, as King Silver needs must fight so long and so hard to gain any ground with you at her side."

Jay and Cor exchanged a long look.

What do we tell them? That the Board decided not to risk arming a telekinetic race whose world contains who-knows-what powers that they might still be able to use, even if all they have are superstitions to guide them? Somehow I think we'll lose even Heart's support if I come across with that.

"I shall tell the King." Jay straightened up. "I shall also tell my masters, be assured."

"Thank you." Heart stood. "I need to get back to my chambers. My wife, you know." He turned back to the threshold and Jay walked beside him.

"Heart," he whispered as he lifted the door-curtain, "the King told me a garrison of one hundred troops has gone missing from the ranks of First City. Do you know where they may have been sent?"

Heart looked startled. "I have heard nothing of this. I will see what I can find out for you."

"You have our thanks, Heart." Jay let the curtain fall back into place and waited until he heard the Teacher's footsteps fade down the hall.

"We've got to see them armed," he said to Cor's back. "Silver's losing support, even though she's winning. We're losing support because we're not stronger than the myths. The Vitae are going to show up soon. If we don't have this place locked down before then, then all our time and effort, it's for nothing and the Vitae will let these . . . people loose on the Human Family."

"The Vitae might just kill them," said Cor without turning around. "They don't think much of genetic engineering on humans."

No, thought Jay. *I don't think they'd kill this crowd.* But he said nothing. Cor was trying to convince herself they were doing the best thing possible, and he needed to let her succeed.

"All right." Cor faced him and folded her arms as if she were trying to keep out a chill. "Tomorrow we can go back to the shelter. Find out what luck Lu's had with the Notouch. If there hasn't been anything, then I'll back you on the call for arms. I mean, there's not that many power-gifted and it's becoming very obvious that without Stone in the Wall and her family, no one knows what the story is with the arlas."

"Thank you," said Jay seriously.

Cor gave him a watery smile. "Keep well 'til then, Jay."

"Keep well."

She left and Jay sagged onto the bed. *There's a chance we can still take this place. A good chance.* He stared out toward the window and fingered his torque. *If we can just get moving.*

The torque beeped. Jay's heart leapt to his throat. The torque beeped again, and again, and once more for good measure.

Blood and bones. Jay pulled the translator disk out of his ear. *It can't be time already!*

With his free hand, he undid the catch on his torque. The signal said this transmission couldn't be handled with the usual setup. It would be coming from too far away, at too high a frequency. He slid the disk into a barely visible socket on the torque's side and waited.

"Jahidh, this is Kelat. The First Company has landed in the Home Ground and I am with them. You have about two hundred hours left before Second Company comes down to reclaim the populated regions. What is the state of your operations?"

Jay stared incredulously at the torque. "Kelat, I don't know," he said. *What do you think I'm doing?* he added silently. *Running a lab experiment? Controlling a team of Beholden?* "The Unifier cause is a mess, I've managed that much, but I'm also standing in the middle of it. We may have finally found another artifact like Stone in the Wall, but I won't know for sure until I've heard from Lu."

"Contact me directly when you have more news." The torque fell silent.

Jay refastened the torque around his neck. Their conversations had to be brief, he knew that. Lu might not be the most conscientious systems handler alive, but he had designed some highly efficient watch programs to make up for it. But somehow, knowing Kelat was within reach made his isolation that much sharper.

We weren't meant to work alone, he sighed. *Father was right about that much.*

Jay lifted the lid on the chest beside the bed with one hand and loosened the belt on his overtunic with the other. He peeled off the stiff cloth and pitched it onto the chair for the Bonded to pick up for washing. He unstrapped the gun belt next. His gun was the only one the Unifier committee had voted to allow onto the planet. It was a barbaric projectile weapon. It made too much noise and too much blood, but it was impressive. It was for an emergency, if they needed to scare these people who could kill with a touch.

Jay remembered the first project he'd ever worked on as an apprentice engineer. The Vitae had been contracted to create a security network for Eispecough, one of the countries of an embattled world called Toth. Basq, proud of Jay's engineering aptitudes, or maybe just seeking the extra status that would come from proving his son was brilliant, had gotten him assigned to the job of designing the module links. He'd worked hard, almost fanatically, and watched the network grow. He remembered his pride, both of place and accomplishment.

Then, there'd been an election in Eispecough and a new government moved in. They canceled the contract and told the Vitae to leave. The Vitae did leave, because that was their way. Work for hire only and when told to go, take the severance payment and go. Jay had kept a surreptitious eye on his work, just to see how it held up. He'd even done a little remote repair work on the code. Basq had known about it and kept it quiet. Contractor Kelat had found out, however, and had Jay removed from Basq's custody, citing that Basq, by overpermissiveness, had allowed his child to become a danger to Vitae public dealings.

Three local months later, there was a civil war in Eispecough and the network was destroyed. The Vitae did nothing. Their work wasn't theirs. Their vision wasn't theirs. They'd abandon it all to chaos, because they would not take responsibility for their vision.

The Imperialists wanted to change that. They saw the change that was happening in the Quarter Galaxy. The Vitae in their fearful isolation had made no friends, established no colonies, and claimed no servants. They survived because many civilizations in the Quarter Galaxy considered them useful, and so they were used. But that could change as colonies and stations grew ripe with their own histories and technologies. There might just come a day when the Vitae went from being respected experts to being beggars, unless they established real power. Unless they began issuing contracts instead of just obeying them.

That, no matter what his father said, was the real work.

Jay weighed the weapon in his hand for a long moment before he laid it carefully in the chest. He couldn't see the angle on any of the shadows from here, but he had the distinct feeling tomorrow was still a long, long way off.

Cor left Jay's room without looking back. Her thoughts crowded around her like a cloud of biting flies and she was so busy trying to shoo them away so she could find some kind of understanding, that she lost track of where she was going. She looked up, blinking at the shadows and squinting at the stonework. The relief carving of the three Crooker trees told her she was almost to the dining hall. Her stomach rumbled. Food would help clear her head and warm her cold hands.

The hall itself was a broad, solid, graceless chamber. The space between the tables and benches was taken up either by stone pillars or by coal fires carefully banked in their own ashes. When she'd first gotten here, Cor had found the acrid heat suffocating. Now she breathed it into her lungs as a source of comfort and reassurance. This far into the house it was never warm. The day's heat was not strong enough to penetrate the stone, but the night's cold never seemed to have that problem.

And it'll do nothing but get worse, she thought. *The Dark Seasons are coming.*

Averand, her homeworld, could zip around its sun forty times in the time it took the Realm to skulk once around the Eyes of the Servant. She remembered when she first saw the simulation of the Realm's orbit. It circled the binary warily, swinging in almost too close, then backing off almost too far, always riding the bare edge of tolerance as it made its long, slow way around its stars. It was on its way out to the far, cold edge now.

Ceramic pots stood in the ashes at the edge of the fires. Cor snagged a red clay bowl off a table she passed and dipped it into the nearest jar to shovel out a helping of porridge, mushrooms, and overcooked chicken meat. She glanced over the jar, looking hopefully for a flat dish of baking bread, but didn't see any. She sighed at the porridge. It'd keep her from starving, but not do much more than that. Even the Nobility kept barely at a subsistence level in the time when there was more day than night.

She thought about Raking Coals, who brought his sledge in every tenth day and kept asking her what price she set her own hands at with a broad wink and a happy leer. And the Oilbrake sisters, who carried fifty-pound sacks of grain on their backs when their pair of oxen went lame and still whistled at the stable boys who crossed the courtyards. And the Notouch daughters who scrambled this way and that in the courtyard, grabbing up the feathers that came down like snow when the house's Bonded sat on the roof and plucked chickens.

It was a filthy, hard, stupid life, and if the Vitae got hold of them, it would vanish.

And if the Family gets hold of them? Cor dropped onto the bench and stuck her fingers into her bowl, shoving the food into her mouth before it went cold.

She'd been sent down with the team when the Unifiers still thought these people were Family. She'd hunkered down and learned the language and the customs and made friends as fast as she could. She learned to tell jokes and to laugh at them. She learned to pitch in with the work of the Bondless and to defer to the Teachers and the Nobility. She could recite the Words of the Nameless in the Temple on the tenth day and navigate using nothing but the walls around her. She'd deliberately set out to find anything and everything she could admire and respect about the culture. It was her job. She'd trained for it specially for years.

Then the word came down. These weren't Family. These people were artificially created. Nothing like this had ever been found before. New policy would have to be formulated as soon as the extent of the engineering could be understood.

Policy? She scowled at her bowl and her porridge-spattered fingers. Jay's voice had been flat and unquestioning when he delivered the message. As if there could be any policy for this world except getting them some decent food and a way to keep warm and dry through a twenty-year winter. These people who worked and starved and slaved and still sang and loved and told really, really obscene jokes.

Behold the noble savage, she thought grimly. *Cor, Cor, Cor. They're dirty and ignorant and so enslaved to their superstition that they don't even know what they're standing on top of. Come out of it, woman. It's a raw deal, of course, but the worst the Family does'll be better than the best the Vitae'll do.*

Cor scooped up another mouthful of porridge.

Of course it will.

A sharp ringing in her ear made her jerk and Cor nearly sent her bowl crashing to the floor. After a moment she realized it was her translation disk. She balanced her bowl in her dirty hand and tapped the disk twice.

"Cor, Jay," said Lu's voice. "Get yourself back here and move it like you mean it."

Cor shot up straight and shoved the heel of her hand against the torque. "What is it?" she demanded, forgetting to whisper like they usually did over the e-comm links.

"We hit diamond. I think. I . . . look, just get back here."

"On our way," came Jay's voice.

Cor sucked the last of the porridge off her fingers and deposited her bowl on the table for the Bonded to find later. She hurried through the halls and across the walks of the High House, shouldering past anyone who didn't get out of the way fast enough, barely pausing to raise her hands to them. Something could have happened down in the smooth shadowy tunnels under the shelter. Maybe something finally switched on or came alive. Something real and comprehensible. That idea shone like a freshly lit lantern.

"Jay." Cor slapped his threshold and pulled the door-curtain back at the same time. He was sitting on his bed, shoving his right foot into his boot.

"Where's your gear?" he demanded. "Come on, we've got to get moving. We've only got a couple of hours until nightfall."

"Have you got us leave from the King?"

A spasm of distaste crossed Jay's features. "I'll get it, I'll get it. You get the sledge ready. We need to move it!"

"All right, all right. I'll bring everything round to the main courtyard." She let the curtain drop. She was halfway down the corridor before she was able to put a name to the strained, stark expression on Jay's face. He was scared. No, he wasn't just scared, he was so panicked that he didn't care what she saw.

What in any hell could panic a Vitae? Even an ex-Vitae?

Her throat tightened but she didn't let it slow her down. Jay needed to get back to the shelter. They needed to find out what was going on and get that information back home. That was her other job. She was to learn everything, immerse herself in everything, and at the very end, it was her absolute responsibility to get out with what she knew.

In the back of her mind a voice said Jay was not going to make that easy. She gave a mental shrug to silence it and concentrated on not skidding on the slick flagstones of the open walkway that led to the stables.

"Skater! Sight!" She shouted the stable keepers' names imperiously and added a loud whistle. The pair of squat, Bonded men scrambled into view from between the oxen's fat bodies. "I need the sledge. Let's get it done."

They passed their hands briefly in front of their eyes and sprang into action. With whistles and wordless shouts, they bullied a quartet of oxen into place and started strapping them to the yokes while Cor knotted and buckled the leather reins into place. She tried not to think about how the oxen's eyes looked so much like Skater's, or how once upon a time she never would have ordered another person around like that.

I am not here to judge. I'm here to learn and get the news out so they can all join the Family.

Except they're not going to get to.

It's still got to be better than this. She caught up the driving stick and slapped the rump of the left, rear ox.

"Move, you lumps!" she hollered. The sledge scraped forward over straw and mud out onto rutted dirt and rock.

Jay jogged up to the sledge and swung himself clumsily up next to the driver's stand before she could call the team to a halt.

"Keep going," he said, clambering back to sit on the crates.

Cor managed to keep the reflexive jerk in her arms from tightening the reins. The oxen plodded forward toward the main gate.

"What's with you, Jay?" She tried to catch sight of him out of the corner of her eye, and still keep her other eye on the approaching gate.

"I think I know where that missing hundred went." He was looking past her shoulder, toward the heights. His face was still strained as he scanned the tops of the roofs and the distant walls.

"Are you going to tell me, or are you seeing scars on my hands?" The saying popped out before she could stop it. Her knuckles tightened on the reins and she had to just nod at the guards at the gates. Only one of them looked up. The other five had their eyes fixed on the commander coming down from the staircase alongside the wall.

The sledge jostled through the gate and Cor had to keep her eyes on the ruts in the half-dry road as well as the walls of the houses that defined the narrow streets. She pulled on the reins and whistled to the oxen to steer the sledge in something approaching the right direction.

"They're here," said Jay.

"What!" Cor glanced wildly from the street, to Jay and back again. She meant to tell him he had lost his mind, but her surroundings were beginning to penetrate through acclimatized eyes and her brain was starting to realize something was wrong.

Narroways was a noisy place, and this afternoon was no exception. There was noise and plenty of it. Shouting and hollering bounced off the close-packed buildings and cut through the steamy wind. Every blacksmith in the city seemed to be at his forge, hammering away. But there weren't any children on the stairways, just the tops of heads and glimpses of faces bobbing to and fro on the roofs. No pedestrians crowded the streets. No soldiers on their oxen jostled them aside. There was just the shouting and the clattering and . . .

"Skyman!" shouted a voice.

A stone whizzed past and Cor ducked. The oxen halted in confusion. Jay hauled open the sledge's canvas cover. The missing people spilled into the street like a flood down a canyon, driven by soldiers in the First City uniform. The noise hadn't been blacksmiths, but swords. People ran into the houses, trying to get out of the way of the fray, but some were making a stand, with whatever they had at hand. Bodies draped in ponchos so she couldn't tell if they were men or women surged around the soldier's oxen waving sticks and

hatchets. The soldiers flailed with swords and clubs. Stones
from slings shot through the air indiscriminately.

The lead oxen bellowed and reared, giving Cor something
she could concentrate on. She hauled hard on the reins and
whacked their broad backs with her stick, poking and shouting,
reminding the stupid beasts that they were more afraid of her
than of anything in front of them. The sledge lurched forward.

But there's a truce! her mind cried.

First City is a bunch of sticklers for . . .

*First City is losing. Badly. But they knew Narroways
couldn't afford to prolong the war. They were ready to risk
two minor members of their Noble house in a gambit to knock
what was left of Silver's support out from under her.*

*And they wouldn't feel it was much of a risk if they knew
that Heart of the Seablade was a Heretic.*

Cor shouted at the oxen and smacked at them with the
reins. The big, stupid beasts bellowed and stamped forward.
Hands grabbed her arm and for a split second she saw an
angry round face and felt herself dragged off-balance. Jay
almost fell forward and smashed a heavy fist across the stranger's mouth. The hands fell away and Cor regained her footing.

The oxen were panicking now, all of them fighting through
the surging, clamoring mob to try to find enough room to run.
Cor gave them all the rein she could. Animal instinct and a
ton of mindless fear might just clear the way for them. Another
pair of hands snatched at her. She smacked flesh with her
driving stick and heard a voice howl. More hands. She struck
out again. More screams, more white eyes, more confused
colors on earth brown skin. She lashed out again and again,
the noise of battle fading fast behind a ringing in her ears
and a sick swirling in her head.

Jay loosened his jerkin and pulled out the gun.

He hunched beside Cor, drew a bead on the thickest ranks
of the First City soldiers, and squeezed the trigger.

The soldiers of both sides exploded. Blood and flesh
sprayed everywhere with the sound of the shots echoing
between the houses. The fray turned into a stampede as they
screamed and fled. Cor urged the oxen forward and they tried

hard to break into a run to get away from the noise and the blood.

"Brilliant!" she shouted hysterically. "Now you'll have half of Narroways convinced we're the Aunorante Sangh!"

Jay didn't answer. He just leveled the gun toward the fleeing backs and fired again.

"Over their heads, you animal!" Cor shrieked, but she didn't have the luxury of turning to see if he'd done it. The oxen had spotted the gates and they were barreling forward. It was all she could do to keep a grip on the reins. The maddened beasts were about to yank her arms out of their sockets. She couldn't slow them, couldn't steer them. A river of would-be refugees clogged the gateway in front of the wagon, but the oxen were beyond caring.

"Outta the way!" she screamed. "Runaway! Runaway! Get outta the way!"

The walls closed in too tight and her voice rode too high and thin over the incoherent crowd. Backs fell into the mud and more screams rang through the air. All she could do was keep her numb fingers wrapped around the reins and pray they'd get out of the crush soon.

They made it through the gates in a blur of light and shadow and burst out onto the open road. The oxen stampeded down the flattest path through the crowd that was surging out in all directions. Sleighs and sledges rocked and swung to get out of their way, people scattered as if a wind blew them apart. Pain began to creep up from Cor's clenched hands and down from her clenched jaw.

They were ahead of the crowd now, with the worst of the noise and riot pounding at their backs. Cor could separate out the bellows of the oxen from the screams of people. The sledge lurched and jumped badly as it hit the unyielding ruts in the road. She gathered nerve and muscle, braced her feet against the slats on the floor, and threw all her weight backward, dragging the reins up against her chest.

The oxen bawled and the left lead tossed his head hard. Cor gritted her teeth until she was sure they'd crack and hung on. The sledge skipped across another series of ruts, but the team slowed down and stopped.

"What're you doing!" shouted Jay, dropping into Standard.

"Shut up!" Cor snapped back. "Just sit down and shut up!" She ran her hands across the oxen's sides, feeling the way they trembled and how their lungs heaved. She jerked on the harness, checking the knots and straps to make sure everything was tight. She closed her mind against the sight of the rust brown blotches that soaked up the layers of dust on the team's bald, pale legs.

When she was satisfied the tack wouldn't come undone, she resumed the driver's stand and slapped the reins. The oxen obeyed the gesture and lumbered forward. The country-side was deserted. In the brush and trees Jay saw knots of oxen and people, fleeing from the city. Word must have spread that there was fighting in Narroways and they were all clearing the road. Cor set her teeth gingerly to avoid reawakening the ache that ran all the way down to her shoulders and pressed the oxen's pace up the rise toward where the world bent. She tried to forget that Jay was sitting at her back with the gun resting on his knees. She tried to tell herself that he had just done what he had to. They had to get clear of the crowd. If she'd been dragged down, she would have been killed and he would have been trapped. She had to get out. It was her job. She had to get away. And they weren't Family anyway and they weren't ever going to be and whatever they did now was better than what the Vitae would do later.

She tried to pray that King Silver's troops were mustered and giving the First City troops all the hell there was to hand out. They had to win so the Unifiers could win.

In the end, all she had the strength to try to do was not be sick.

Up ahead, the canyon had gone black. The oxen dragged them past the shadow line and Cor squeezed her eyes shut. She opened them and peered through the murky night. She didn't look back. She'd never learned to enjoy watching the daylight get swallowed up.

Jay was rummaging around in the cargo boxes. The noise stopped and he came forward to hook a pair of powered lanterns to the sledge's awning, one on either side of Cor's head. He looked at her, but neither one of them said anything.

The lanterns made a clear puddle of light to show her which way to drive the oxen, but did nothing to draw the teeth of the wind that had turned vicious in the darkness. She tried to read the mottled clouds. No breaks in the sky meant rain all too soon. Just enough light touched the Wall ahead to show her the jag and split that marked the entrance of the thread canyon where the shelter waited.

She halted the sledge and, even though she could feel Jay's impatience like a weight on her shoulders, she unhitched the oxen. If the gods knew what was going on or how long it would take to clear it up, they weren't talking. She slapped the oxen alternately with her hand and her stick until they ambled away. Somebody'd find them and take them in. Left tied up to a tree, they might just freeze before sunup. The Realm held no warmth at all after dark. No one was sure why. Cor had a theory, but she kept it to herself. Theorizing wasn't part of her job.

Jay had both lanterns in his fists and handed her one. He'd stowed the gun out of sight. The numbing horror of watching him fire so calmly on the crowd was beginning to thaw, but she still couldn't make herself speak. She motioned for him to go ahead of her.

He grunted something she didn't try to hear and started up the crevice in the wall that held their little, domed base.

The cold had gotten its teeth well and truly into her bones, as they said, by the time Jay opened the shelter's door and they stepped, blinking, into the light and warmth. Lu was nowhere to be seen.

"He must be downstairs," said Jay.

He said it very casually, but that casualness vanished as soon as they peeled back the hatch that covered the tunnel entrance.

Once the silicate had been discovered, she and Jay had paid half a dozen Bondless to take them around to all the exposed patches they could find near Narroways. They'd carried on for only a week before they'd found the hatch.

It had taken Lu three times as long to pry the thing open. At the bottom of the well, a corridor ran straight into the canyon Wall, smooth-sided with an arching roof and level

floor and no lighting fixtures at all. The surface of the walls
seemed to shift and flow wherever their lights touched them.

About twenty yards past the entrance, the tunnel under the
wall turned into another shaft. The platform that covered half
the tunnel mouth and was obviously supposed to be used to
navigate it was even more stubborn than the hatchway had
been. Since they had used the ladder they were issued to get
down the first shaft, they had been forced to commission
something the people of the Realm actually excelled at. A
native-made rope ladder dangled down into the darkness.

Ladders and rope bridges were a part of her daily life now,
but it had taken Cor a long time to get used to climbing
the thing. It swayed and wriggled under her hands as she
descended. Although it was really only ten meters or so to
the next level, it always felt like a hundred. She breathed a
sigh of relief as the tunnel's lip came within reach of her toes
and she could stand on her own and pry her fingers off the
braided rungs. She waved up to Jay's silhouette so he could
start down.

Light shone softly from down the end of the tunnel, too
much light for it to be just Lu's lanterns. Eerie shadows shifted
on the wall, even though the light burned steadily. Voices
echoed unintelligibly off the walls, but someone was crying.

"Lu?" Cor hurried forward.

"Here." Distance and echoes made the word ring around
her ears.

The light grew and enveloped her as she reached the threshold of the room they'd dubbed "Chamber One." The curved
walls were all made of the same strangely shifting stuff as
the tunnel. The frames of the furniture, chairs presumably,
were thick with dust from rotted padding. In the sockets on
tables set flush to the wall waited fifteen of the gleaming
white stones, which the People called arlas.

The really unnerving thing was the tanks. After who knew
how many thousands of years, there was still liquid in them
and in the liquid, there were shapes of things. Whether they
were grown things or manufactured, Cor couldn't have said,
but they moved sometimes, sluggishly and without purpose,
waiting for commands she didn't know how to give. She

couldn't help looking at them now, and was relieved to see
that the liquid turned smoky in this new, bright light, and she
still couldn't tell what was in there.

Lu stood over the two Notouch waving his hands helplessly,
like a father who didn't know how to comfort a crying child.
Trail had her head cradled in her hands and was weeping—
long, shuddering sobs that shook her whole body. Cups had
her arms around her and crooned to her softly.

"What happened?" asked Cor as she felt the blood drain
from her cheeks.

"The lights came on," said Lu, still gaping down at the
Notouch.

"What?" Jay came up behind Cor, breathing hard from his
climb.

"The lights came on," said Lu again, gesturing around the
room. Cor saw that the ceiling was glowing in random patches
as blobby as the shadows behind the walls, but thankfully,
they stayed in fixed positions. "It seems Trail here really is
related to Stone in the Wall. She touched the stones"—he
waved one hand back toward the banks of holes and arlas
without looking at them—"and poof!" He spread his hands
helplessly.

Cor knew what he wanted to do. He wanted to touch the
crying women to comfort them with a friendly hand and kind
words. He also knew what would happen. They'd flinch and
cower and try to get away. They didn't know how else to act.
They were Notouch.

And if the gods know what else they are . . .

"You'd better see this, too." Jay took two hesitant steps
toward Chamber One's "back door," another threshold leading to a tunnel that was indistinguishable from the one they
came down, except for the sign Jay had painted over it saying
NOT THIS WAY.

Cor leaned into the corridor. Instantly, a flash of ruby light
dazzled her eyes. She blinked hard. Another flash bounced
off the tunnel walls, and another.

"Gods in Earth and Hell," she whispered. "What's doing
that?"

"I haven't had the guts to go look," said Lu. "I've got a feeling those cables we found got switched on, too."

Jay slammed both fists against an empty table. "We don't have time for this!"

Startled, Lu jerked his head up. "What's with him?"

"First City broke the diplomatic truce," said Cor. "The war's going on in Narroways' streets now." She gazed around at the arlas in their control boards and the creeping things in their transluscent tanks and the shifting, meaningless shadows on the walls.

Lu'd spent days, weeks, recording and cataloging every feature of Chamber One. They'd all spent months entertaining themselves with speculation about what it all meant, and not once did they even come close to understanding it. Then, a superstitious, enslaved woman touched a stone and this room of shadows and riddles lit up like morning itself.

I wish I was Lu, she thought suddenly. *I wish the important things were wires and generators and transmitters and keeping everything up and running. I wish I thought people were all basically the same and that if they weren't acting like it, they would as soon as they had things properly explained to them. I wish I didn't think we were in way, way over our heads.*

"Hey, Diajo-Cor." Lu made her name into the Averand diminutive. "Are you all right?" He wrapped a skinny, cord-muscled arm around her shoulders and she thought she felt him relax for simply having someone he could touch without panicking them.

She squeezed his hand. "Yeah. Yeah."

Except that I'm too tired for this. I'm too cold, and all the gods come to my aid, I am too scared.

She walked out from under Lu's arm and stood over Trail and Cups. Trail's sobbing had quieted to a hoarse, intermittent noise.

"Notouch," said Cor. "Get up that ladder into the white room. You can sleep by the fire until she's well enough to talk. Get out of here."

"As you command, this despised one shall do," said Cups and there was no mistaking the relief in her voice. Trail

moved, jerkily, reflexively, but at least she moved. A lifetime
of following whatever orders she was given got her to her
feet so she could walk out into the dark tunnel behind her
cousin.

Lu watched them leave. "I don't know for sure what happened to her, but she didn't like it and I don't think she's
going to do it again."

"She's going to have to," said Jay.

Cor felt a cold flare of anger go through her. She remembered the sound of gunfire and the sight of blood. "I don't
care who you think you are, Jay, but you can't make this
decision without orders from May 16."

Jay stabbed a finger down the tunnel. "If King Silver can't
hold Narroways, we're going to lose any chance of creating
a coherent power base before the Vitae arrive. The only other
thing we can do is get control of this place." He leaned
forward and Cor saw his jaw shake. "If we don't, we're lost.
Everything is lost!"

The force of his blunt statement took Cor back. "We
have to get the go-ahead. We don't know what we're dealing
with—"

"We're dealing with the Vitae." Jay cut her off. "Listen
to me, Cor. Listen hard. Do you know what they're going to
do? They're going to come in here, round everybody up, sort
out the useful ones, and pen them up. While they're doing
that, they'll be analyzing everything they can get their hands
on down here. When they're done with that they'll put the
two together and see what happens. They'll measure and
they'll record and they'll study until they understand it all.
Then, while the Unifiers are flailing around out there trying
to make political hay in this particular patch of sunshine, they
will bring what they've learned out into the Quarter Galaxy
and do whatever they please!"

"Cor," said Lu gently, "I don't like this either, but I've
got to agree with Jay." Lu shook his head. "There's too much
power here. But what we need to do first is get those two to
introduce us to the rest of Stone in the Wall's family."

Cor hadn't been expecting that, and neither had Jay. His
brow furrowed.

Lu sighed exasperatedly as they both obviously failed to comprehend his reasoning. "You both talked to her. Her family's got an oral tradition handed down from oldest daughter to oldest daughter along with those three arlas they carry. It's garbled as all hell, but we could probably interpret it with a little work." He paused. "It probably won't be a whole lot, but it'll be the closest thing we're likely to get to an operator's manual for this . . ." He waved his hand vaguely toward the tanks and the gleaming arlas. "Maybe we can figure out how to get it to work without jumping the people we need straight into shock."

Jay's shoulders sagged. "All right," he said at last. "But we send a message out to May 16, right now, and explain the situation. We get permission to go ahead with what needs doing, no matter what it is or who we need to drag down here."

There was danger in his voice, almost fanaticism. Cor swallowed her fear because she knew he was right. The war they'd started was going to swallow them up if they didn't get it settled. The idea was making her sick to her stomach and weak in the knees, but they were running out of merciful options.

Jay still looked grim. "You're going to find the rest of Stone in the Wall's family, Cor, so we're ready when word comes. I'm going with you. I don't like the way you've been talking."

Cor just nodded. This was wrong. This was not the way it went. If it was necessary to ride out a civil war, that was what you did, ride it out. You didn't slam your hand down over them. But there was too much at stake here.

Whatever the Family does with the People will be better than what the Vitae will do, she reminded herself.

It has got to be.

6—May 16, in the Net, Hour 22:34:34, Planet Time

. . . They say nothing will happen if the Human Family remains divided. This is true. The cycles of rise and fall will continue unabated and we who have lost our Evolution Point will remain at the mercy of a universe that does not and cannot care for the children it has spawned.

Dr. Sealuchie Ross, from her investiture speech, given 6/34/376 (May 16 dates)

*W*alls towered solid and insurmountable on all sides, leaving only one tiny chink for Dorias to squeeze anything through. He extended his arm, slowly and painstakingly. There was barely enough room inside to grope for useful pathways without disturbing the existing network. Still more walls hemmed him in. Dorias strained, stretching out his fingers as far as they would go, carefully feeling his way along the quivering veins that carried packets of information. All of the veins threaded their way straight into the walls. They left no space wide enough for Dorias to even attempt to fit through.

Dorias withdrew his arm and sent a probe back to the storage space to see if there were any explorer modules ready and waiting. Dorias seldom moved his entire self. It was an uncomfortable, unwieldy process. He had to squirm his way into fibrous paths and drizzle his consciousness into processors that were so loaded with their own data that each thought would become a leaden weight dropped without any accuracy. As he let his thoughts go, they would vanish completely, and he could only hope for their return.

Instead of enduring that, Dorias had designed a retinue of mobile parts that could travel the networks for him. Smaller and quicker than he was, they could bring back information, or perform tasks that required the manipulation of machines and datastreams light-years away from the direct line of thought from his den.

The probe came back. Luck. A module had returned today and its information had been emptied into storage, waiting for assimilation. Dorias sent the probe to fetch the explorer. When it arrived he lifted it into the newly discovered space. The explorer was smaller than his hand, but it was still a tight fit. As Dorias watched, the explorer began to methodically catalog and examine each vein where it met a wall, looking for patterns, vulnerability, usefulness. The explorer automatically posted a sentry for itself. If anyone watched it too closely for too long, it would withdraw to storage with its report.

PING!

Dorias shrugged aside to make room for the incoming signal.

PING!

The signal shot into his path and Dorias caught it neatly. It proved to be one of his wanderers. Wanderers piggybacked out on ships or stations, sometimes with preassigned tasks, sometimes just to wait quietly in case he needed a presence there.

This one's home was aboard the *U-Kenai* and it held a new message from Eric Born in its teeth.

Dorias drew the wanderer into himself and waited while the message it carried dispersed into his working consciousness. The message said only that the *U-Kenai* was finally on its way to May 16, and that Eric was on his own. Bare facts, thrown together without much thought. Eric in a hurry, and more than likely, Eric worried.

About the Vitae, thought Dorias. The name brushed against

old sores. The Vitae built walls that enclosed whole worlds and left him clawing at the entrances. They blockaded old pathways, dropping barriers between him and the wanderers, so he had to design searchers to retrieve them. The rescues could take years, or never happen at all.

Dorias didn't mind that the Vitae made life difficult for him. Challenges were stimulus, not obstacles. What he did not like was the nagging idea that they might manage to make life impossible for him, or anyone else like him.

He was also worried about the fact that Eric hadn't told him where the woman, Arla, was. It didn't take much work to guess that if she wasn't with him, Eric had probably taken her to Perivar as contraband. But the fact that Eric hadn't volunteered that information spoke volumes about how little he trusted Dorias's offer to help.

Dorias sent the wanderer back to storage. He could replace it aboard the *U-Kenai* when Eric arrived. Dorias activated the monitors surrounding his den. All communications would be checked, categorized, and stored for the duration. Projects in progress would be monitored and he would be alerted if any strayed too far from the herd.

He called for a talker and a dancer and attached leashes to them. Then he opened one of the dozens of lines that ran out of his den, shot the explorer down its length, settled himself at its mouth, and waited.

Seventy-six seconds later, the leash jerked into life, humming and tingling with the myriad signals that made up a human voice. Dorias drank them in.

"Ross, here."

"This is Dorias, Madame Chairman." Holding the end of the leash, Dorias felt the talker relay his signal while the dancer began to move, painting and repainting his portrait across Ross's video screen.

"What can I do for you, Dorias?"

"I have just gotten a message from Eric Born. He is on his way to May 16, but he is not bringing the woman."

"Damn." She followed the curse with a five-second pause. "Well, we knew that was a danger, didn't we? Has he said how much the Vitae found out?"

"This is what I have from him." Dorias shook the leash so a copy of Eric's message spilled itself along the line. The dancer took up the new pattern and repeated it on the screen and waited while Ross assimilated it for herself.

"Not a lot there."

"I believe he had other concerns at the time."

She chuckled. "Can't argue with that, can I? And before you have to ask, yes, I'll see he gets landed as soon as he gets in-system." Another pause. "And, of course, I'll extend our offer in person. What do you think he'll say?"

Dorias felt through the places where his memories of Eric Born lay stored, looking for the right answer. "It's difficult to say," he admitted at last. "I think he'll be more likely to agree, as long as he doesn't know his brother-in-law is helping our team in the Realm. He's never said what grudge he holds against Heart of the Seablade, but it is a strong one."

"Mmmmph. How does he feel about the war, then, do you suppose?"

"He's concerned. Eric works very hard to make it known that he does not care what happens in the Realm, but much of that is bravado. It is my guess that he did not wish to bring the woman, Arla Stone, to May 16 because he didn't know if it was safe for her here. Teachers, you see, are bound to protect the lives of the People."

"Mmmmph," Ross said again. "Important considerations, but at this point, he can't have any wish to see the Vitae in the Realm, can he?"

Dorias didn't answer.

"Is there anything else you think I should know?" Ross asked finally.

"Yes. Eric will almost certainly be in need of sanctuary . . . and I will be helping him, even if you decide not to."

"Even if he decides against the Unifiers?"

"Eric probably will not decide for or against the Unifiers. He will be deciding for or against what will allow him to live as free as he can for as long as he can. I owe him for past favors and I will help him do this."

"I am at least glad you let me know, aren't I?"

"I owe you for my own sanctuary, Ross."

"I can't stop you from helping your friend if that's what you need to do." Ross's signal became heavier and a bit slower. "All I ask is that you remember your cause is still our cause."

"I would not choose to forget something so important."

"Just wanted to hear you say it, didn't I?" Ross's signal lifted itself back to normal. "I'll meet Eric Born at the port if he's not likely to raise objections. Talk. Show him a few things. Hand over our offers. Try to find out what he really cares about and how much. Then . . ." She decided not to finish the sentence. "Thanks for the news, Dorias."

"You're welcome to it." Dorias reeled in the leashes for both modules and sent them back to storage.

They did not talk about debt. They did not talk about blackmail or the damage they could do to each other. It was the same with Perivar, and with Eric. Without each other they were alone, and the fact was, alone it was impossible to survive. Dorias knew. He had tried.

Schippend leveled his drooping eyes at Eric. "We're processing three hundred new arrivals right this minute. Your information will have to wait in the queue with everybody else's." Without another word, he resumed his meticulous poking at the *U-Kenai*'s control keys, looking for viruses or contraband software before he issued Eric a permit to hook into May 16's communications system.

Eric bit down the urge to order the bureaucrat to move his lumbering body like he had a brain under his skull. Instead, he brushed past Cam, who stood motionless in the back of the bridge, and stalked toward the open airlock.

May 16 was an impossibility. May 16 had a stable, planetwide climate, something which was about as likely to occur naturally as fiber optic growing on an evergreen tree. In a feat of engineering that had even made the Rhudolant Vitae blink, somebody had given the planet a solar-synchronous orbit and a perfectly adjusted tilt and rotation. It was always spring, wherever you went and whenever you arrived. A lot of planetologists spent a lot of time arguing about how it had been done. No agreements had ever been reached, because whoever was responsible for the place had neglected to leave even their name behind.

The Alliance for the Re-Unification of the Human Family had discovered it, unpopulated, and had promptly adopted it as their base. They said it was a symbol of the need for the establishment of the universal Human Family. Once, here, on this spot, someone had been able to engineer an entire planetary orbit, not clumsy terraforming or even more clumsy domed colonies, but an entire orbit and possibly an entire planet. Now they were dead and dust and all the current inhabitants could do was try to recover old knowledge.

Eric leaned against the outer threshold of the airlock and breathed the fresh, moist air. His eyes restlessly scanned the port that surrounded the *U-Kenai*. The vast, bleak expanse of concrete under the cloudless sky made it impossible for him to really relax, even in the soothing warmth of the day. Other ships sitting in their own bays broke up the horizon and the cargo haulers that chugged between them helped fill up some of the space, but there was too much left over. He could barely see the sharp, artificial lines of the Hangar Cliffs in the distance. Pride kept him from circling to the other side of the *U-Kenai*, where he could stare at the City of Alliances. Its carefully planned and meticulously maintained buildings made a border wide enough to fill in the ten-mile-wide plain that had been leveled by whoever had originally owned May 16.

It wouldn't have been enough, anyway. Nothing was ever enough to kill the last trace of agoraphobia that nibbled at the edges of his mind. Eric had been secretly grateful that his assignments from the Vitae kept him mostly on space stations. He frowned at the port and his thoughts at the same time as he remembered tearing through Haron Station with Arla on his heels.

I wonder what she's looking at right now. Eric's gaze traced the orderly forms of the distant cliffs. *I hope she's got the sense to listen to Perivar and do what she's told. I hope . . .* His thoughts pulled themselves up abruptly as he realized what he really hoped was that he'd get the chance to find out what had happened to her.

If I live so long . . . Eric cast another glance back toward his bridge. Schippend was muttering something into his torque.

I hope whoever Dorias drafted to get me into the city can wait awhile, he added sullenly. He could appreciate, in theory, the Unifier philosophy that living human beings ought to deal with living human beings. He could also understand their desire to keep both their people and their machines free of ailments caused by contact with outside sources. He ruefully rubbed the spot where he'd been injected with an armful of antivirals and antibiotics. In practice, however, their philosophy combined with their caution made for a customs process that could stretch on for hours.

One of the smaller, open port cars whirred up to the *U-Kenai*'s bay. A squared-off woman from a cold climate climbed out of the driver's seat.

"Sar Eric Born?" She squinted in the bright morning sun.

"I am." He straightened himself up.

"You'll be accompanying me once your processing is completed."

Eric managed to keep his voice smooth and patient despite the abrupt goading her tone gave his strained patience. "Thank you, but a friend of mine has . . ."

Her broad mouth smiled in jerky stages. "Sorry. Used to people knowing me on sight, aren't I? I'm Sealuchie Ross and I am the transportation your friend arranged." She must have read the look on his face as skepticism because she added, "We could hunt Dorias up and confirm it, if you want to."

Eric studied Ross for a moment. That was the name he had from Dorias. It also stirred a separate, vague memory in the back of his mind that he couldn't make show itself clearly. She was not a young woman. The blond color of her hair was faded and streaked with grey. Time had pressed her rose-and-white skin close to her bones and the wrinkles around her eyes proclaimed she had a serious outlook on life. She certainly did not have much use for ceremony. Or fashion. Eric looked over her loose green shirt and trousers and flat-soled boots. Her torque had several thread-fine cables that adhered to her flesh, one led to her translator disk, one to a pad pressed against her temple, and two others to pads pressed against her wrists, where her pulse could be measured.

Security wired. Eric dug harder in his memory. Whoever she was, she was important.

"I'm sure that won't be necessary," he lied, and looked over his shoulder toward the *U-Kenai*'s bridge again. "I'm just waiting on my IDs and communications clearance."

"Are you?" Without asking permission, Ross climbed past Eric through the airlock. Eric followed her, at a loss for the words to ask this woman who she thought she was.

"Who's processing this arrival?" she asked as she reached the bridge.

Schippend turned laboriously around with his mouth open. When he saw who came through the doorway, his mouth stayed open and he jumped out of his chair, holding himself rigidly at attention.

"Madame Chairman. This is ah . . ."

"Unexpected would be a good word, perhaps?" she replied without smiling. "This arrival is now to be given priority. Do you require my authorization?"

"I may, ah, Madame Chairman," stammered Schippend. "There are delays in the . . . um . . . background check . . ." His eyes shifted restlessly to Eric.

She nodded. "You will tell me personally if there's anything requiring special handling. I shall leave a line open from this ship." She tapped at her torque and her mouth moved as she added a subvocal command. She turned to Eric with a hint of real apology in her manner. "I am sorry about this, Sar Born."

"Thank you." Eric found himself struggling through a mental readjustment. This, at least, explained why her name had struck a chord in him. Madame or Master Chairman was the title used for the appointed head of the Unifiers.

Sealuchie Ross, Madame Chairman Sealuchie Ross, he corrected himself, ran the planet he was standing on.

What this did not explain was why the person who ran the world was running errands for Dorias.

"Dorias forgot to mention your position when he said who was coming to meet me," Eric said over the sound of

Schippend demanding to know where arrival Eric Born's IDs were, damn it!

Ross's mouth twitched. "Very like Dorias, don't you think? Not one to care much for a person's rank." Eric couldn't tell whether this amused or annoyed her.

"No, he's not," Eric agreed, trying to haul together an appropriate set of manners. "I should perhaps apologize for taking up so . . ."

She cut him off with a wave of her hand. "One of the prerogatives of the job. I get to decide what I spend my time on, don't I? Now, if you're ready, we can go talk somewhere more comfortable." She started toward the airlock.

Eric hesitated. Beside him, Schippend was sweating and swearing quietly into his torque. Cam stood motionless waiting for orders, and Madame Chairman waited for Eric to make some move.

The idea of leaving a stranger aboard the *U-Kenai* made Eric uneasy. He wanted to talk to Dorias and get his side of this story, but until he had his May 16 IDs, there was no easy or legal way for him to get into the system. He certainly wasn't going to use his power gift with so many unknown factors surrounding him.

"I'll be joining you in a moment, Madame Chairman." Eric gestured her politely toward the airlock and walked back to the common room. He picked up the satchel he had packed with a change of clothes and a few pieces of communications hardware in case his visit became . . . complicated. Then he hit the combination of keys on the comm board that opened a line straight into Cam's private ears.

"Cam," he whispered, "once the inspection's complete, seal the ship. Keep everything up and running."

"Yes, Sar Born," Cam acknowledged.

Eric nodded to himself. Some things, at least, were predictable. He shouldered the satchel strap and made his way back outside.

Madame Chairman Ross waited in the port car. Eric climbed into the empty seat beside her. "Whenever you're ready, Madame Chairman."

"Ross," she corrected him. "The title's for Unifiers and formal occasions, isn't it?"

"As you prefer." Eric stowed his pack under the seat. Ross released the brake and steered the little car into the main traffic lane that crossed the port. Eric kept his eyes on her to avoid having to acknowledge the stretch of empty space around the port or the open sky overhead.

Ross, it turned out, was not one to make small talk. She drove with her gaze on the shifting traffic, projecting an air of intense concentration. It was not from lack of skill, Eric decided. She handled the car well, sliding smoothly in and out of the stew of maintenance, transport, and private vehicles that flowed through the port. She was just extremely single-minded.

They left the port car at the free-standing arch that was the gateway to the main roads and transferred themselves to one of the automatic cars that waited there for hire. While Eric took his seat, Ross punched in her ID code and the address of their destination on the keypad and the car rolled into traffic.

"You have a room reserved at one of the diplomatic hostels, Sar Born," Ross told him. "Once we have you cleared for the networks, you may use it for an hour or a year, if you require."

"You have my thanks, Ross."

"I hope you won't mind if I also have your company for a while yet." She released a catch on her seat so that it swiveled around and let her face him. "There are a few things about the City of Alliances I want to show you, and some questions I'd like to ask you."

"I'll be happy to be of service if I can," Eric said. *I'll need new employers, after all,* he added to himself, *that is if your crowd is even marginally more trustworthy than the Vitae.*

The cityscape they moved through struck Eric as highly organized. The low brown-and-green buildings clustered around common courtyards. Ruler-straight streets crisscrossed the plain under the raised tracks carrying the monorail trains that provided most of the public transport.

The place had clearly been designed to provide comfort

and convenience for its citizens. Eric couldn't work out why it made him feel so uneasy.

Ross's car had precedence on the streets. The roadway pulled other cars out of the lanes to give the chairman clearance so her transport could breeze through the traffic. Eric guessed they were probably moving five to ten miles an hour faster than the other cars.

Madame Chairman may not go in for formalities, but she's got no problem using her privileges.

"Dorias said you're a friend of his," Eric ventured.

"Select circle, isn't it?" she said in a voice more relaxed than anything Eric had heard from her yet. "I think it's just you and me."

"No, there's a couple of others." She waited for him to name names, but he didn't.

She shook her head. "We're almost to my offices." She glanced at the readouts on the car's dashboard.

"But he is working for you?"

She nodded.

"As a Family member?"

Ross considered this. "Strictly speaking, no. But I'm not a xenophobe, Sar Born. I don't think that the creation of the Human Family means we should become isolated from the other sapient beings who share our galaxy, especially those we have created. Dorias is dedicated to the idea of a stable Human Family and I welcome him into the Alliance."

Well, she certainly speaks dogma fluently, and she knows how to talk without saying much.

He tried another tack. "I got a message from Dorias telling me to contact you."

"Part of a message, you mean," Ross's mouth twitched. "He told me the transmission didn't arrive intact. Yes, I asked him to get in touch with you. We wanted to offer you a contract for your services as a systems handler. Dorias says you're even better than he is." She lowered her eyebrows. "It's difficult to believe anyone could be better than a living piece of netware."

What do you want to hear, Madame Chairman? Eric wondered.

"Dorias has some limitations I don't," he said, watching her face closely. "Then again, I have some limitations he doesn't. Who's better depends on the job you have in mind."

"That will come when I present the formal contract." She pulled her gaze away from his and set her jaw at a different angle.

"Dorias also said it was the Unifiers who originally removed Stone in the Wall from the Realm."

"Stone in the Wall?" Ross repeated the syllables awkwardly. "Is that her name?"

"One of them." Eric ran his hands down his thighs. His palms were itching where his sun tattoos had once been.

Ross turned her bland face toward him. "Yes, we asked her to come to us as an emissary. The Vitae kidnapped her en route."

You've had that line ready for hours, haven't you, Madame Chairman? The itch in his palms intensified and in the back of his mind an outraged voice demanded to know where she had the gall to interfere with the life of one who had been named by the Nameless?

"Here we are." Ross pointed toward a domed, green glass complex behind a wall of milk-and-coffee stone. "I should warn you, Sar Born. There's going to be a bit of a scene when the car stops."

The car turned a corner smoothly and rolled through the slated, iron gates into a walled courtyard. The car stopped and the door opened itself.

The "bit of a scene" turned out to be a small army of assistants and security personnel that swarmed out of the grandiose buildings that fenced the yard.

"Madame Chairman, I've got the report on the . . ."

"Madame Chairman, you have an appointment with the . . ."

"Madame Chairman . . ."

"Madame Chairman . . ."

Ross stood like a statue in the middle of the zoo and let a big man in a grey uniform peel off her security patches and replace them with fresh ones. She seemed to drink in everything at once, occasionally rapping out a monosyllabic reply. "Yes." "No." "Go."

"Sar Born, if you please?" One of the security men stood at his elbow with a set of patches in his hands. Eric nodded briefly and let the man press one patch against his translator disk and the other against his temple. The wires tickled briefly as they adhered to his flesh.

Ross's mouth bent in what might have been a smile of approval or smug satisfaction. The expression passed too quickly for Eric to read.

"With me, if you please, Sar Born," she said. The crowd parted quickly as Ross strode toward the nearest door.

Eric gathered his wits. He followed Ross through the arched doorway flanked by a contingent of administrators and guards who had been selected from the army either by prior arrangement or telepathy.

The halls inside the complex were a combination of history lesson, bureaucrat's nest, and academic monument. On this side, the green glass was stained with a myriad of colors to depict the cities of a hundred different branches of the Human Family. Guides in black-and-blue coveralls pointed out individual scenes for gaggles of onlookers, lecturing them on the derivation and significance of each. The public access terminals were as much sculpture as they were information sources, each one done up as a different style of architecture. The Unifier administrators hurried around these obstructions without giving them a glance.

Security herded family tour groups to the side as Madame Chairman and her entourage breezed past. The professionals stepped aside, occasionally remembering to give some kind of salute in acknowledgment of their leader.

Finally they reached a lobby fenced by walls of translucent silicate. Half the entourage stayed respectfully outside while Madame Chairman and her most select group funneled themselves through the doors. The lobby was filled with worktables and around them clustered Unifiers and petitioners gabbling away in a dozen languages.

And unmistakably waiting for Madame Chairman stood two Rhudolant Vitae.

Eric froze. The Vitae leveled their attention on him like a lead weight. They marked him. No question. Ross did too. She was watching him.

She had known. She had known they were going to be here and she'd paraded him right up to them.

"You're with me, Sar Born," she reminded him as her security men opened up the doors to what Eric assumed was her inner office. One of her nameless assistants stepped up to the Vitae, explaining in cool, polite tones Madame Chairman would be with them as soon as possible.

The doors swung shut behind them, leaving Eric and Ross alone together in an airy, comfortable office. It had two walls' worth of windows and a third full of monitor screens that showed scenes from the City of Alliances, maybe real-time, maybe historical. Eric wasn't sure.

"Please, sit down." Ross gestured toward a stuffed, stationary chair and took her own seat behind a desk that looked as though it had taken a half acre of forest to build.

Eric ignored her invitation. "What do you want from me?"

"Your help," she said simply.

"And you had to show me the Vitae to make sure you'd get it?"

She didn't even miss a beat. "I had to show the Vitae you had come to meet with me. I'm hoping it will help slow them down." She ran her hands across the desk top. "Have you seen this yet?" She pressed a silicate key inlaid in the natural wood.

The video on the center monitor blurred until there was nothing left but a mottled grey background. Eric's spine stiffened. The greyness shifted and stretched until it became a pair of Vitae, one about ten centimeters and four kilograms heavier than the other.

The shorter one dipped his, if it was a him, chin in acknowledgment toward whatever camera had made this recording. Eric's brow furrowed. The Vitae did not use gestures like that, in public anyway.

What is this?

The taller Vitae spoke. "I am Ambassador Ivale of the Rhudolant Vitae. With me stands Ambassador Asgaut. We have been authorized by our representative assembly to make this recording and see to its distribution across the Quarter Galaxy.

"We are asking any and all individuals who hear this in their official or private capacities to respect the Rhudolant Vitae's claim of the world designated MG49 sub 1 by the Meridian system of Coordinates."

Eric felt the lids on his eyes pull themselves back as far as they would go. He was vaguely aware that the harsh, ragged sound under the sudden ringing in his ears was his own breath.

Ambassador Asgaut spoke. "We do not ask for any group's approval. We are not requesting permission for this endeavor. We are publicizing our intentions so that, in future, the system may be treated as Vitae territory subject to our laws and governance."

"We thank you for your attention," said Ivale.

The image faded to black.

Eric's knees shook. His eyes couldn't focus properly on the still, dark screen in front of him, and he had to fight to even keep them open.

"They've never done anything like this," said Ross coolly. "The Vitae don't claim worlds. They buy or trade for what they want until a culture's under their thumb, in case they need its resources for something.

"I was hoping you could tell me what's so fascinating about a place that is so old and decrepit it doesn't even have a proper atmosphere on three-quarters of its surface?"

Eric turned around as quickly as his weakened legs would let him and raised his eyes so he could see her.

"What is being done about this?" he asked hoarsely.

"Not much." Ross leaned back, resting just the tips of her fingers on the edge of her desk. "I wonder, Sar Born, if you have any idea exactly how powerful the Vitae are? They do a significant percentage of the building, maintaining, and managing for the known members of the human race. Most of their clients are willing to simply let them have MG49 because they can't afford to upset them. Some of them are even eager for them to get it, because they think whatever it is the Vitae found there will eventually be up for sale." She eyed him carefully. "They don't even care whether it's contraband or not."

Eric's gaze drifted toward the blank screen again. Faces flashed in front of his mind's eye. Lady Fire. Heart of the Seablade. Arla.

Ross sighed. "Sar Born, whether or not you understand that it's in your interests to cooperate with the Human Family, I can't say, can I? But you should see that both our kind have an enemy in the Vitae."

Eric's eyes widened again. "What do you mean, both our kind?" he croaked.

Ross kept her gaze focused on him. "When we discovered what seemed to be a culture of the Family on MG49 sub 1, the Alliance sent a delegation to begin the process of reunification. We were extremely startled to discover for all the superficial matches, your people aren't really Family. Telekinesis, for example, is not something that has ever evolved naturally for any branch of the Family, although several have managed to induce very weak forms of it through genetic engineering." She paused. "Whoever worked with your ancestors was rather more successful, I gather."

Eric jerked backward half a step. "How did you . . ."

Ross waved dismissively. "It was one of the first things our observation team noticed. Everybody's got legends about telekinesis, or telepathy, or any of a whole host of extrasensory perception and skills. But nowhere, except on MG49 sub 1, can they be performed on a macroscopic level, on command, by a significant portion of the population. There're other proofs, too, if you want them. Your people were not born, Sar Born. They were made ."

No! shouted a voice in the back of his mind. *We were named by the Nameless! "The Nameless spoke of the People then. They named Royal, Noble, Bondless, Bonded, and Notouch. Each life they named became Truth and took up its place in their Realm . . ."* He silenced the voice harshly.

When he could finally speak again, he said, "If we're not Family, what are you doing there? Why don't you leave us . . . them in peace?"

Ross leaned across her desk. "Because while you yourselves are not Family, you are part of the family legacy, like Dorias. We need to understand you so we can welcome you properly." She looked at him and her eyes were intense. "And you can be sure we will welcome you, where the Vitae will only enslave you."

"You really are a believer, aren't you?" His voice was heavy with exhaustion. This was too much all at once. Far too much.

"Yes," she said without hesitation.

"Even though you know you've started a war?"

"I didn't start the war. Isolation from the Human Family started that war." Ice glittered in her eyes. "Reunion will end it."

Eric's head drooped. "I'm going to ask you one more time, Madame Chairman," he said toward the carpet. "What do you want from me?"

"I want you to speak for the Realm. I want you to say you do not want the Vitae there and that you protest the invasion. I want you to repeat it for broadcast to the Family members and attendant governments. I want you to make life difficult for the Vitae." She paused. "You know you can see it from here."

"See what?" asked Eric, confused.

"MG49 sub 1. The Realm of the Nameless Powers. Your sun and its companion are one of the stars in our sky."

"And?"

"And it's a crashing funny-looking place, isn't it?" She touched the inlay on her desk again and Eric, almost involuntarily, looked toward the central screen. The monitor showed an extremely out-of-scale representation of a binary system; a golden primary star looming over a white dwarf. Eric watched their gentle motion. He could remember his father's stories of *his* father's delight at the discovery of that companion. It confirmed the Teacher's assertion that the sun, the suns, were Garismit's Eyes watching the Realm, as the stars were the eyes of the Nameless, watching from afar.

At the edge of the screen hovered a lopsided planet, rotating gently to display a surface of bare, radiation-burned rock. If he watched long enough, Eric knew, it would eventually display a blur of cloud cover held in place by a ragged circle of mountain. The Realm of the Nameless Powers.

"Just sits there, doesn't it?" said Ross, resting her elbows on the desk. "All on its own, in a steady orbit around a binary star. No moon, no other planets, not even a gas giant or two for company."

"Madame Chairman, what are you getting at?" Eric said in a strangled tone.

"I mean the Unifiers make it their business to hunt down unknown worlds. We're very good at it . . . but your world . . . this arrangement is so manifestly unlikely for the production or support of human life that we didn't even bother to look at it. It was an accident that we found your people at all. One of our spotters calibrated a probe incorrectly."

Her voice was steady but her eyes practically glowed with eagerness. "You know, there's only one world we've searched for that we couldn't find."

"Which is?" Eric tried to keep himself under control. Let Madame Chairman lead him along. Let her play her game out. When she was finished, he would still be standing here and she would have his answer in full.

"The Evolution Point for the Human Family," she said. "We have been looking for three centuries now and we have come up empty, haven't we? After three centuries." She spread her hands. "I think I know why."

Eric said nothing, he just let her go on.

"Dorias told me that your mythology is founded around the idea that a servant of the gods moved the world to a safe location." She smiled so wide that he could see her teeth. They were white, clean, and as even as the lines of the Hangar Cliffs. "I think they didn't just move it, I think they hid it." She nodded toward the screen again.

"Madame Chairman"—Eric did not let himself look at the screen—"why would anybody want to hide the Evolution Point?"

"To keep it from the Rhudolant Vitae?" she said archly. "Or their ancestors. I can't say for certain, can I? We haven't got an overall history of the Quarter Galaxy for ten years ago, let alone three thousand. We do, however, know that engineering a planetary orbit was possible for someone, at some time." She pointed meaningfully at the ground.

Eric could feel her assurance reaching out to him, as palpable as the touch of a hand.

"You see what it means, don't you? No one even vaguely connected with the Family would willingly let the Vitae lay sole and whole claim to the Evolution Point and the people on it. Since the Shessel were discovered, safe and sound on their own Evolution Point, there has been a reemergence of interest in the Family for finding ours. Sar Born, speak for your people, the Guardians of the Evolution Point, and you give us all a real fighting chance against the biggest stopping block to the reunion of Human Family. You could put the Vitae back in their place, just by speaking out."

"And if I don't," said Eric, "then what?"

She spread her hands. "Then nothing, Sar Born. You have the use of the room and will have use of all the nets as soon as your IDs are cleared. You are my guest. I, on the other hand, am Chairman of the Unifiers and I will harry the Vitae in whatever way I can until I find out what it is they are trying to do. Why, for instance, they are kidnapping natives from MG49 sub 1."

Eric's mind reeled and his sense of balance finally failed. Forgetting pride, he collapsed into the nearest chair. Ross didn't take her attention off him. Despite that, he curled his fists around his palms and pressed his knuckles against his trouser legs. He remembered looking toward First City's walls and thinking *if you will break the law, I will break it more grandly and more permanently than you ever could*, and wishing his father could hear him, and then he remembered the tears that mixed with the icy rain, because part of him still wanted to run home and find out that none of what he had seen had happened.

He stared at the smooth, unmarked backs of his hands and fought to remember it had been ten years since he had told the Realm to go drown itself. Ten years of making his own life unburdened by the laws of the Nameless and the conflicts they bred. It was a freedom he could not, would not, just toss aside.

"Madame Chairman, I don't speak for anyone in the Realm. I left there and I have no intention of going back, or of getting myself caught up in whatever war you want to fight with the Vitae. I have business of my own to take care of that will use up my personal resources. I thank you for your hospitality and I hope I shall not have to impose on you for long. I shall pay for what I use, I assure you." He stood and found his knees held steady.

Ross pressed both palms flat against her desk top. "There is one other thing of which you should be aware, Sar Born."

Eric held himself still. "Which is?"

"Two unifiers, good people, friends of mine, died when the Vitae kidnapped your kinswoman."

Eric almost said "she's not my kin," but he stopped himself in time.

"There are Trustees and Board members here who want to publicize what those two died for. Do you have any idea what will happen to you, and to your world, if I let them?"

"I am sure, Madame Chairman, you will do exactly as you see fit whenever you see fit," said Eric. "And that there is nothing I could do or say to stop you.

"May I go now?"

He had to give her credit; she had obviously prepared herself for this possibility. She did nothing more than lean back in an attitude of resignation and wave toward the door.

"You are a free individual, Sar Born, you may come and go as you like. I have no claim on you. Especially since you say you will pay for what you use. One of my clerks will see that your debts are totaled and sent to your room."

Eric left. Behind him, Ross must have given notice that he was coming out, because the security man was waiting to remove his patches and the floor indicators were lit up with the way back to the courtyard clearly marked. An auto waited for him with the door raised.

He climbed in. The door closed. It was then he realized he had no planet ID to enter to make the thing move.

Eric leaned back in the seat, closed his eyes and began to curse. He did it slowly and methodically, using all the blasphemies in all the languages he knew. He even added some he hadn't heard since he'd been a student in the Temple. By the time he was finished, the entire complement of the Unifiers, and the Rhudolant Vitae, and their ancestors back seven generations had been maimed, rendered impotent, ripped away from the shelter of any divinity, accused of bestiality, and blasted headfirst into the marshes the Notouch used for toilets.

A slight vibration trembled the soles of his shoes and the car began to move.

Eric's head jerked up. A voice spoke over the intercom. "Can't leave you alone for a moment, can I?"

"Dorias." A wave of relief washed over him followed fast by a wave of anger. "Dorias, were you listening to what your Madame Chairman said?"

"I was. We'll talk when we get to your room. I'm making it safe for us now."

They gave me a bugged room? Eric began cursing through his teeth. *The Vitae first, now the Unifiers. Who do these people think they are?*

The car traveled three kilometers' worth of tidy city blocks and finally parked itself in front of a three-story, brown brick building built like an abstract sculpture made of uneven blocks. The silver cables of access elevators stretched between its widespread wings. The car door raised itself and Eric picked up his bundle. As soon as he stepped onto the pedestrian walkway, the car door closed itself up and the vehicle drove itself away.

A second car pulled up in the spot his had vacated. Eric looked back automatically and saw Schippend heave himself out of the vehicle.

"Sar Born," he puffed. "I have your IDs, Sar."

Schippend held out four flat squares of shiny polymer embossed with his name, the location of his ship, and his arrival date. One was labeled for access to public transportation, one for the libraries and other public buildings, one for automatic access to communications networks outside his ship, and one for drawing on the credit he'd been required to transfer to a May 16 account.

Eric tucked the squares into his tunic pocket and sealed it. "Thank you for your help, Sar Schippend."

"I apologize for the delay." Schippend's eyes glittered. "Madame Chairman frequently makes things difficult for people who don't give her her own way."

"Does she?" said Eric carefully.

"And if she is making things difficult for you, Sar Born, I'll be glad to help you leave May 16. Immediately."

Eric's back stiffened and he wasn't able to keep his surprise from showing. He also couldn't help noticing the greedy look in Schippend's little blue eyes.

"Thank you for the offer, Sar Schippend," Eric said. "I'll have to consider it."

"I am on the public lines, Sar Born. One is open for you." Schippend climbed into his car and was gone.

Garismit's Eyes! Eric rolled his own toward the heavens. "Anyone else?" he demanded. The street remained quiet, except for the traffic rushing past.

The hotel did not have a main doorway. Instead, the hatches for six separate access elevators faced the sidewalk. Eric slid his ID card into the labeled slot and a door opened to let him inside. He watched the shiny, gold walls as the elevator rose for about thirty seconds, glided sideways, then forward, then rose again. He did not touch the key that would have turned the cabin translucent and allowed him to see the panorama of the City of Alliances spread across its perfectly flat field.

When the door opened, it led to a comfortably furnished room, about twice the size of the common room on the *U-Kenai*. Instead of a window, the outer wall was taken up by an elaborate comm center, with all its keys labeled in three different languages.

"Very nice." Eric dropped his pack on a table.

He sat in the comm screen's chair and tried not to squirm while it adjusted to fit the contours of his body. He opened the line to Dorias's home space.

The screen filled with the blur of shifting colors cut by rippling, horizontal lines that was Dorias's idea of a self-portrait.

"Hello, Teacher Hand," Dorias said, and the lines jumped,

matching the frequency and intensity of his voice. Dorias had never completely dropped Eric's title. You taught me I could make my own choices, Dorias had said. I choose to remember your earned name.

"Hello, Dorias. I hope you're doing well," he added with more than a trace of irony to his tone.

"Quite," replied Dorias blandly. "Better than you are, I think." He paused. "Eric, I'm sorry. I didn't know this would happen."

"I'm sure you didn't." Eric slumped and the chair undulated against his spine. "I'm sure Madame Chairman didn't give you any reason to be alarmed about what might happen once I got here."

"Teacher Hand, that is unfair."

"Is it?" asked Eric bitterly. "Your friend is a schemer and a fanatic, Dorias."

"Of course she is," replied Dorias calmly. "It's fanatics who get caught up in events like this. Normal people know when to give up and go home."

"Thank you very much," Eric muttered.

"You were the one who told me the power gifted were trained to be fanatics in the Temple."

"I know. I know." He sighed. "What are you doing here, Dorias? What could you possibly want with these people?"

"They're the only ones around who have even a small chance of making an effective block against the Vitae. They are interested in establishing a permanent, open communications network. If I help Ross with . . . Family matters . . . she works on making sure that network is one I can use and the more space there is, the more chances there are that there'll be others like me found, or made."

Eric blinked. "Does Madame Chairman know about this grand scheme?"

"Of course she does."

"Dorias." Eric leaned forward. "I don't know how safe you are here. I don't think Madame Chairman approves of people who are either not Human or not under Family control."

"Never fear, Teacher, I've made myself extremely useful to her. She has a lot riding on my continued goodwill."

And you've got a lot riding on hers. It was easy to forget that Dorias was only six years old. His experiences and memories were mature and complex, but his knowledge of human duplicity, while it existed, was limited. He hadn't had to plumb many depths yet. Eric debated telling him about Schippend for a moment, then decided against it.

Who knows what kind of pressure Madame Chairman would lay on Dorias if she found out he knew about a member of . . . Of what, a conspiracy? Political opposition? Black market? What?

Eric's shoulders started to ache from the weight on them. "Dorias, I have a feeling things are moving double-quick around me. I've got to get going."

"What are you thinking of doing?"

"I'm going to try to tap into the Vitae private network so I can find out what they're doing in the Realm."

"You don't pick the easy targets, do you?" A pair of lines arched in an imitation of raised eyebrows. "You know it's physically impossible for me to get inside their net, don't you? It's like you trying to walk through a brick wall."

Eric grimaced. "I know. I'm counting on being able to use my power gift to at least open a line in there. I might even be able to work the data retrieval commands. But I won't be able to interpret anything I pull out."

"Ah, and that would be my job?" said Dorias.

Eric nodded and then remembered Dorias couldn't see him. "Yes. The only real problem is I can't do my part from here. I'll have to get close to a station or terminal that's got access to a Vitae system. But I can't risk a transmission from the *U-Kenai* to May 16. I've got no idea who the Vitae have watching for me. I need . . . I need to ask you to come with me." He said it carefully. Dorias did not like data boxes. They could be picked up and carried away too easily.

Dorias's frequency lines wriggled and bunched sharply. "There's another possibility." His lines smoothed out. "I could, if you can give me time, provide you with a copy of myself."

That took Eric aback. The idea sank in and he smiled. "You'd give me your firstborn? Dorias, I'm honored."

The frequency lines bowed upward momentarily to parody a human smile. "It would not be my firstborn, although it is certainly not something I do frequently, but yes, that is the idea. I'll estimate the required storage space."

Eric mentally ran through an inventory of his ship's information systems. "I haven't got a whole lot of the dynamic storage to spare, Dorias. I run pretty close to capacity." He stopped. "Unless you could fit a new program into Cam."

"The android?" There was a split-second pause. "Yes. I could do that. In fact, it would be easier to fit a program based on my own makeup into the android's network than the normal ship systems. It's much more flexible. I am beginning work on it now." A section of waves and colors fenced itself off in the lower right-hand corner of the screen.

"Thank you." Eric watched his friend's fluctuations for a moment. "How long do you think this will take?"

"Until tomorrow morning, I'm afraid. This is a precise job."

"That'll do fine. I have some other . . . inquiries I want to make. I'll call back later, all right?"

"And I'll keep an ear out for anything new about . . . you."

"I'd appreciate that. Good-bye, Dorias."

They broke the connection and Eric sat staring at the blank screen for a long time. *Why didn't I tell him? He might even know what Schippend's up to, or who he's working for. Garismit's Eyes, what're things coming to when I won't trust Dorias with what I know . . .*

Rather than think about that, he opened his satchel and pulled out a cobalt blue box, six inches on a side, with a small display screen on the top. A hardwire jack had been set in each side. The box could have been anything at all, from a storage box to a private data recorder to a virus apiary.

Actually it was a couple of ghosts.

Eric put the box on the chair and fished a coil of cables out of his pack to lay beside it. Then he knelt in front of the comm board. He ran his fingertips around the edges until he found the catches for the circuit cover. After a moment's scrabbling, he managed to snap them open and lift the cover away.

In some ways it would be safer to do this aboard the *U-Kenai*, but from there it would be harder to hide the point of origin for his signal.

Eric opened a flap on his tool belt and laid a pair of small screwdrivers and a delicate knife on the floor. Then he sat cross-legged in front of the board and did nothing for a long moment but study the circuits. Some of the major blocks were labeled. Some were color coded. He noted with a certain amusement that the Unifiers were using a coding system derived from the Vitae's public standard.

He located four of the major transfer points. After that, it was only a few minutes' work with the knife and the screwdrivers to splice a quartet of cables into the existing system.

He looked back at the squirming chair in disgust and dragged a single-phase seat over from the table and sat down in it.

He retrieved the box and plugged the free ends of the cables into its sockets.

Perivar had made this box. As soon as he had been able to pick himself up off the deck where Tasa Ad and Kessa had died, he had ordered Dorias to ransack the ship's data-holds and gather together anything and everything about its owners. Fighting the sickness spreading from his wounded arm, he had taken the readings from Kessa and Tasa Ad as they lay dead on the deck. He had almost lost their chance of escape, but he knew he'd need their retina and finger scans, their DNA echoes, and their images. When he and Eric had ducked the other runners and climbed aboard the *U-Kenai*, Perivar had dumped all that information into this box. Eric remembered how he had paced between the airlock and the common room while Perivar bent over the box, selecting, organizing, creating. Eric laid his hand on Dorias's carrying case and, for the first and last time, he pleaded to the Nameless for a Skyman. Perivar jacked the box into the comm board and, using the ship's intercom, sent orders to Cam to get the *U-Kenai* under way. The android verified that the orders came from its owners and obeyed.

When Eric got onto Schippend's line, Schippend would not see him. His screen would show him Tasa Ad standing a little in front of Kessa, who would be hanging back to act as his backup and advisor. Just as they had appeared when they lived. He could scan their retinas, if he had the equipment, and verify the DNA records of their arrival and registry on May 16. As far as the network was concerned, they were alive and well and in residence in the City of Alliances. Eric could view the runner's images on the box's display screen and control them with a touch.

Their projected behaviors had been so like what he had seen from their living counterparts, Eric had once asked Dorias to analyze the processes inside the box to see if he could find any sign of independent consciousness in them. He still did not know what he would have done if Dorias had said yes.

Eric cradled the box on his lap and, with one hand, called up the public directory to trace the open line Schippend had reserved.

Schippend's face appeared on the main screen, and he was obviously none too pleased to see a pair of strangers on his screen. "This is a reserved line, and I . . ."

Eric touched the image of Tasa Ad and said, "Your pardon, Sar Schippend." on the box's display, Tasa Ad's head inclined smoothly. "I just wanted to be certain that I would reach you," he went on. "We have a mutual acquaintance, I believe. Sar Eric Born."

Schippend stiffened. "Sar Born is no acquaintance of mine. I was assigned to clear his planetside IDs. That's all."

"He told me that you also offered to help him leave the planet if things got . . . difficult for him." Tasa Ad's face took on a knowing smile. Perivar had done a great job programming the body language. Not surprising, Eric supposed, since ghosts had been his specialty as a revolutionary.

Eric tapped the screen over Kessa and mouthed the words for her. She straightened up. "Or if Madame Chairman made them difficult."

"What do you want?" asked Schippend.

"Credit," said Kessa. Eric touched Tasa Ad and gave him his lines.

He waved his sister back. "If there's someplace you or your employers want Sar Born to be, or not to be, we can take care of it for you."

Schippend's expression became wary. "And how is it you can manage that?"

"We are the ones who gave him passage off his home-world," said Tasa Ad. "He owes us for a few things."

"And we owe him," added Kessa darkly.

"I need to clear this line," said Schippend.

"Of course. We can be contacted at this space." Eric cut the line, leaned back, and waited.

He didn't have to wait for long. The box screen lit up in less than a minute. Text lines spilled across it, reporting that Schippend was running his checks. He was making sure that Tasa Ad and Kessa had actually landed, that they had been checked in and verified. As long as he looked in the May 16 network, all his calls would be routed to the ghost box. If he started checking outside, he would find that Tasa Ad and Kessa had vanished six years ago. And then Kessa would just explain that being driven underground was what they "owed" Sar Born for.

Eric stretched. Between checking up on Tasa Ad and then contacting his employers, Schippend could be at this for hours. Eric used an unaltered line in the corner of the comm board to order a meal from the kitchen. He yawned. Some sleep would be good, but he couldn't risk it. He had to be awake in case something went wrong with the ghost box. He called up his account from the clear line, saw the negative balance, and choked. If he wanted to keep his word to Madame Chairman, he'd have to drain his own accounts to the bone. The credit listing flicked over as he watched. Now, he'd have to go into debt.

When it only took Schippend three hours to open the line to Tasa Ad again, Eric was surprised. The man was nowhere near as slow as he pretended to be.

Eric activated the ghosts and tapped Tasa Ad. "Sar Schippend, I did not expect to hear from you so soon."

"For this particular project, there is not much time to waste." Schippend leaned forward.

"We'll keep that in mind," Eric said for Kessa. "Is there a way we can help you?"

"Yes. You can get Eric Born off May 16 and take him to the ship the *Morning Glory*, docked at Orbit one."

"We'd be glad to," said Kessa. "If the pay's good."

"Oh, very good. It's Vitae pay."

Eric almost swallowed his tongue. The ghosts froze for a dangerously long pause. He jabbed a finger at Tasa Ad and choked out the words. "I should have guessed."

"Is there a problem?"

Kessa laughed. "No. I just prefer working with men with hair, that's all." All three of them laughed.

They haggled over prices then and delivery of credit, which went straight into the ghost box. Eric smiled grimly to himself as he realized he now had an easy way to pay off the outrageous bill he was running up.

He cut the line to Schippend and opened a new one to Dorias.

"Dorias. Is the copy done yet?"

"I told you, tomorrow morning, Teacher."

"Dorias, I have got to get out of here." He explained the conversation he had just finished with Schippend.

Dorias was quiet for a long time. "All right, Teacher. I'll move as fast as I can. Get back to the *U-Kenai* and get Cam ready to receive a transmission."

"Thank you, Dorias."

Eric called for a car with a preprogrammed destination. He dropped most of the credit Schippend had sent Tasa Ad into his May 16 account.

The car arrived and Eric climbed inside. He spent the ride trying not to fidget.

It was all so ridiculous. The Realm was a dead world and a dying people and all of a sudden empires were ready to go to war over it. If they wanted the power-gifted, they could just hire a few contraband runners and take them. They weren't exactly hard to spot. And if they just wanted the genes, Eric forced the thought through, the Vitae had had plenty of opportunities to get them from him. And if the Vitae wanted the planet? That was the most ridiculous part. There were plenty of dead rocks in the Quarter Galaxy that they could have laid claim to without anyone kicking up a ruckus. Almost as ridiculous as kidnapping a Notouch.

What would the Seablades say if they knew? he wondered. *What would Mother say? Nameless Powers preserve me, what would that old goat First Teacher Signed to Still Water say?*

That's if they're still alive. He bit his lip.

The auto pulled up to the port and Eric transferred into one of the port cars. It was a good thing there was little traffic at this hour. He drove with only half an eye on where he was going.

The *U-Kenai* waited undisturbed for him. Eric boarded his ship and sealed the airlock. He let out a long breath. *Home*, he thought. *And as safe as I can be anywhere.*

"Cam," said Eric as he walked onto the bridge. "Sit down. Open interface."

The android sat in the pilot's chair and stretched one arm toward Eric. With the other hand, it lifted back a socket cover on its wrist.

Eric pulled a single cable out of a storage compartment under the main boards. He plugged one end of it into the comm board socket and the other into Cam's wrist. The android did not move.

Eric opened the line to Dorias.

"All ready, Dorias." Eric stood back.

"Eric," said Dorias's voice. "I am not happy about this. I have not had time to fine-tune the copy. There may be flaws . . ."

"Dorias, I can't wait. Please," he added softly.

There was a measurable pause. "Sending," said Dorias.

Eric waited. The only sound on the bridge was the vague hum of machinery. Then Cam turned its head toward Eric and blinked twice.

"Hello. I have been sent by Dorias to help you retrieve the data from the Vitae system." For the first time, Eric heard intonation in Cam's voice. The android held out one smooth hand.

Eric stared at it for a minute, before he reached out and

shook its hand. "I am honored to meet you . . ." he stopped. "Dorias, what's its name?"

"I hadn't thought of one," said Dorias. "That is part of your ceremonial role, isn't it? I thought you'd give it one."

Eric considered the android for a moment and then took the hand he had shaken between both of his and spoke in the language of the Realm. "I speak for the Nameless Powers. I see for the Servant Garismit. In so doing I name you. Your name is Adudorias."

"Adudorias." The android nodded. "Does it mean something?"

"Just 'Son of Dorias.'" Eric tilted his head. "Is it all right with you?"

"I find it quite appropriate," said the android. "My parent informs me that 'Abassyd Station would be an optimal site for our endeavors. You will be able to open a direct line to a communications terminal that has a hardware connection to a Vitae junction box." Adudorias reached across to the comm board. "Excuse me," it said as it unfastened the cable.

"Nice manners," Eric remarked toward the comm board, feeling a bit strange. Dorias he was used to, but polite phrases coming from Cam were unsettling. "Thank you, Dorias. I'll be back as soon as I can." He reached for the shutoff key.

"Eric?"

"Yes?" Eric pulled his hand back from the board.

Dorias hesitated. "I think it would be better if you did not trust anyone else more than necessary. You are right. A war is brewing."

Eric felt his eyes narrow. "I'll remember that. Good-bye, Dorias." Eric closed the channel down and eyed the android sitting in the pilot's chair. Cam had been the one fixture in Eric's life since Perivar had left. Cam didn't move unless it was ordered to. Cam didn't quest or question. Cam did exactly as it was ordered to and no more.

Adudorias ran Cam's hands across the pilot boards, checking their layout and display sequences. It scanned the bridge, taking it all in with something that appeared to be interest.

"Adu," said Eric. "We need to get going. Can you head us out for 'Abassyd Station?"

"As soon as we're clear," it answered.

Eric went into the common room and laid himself down in the landfall alcove. He felt a twinge of obscure remorse inside.

How was I to know I'd miss a nonsentient machine? He set his jaw and stared at the wall. *Garismit's Eyes.* He rubbed his hands together. *I will be glad when this is over.* Shaking the thoughts away, he fastened the webbing over his torso. He'd left the view wall on and through it he could see the nighttime stealing in its strange, slow way over the City of Alliances. A few stars were visible over the tops of the distant cliffs.

He couldn't stop part of his mind from wondering if one of them belonged to the Realm.

7—The Home Ground, Hour 08:19:19, Settlement Time

It does not matter if you know the enemy when you see him, but you must be certain that you will fight the enemy when you know him.

From "The Words of the Nameless Powers," translated by Hands to the Sky for all who follow.

CONTRACTOR Kelat looked down at his hand and flexed the newly grown finger. He smiled and felt his chest swell. He had never really believed he would be able to have it regrown. He had never believed he would really walk on the Home Ground.

He looked about him. And he had certainly never dreamed it would be like this.

They had had to seal the building, if four walls of patched cement with a polymer sheet for a roof could be called a building, and install an atmosphere-processing plant. The Beholden and the Engineers worked with zeal and the whole process took only a few hours. The inside was a wreck. Everything was preserved, certainly, but it was also vacuum welded and corroded by dust and radiation. There had been liquid in a lot of the mechanisms that had evaporated centuries ago, allowing the circuitry to collapse into incomprehensible jumbles.

So much gone. So much stolen.

But so much left, he reminded himself. So much that can be done. Outside, the thin atmosphere just barely carried the rumble of the excavation machinery. The Engineers were carefully digging down around the base of the pillar Baiel had found. The Engineers' scans indicated it was a part of a network that extended . . . everywhere. Kelat allowed himself a smile at the bewildered look the Engineer gave him.

Kelat glanced toward where he knew the mountain range lay and wished, fervently and irrationally, that Jahidh would signal with more news of the artifact he had found. If the theories were correct, they were holding two halves of the Ancestors' system, the human-derived and the mechanically derived, and until they could bring them together, they would never understand how the Ancestors' world worked.

What bothered Kelat was that there did not seem to be any obvious interface between the two. There were control boards and readouts and other input-output sources that were perfectly comprehensible to the Historians and Engineers, but there was nothing that seemed to justify the enormous effort it would have taken to breed human-derived artifacts. Kelat could not bring himself to believe the Ancestors had created them to no definite purpose, not with the cost their creation had entailed.

"Contractor?" One of the contract apprentices made obeisance. "There is a message for you from the artifact reclamation subcommittee, 196."

Kelat made his way over to the portable board and sat on the stool in front of it. He was ashamed to admit it, but he was looking forward to having a few more trappings of civilization installed.

The touch of his fingertips on the screen opened the channel. Caril's face appeared against the grey background.

Kelat glanced sharply left and right. No Witness was in the room. They were occupied watching the activity outside, not the administrative details. His mind began the First Grace in thankfulness.

"What news?" he asked.

"The *Grand Errand* is being moved to the encampment in orbit around Kethran Colony," said Caril. "Stone in the Wall has been located there, in one of their gene-tailoring facilities."

The work of the Ancestors in the hands of outsiders! Kelat was aghast. He hoped it did not show. Caril was easily impressed or repulsed by appearances.

"What do we know about her circumstances?"

"Basq's committee is expecting difficulties and has requested to be put on the Assembly docket to authorize a bribe for the colony officials to recover her. Kethran feeling is hostile to the Vitae presence and her contract is being held by a member of one of their first families. We may offer to withdraw. The projections show that if we did, the local government would request our return within fifteen years. The trade-off will probably be deemed acceptable."

Kelat's newly grown finger began to twitch. He stilled it. "Is there any way we might recover her first?"

"Paral is reconstructing an activity trail. Outside the Amaiar Gardens, she appears to only have had brief contact with a Shessel-held communications firm."

Kelat thought. "Would you say it is a safe prediction that if the artifact felt threatened, she would attempt to run away?"

"That is certainly her observed behavior."

"Then our course of action seems clear." As he spoke, a measure of calm returned to him. "We induce her to run. Have we any of our own people on Kethran?"

Caril paused, considering. "A few. It will be possible for me to send Paral down to coordinate."

"Paral . . ." Kelat hesitated. "He's very young, Caril."

"He is dedicated. He will do what is necessary."

As does Jahidh, but that does not mean an efficient operation. Kelat tried to see alternatives, but could not. "Just impress upon Paral that he is to do no more than necessary, Caril.

"What about Eric Born?"

"He was seen on May 16, but his ship left orbit before any movement could be coordinated to recover him. Basq's network traces have been put in place, and we are waiting."

The hum from the excavation changed pitch and Kelat made an abrupt decision. "If you are forced to make a choice, Caril, the female artifact has priority over the male."

"Understood, Contractor."

"And let me contact you next time. The Witnesses here have no fixed posts. Bad timing could see us added to the Memory prematurely."

"Also understood." With that, she closed the line and the screen went black.

Kelat sat watching the blank screen for a long moment. His new finger twitched spasmodically against his thigh.

This was bad, this was wrong. There were too many factors too far out of control. But what could be done? The Imperialists were committed. The dependence on service could not continue. The power in the Quarter Galaxy was shifting with the rise of the Unifiers and the discovery of the Shessel. The Vitae were in danger of losing their footing. The rule had to become open and firmly established. The artifacts and the Home Ground were the keys to the Imperialist success. They had to be recovered and understood.

Kelat bowed his head and began reciting all six Graces. There was nothing else to do.

'Abassyd Station was so new, even the Vitae hadn't had a chance to get themselves organized on it. No comet-branded ships waited in its docks. Its personnel roles had only half a dozen Vitae designations listed. The construction records showed the Vitae's private area was yet to be built.

But they were in there. Eric leaned forward in the copilot's seat and stared at the view screen showing the station's skin. Its cylindrical modules gleamed silver and gold in the light of a distant sun. The Vitae were under there, supervising, devising, scheming.

It had taken 172 hours to get here from May 16. The *U-Kenai* had been hanging from the docking clamps for an additional eight hours, and so far, nothing had happened. If the Vitae had noticed that his little ship didn't match the transmission that described it, they weren't making an audible fuss about it. He glanced at the comm board. There hadn't been a twitch or flicker since the initial recorded docking message.

Eric stared at his fingertips where they rested against the board's edge.

What are you waiting for, Teacher? Permission from the Nameless? Or just from the Rhudolant Vitae?

During the flight time, he'd arranged a small shipment of microchips and equipment for himself. It wasn't due to arrive at the station for another forty-eight hours. Ostensibly to save money, he'd listed his decision with the dockmaster to bunk in his ship rather than rent a room. Right now, Adu was linking the ship's computers into the station's communications network so that he could catch up on the news and be notified as soon as his shipment arrived.

The Rhudolant Vitae were also hooked into the network.

"Time to go swimming," he muttered as he stood up.

"What do you need me to do?" asked Adu.

Eric started and stared at the android. "Sorry. I'm used to Cam. He never volunteered information if it wasn't an emergency."

"Understood." Adu puckered the android's mouth in a gesture that Eric guessed was meant to be a smile. "But what do you need me to do?"

"Wait," said Eric. "And when the information starts coming in, make sure it gets into the datastores. I'm not going to be able to be very discriminating about how I shovel in what I get. When the data comes in, I'm going to need you to siphon out the useful segments, any references to MG49 sub 1 or the Realm of the Nameless Powers, Eric Born or Stone in the Wall. And keep Cam's security programs up and running." He stopped. "You might also make sure the emergency beacon is primed to send a message to Yul Gan Perivar in the Amaiar Division on Kethran Colony. If something happens, Perivar should be told." Adu was looking at him with a disturbing steadiness. "He's a communications professional.

If the Vitae are watching us, he'll be able to get a message through to Dorias with a lot less risk than we could."

"Do you think . . . something will happen?"

The tone in Adu's voice was soft, almost like a child's fear. With an odd twinge, Eric realized that was exactly what it was. He gave Adu the smile he reserved for hand-marking days.

"Not really, but I want to be on the safe side."

"Also understood." The android turned back to its work and Eric retreated to the common room's work station. Tapping the line from the common room would leave Adu more room on the bridge to work.

Eric sat in front of the work station just as the green light blinked on above the main board. The line to 'Abassyd Station was open and clear, waiting for his signal. Eric stared at the board for a long moment, trying to find the nerve to begin his task. If this did not work . . . if this did not work . . .

The Nameless speak of this deed. The words of consecration surfaced in his mind, startling him, but he let them continue. *Their Words give it substance. It is true and cannot be denied. The Servant watches this deed. His eyes see my path. It is true and cannot be denied.*

He swiveled the comm chair around so the board was at his right side. Then he lifted his hand and laid it on the keys.

Once, he'd heard Perivar and Tasa Ad trying to find words to fit the power gift into the way they saw the universe. They had eventually settled on something like "resonance fields which manipulated quantum effects."

Kessa, on the other hand, had said, "It ain't natural, but it works, what more do you need?"

Kessa had a very direct approach.

Eric couldn't read a computer's mind any more than he could read a human being's, but his gift could give him a feel for the workings, both mechanical and logical. Once he knew that, the only way to keep him out of a system was to shut the power down, or incapacitate him.

The board's smooth polymer pressed against his skin and quickly became slick with his perspiration. He closed his eyes.

What I do is true. What I do is seen and spoken. It cannot be denied.

I cannot be denied.

He let his gift flow from his hands into the console. Familiar territory. He knew its shapes and nuances. With the barest effort, the blind fingers of his power made sure the configuration of the gate between the board and the open line was the proper shape. Then they scuttled down the clear channel, playing his consciousness out like a rope behind them.

The open terminal on the station was easy to find. It almost pulled him straight to it, funneling his senses down into the lines and etched pathways. The fingers of his power divided themselves to probe for the open paths between the closed ones. He moved patiently, feeling the walls to determine the shape of the place he worked in. He activated nothing. He changed nothing. He just touched the walls and remembered.

Eric found the pathways reassuringly familiar. It was all standard terminals and standard gates. Standard means to standard ends. The datastream pulled him along and Eric rode the current. His power gift divided, and divided again until he found a major routing station. Eric explored the paths leading out of it, ten at a time, until he touched a place that made his skin curdle because it felt completely strange.

He probed the strangeness carefully. It was an open portal, no question there. Information flowed steadily through it like water through a sluice gate, but the shape of the gate was undefined. It shifted minutely under his delicate touch. He recalled the other fingers, consolidating his power into a single probe and slid it across the yielding surface into the datastream.

And there was nothing there.

Eric fell into formless vacuum, the thread of his consciousness streaming out, lost and flailing. There was nothing to hold on to, no paths, nothing to do but fall.

Too far! Too far! Stop it! Pull back!

No!

His power gift slammed against a surface and lay still. Gradually, Eric recovered himself enough to move it again, searching to find a shape in this new place. Like the gate, it yielded to the lightest touch. It held its shape only loosely. It reminded him of something else he knew the touch of. It felt like . . . a living body.

The realization jolted through Eric and almost broke his concentration. This wasn't silicate and current he was dealing with. This was a realm of synapses and diffusing chemicals. Eric let his power's fingers spread out, encompassing as much of the new space as he could reach, trying to understand the ebb and flow of the new medium. The logic of it came to him slowly. This was a place to filter and organize and redirect. The gates made of nerve fibers weren't laid out in tidy lines like silicate gates, but there was a pattern there. It was subtle and easily disturbed. Eric lifted his power's fingers from the surface and let them drift, trying to understand the scope of the system. He wished in vain for a way to see the surroundings, but the best he could do was imagination. His mind's eye showed him a web of synapses stretching out to make a taut network of nerves. His power found holes in the net. Channels to other places that opened and closed in response to the system's need.

Eric held his power gift in one place, feeling the triggers and responses that moved around him. Pins and needles began to prickle his physical hands and a cramp started in his left foot. He ignored the discomfort. He had to. He had to concentrate on understanding what he touched.

Eventually the pins and needles faded away. Eric could no longer feel his physical hands at all. He didn't care. He could feel the shape of the commands that flowed through the synapses. He touched the places where the commands were fabricated and he knew how they were generated and which channels they opened. He understood the system. Maybe not everything, but enough.

He let his power slide down an open channel to see where the commands went.

He fell again. He clenched his jaw and held his panic in check. When he landed, the surface was firm and orderly. Silicate channels with orderly gates and switches waited at right angles nearby.

Now that the basics of the system had been defined, it did

not take Eric long to understand the specifics. There were only so many ways you could store data, and only so many ways you could retrieve it, no matter what the shape of your container. A Vitae system would be ruthlessly logical and efficient. He could feel their data in tidy little packages, lined up and blocked together, all of it uniformly and exhaustively labeled.

Don't say "exhaustive." He swallowed. His throat was completely dry. His lungs strained to drag in enough air to keep him conscious.

He could feel the shape of open gateways and command protocols that led to more distant storage areas. Places he couldn't possibly reach directly. It didn't matter. They would be reached for him.

Eric withdrew to the shifting, organic layer. He found the nerves he needed and pressed against them until they yielded the commands he required. Then he followed those commands down into the silicate layer. Closed gates blocked his commands, preventing their execution. His power gift forced the channels open and sealed their gates in place. When all the data was flowing freely, his power doubled back on itself and followed its own length back to the *U-Kenai*. Back to him.

Eric's hand slid off the board and dropped to his side. He could not lift it. All he could do was shake and gulp air like a man who has nearly drowned. Perspiration flowed into his eyes, making them sting and water. The pounding of his heart shook his whole body.

Nameless Powers preserve me. Never been this bad.

He opened his mouth to try to call for Adu, and gave up. He couldn't force any noise from his throat but a sickly wheeze. His head fell back against the chair.

I'll be all right in a minute, he told himself as his eyes closed. *In a minute.* Time passed, he knew that, but he didn't know how much. Awareness came and went. He did not have the strength to interfere with its whims. Eventually he was able to breathe normally and the perspiration dried on his neck and face, even though his tunic remained soaking wet. So did his trousers. Eric tried not to think about that.

With an effort, he was able to reach across the boards and

stab the request key on the food dispenser for water. He gulped it desperately, spilling half of it down his shirtfront. His stomach rebelled at the invasion of fluid and almost rejected it. The strain of keeping the water down nearly cost Eric his ability to stay sitting up. He felt better, though. He could think enough to open the intercom to the bridge.

"Adu," he croaked, "are you getting anything?"

"Lots," came the reply. "I'm processing it now. I'll find the most recent references and route them back to your screen as soon as I can."

"Good. Good." Eric swiveled his chair around so he faced the drawer of ration squares. Hunger burned in him with nauseating intensity. Even the ration squares smelled wonderful. Eric forced himself to eat slowly. Exhaustion and trembling hands helped. He consumed three whole bricks before the edge of his hunger blunted and he felt some real measure of strength return to him, enough, at least, to muster some disgust at his filthy condition.

He got to the cleaner stall by leaning against walls and doorways. He sat on the tiles while the sonics shook the grime from his skin and clothes. His eyelids drooped. He wanted sleep, badly. Sleep would take care of the ache in his head and in his eyes. Sleep. Yes. That would do it.

Not yet. Eric jerked his sagging head back up. *Need to make sure we've got what we came for, first. Nameless grant that we've got what we need. I couldn't survive using the gift again anytime soon.*

He stumbled back to his chair and fell into it. The message DATA WAITING glowed on the main screen. Eric hit the PLAY key and slumped back, forcing his eyelids to stay open until the screen cleared and the information Adu had retrieved began to unfold for him.

What appeared was a video recording of a gathering hall. Despite his fatigue, Eric sat up straighter. The place was filled with people standing on broad, flat tiers that rose from a central platform. Here and there he saw the scarlet robes and bald scalps that were the defining traits of every Vitae he'd ever seen, but they were the minority. Over a hundred men and women, robed in every color he could have imagined, stood in that room. Their skin was tinted solid black or clear pink, and every shade in between. They were bald, or bearded, or carefully coiffured. Metal and jewels dangled from wrists and necks and pierced skin. Some were missing appendages, ears or fingers or . . . Eric winced as he saw one old man with a hollow eye socket. There was something else. Eric leaned closer to the screen and squinted. Around each human form hung a vague corona of ghost white light.

They're holograms. I'm looking at an assembly of holograms.

A hole opened in the central stage. Five figures, the only real people in the room and all clothed in solid black robes, mounted a sunken staircase. Behind them walked five more people. These wore green and all had camera sets mounted over their right eyes. The procession ringed the stage, facing the assembled holograms with the people in green standing a little behind the ones in black.

"The Reclamation Assembly is called to order and sealed to its purpose," said the black-robed man with his back toward Eric's point of view. "Because of the critical nature of what we must discuss, I call for the assembly to agree to allowing a mechanical tally of attendance and transmission of the records of the previous meeting to personal data storage for review and confirmation at a later date. Do any here wish to register objections?" There was silence.

The square-jawed woman who stood facing Eric spoke next. "There are three items of business that must be approved immediately. First is the proposed method to counter the current activity of the Unifiers regarding the status of the Home Ground in the view of the client governments of the Quarter Galaxy."

Home Ground? Eric frowned. *I didn't think the Vitae had a home.*

"Second is the procedure for seizure and control of the artifacts on the Home Ground."

The translation must be mucked up. That can't be what she said.

"Third is the procedure for establishing habitable zones for the main body of Vitae emigration."

The man standing to her immediate left spoke. "Historian Masselin of the *Guardian Voice* will present the first proposal."

The crowd of holograms faded from view, leaving a single figure, a bald Vitae in an amethyst robe, standing on the third tier from the stage.

"We still do not have a reliable model of how the Aunorante Sangh accomplished the theft of the Home Ground . . ."

"Adu!" Eric started to his feet and slapped his hand down on the STOP key.

"What?" came back the android's voice.

Eric backed away from the screen. "Where are you getting this translation from? It's screwed up eight-eight ways." He stabbed a finger toward the keyboard.

"The translation is accurate."

"It can't be!"

Adu stepped into the doorway. "Why not?"

Eric stared at the blank screen and realized he was still pointing. He lowered his hand slowly and swallowed. "Because," he said as if he could force reason into his words, "*Aunorante Sangh* is a term from the Realm, not from the Vitae. This translation is coming through in Standard, and it must have gotten cross-fed with the . . ."

He suddenly remembered Basq's sharp response when he had used the term. A slow, sick sensation closed in on him. Fear, with unwanted comprehension following fast behind.

They thought they'd be able to talk to Arla without help. Why did they think that?

"Adu," Eric croaked, "do a data sort for me. The cross-reference is *Aunorante Sangh*."

"Right." He turned away, then turned halfway back. "Are you all right?"

Eric didn't answer; he just sank back into his chair.

What's the matter with me? I left that all behind. I left! I . . . Eric looked down at his hands and watched the smooth, blank, brown skin stretch and relax as his fists clenched and unclenched.

Right. I left. But I haven't forgotten anything. And I still go back. First sign of trouble and I'm right back where I started.

Oh Nameless Powers and Metthew Garismit, let me be wrong. Let me be sick and tired and completely wrong. Eric pressed the heels of both hands against his eyes. *Garismit's Eyes! How could I have hoped to get away!*

". . . recording the statements of Bio-technician Uary of the *Grand Errand*. Proceed, Technician."

Eric lifted his hands away from his eyes. On the screen, a pinched young man in a bright purple robe was unbending from a deep bow. At a table in front of him sat a man and a woman both robed in black. The man's hand lay on the table and only had four fingers on it.

"Contractor Avir, Contractor Kelat, I have entered the data from the DNA analysis on Eric Born into data storage, but my findings are . . ."

Eric's throat closed. He swallowed to clear it, but could do nothing to move his frozen gaze, or close his opened jaw.

The purple-robed man, Uary, leaned against the tabletop. Above the table appeared a holographic representation of two beaded, twisted strings.

"This is Born's DNA construct. It is between one-half and one-third the length of the DNA sequence of any other race from the Evolution Point that our databases have on file. This brevity and lack of redundancy attests to his artificial genesis as much as his extramechanical ability. But within this short stretch, his Engineers"—Uary paused—"left no less than three hundred nucleotide sequences that can be identified as unique to the Rhudolant Vitae."

Avir rose slowly. "Be very, very sure about what you are saying, Technician." There was a tremor in her voice that sounded to Eric like eagerness.

"I am, Contractor," said Uary with absolute finality. "Eric Born's ancestors must have been engineered from Vitae DNA. If we know where his world is, it is likely we have found the Home Ground again. There is no question in my mind but that he is Aunorante Sangh."

No.

"We will have to confirm . . ."

*The Nameless sent their Servant, who saw a way to move
the world* . . .

". . . will authorize a probe . . ."

Funny-looking place, isn't it? Out there on its own.

"I cannot at this time offer congratulations . . ."

It ain't natural, but it works . . .

"No!" Eric shouted aloud.

It couldn't be. The Realm could not really have been moved.
It was not possible. There could not have really been Nameless
Powers who walked the world and created their people. They
could not have really sent their Servant, who understood how
to move the world to get it away from . . . Eric stared at the
robed figures in their bare silver room. To get it away from
these people in their ships.

"If this is true, though, Technician," the black-robed man
with the mutilated hand was saying, "your name will be
remembered in every chapel on every ship on every day of
worship. You and Basq will have brought us home."

*It's nothing! The Words are just lies and air and a way to
maintain power! There were no Nameless! There can't be!
Because if there were* . . .

*If there were, I've sinned. I went over the World's Wall and
I led the Vi . . . the Aunorante Sangh back to the Realm* . . .

Have to get out of here.

"Adu!" he called to the bridge. "Get us out, head anywhere, break the limits and go!"

"I can't."

"What!" Eric staggered down the corridor to the bridge.
Adu sat motionless in its chair, watching the screens.

"This ship has been placed under a quarantine lock."

"Quarantine lock?" Eric repeated, trying to force his mind
to understand. He knew the term, but his mind wouldn't define
it for him.

"Standard precaution built into space traffic hardware and
software, so that in case of a computer or biological virus the
ship can be held in isolation. While the quarantine is active,
the docking bolts will not release the *U-Kenai*."

They'd be coming for him. Now. At once. They were on
their way. They'd been waiting for him.

"They won't have me."

And what am I going to do to stop them? I can barely stand up.

"They won't have me," he repeated through clenched teeth. "Adu, find a way to override the quarantine."

"It will take . . ."

"I know. Release the beacon and get going on the lock." Eric returned to the common room.

No time for hesitation. He was under siege. He had to buy all the time he could and worry about any damage he did if he survived that long. He hit the seal for the door and tore out the wires in the lock. Ignoring the sting on his palms, he jammed the manual bolt home. He dashed across the common room and sealed both cabin doors.

Make them hunt.

He lifted the hatch under the view wall and climbed down the ladder to the drive room. Dizziness made the walls sway drunkenly as he reached up to shut the hatch and slide the locking bolts shut.

Make them dig.

The drive room was sterile, brightly lit, and cramped. Most of the room was taken up by the curved, ceramic drive housings with their meters and input terminals and warning labels. Heat exhaust and fuel intake pipes ran fore and aft overhead, or rammed themselves into the floor like pillars. Anybody who wanted to take him here would practically have to get up close enough to lay hands on him. If they get that close . . . Eric flexed his hands. There was some strength left. Some. It'd be enough. The Vitae were little creatures. Sorry, pale, flabby little creatures.

The Vitae were the Aunorante Sangh, no matter what name they had bestowed on the People.

Nameless Powers preserve and forgive. I didn't know. I didn't know. How could I know?

He'd led them to the Realm. To the Temples and the Kings. To his family. To Lady Fire.

I didn't know. I didn't know.

The compartment walls were thick, shielded, insulated and shielded again. He couldn't hear anything. He raised his hand to his translator disk to hail the bridge, but stopped. The Vitae could trace that signal straight to him. He pressed himself into the corner. No way out from here, but only one way in. When they came for him, he would see them before they saw him. It was his only advantage. It would have to be enough.

I am Teacher Hand. I am dena Enemy of the Aunorante Sangh. They will know that. They will not forget that.

I will not forget it again.

I didn't know. I didn't know.

Metal and ceramic snapped over head. Eric pressed his back against the smooth wall. The hatch lifted away from the ceiling. Boots lowered themselves through the hatch and a human form, completely encased in a scarlet vacuum suit, dropped to the floor, landing steadily on both feet. Eric saw his own reflection in the blackened faceplate as it moved aside so its partner could drop down beside it. He faced them both. They could see him perfectly. He could tell by the way his distorted face shone on their visors. They both carried dart guns in their gloved hands, he noticed. Tranquilizers, probably, but maybe poison if they were done using him.

"I deny you. I defy you. I stand against you as the sun stands against the Black Wall." Every Teacher knew the words of resistance. They were told the Aunorante Sangh might return at any time, maybe even before the Nameless did. He held his hands up so that his palms reflected in their faceplates and braced himself against the wall.

Nameless Powers, grant me strength to fight for you. Grant me strength to live up to the name you have given me.

The first one raised its gun and fired. The dart sliced through the air straight toward the hands Eric offered up as targets. Eric released his gift and it felt like a fist squeezed his heart. The dart touched his palm, and fell to the floor at his feet.

Got to stay standing. Can't let them know what it cost me. I am their enemy. Can't let them know.

Hurry Adu!

The second one fired. Then the first fired again. The darts clattered to the floor and Eric's breath came out in ragged gasps. They knew now. How could they not know? He saw

his own bulging eyes and gaping mouth in their visors. One
more volley and he was gone.

He screamed like a madman and lunged for the first of
them. His arms and legs were weak as water, but he still
outmassed the Vitae. They toppled onto the deck together.
The fall loosened the Vitae's grip on its gun just enough. Eric
tore it from its fingers as the Vitae shoved him aside. Eric
squeezed the trigger and shot his target in the torso, only
because there was no way to miss.

The Vitae dropped onto the deck plates and Eric looked
wildly around for the other one. Nothing. No one. Then, the
drone of the engines died away into silence. The Vitae stepped
out from behind the second level drive.

Eric fired and dropped. The Vitae fired and then it fell with
Eric's dart in its arm. Eric felt the sting and the shock as the
dart drove its tip into his shoulder blade. Arms, legs, torso
were all gone in an instant and his eyesight left him before
he hit the deck.

The Vitae maneuvered the support capsule out of the airlock.
Adu sat frozen in place on the bridge, doing nothing but
absorbing the information about the *U-Kenai*'s status through
Cam's eyes. The quarantine lock was gone, but not through his
doing. The Vitae had reported that the source of the contamina-
tion had been removed. The station had downgraded the alert.

The airlock door closed with a rush of canned air. Adu still
didn't move. Eric Born was gone. There was nothing left to tell
him how to act. He opened all the instructions he carried in his
makeup and examined them all minutely. Nothing there. Nothing
to tell him what to do if the Vitae carried Eric Born away.

The comm board flickered and shifted again. Adu read the
new status. The *U-Kenai*, formerly owned and commanded by
Eric Born was now officially salvage, with ship and contents to
be claimed by the Rhudolant Vitae.

Ship and contents. Adu's attention froze on the phrase.
Him.

The instruction sets were very clear regarding the Vitae.
Interaction with them, unless supervised by Eric Born, was
to be strictly avoided.

Adu pushed the android body into action. The quarantine
lock had been lifted and only the normal security precautions
held the ship in place. He had already established access to
the security database. With less than a dozen key changes, he
overwrote the holding order.

A regulatory override cycle kicked into play from Cam and
Adu squashed it. The docking clamps lifted back and the *U-
Kenai* fell away from the station.

Adu rolled himself to one side and prodded the Cam program forward to take charge of the flight calculations. As a
precaution, he settled himself at the gateway between Cam's
flight instructions and the regulatory overrides. It wasn't long
before the alarm bells began ringing. The Vitae had already
detected his ruse. The signals activated a swarm of overrides
and cutoffs in Cam's programming that charged toward the
gate. Adu sat like a stone wall between the security programming and the flight programming. Cam continued measuring,
calculating, and planning in a smooth, unbroken chain. Eight
kilometers from the station, he lit the *U-Kenai*'s first level
drive and shoved the ship toward the vacuum at its top speed.

No ships approached them, although Adu was certain the
Vitae would be tracking them. He tripped another switch in
Cam's programming and although they were still too close
to the station and all the security overrides battered at him,
Cam cut in the third level drive and the *U-Kenai* leapt into
the empty realm past the light barrier.

The security cutoffs fell back and Adu was able to move
again. He threaded his way around behind Cam and made the
android's hands work the comm boards. The beacon was on
its way to Perivar. The *U-Kenai* could overtake it and scoop
it up on the way, and then the whole ship could fly toward
this Perivar, who Eric said could get an undetected signal to
Dorias. He could tell Dorias what had happened. Dorias had
given him his original instructions. Dorias would give him
more and they would be correct and they would erase the
lingering image of Eric Born being removed in the support
capsule, the image that hung inside Adu and would not go
away.

8—Amaiar Gardens, Kethran Colony, Hour 05:12:56, City Time

*The first and best occupation of the mind is to fight destiny.
I do not mean run away. I do not mean trick it, or cheat
it. I mean to face it on open ground, to raise whatever force
is at one's command, and to wage open, unflinching, and
total war.*

Zur-Ishen *ki* Maliad, from "Upon Leaving Kethre"

*E*vran was beginning to get on Arla's nerves. Most of the
other students had adopted a normal speed for talking around
her and had begun to assume she understood what they were
saying unless she told them otherwise. Not Evran. He talked
to her like he might to a three-year-old, and when she bothered
to respond long enough to let him know she thought he was
a fool, he'd smile indulgently and say she just didn't understand yet.

He'd taken to following her around the lab, lecturing as he
went. Right now he was leaning his buttocks against one of
the unused analysis tables, delivering his unbroken stream of
philosophy, or science, or whatever it was, and trying to touch
her on her arm if she was stupid enough to get close to him.
It was just about enough to drive her insane. Not because the

tasks were particularly difficult, but because she was still learning how to read without help and she needed all her concentration to get the notes of new instructions that Zur-Iyal and the others had left for her.

She cast a longing glance out the window toward the fields and cattle pens and then a quick one at the clock. Two hours before her shift was over. Two more hours for this fool to sit there and yammer.

". . . I know Allenden and the others are trying to tell you that your genetics, your body, you understand, Arla? are the final determination of your existence, I mean, that you've got no choice, you understand, because you were so carefully built, but in reality you've got more choice than we do, you understand, because . . ."

Arla bent more closely over her notepad display, trying to decipher the instructions Myra Lar *ki* Novish had left for her.

. . . check the monitors on the B series protein cross sections. If any of them read over . . . Her lips moved while she read on her own, a habit she was trying to break. Her free hand dropped down to her pouch of stones, as if just touching the leather could help her. She pulled her hand away.

". . . You aren't carrying the excess genetic baggage that the rest of us are, you understand? The survival instinct, the macrogenetic tribal survival instinct, I mean, it's not natural for you to want to pass on exclusively your genes, I mean, you are not naturally inclined to warlike behavior the way we are, you understand?"

. . . Sixteen to the twenty-third power, is that what that says? Nameless Powers preserve me from this idiot. Yes, that's what that says . . . For the HT6E enzyme concentration, call me immediately. I'll be on line at . . .

". . . that means, Arla, that you aren't motivated by, I mean, you understand, you don't cling to irrational, instinctive behavior, like we do. You make your decisions exclusively, you know that word, right? On the basis of personal experience, and that means that . . ."

"If you're going to try to corrupt impressionable young minds, Evran *ki* Kell, you really ought to do it in a lower tone of voice."

Arla almost cried out in relief. Zur-Allenden *ki* Uvarimaya-nus strolled through the doorway. As usual, mud covered his boots and breeches. A smile glowed on his pointed face, but it didn't reach his eyes while he looked over Evran. For reasons Arla hadn't gone out of her way to understand, the pair regarded each other as Heretics and would avoid each other whenever possible.

Evran stuck his chin out toward Zur-Allenden. "We're not on *Quapoc* ground, Zur-Allenden. There's no law against my talking to her."

"But I'll bet she wishes there was." Arla turned away to hide her smile. "And face it, Sar Evran, Manager *ki* Maliad catches you trying to make her into a Determinist, she'll boot you off-planet so hard you'll reach Station Eight without a shuttle."

Evran sniffed. "You are the ignorant child of an ignorant people."

"And the Balancers decided there weren't enough self-satisfied little shits in the universe so they sent us you." Zur-Allenden stumped over to his corner table, leaving a whole trail of squashed leaves and earth behind. Arla groaned inwardly.

Why can't he use the clearing room like everybody else? she thought as Zur-Allenden began stripping his boots off and leaning over the tabletop to check the results of whatever experiment he had brewing under the glass, showering more dirt everywhere.

Fortunately, Evran's stock of insults was smaller than his stock of pedantic speeches. "Arla, think about what I've said and come find me when you've got any questions." And he stalked out.

Zur-Allenden shook his head. "What amazes me is he says that like he thinks you'll actually do it. Like he thinks you don't have a brain in your head."

"Used to it." Arla ran her thumb along the bottom of the monitor display to make sure she got the numbers right. *I hope I get faster at this soon.* Her hand dropped to her pouch again, and she stopped it midway. She stuck the pad into the feed-out slot on the edge of Myra Lar's table so the two machines could talk to each other.

"Wouldn't have thought so." Zur-Allenden planted his stocking feet on the tile floor and folded his arms across his skinny chest.

Arla bent over the table and ran her finger down the line of glowing figures, slowly reading each one. Myra Lar had been overly diligent in explaining the importance of a manual check. "Be surprised, you would."

Zur-Allenden sat silently for a moment and Arla tried not to wonder what was going on inside his head. She'd used every trick she knew to try to get him to drop his guard around her. She'd worked diligently. She'd volunteered to run extra errands. She'd been overflustered and profusely apologetic when she'd made mistakes. She'd occasionally "let slip" remarks about her children and her sisters. The performance had gained the confidence, even the friendship, of almost everyone else in the lab, but not Allenden, and Arla was beginning to wonder why.

Blasted Skymen. You all look alike but you all act differently. There's no way to tell who's going to do what. Why can't you just mark your hands so a person can tell who you are by looking? Her hand twitched like it wanted to move to her pouch. She pressed it harder against the tabletop.

She had asked Iyal if there were other places where the people were marked so they could be told apart, and had received a strangely sad smile from her. "Almost everywhere has a social hierarchy, Arla. It seems to be part of being human. Some places use tattoos, or natural appearance to enforce it. Some places use family names or histories . . ." Her sentence had trailed off, and her face had turned thoughtful. "I'd be willing to speculate that maybe your world's hierarchy came from genotype . . . family . . . but if that was it, what're you doing on the bottom?"

"Oh, I forgot." Allenden snapped his fingers, interrupting her reverie. "Zur-Iyal wanted me to remind you to make sure you've got the lab cleaned and locked down by hour six. Maintenance is running the building check tonight and we all have to clear out early."

Blast, blast, blast. I had work I wanted to do tonight. Her eyes flickered involuntarily toward Allenden's keyboard. Arla was glad she had her back to him so he couldn't see. "Thank you, Zur-Allenden. I'll have it done."

"Good enough." Boots under one arm, computer pad under the other, he shuffled out, trying to keep himself from sliding on the tiles.

When the door swung shut, Arla let her shoulders sag. She couldn't have said who wore her out more, Allenden or Evran. *At least Allenden tries to keep a lock on it.* She sighed and started on the next set of numbers. *Why do they nag at me like this? The Nameless Powers have seen me deal with worse, most of my life, in fact. The Skymen just give me words.*

Words and plenty of them. Iyal and her cohorts honked like geese sometimes about the contents of Arla's blood and bones.

"You are saying that some person decided how I should be?" Arla had asked Iyal once.

Iyal had come into the lab just to stare at her. A recent analysis had just come out of the machines and Iyal was more confused than usual.

"Basically, yes. Not you, personally, of course, but at least one set of your ancestors. Probably more than one."

And the Nameless Powers spoke the names of all the People that would be and in each name declared the soul and life that it would have . . .

"That's not unheard of." Iyal leaned against the wall. "I've met GE descendants before. What's incredible about you is what your . . . engineers bred for."

"What is that?"

"I don't know." She threw up her hands. "That's the problem. Usually it's obvious. Strength, speed, intelligence, creativity. You, though, you make no sense."

Neither do you, but she didn't say that.

Zur-Iyal spread her hands. "Let me try to explain this. We've talked about cells, right? Cells in a body communicate via a series of messengers. Chemicals emitted by one cell cause a reaction in second cell. That second cell might undergo an internal change, or it might send off its own messenger.

"That's extremely simplified, of course."

"Of course," said Arla humbly.

Zur-Iyal's eyebrows went up. Her puckered mouth twitched into a half smile. "Deserved that, I suppose." Iyal was quicker than most of them to pick up on when Arla was acting. Around Iyal she had to be extremely careful how she played the Notouch.

"All right," Iyal went on, "your people are, obviously, from the same Evolution Point as mine. That should mean you have the same messengers in your cells, plus or minus three or four to allow for your native environment.

"As far as I can tell, your cells will react to twenty separate messengers that aren't present in any other known Human variant. Then there's your brain." She shook her head. "The brain, as we know it, is a complicated, disorganized organ with three or four backups for every function. It stores information, but it stores it wherever there's room and reacts according to a branch of chaos theory. That doesn't even begin to cover how it decides whether the information gets stored as short-term, or long-term, or muscular memory." She scowled at Arla. Arla didn't flinch. She had learned fairly early on that Zur-Iyal's scowls had nothing to do with her personally. The woman was annoyed with her cells, or her brain, or whatever it was that she couldn't understand today. "Your brain, on the other hand, is more tightly organized than a Vitae datastore. I can predict, PREDICT, where a given piece of information is going to end up, down to the cell. Your short-term memory is ridiculously huge, and your long-term memory defies description, and you've got no backups." She frowned even more deeply. "You should be a flipping genius, but you're not. You should be totally impossible, but you're not. Although for the life of me I don't know why." Again she shook her head. "I find it hard to believe that someone so carefully constructed has no idea of her function." Zur-Iyal looked at her very hard, as if trying to pull the ideas out with her eyes.

"Would help if I could, Zur-Iyal," Arla told her honestly. "But there's too much I don't understand."

"I was afraid you were going to say that." Iyal had sighed
and stumped out again.

*I could tell her the apocrypha, but, Garismit's Eyes, how
would I make her understand it?* Arla stared out the laboratory
window. There were fifteen separate stories about the Nameless and the Servant that the Teachers had declared to be lies.
One of them told about her family and her namestones.

The gardens' flat, cultivated land spread out in front of her.
The window frame gave it just enough shape to keep her
leftover fears quiet. Silver drones bobbed between the long
rows of plants, checking soil quality, watching for parasites
and fungi, administering fertilizer or pesticides as necessary,
or harvesting the mid-season crops. Not all of what they
harvested would be used as it was. Even through the window,
Arla could catch the faint green scent of the processing sheds,
where the raw organic materials were augmented with artificially produced animal products and turned into a variety of
unpronounceable things that had mechanical or medicinal
uses.

The cleanliness and precision of the place was the most
completely and utterly alien sight for Arla on the entire world.

She leaned her hip against the counter and watched the
drone's movements. She remembered the smell of animal pens
where she spent what felt like half her life in the Realm. She
remembered the ache in her shoulders as she dug out the
manure and mud. Chilblains broke through her hands from
spending hours up to her knees and elbows in water harvesting
grain. She lived with the rain, the stink, the ache, and the
Teachers coming once a month to her village to tell them all it
was what the Nameless meant for them. And she had believed.
From the time she could hear and understand, she'd believed
because everyone around her did.

Then came her Marking Day. At the end of that day, she
lay on her mat, her hands wrapped in bandages and throbbing
from the pain. The leather belt her old grandmother had fastened around her chafed her waist and legs miserably. Outside,
the night's hail clattered against the roof. The wind rocked
the house on its stilts. Its fingers found their way through the
cracks in the walls and drew themselves across her. She stared

into the darkness, hearing the sounds of her father and little sisters breathing and snoring all around her and wishing for sleep to come.

The floor had creaked from gentle steps and she smelled her mother's musky breath.

"Get up, Arla, I've something to show you."

She'd sat up, blinking. Mother had taken her by the arm right above the ragged bandages and led her out into the other room. The fire on the central hearthstone was nothing but red coals buried in ash. Mother poked them carefully with a stick until the tiniest flames flickered up. The dim orange light showed up her wrinkled, leathery face and Arla wondered why her mother was smiling. She never had before.

"Now that you've lived to be marked, Arla, I can start telling you about your name. Stone in the Wall. Arla Born of the Black Wall. What I say is true, daughter of my blood, but you must never, ever tell anyone. If someone comes who has need of you, they will already know. If anyone else hears, you'll be killed for a Heretic. What I say is from the Nameless Powers to our family, do you understand?"

Arla didn't, but she'd nodded anyway. Mother's anxious tones sent chills through her that were worse than the ones the wind brought.

Mother sat back and folded her hands like she was making a vow or a curse. She stared at the moss-chinked wickerwork that made up their house walls. She spoke in measured cadences like she did when she was reciting the Words. "When the Nameless Powers left the Realm for the place beyond the Black Wall, they knew that the people would have need of aid and protection. So they gave their Words to the Teachers and their authority to the Royals. They set the seasons and the days in motion so that the people would have time and life.

"But they knew the Aunorante Sangh were waiting with their tricks and their traps. They knew, for they were the Nameless Powers and nothing is hidden from them, that the Aunorante Sangh might send servants to disrupt the workings of the Realm, which would kill the People.

"To prepare against this, the Nameless Powers spoke new

words and these words became jewels. They took each jewel and they spoke its name over it. As they spoke, the jewels split into four parts. Three parts remained stone, but the fourth became a person.

"The names that the Powers spoke for the jewels gave the stones the power to hear and understand the workings of the world, but only in the hands of the people who had been made from the jewel's substance. The Nameless scattered the people across the world. One became a Royal, one a Noble, one a Bondless, one a Bonded, and one a Notouch.

"The years passed and the stones and their names were handed from parents to children. But the names became corrupted and garbled by the speaking of men and, gradually, the truth was lost by all, except the Notouch. For we who cannot touch power or coinage cannot be distracted by the ways of the world.

"The Nameless Powers, where they watched through the Black Wall, saw the Aunorante Sangh breeding their servants the way a farmer breeds pigs. They saw, too, that they were building their own Realm that their servants might have a fortress from which to launch attacks upon the People. The Nameless knew those servants would one day be sent into the Realm. So the Nameless Powers spoke new words. Metthew Garismit, they said, and they created their own servant and opened the Black Wall so he might walk down to the Realm.

"Garismit knew his name from the beginning and he knew that to save the Realm from the Aunorante Sangh, he would need to move it to where the Aunorante Sangh could not reach it.

"The Teachers say that Garismit went into the belly of the Realm and spoke to it with its own name. That is not all he did, Arla.

"To make the world hear him, and to hear it, he needed the stones and their keepers. He went first to the Royal and the Noble. But they had hidden their stones in their money houses and would not dig them out. He went to the Bondless, but they had gambled the stones away years ago and did not know where they were. He went to the Bonded, but the slave had given the stones for a master's favor and did not know where they were.

"So Garismit went to the Notouch. He called her by her name—Clear Sight—and Clear Sight took her stones into her hands. Garismit opened the ground for Clear Sight and he led her down the paths to the center of the earth. The stones became eyes and ears and the Realm saw Garismit and heard him as he spoke its name and it moved at his command."

Mother had fumbled with the thong of a leather pouch then. Arla could still remember the musty smell that rose from the leather.

"Hold out your hands, daughter."

Feeling like she was dreaming, Arla had held out her bandaged hands. Her mother laid the stones in them and Arla gasped, partly from the pain of their smooth weight against her fresh hand marks, but mostly from their beauty.

"These are Clear Sight's stones," Mother said. "We are her daughters, named by the Nameless and born of their substance. We serve the Nameless by keeping them safe and close. The Aunorante Sangh still seek us. The Nameless Powers may send another servant to save us from them again. The Nameless themselves may return. When they do, they will need the stones and we must be ready with them." Mother tucked her hand under Arla's chin and raised her daughter's eyes away from the beautiful spheres. "This is the beginning of the truth, daughter of my blood, Arla of the Black Wall. There is more, and I will teach it to you. We can only speak of these things when the world is protected by the Black Wall. When the sun comes again, you cannot let anyone know anything has changed for you."

Mother'd taken the stones back, then led her daughter back to her mat. Arla spent that night shivering in the dark, but now from wonder rather than cold.

Arla kept her silence as she traveled with the other women and children to the cities and she did not show anything had changed. But something had. She knew it when she listened to the Teachers. Thoughts crept unbidden into her head when she was supposed to be filling it with the words of the Nameless Powers and Metthew Garismit.

. . . the Notouch are the dirt and stone of the world, but I'm not Notouch. I'm born of the stones and born of the Black Wall. If the Teachers could lose the story of the stones, what else could they lose?

If names given by the Nameless can become corrupted by the speaking of men, what else can become corrupted?

And always, always, through the other thoughts, through the anger that blossomed and the rebellion that grew into willful and deliberate heresy she remembered that the Nameless Powers had condemned their best to be Notouch. The knowledge of who she was and how she had been wronged by the Nameless Powers and all their servants shaped her life from her Marking Day to the day she'd walked unafraid up to the Skymen and asked to know how she could be of use.

She caressed the pouch that held her namestones. All her life she had longed to be recognized for what she really was, and now it was happening. These Skymen with their naked hands and their ignorance of the Words of the Nameless treated her like a trophy. She should have been reveling in it, using it for all it was worth. But all she wanted to do was get home, get the stones back to her home and her daughter, where they belonged. There wasn't a minute that went by that she didn't wonder what would happen if she lost her life, lost the stones out here. Then she would not only have lied to Little Eye, she would have taken away her children's only hope of getting out of the mud.

Arla realized her knees were trembling. She turned away from the window and strode across the room.

Counters. Floors. The terminal. I'm not sure how much longer I can deal with these Skymen. I don't know how much longer I've got before whatever plans they have for the Realm come true. I've got to find out what they want and get back home. She saw all her children lined up before her mind's eye and swallowed hard against the pang of homesickness.

She slid the door for the sanitation cupboard and dug out the sponges and canisters of solvent. *Can't go yet. Too much I don't understand.* Her own words came back to her. A wave of exhaustion washed over her. *Just too much. How has*

Teacher . . . Eric Born . . . managed to live out here for ten years without losing his mind?

Thinking of him was a mistake. His name brought the image of him to her mind, along with an absurd longing she'd managed to avoid finding words for.

Scowling at her hands, she bent to her work.

"G'wan! Get outta here! Move it!" Iyal swatted the backsides of the sandy brown cows indiscriminately with her prod. The beasts bellowed and jostled each other but they moved steadily toward the narrow gate where Jexid, the new intern from the Nuot Division, gave any of the balky ones an extra prod to funnel them up the ramp of the transport. Old Keyenar *ki* Oruat tapped each of the fat, stupid, carefully engineered beasts between the ears with the signature wand and checked its number to make sure only the cattle that had already passed inspection made it into the shipment.

Loading and herding the big animals was one of the things people still did better than the automatics. Nobody'd yet been able to program a cheap automatic with enough self-preservation instinct to get out of the way if there was a stampede.

A sharp whistle jerked Iyal's head around. One of the cows bawled and stamped its foot down. Iyal felt the shock up to her ankle, despite her steel-toed boots. She whacked the cow and cursed and at the same time she tried to see who the idiot was who didn't know they still hadn't managed to breed all the nerves out of the mountain-specific cattle.

Outside the fence Zur-Allenden waved at her frantically and beckoned, while pointing at her sedan chair unit with his other hand.

Ground beneath my feet, what does he want now and why can't he call me over the crashing terminal? She gave the cows in front of her an extra shove and hit the TRANSMIT key on her torque.

"Get an appointment, Allenden," she muttered through clenched teeth as she leaned sideways to try to keep a nervous yearling from squashing her side. It stamped edgily, missing her toes, thankfully, and moved forward.

Got to calm these critters down. Well, with the new configuration in the next batch . . .

"Iyal, I need to talk to you about your new . . . acquisition," came Allenden's voice through her translator disk.

"What acquisition?" Keyenar was cutting one of the cows out of the herd and prodding it toward the side holding pen. Iyal hooked her prod onto her belt and waved both fists in the inquiry sign and he held up three fingers. Wrong number. Nothing major.

Iyal brought her hands down. Understood. She snatched up the prod again to urge the cows forward. The press was easing as most of the cattle lumbered onto the truck. There was always a mild relief in being able to breathe freely again. Allenden was not allowing her to enjoy it, however.

"You know," said Allenden. "The woman."

"It shouldn't be that tough for someone named Zur-Allenden *ki* Uvarimayanus to pronounce Arla Stone." The torque picked up her subvocalized words and relayed them to Allenden's translation disk. She hoped it also managed to accurately transmit her tone.

"Zur-Iyal, I can't talk about this over the air. Give me ten minutes. Please."

For a moment, Iyal considered telling him to go bury himself in manure, but Allenden was capable of making himself extremely unpleasant if he felt ignored, and she didn't feel up to being called into Director *ki* Sholmat's office and read the employee relations section out of her supervisor's contract.

She waved to Jexid to come take her place at the back. The intern, to her credit, unhooked her own prod from her belt and waded into the thick of the herd, slapping and cursing like an old pro.

Iyal squelched through mud and debris to the side gate and palmed the latch. It registered her sweaty, muck-stained hand and let the gate swing open for her. Iyal stomped up the path, showering the concrete with dirt at each step until she reached her sedan chair. She plunked herself down in the seat and immediately switched on the monitor boards to check the input from Keyenar's wand against the manifest. This was a big order and an important one. Since the Vitae had taken

over Kethran's gene-tailoring industry, there had been far too
few of those. The last thing she needed was Allenden bothering
her about his pet trivialities.

But then, he probably knew that. He never picked his fights
randomly.

The summer heat and pent-up annoyance broke a fresh
sweat on her forehead and cheeks, despite her broad-brimmed
hat and screening lotion.

"I'm serious, Iyal." Allenden squatted down beside the
front legs of the sedan. "I think we've got a problem."

"You mean a new problem." Iyal watched three new regis-
tration numbers appear on the list. "So let's have it."

Allenden glanced this way and that. Iyal sighed. Allenden's
penchant for dramatics never failed to get under her skin and
stick. "Get it out, Allenden, I don't have all year. We've got
260 head to get inspected, loaded, and delivered." She
squinted at Allenden out of the corner of her eye. The sun
was behind him and it took a minute for her new lenses to
adjust so she saw something other than a black blob where
his face should be.

"Iyal. Your . . . Arla, she's a Vitae spy."

Iyal felt her eyes swivel all the way toward Allenden. Her
gaze followed a second later. "What?" Almost no one on
Kethran, from First Family members on down to Fourth
Wavers, liked having the Vitae around. Most recognized them
as an unpleasant necessity. Some were waiting for a chance
to kick them offworld. A few, like Allenden, were actively
looking for ways to force them off.

"Somebody's been using my access codes to get into the
datastores after hours."

Iyal finally took her attention off the herd and the boards
and turned all the way toward Allenden. The man was built
like a sun-bleached beanpole on stilts. Even on his knees in
the grass, the top of his head was level with hers.

Iyal snorted. "Arla can barely type her name or understand . . ."

"She's got a Vitae gene sequence, Iyal. For all we know
they created her as a way to get in here."

"Don't be stupid, Allenden. Should that sequence turn out

to be exclusive to the Vitae, which I doubt, even the Vitae aren't that good at genetic engineering.''

''We don't know exactly how good the Vitae are,'' he said levelly.

Who's paying Perivar's bills these days? The thought slid into her mind. *No. Not Perivar. Bones and breath, he works with a Shessel. He . . .*

Who is paying his bills these days?

''You want to talk about this inside?'' Allenden glanced across toward Keyenar, Jexid, and the herd.

''No, I do not want to talk about this inside.'' Iyal heaved her shoulders back. ''If you want to insult my judgment, Assistant Researcher, you can do it in writing to Director *ki* Sholmat.''

Allenden leaned close enough for her to smell his fruity breath over the scent of the cows and the summer grass. ''I saw her Iyal. Security's got her recorded. Reading the lab notes. Senior research level lab notes.''

No. I won't believe it.

And if security really has got her recorded?

No. Some of those rented eyes haven't got the brains we gave the cows. There's been a screwup. There must have been a screwup.

Allenden waved his hands toward the sky in a gesture of helplessness. ''Iyal, you brought her in here just before the Vitae made their announcement about taking over MG49 sub 1. Everything's changing with them, don't you see? We've got to look at everything in a new light. Now that they've picked a single base, they're going to be moving to centralize their influence. They'll be tightening the screws and closing the locks. The only reason they haven't done it before is that they've been too scattered, too busy maintaining control over themselves to spare resources for consolidating an empire out of the rest of us.''

Iyal blinked at him. She tried to take her time to formulate a decent reply. That was a mistake, because it gave Allenden's little speech time to sink in. He'd obviously rehearsed it several times. Maybe he'd even talked to some people who had better sense than he did. If you believed in conspiracies, the formula made too much sense, and if you'd ever seen the Vitae organize a project, you believed in conspiracies.

It would still mean that Perivar had lied to her, and that Arla had lied to her, and that Zur-Iyal *ki* Maliad had seen the chance for profit and advancement and had lost track of the overall situation.

That was not acceptable.

"I said, if you want to question my judgment, you take it to Our Cousin Director. Until he fires me, I'm your supervisor, and I say that Arla Stone is my responsibility, not yours." She folded her arms and directed her attention to the cattle pens. Keyenar slammed the truck's gate shut and waved to the driver. The transport rolled across the grass. Its balloon tires molded to the damp ground so the turf would be disturbed as little as possible. The labs only had an allotment of ninety-five acres of chopped ground and they needed all of that for gardens and pens. They couldn't afford to go hacking up the fields.

Allenden reached across the chair's boards and with one, bone-thin finger tapped six keys, one after the other. The manifest cleared from the main screen and in its place appeared a view of Lab #20. Arla Stone hunched in front of the comm screen on Allenden's research table. Iyal squinted over the dark woman's shoulder and saw nothing but a blur of gold light on a black screen. Allenden keyed for the security camera to zoom in closer on the text. Arla had the screen set for the fastest scan level and the words flashed by too fast for Iyal to do more than pick out one or two at a time, but she did catch the gold logo of the First Families and the green-and-blue globe of the Kethran Diet.

Seven screens of information flashed past before Iyal realized Arla was reading transcriptions from the Diet sessions. Reading high-formal tense, legally extensive and twisted documents restricted to First Family access. Iyal touched two keys and brought up a profile from the second security camera. Arla's black eyes flickered back and forth. She was really reading them, and reading them faster than Iyal could.

Iyal sat back in the chair, not caring what Allenden made out of the bewildered look on her face.

Impossible. Ridiculous. She had only started learning the language four weeks ago. She didn't even have full command of one level of grammar yet. She barely knew where an ON switch on a view table was. How in all the worlds that lived had she gotten into secured files?

Allenden planted both hands on the edge of the board. "We've got a spy in the ranks, Cousin Manager."

"No."

"What do you mean no!" Allenden reared up like a startled cow. "Look at her!"

"Yes." Iyal gestured at the screen. "Look at her. Right in front of the security camera. Clear as all outdoors and solid as dirt. You're telling me a spy, a VITAE spy, is going to tap the secured network from the lab in front of a camera?"

Allenden's mouth opened and closed three or four times before he finally said, "Then what else could she possibly be?"

"I don't have any idea." Iyal hit the HOME key on the chair's control board at the same time. "But I'm going to go find out."

"You can't just . . ." began Allenden as the chair's legs telescoped up to their active length.

"I can, and you'll wait until I have before you say another word to anybody." The chair rocked forward, picking its quick, mincing steps over the grass. Iyal twisted around to see if Allenden understood. "We need to know what we're dealing with before we make a fuss."

Allenden nodded. Iyal took that as a good sign and settled back into her chair again. The sedan carried her down the paths that bisected the beds of medical plants and grains. The lab section had been laid out for efficiency, not aesthetics. Domes of white polymer skins alternated with square, white concrete buildings that sat in the middle of squared-off plots of plain grass. A quarter of an acre of grass had to be reserved for every cubic meter of building so that solar reflection and environmental absorption would balance each other out.

People and drones hustled to and fro down the prescribed paths. One or two raised their hands in greeting, but Iyal only nodded absently in return.

Arla Stone. Arla Stone. Iyal had been all but breathing Arla Stone since Perivar had brought her to the lab. For weeks now, Iyal had wished in vain that she could find whoever had designed the woman's ancestors so she could shake their hands, and then pick their brains, even if they were the Vitae.

She'd told Perivar that Arla was a walking work of art, but now Iyal was ready to revise that interpretation. The woman was nothing short of a miracle.

Iyal was used to the idea of genetic engineering. Every piece of flora and fauna on Kethran had been built to fit into the tailored biosphere. Her own work carried on the family profession and she was proud to do it. But there wasn't a soul alive on Kethran, or anywhere else she knew of, that could design a DNA string that contained nothing but the bare essentials organized to express themselves in a totally predictable fashion in a human being. In a strain of yeast or algae, maybe. But not a human being. She had learned more about neurochemical regulators in the three weeks she'd known Arla than she had in ten years of active study.

But not everything about Arla made sense. Who would design an organism that did not have enough room left over in its DNA to allow for adaptation or compensation for changes in environment? The rate of birth defects would be astronomical. Arla was perfect, but if one or two of her perfect traits hadn't expressed themselves because of environment, she could have been in trouble. Iyal was surprised Arla had even managed four living kids out of a total of seven births. If you wanted to keep her branch of humanity alive, you'd have to do an incredible amount of outbreeding, which would negate all that careful engineering, or you'd have to be able to check each fetus to make sure conception had worked, and then you'd have to monitor each child to make sure they grew up all right, and tinker with them all as necessary to keep weaknesses from creeping in.

No. It made no sense. A group like that would require more maintenance than . . . Kethran Colony.

The comm screen still showed Arla hunched over Allenden's table, reading the documents flowing past. Nothing in those short, perfect strings she carried around inside her explained this. Nothing at all. Not even the incredible organization inside her skull.

Iyal's translator disk beeped and she winced.

"Cousin Manager Zur-Iyal *ki* Maliad," said Director *ki* Sholmat's voice, "I require your attendance at my office immediately."

Iyal felt her forehead wrinkle. The Director hadn't chosen to acknowledge their First Family connection since Iyal'd deigned to marry a third wave colonist.

She touched the TRANSMIT key on her torque and whispered, "With respect, Cousin Director, I have an emergency in the lab." Arla had moved on to a new set of documents. These had the lab's privacy logo on them.

"Delegate it," said the Director. "I have an Ambassador from the Rhudolant Vitae sitting in front of me. The Vitae want to talk to you about some property of theirs they say the lab has wrongfully appropriated."

Iyal's eyes bulged in their sockets as she tried to keep from gagging audibly. Under her gaze, Arla went on reading, completely undisturbed.

"Cousin Manager?"

"I'll be there in five minutes, Cousin Director." Iyal shut the connection down.

Iyal ground her teeth together and, at last, touched her torque and whispered Allenden's name.

"Zur-Allenden," she said. "This is Zur-Iyal. There's trouble. I need you to get Arla out of the lab. Send her to sweep the attic, anything, just keep her out of the way of the management halls for at least the next hour."

"But . . ." came Allenden's hesitant voice.

"The Vitae are sitting in the Director's office," she said. "Get Arla out of sight."

"Done and done." Her translation disk buzzed as he closed the connection.

The sedan halted in front of the double doors labeled CENTRAL RESEARCH FACILITIES BLOCKS 6–12. AUTHORIZED PERSONNEL ONLY and froze its legs, settling toward the ground so she could climb out. Iyal cut the comm board off and shut the chair's power off.

She rubbed her temple as she pushed through the facility doors and walked down the bare, tiled corridors. Her gaze strayed to the portrait of Killian that she wore on her wrist. He was off-shift tonight. She could put in a real-time call. It'd be good to talk to him. It'd help sort out the jumble of problems swirling around inside her mind.

Director Zur-Kohlbyr *ki* Sholmat's office was a three-room suite at the east end of the building. Kohlbyr was an entrepreneur, an aspiring politician, and the oldest child of the first of the First Families. As a result, he knew all about the importance of appearances and he used all that he knew when creating his workspace.

Iyal entered the waiting room, a comfortable lounge that had been partitioned off to accommodate both Human and Shessel visitors. It gave the impression that the Director was an open-minded man.

The door to the meeting room stood open. Iyal stepped in. It was a greenhouse-style room with transparent silicate walls that let in the view of the medical compound and the clean fields. The ceiling was also transparent, so she could see the clouds building up for the weekly heavy rain that this longitude required to keep the vegetation healthy.

At the moment, the room was furnished with clusters of small tables and padded chairs. It was a casual atmosphere where people could meet, drink, circulate, and chat. Director *ki* Sholmat sat at the table in the sunniest corner, sipping something gold out of a long-stemmed glass. Next to him, a Vitae Ambassador sat like a statue carved of ruby and marble.

Iyal clenched her teeth and forced her mouth to smile.

"Zur-Iyal *ki* Maliad." Zur-Kohlbyr bowed his head but did not stand. "Sit and know yourself welcome, Cousin." Iyal's stomach turned over at the hypocrisy but she drew back a chair and sat, ankles properly crossed and hands neatly folded on the table. If she was going to be treated as a dignitary, she would put on the show, even if her coverall was dirt-spattered and she smelled strongly of cattle.

"This is Ambassador Basq from the Vitae ship *Grand Errand*."

"Ambassador." Iyal briefly touched her fingertips to her

forehead to salute him. At least she assumed the person under the draping of cloth was a him. The only feature he had to distinguish him from any of the other Vitae she'd seen was a blister over his right eye.

Zur-Kohlbyr took another sip out of his glass. "The Ambassador came to me asking about the location of the Subcontractor Arla Stone. I informed him we would have to consult you, since you were funding her contract out of your own accounts."

And you didn't bother to tell him that the lab's refunding me for it.

"Zur-Iyal," said Ambassador Basq in the smooth, even voice that the Vitae seemed to be born with. "If you'll permit, I would like to clarify the origin of the individual you call Subcontractor Arla Stone."

Iyal raised her eyebrows to indicate gentle inquiry and managed not to let her hands twitch, even though her nails were ready to dig into her own skin.

"You have heard our announcement of the Vitae claim of the world MG49 sub 1?"

Iyal inclined her head. "The city council held several public briefings on it. Being under Vitae management, we are most interested in the shifts in status of your people." Her high-formal grammar was rusty. She didn't go home much and she never went to First Family celebrations. She hoped the translator disks were compensating.

"Then you know that the Kethran Diet and Executors have already agreed to honor our claim to the planet."

Iyal nodded again. She'd paid very close attention to both the video clip and the vote that had followed its screening, and had sworn profusely at the result.

The Vitae's little blip didn't tell us anything! How could we make that kind of decision without taking a look at the place?

Who's we, Iyal? Killian had asked quietly. *Your opinion's not on the register.*

In case you've forgotten, I gave up my vote when I married you. She'd said it sourly and regretted it immediately. But it was Kethran law. You couldn't marry up, you could only marry down. She could have kept her vote only by making a partnership bond with a member of another First Family, or a selected Parent World family who wanted to emigrate. Killian's name didn't appear in any of the proper files.

Your vote, yes, but I hadn't noticed you'd lost your voice. The cool exchange was the closest they'd ever come to an actual fight.

"I now make confession, Zur-Iyal," said Basq. "And I trust to the discretion of yourself and your Cousin Director. While we were deciding whether to press our claim, MG49 sub 1 was raided by contraband runners. Arla Stone was one of the things taken from us.

"It is not an independent human being, Zur-Iyal. It is a genetically engineered artifact and the Kethran Diet has acknowledged that it is Vitae property." He paused as if to let his statement sink in. "Of course, you could have no way of knowing this. I'm sure you picked up its contract in good faith and had no idea you were hiring contraband."

Of course not. Iyal shook her head. *That would be illegal by Kethran law. Vitae-enforced Kethran law.*

Zur-Kohlbyr set his glass on the table with a click. "I informed the Ambassador that since the subcontract was legal and since no accusations of contraband running had yet been filed, you were the one who would have to release Arla Stone to Vitae custody." He gave her a look that tried to rivet her to the back wall. "Formalities need to be observed, particularly in times of flux."

"Particularly in times of flux." Iyal shoved tones of agreement into her voice. Inside she wondered, *what are you trying to tell me, Zur-Kohlbyr?*

"A state of affairs the Vitae appreciate, I can assure you," said Basq. "I trust, however, Zur-Iyal, that you will not be hesitant to expedite matters as much as possible."

The image of Arla at the research table flashed in front of Iyal's inner vision.

"Naturally," she answered, attempting to match Basq's fluidity of speech. "So, as soon as you, Ambassador, submit documentation supporting your claims to my office, I'll recall Arla Stone from field assignment and nullify her contract before witnesses." Her stomach tightened as Zur-Kohlbyr smiled.

No, I haven't forgotten any of the legalities, Cousin Director. Now why are you so glad about that?

"I wish to be perfectly clear and candid about the Vitae position at this time, Zur-Iyal," said Basq. He leaned forward a very little, but even that much body language surprised Iyal. The Vitae usually moved like freeze-frame videos. One sharp, separated motion at a time. "When we have the artifact in our possession, we are leaving Kethran Colony. The reclamation of MG49 sub 1 will be absorbing all our resources. We will be forgiving all debts and contracts that tie Kethran to the Vitae."

Iyal's breath caught in her throat. *Leaving? We hand you Arla and you're away from here?*

"We will, of course, be leaving all our hardware behind in payment for unfulfilled obligations on our side. We will also provide training manuals and AI software guides for the continued health and management of your colony, which has been our good client for over a decade."

We'll be rid of you? For good and all?

"My failure to reclaim the artifact will delay this operation," added Basq.

"However, as I said, Ambassador, formalities must be observed," cut in Zur-Kohlbyr. "Zur-Iyal will require supporting documentation before the contract is nullified."

Basq was silent for a long moment. "She'll have it," he said at last. "I'll contact your administrative assistant, Zur-Iyal, if I may, for the details regarding the extent of the documentation you will need and all the points it will have to cover."

"Certainly," said Iyal.

Basq rose and saluted her stiffly. "You'll have what you require before tomorrow morning. Perhaps you should recall the artifact today?"

"When I have your documentation, Ambassador, I'll proceed." Out of the corner of her eye, she saw Kohlbyr nod once. Again, he approved of her move. What was going on? His master-in-council had voted against the Vitae takeover, and here she was thwarting their removal with bureaucratic formalities and he was happy about it.

"Very well." Basq saluted the Director. "We will continue this conversation tomorrow then."

"My line will remain open for your message," said Zur-Kohlbyr. The Director did not even stand. Basq's scarlet robes fluttered as he left the room alone. Iyal wondered if the Vitae Ambassador knew he'd just been insulted.

I'll bet he does. If he knows enough about my private politics to come across with the fact that I'm holding up their pullout, he surely knows about our manners. Killian's calm, blue eyes gazed up from his portrait. She laid her hand across it to keep herself from seeing his face. She did not need a reminder of how alone she was right now.

Zur-Kohlbyr touched a key on the wall and the door to the waiting room slid shut. He leveled a wide grin toward Zur-Iyal. "I knew I could count on you, Cousin."

"Forgive me, Cousin Director." Iyal took her hands off the table and folded her arms across her chest. "But this sudden reacknowledgment of our family connection has got me a little confused." She shifted her expression to a glower and her tenses to across-table casual, which was one step from insubordinate. "Are you going to tell me what's going on?"

Zur-Kohlbyr's smile was indulgent. "Iyal, these are serious events here. We have the chance to take the lead with them and shape Kethran's future as a power in the Quarter Galaxy."

Uh-oh. A gleam shone softly in the Director's eye. He was smelling power and he had a keen instinct for it. It was a genetic tendency reinforced by the First Family environment. His branch had been particularly successful at applying it for a hundred years.

"The Vitae want our Arla." He settled back and lifted his drink. "They want her more than I've ever seen them want anything since that business with passing the anticontraband measures. Now, why?" He sipped his gold liquid. "Would you like a drink?"

"No, thank you." *I don't think my stomach could handle it right now.*

He swirled the liquid in the glass meditatively. "She must

be unique in some significant way." He smiled at Iyal again. "If we knew how, we, you and I, Cousin, could give Kethran what the rest of the Quarter Galaxy would sell their lives to have, a step up on the Vitae."

"Well, it's not like we haven't been trying to work on it, Zur-Kohlbyr," Iyal reminded him.

"We've been trying within very strict boundaries." He swallowed the last of his drink. "I suggest that the importance of speed in this matter removes those boundaries."

Iyal felt the blood drain out of her cheeks. "What do you want me to do, Cousin Director? Take a sapient woman apart to see how she ticks?"

"Zur-Iyal." Zur-Kohlbyr rested his hands flat on the table. "We need this. Things are building quickly in the Quarter Galaxy. The Unifiers are becoming a real force, and we don't know how power will go to their collective heads. The Shessel are beginning to colonize and spread in their own right and we don't know what they will do either. The Vitae are pulling back to this little world they've found, perhaps permanently, perhaps not. Without some leverage, Kethran, this world our parents built from a dead rock, is doomed to be tossed around the political storm like a feather in a stampede."

Iyal said nothing.

"Cousin, I know you have limited your considerable talent for intrigue and manipulation to the occasional interaction with contraband runners. Since it was proper to your postmarriage status and beneficial to the labs, I've never said anything about it. Now I'm asking you to remember your birth family and your place in the soul-politic and do not make me force you to hand this artifact over to me after I've seen to your arrest.

"Where is Arla Stone now?"

Iyal gripped her wrist until the edges of the portrait bracelet dug into her palm. She saw Arla in the lab, reading. She saw her, narrow-eyed and plainly frightened, as she arrived by Perivar's side. She heard her own voice talking to Perivar: *And I'm not crazy about the idea you'd think I'd get her in here and put her in a processor . . .*

And she heard Basq promising to leave as soon as they

had Arla, and she saw Kethran forced to crawl back to the
Parent World because they couldn't manage on their own.
And she heard Cousin Director's threat again and she knew,
she knew, that he meant it. And she saw Arla in the lab.

Iyal stood up. "Arla Stone is on field assignment, Cousin
Director. I'll have her recalled immediately. You'll have to
give me eleven hours, though."

He nodded. "I think I can give you just that, Iyal. Remember, we need her alive, but I'm sure we can explain away any
other . . . aspects . . . of her physical condition." His smile
grew conspiratorial. "I knew, I knew, you would hold true
on this."

"We will also have to talk further, Cousin Director," she
said with what she hoped was a knowing leer.

She let him walk her to the door and salute her as she left.

Back out in the corridor, she used her torque to call
Allenden.

"Where is she?" she asked under her breath as she skirted
two interns who were deep in their own discussions.

"Sweeping the attic, actually," came Allenden's reply.
"Iyal, what . . ."

"I'll tell you later. Just sit still for now, all right?"

"All right, Iyal, all right." There was a peeved note in his
voice. Iyal swallowed. She couldn't risk getting Allenden
angry right now. There was too much she might need him for
later.

"Allenden," she said. "We need to move with extreme
caution on this. It could shape up into a family war if we
don't."

She could tell by the length of the pause that she had gotten
to him.

"I'm waiting on the news, Iyal," he said, and shut the
connection down.

In no mood to wait for the service lift, Iyal ran up three
flights of stairs.

The attic was actually a lab that had been shut down three
years ago when the Vitae had finished implementing their
plans for controlling the genetic engineering industry on
Kethran. The loss of business had forced Amaiar Gardens to

cut its staff. The unused lab had never been officially converted into storage, but unused equipment, broken furniture, and anything else that anybody wanted to get out of the way turned up there. Every now and again some intern in trouble with his supervisor would be sent up there to clean it out and organize it.

Inside, Arla was lugging a polymer crate full of anonymous cables from its spot in the middle of the floor. Iyal stood in the threshold and watched her for a moment. Arla wore the plain moss green shirt and trousers that most of the interns favored when doing heavy jobs, but she still kept her spill of dark hair wrapped under her black turban. The thick tool belt around her waist had a cattle prod dangling next to the bumpy leather pouch she always carried, because even though they weren't supposed to, the newer handlers had taken to quietly getting Arla out into the pens to help deal with balkier specimens. She had, as near as Iyal could understand, been some kind of animal handler back on her homeworld. She never complained about the extra work. She never even asked why she was being tapped. She just waded in and did whatever she was told to with an eagerness to please that bordered on groveling sometimes. For the past couple of weeks, Iyal had been wondering what all that ingratiation was covering up.

Now she was still wondering.

Arla stacked the crate on top of a container of silicate blocks and turned around. She saw Iyal in the doorway and flinched.

"Zur-Iyal," she said as she recovered. "Sorry. Was . . . I was startled."

"Don't worry about it." Iyal stepped all the way into the room and let the door slide shut behind her. "I need to talk to you, Arla."

"All right," said Arla, without hesitation, like she always did. Sometimes, Iyal had the feeling she could tell the woman to go jump off a cliff, and Arla'd still say "all right."

Sometimes. Other times, out of the corner of her eye, Iyal caught Arla studying her with her innocent, brown eyes turned to black slits like she was memorizing Iyal's motions, and calculating . . . calculating what?

Iyal shot the bolt on the manual lock. "Arla Stone, you've got two minutes to explain why I shouldn't hand you over to the Vitae Ambassador who was here looking for you."

Arla blanched until she was nearly as white as a Vitae herself, but her voice remained steady.

"Do you understand what you are saying, Iyal . . ."

"You're lying." Iyal said. "Now you've only got one minute."

For a moment, Arla did nothing but rub her hands together and stare at their scarred backs. She murmured softly in her own language. Then, abruptly, she switched to Iyal's. "I should've known," she said, without a trace of accent or awkwardness. "You're not like the Nobles in the Realm. You've got no expectations about what I can and can't do. You're not so easy to bluff." She faced Iyal. "The Vitae. What is it they want from me? Did they say?"

"Yes. They say you're their property. That you're an artifact that was stolen from them and that they want you back."

Arla sank into a rickety chair, wrinkling a short stack of polymer sheets that rested on the seat. "You do not like them."

"No." Iyal folded her arms. "But right now I'm trying to decide if I like you less. I've got security footage of you breaking into secured documents, Arla."

Arla's head jerked up. "You've got what?"

"Don't try to go back to the country girl act, Arla Stone . . ."

"No! No!" Arla waved her hands violently. "I don't understand. Security footage. What is that?"

Iyal stabbed a finger toward the boxy camera over the doorway. "Pictures from a camera like that one. Security surveillance. Yards of tape with your picture on it, pulling off ninety-nine different illegal maneuvers."

Arla stared at the camera. Her mouth moved silently and her face went from white to green. For a moment, Iyal thought she was actually going to be sick. Then, Arla let out a cluster of syllables so bitter and explosive that Iyal couldn't imagine them being anything but curses.

"No more time," Iyal said. "Start talking."

"All right." Iyal didn't have to strain to hear the new tone in her voice. This was not innocent trust. This was considered acceptance. "What do you want to know?"

A dozen different questions leapt to the front of Iyal's mind: What are you? Why do the Vitae want you? How did you learn to read so fast?

At last, she said, "How did you manage to access the Diet transcripts?"

"I saw Zur-Allenden do it once."

"Once?"

Arla nodded. "That is all I need. I was resetting one of the research tables and he was paying no attention to me."

"So, you've got a photographic memory?"

Her lips moved, repeating the term, and her brow wrinkled. "Something like that, yes."

"So you can read. The illiteracy was an act."

"Sometimes, now. It wasn't when I first came here."

"Then how . . ."

Arla fumbled with a pocket on her tool belt and pulled out a pair of gloves; then she opened the leather pouch she carried with her and drew out an ice white sphere.

"This is one of my namestones." She kept it cupped in her hand as Iyal leaned over it. "They give me the ability to remember everything I have ever seen, or ever heard. But they also let me have a base for those memories . . ." She frowned. "They correlate what is in my head so it makes sense to me. If I have a question, I hold the stones and they find the answer in my mind and give it to me. The more I have seen, the better the answers get.

"Before I came here, I was in a Vitae holding cell and a ship called the *U-Kenai*. I saw a great deal. I knew something about computers and I'd heard at least spatterings of your language. The stones were able to"—she frowned again—"create relationships for me so I was able to learn very fast."

Iyal felt her mouth move as she tried to form the words "that's impossible." She couldn't get the sounds out, because in the back of her mind she knew that was not a valid argument. Arla was impossible, yet there Arla sat, relatively calm and collected and holding a stone in her hand that was really . . . what?

Can't be an AI, there's no way for her to interface with it. Can't be any kind of computer I know about. Artificial total recall? AND the ability to create contextual relationships? How? HOW?

Iyal stumped over to one of the old research tables and, with one sweep of her arm, dumped a pile of miscellaneous debris and dust onto the floor. She slammed her hand against the ON key and as soon as the screens and boards flickered to life she began activating the scanners.

"Arla, let me see that." Iyal extended her hand and was not surprised to see it was shaking.

After a moment's hesitation, Arla laid the stone against Iyal's palm. It was heavy, smooth, and cool as polished crystal. She cupped her fingers carefully around it. Its surface did not warm up. It was as if it resisted her body's heat.

Iyal set the stone gently into one of the table's scanner pockets and closed the lid over it. Arla gripped the arms of the chair until her knuckles turned white. Iyal said nothing. Arla knew this would not hurt her precious stone, she must know that or she never would have let go of it.

The main screen lit up with the preliminary information. First there was a shell, primarily constructed of crystallized carbon, but there were several trace elements. It had a micro-level capillary construction. Capillaries? In a doped-up diamond? Inside, primarily liquid . . . then how had it not evaporated over time . . . proteins, ribonucleic acids, electrochemical traces, and a filament structure . . .

Iyal blinked up at Arla and down at the screen again. The stone was a hollow, porous, enriched diamond filled with a miniature nervous system and a whole stew of unidentified virus chains.

And I'd bet my marriage contract that each one of them has binders that match that host of extra receptors Arla's carrying around inside her . . . but no . . . the scan only identifies ten variable strings and Arla has twenty-two unused receptors . . .

She's not a tool then, she's a system component. And this

*thing still can't be an artificial intelligence, but it might just
be a real one.* Iyal wished there was a spare chair for her to
collapse into.

"Where did this come from, Arla?"

Arla shrugged. "I was told that the Nameless Powers left
them to my family in case they needed to send another servant
to the Realm. This might be true, but I don't know what it
means."

Iyal lifted the stone out of the scanner and turned it over
in her fingers. This thing should be in the splicing room getting
peeled apart a micron at a time. They should know exactly
what was in there, how it was built, and what made it possible.
Total, context specific, recall in a sphere the size of a small
peach. Who'd need computers anymore? She could buy
Kethran the leadership of the Quarter Galaxy with this thing
and the woman it belonged with.

"You've been very calm about finding out you're not what
you thought you were."

"I haven't found out anything like that," said Arla coolly.
"The Teachers say I came into being when the Nameless
spoke the word that is my name. My mother said I was split
from the same word that made the stones. You say I came
into being when somebody strung together some proteins in
a laboratory. It doesn't matter. I am still myself. My name is
still mine. Only the Nameless can take that away." She held
out her hand. Iyal decided to take the hint and she handed
Arla the stone.

"Are there . . . many people like you in the . . . Realm?"

"I don't know." Arla replaced the stone in the pouch and
drew its strings tight. "I do know there aren't many arlas,
stones, I mean, left."

"How do you know that?"

Arla's mouth quirked up into a tight smile. "About ten
generations ago, the Teachers declared them sacred to the
Nameless and stole them. The ones that exist are mainly in
the Temple vaults. I heard one very highborn Teacher say
he'd only ever seen one set. So there cannot be that many."

Iyal's mouth was dry. There didn't have to be that many.
The Vitae were trying to lay claim to the world where they

existed. What if the Vitae got their hands on even one more person like her? Or a single stone like the one she carried in her pouch? They'd jump so far ahead of the rest of the Quarter Galaxy in technological development, the labs would look like entrail knitters by comparison. There would be no catching them. No countering them in anything. They could have whatever they wanted, whenever they wanted it.

"Arla," Iyal said. "Do you know what world it is the Vitae are laying claim to?"

"No," Arla shook her head. "They've only given an astronomical notation. I haven't got a context for it."

"Arla, it's the Realm. Your home."

Slowly, Arla's hand crept to her mouth. She pressed her palm hard against her lips, as if to stifle a scream, and her eyes squeezed shut. Iyal shifted her weight, uncertain of what to do, but in the next moment, Arla's hand dropped back to the pouch of stones. She whispered something in her own language and swallowed hard.

"Got to find Eric Born," she said, at last. "Got to warn him. Got to get back. Warn my family. Warn . . . warn everybody." The fear that widened her eyes could not have been faked. "The Teachers and the Nobles are bad enough, but those Skymen? We'd never get away. How can the Nameless permit this?" She spit the question.

How can you still believe in the Nameless Powers, whatever they are? Iyal wondered. Then she thought about the stones. *Then again, maybe I should start believing in them.*

"We need to get you off the planet, fast. We've got eleven hours before the Director comes looking for you. Maybe the Unifiers . . ."

"No," said Arla flatly. "They started the war in the Realm. They're too much like the Vitae. I've been listening to their blather. They talk about conquest in terms of contracts and agreements. I must leave Kethran, yes, but I must do it free and clear. I must get back to the Realm, with Eric Born. Then, then I will figure out what to do next." She smiled. "I have plenty to work with." She laid her hand over her pouch.

"What you'll need is credit." Iyal forced her mind back to the practical. "Don't want to risk a transfer to you. The

Vitae have got to be watching me." She glanced reflexively toward the door. "Eleven hours . . . I can get the Diet hopping, create a distraction while you get out of here . . . I might get arrested, too, and they'll freeze my account . . . do you think you can get back to Perivar's on your own?"

Arla nodded. "I know I can, but he told me not to return . . ."

Iyal waved her words away impatiently. "When you get there, tell him I said he'd better help you out or he'll be answering to me. Tell him to give you a loan. Whatever you need. I'll pay it back. Or Killian will."

"I'll tell him." Arla got to her feet. "Thank you, Iyal. I'll remember your name." She spoke so seriously that Iyal could only assume it was a blessing or a compliment.

"I'll get you back to your room so you can pack . . ."

"Pack what?" Arla spread her hands. "I've got clothes and shoes and my stones, and I need to hurry. The public transport runs all night, doesn't it? Is there anyone to prevent me from walking out of the door?"

"No one. Zur-Kohlbyr will be holed up in his office for at least another hour, plotting." Iyal undid the door's lock.

Arla marched out without looking back. Iyal just watched her. When the door closed again, Iyal turned up the power on the old table's comm board and sent a call out toward Killian's ship on the Lous Division Lake, on the other side of the world.

He was sleep-tousled and bleary-eyed when he appeared on the screen, but he woke up fast as he saw it was her. His eyes went round as he read the grim expression on her face.

"Iyal, love, what's happened?"

"Killian . . . I . . . I'm about to find where I left my voice."

"Oh-ho?" he breathed.

"How do you feel about emigrating again?"

He paused for a bare second. "I hear the northern continent of Fresh Dawn has a very unfussy border policy. They need hands and heads."

Iyal's heart swelled. "Love you."

"Love you." His smile was warm as sunshine and almost succeeded in banishing the chill in her soul. "I'll go hand in my leave request now. If there's a shuttle in port, I can be back by ten in the morning and we'll pack, all right?"

"All right."

They said good-bye and cut the signal and Iyal was alone again with her four walls and the silence of an empty room.

"Enjoy it while you can, Zur-Iyal," she muttered as she placed a request for a line to the Diet. "Enjoy it while you can."

Paral wished the Witness would stop looking at him. Even though his gaze was fastened on the monitors and comm boards in front of him, he knew she had her attention fastened on him. He could feel it like a cobweb that had laid itself over his entire body.

Lines 89A and B checked and open for another six hours. Should send the update request for another four . . . He forced himself to think about his job. He had to have the current resources inventoried and updated. He couldn't think about the Witness at his back, watching every movement of his hands, every twitch in his shoulder blades. He didn't have the energy to spare to think about that. He had to get the inventory done and try to find some way to get out to meet Ordeth without looking suspicious, without the Witness seeing an anomaly that could be traced to the Imperialists. It was vital that the Witness be seen to be the only anomaly on Kethran.

Even though the workspace was thoroughly secured and monitored, it held none of the private technologies. It was full of the same kind of consoles and transmission centers that could be seen in any busy clerical office on Kethran. Its security was so it could also hold a Vitae who was not an Ambassador.

It was necessary. Paral knew his lessons like he knew the subtleties of his Master-Ambassador's movements. The Aunorante Sangh had been able to drive off the Ancestors because they knew too much about them. Such power could not be given away again.

That the Vitae had to hide themselves, even from the monstrous Shessel, struck Paral to the core and made it possible for him to plot under the gaze of his master.

If only the Witness would stop looking at him.

The monitor that watched the station's plain, white antechamber beeped, and Paral nearly jumped out of his skin. His eyes flickered toward the Witness before they found the monitor. The door to the outside had opened and Basq crossed the smooth floor to tap the reader for the inner door.

Paral stood and folded his hands, ready for his Master-Ambassador's entrance.

The inner door opened, making the Witness's jade green robe flutter with its breeze. Paral made his obeisance and caught a good look at Basq on the way down.

Basq was not happy; Paral could sense it in the air around him, as palpable as the scent of vegetation and damp concrete that came in with him. Basq moved with the approved amount of decorum, but there was a quality to his movement that Caril had helped Paral learn to read when he first became Beholden to Basq.

"The Manager *ki* Maliad claims that the artifact is on field assignment and will not be recalled until she receives the supporting documentation of our claim." Basq removed the camera patch from over his eye. The Witness moved forward, holding out her hand so Basq could drop the patch into it without doing more than glance at her.

Paral felt a brief flash of envy at the Ambassador's control.

"This is most likely a delaying tactic. We cannot permit the artifact to remain in the hands of outsiders."

Hope and worry both tugged at Paral. If Basq was so far wrapped up in the failure of his excursion to make such a remark in front of the Witness, he was not thinking clearly right now. But it also meant things had gone very badly. Paral suddenly felt how alone he was even more intensely than he felt the Witness's regard.

"We need to contract satellite observation time to locate her whereabouts." Basq sat in the chair in front of the trio of comm boards, but didn't raise his hands to the keys. "Find out if the Gardens can be held accountable to the Diet for misrepresentation, possibly theft."

Inspiration shot through Paral and, just for a moment, the cobweb sensation fell away from him. "A suggestion, Ambassador."

"Yes?" Basq turned toward him so that Paral had to look his master full in the face.

Look humble, Paral instructed himself, *and a little embarrassed*. "It's not entirely proper. I have . . . friends stationed at one of the observation posts. If I relayed the request to them, they might be willing to start the search before the allotment request comes in . . . I could post myself at the station and relay any information to you immediately . . ."

Basq didn't say anything. He was ever mindful of the Witness, even more than Paral was. The camera set over her right eye gleamed even blacker than her skin. Paral's palms began to sweat, but there was nothing to do but wait while Basq weighed propriety against emergency.

Just a little nudge, thought Paral, drawing justification from Caril's comments about how susceptible Basq was to prodding.

"I recognize this is irregular, however, Amaiar Gardens may attempt to transfer her, or she may desert the premises . . ." He let the sentence trail off.

It had been enough. "Proceed, Beholden."

Paral made obeisance, partially so he did not have to look at the Witness. "Yes, Ambassador."

Paral made his escape as coolly as he could manage. One of the station's enclosed private cars waited out on the street. He had an hour to spare, maybe two before Basq wondered what had happened to him. It would take that long for Basq to put together the documentation for Zur-Iyal *ki* Maliad, in case he could find no legal discrepancies in her conduct and was forced to proceed on her terms. Paral could relay his improper request to the station en route to the Shessel Embassy. The plan was in motion. All was working smoothly.

He just wished he could shake the feeling of the Witness's eyes from off his skin for one moment more.

9—Amaiar Division, Kethran Colony, Hour 06:20:34, City Time

"... for when humans see freedom, they lose the will for slavery."
Zur-Ishen *ki* Maliad, "Upon Leaving Kethre"

"*T*hey asked specifically to be allowed to deal with you." Shim, the Third in the Emissary Voice, stretched both secondary arms toward Kiv.

Kiv rippled and sagged and wished for his siblings. He'd thought himself ready for the isolation of off-planet work, but it was not so. The old-timers had warned him. The comfort of his children was not the same as having his siblings and nieces and cousins around him. Even with Ere draped around his shoulders, he still felt alone. Shim, a grounded priest, was a fifth cousin Kiv had never met until he had volunteered to hatch out his children on Kethran Colony. The relationship was not close enough to provide any security. It was frightening to realize he knew Human Perivar better than he knew the cousin in front of him.

We serve, and service has never needed the weak, he
reminded himself. *My daughters will understand these
humans who live like priests and act like madmen, even if I
never do. They will carve out lives safe from the possibility
of bondage with them.*

Among the human enclaves, the Rhudolant Vitae were particularly insane. The thought of them wanting to meet with him
specifically was nerve-racking. The embassy environment,
lovingly designed with its arched ceilings and varying textures
in subtle shadings of blue and violet, was not relaxing him
at all, because he kept thinking about Arla Stone, and about
Perivar's impossible promise that nothing would touch Kiv
or his family.

"We have been in touch with our embassies on Kethre and
on seven of the stations," Shim was saying. "The Rhudolant
Vitae are withdrawing everywhere. The matter of this planet
is of the greatest import to them. We need to understand how
it will shift the power balances of their 'family.' You may be
able to garner some information about this."

"I will . . ."

"Do my best," finished Ere for him.

Shim withdrew three of his eyes. "That is all we ask,
Kivere. They are waiting in the visitor's chamber."

Ere tightened her grip with her feet on Kiv's back as he
bunched his muscles against his inner trembling. They moved
through the series of bubble-shaped rooms that linked the
audience chamber with the visitor's chamber. Perivar had
once expressed his surprise at the fact that the Shessel, with
their horizontal torsos, did not like long corridors, until Kiv
pointed out to him that humans, in general, did not live in
high-ceilinged closets.

Ere's hands kneaded Kiv's shoulders. She was plainly
excited by this new game. Kiv worried sometimes that Ere
loved intrigue a little too much, especially for someone who
had not even started her second growth yet.

The visitor's chamber had been placed under one of the
largest domes. The room was framed with interlocked hexa-
gons of steel struts. Between the struts hung membranes like
the one that separated Kiv's room from Perivar's. The inside

of it held human-style amenities and the outside held the Shessel.

Under the membranes waited two Vitae. Kiv blinked all his eyes and Ere's grip tightened. Two red-and-white children, bald as the adults, flanked the Vitae. The children stood as close to their chaperones as they could. Their eyes were wide and round, a sign of Human fear, Kiv knew.

"What game do they play, Father?" murmured Ere. "Humans do not bring their children to transact businesses."

Kiv stroked her back. "Thank you for the reminder, my first named. What game is an excellent question."

Kiv extended himself all the way; eyes, ears, and head alert and towering over the visitors. The Vitae made no move.

"I am Kivererishakadene. With me is my first named, Ere. I say you welcome and ask to what end you have come?" The construction was formal in the extreme, but the Vitae were not to be greeted lightly.

"I am Ambassador Ordeth and here stands Ambassador Paral. With us are our children Iolphian and Tala. We are come to offer payment for a service you can provide us."

"If you need some communications work done . . ." began Kiv.

"My partner and I have an office . . ." Ere finished for him. Kiv laid one of his primary hands on Ere's mouth. This was not Perivar they dealt with. They would act in the Human fashion here, with either the parent or the child speaking the thought. Not both.

"It is not communications support we need," said Paral. "It is a separate service, and we will pay twice the amount of your average annual income for it."

Nervousness closed down Kiv's ears. He forced them open and whistled. "So much? For what service?"

"You have heard our announcement of claim to the world designated MG49 sub 1?"

"We have."

"On that world there are artifacts which endangered our Ancestors and finally forced them to flee their home. It is imperative that we know all we can of them before our children walk on the Home Ground. Otherwise, the danger will be the same for us as it was for our Ancestors. To mitigate this, we took one of the artifacts to a ship for study. It was stolen from us. We now know that your partner Yul Gan Perivar assisted in the marketing of the artifact. . . ."

"You are speaking of Arla Stone?" Kiv shrank back, sheltering Ere a little in the curve of his neck.

"I speak of an artifact," said Ambassador Paral. "One that might come once again into Perivar's hands. If this is the case, we ask that you return it to us." Paral laid a hand on Tala's shoulder. The child jerked reflexively, but the adult held on. "Two years' pay is a small thing compared to giving my child a safe home. As soon as you agree to the service, you will receive a year's pay. If you enact this service, you will receive another year's pay, which will be given directly to your children if you so wish."

"Why are you not speaking to Yul Gan Perivar?" Kiv asked.

"He has worked against the Vitae in the past," said Paral, without even pausing to consider the question. "We have no reason to expect him to do differently now. Your contract of service will mean that you are ready to respect the laws of the world where you do business, where your partner is not."

"It will mean more yet," said Iolphian. Under the voice of the translator, Kiv heard the piping of an immature human and, against his will, something inside him softened. "It will tell the Vitae that the Shessel are better allies than many of those who call themselves human. Once grounded, the Vitae will have to build a new life and we will need a great deal of help."

"Singsong," Ere buzzed in Kiv's hindmost ear. "The speech patterns are wrong. That one has memorized this speech. They are trying to relax our spines with this."

Kiv winked one eye briefly to indicate he had heard. In his mind, he had his own suspicions. *You would bribe my entire people? For possession of one parent?*

"And if I do not give my agreement?" Kiv asked.

"Then we will take our leave and thank you for your honesty and no Shessel shall again be troubled by a Vitae request," said Ordeth.

Kiv did not even need Ere's anxious buzzing to recognize the threat. He retracted his neck and secondary arms, sinking below the Vitae's eye level. It was a stance that never failed to make Perivar uneasy. There was no reaction from the Vitae.

"Because you are bringing the welfare of all the Shessel into this," Kiv said, "you force me to consult the Emissary Voices before I take what you offer."

Whatever Ordeth said to Paral, it didn't translate. All Kiv heard was "Navin uary ketket ti." Whatever that meant. Paral replied "Iveth mikhain." The children stood like dolls and said nothing at all.

Ordeth faced Kiv again. "Please consult the Voice then. We can wait a short time only."

Kiv had been dismissed by humans before, but seldom so abruptly. *Why would they bribe an entire people?* he thought as he turned on his own length and left the room. *Because they can.*

"It's a charade," said Ere eagerly. "Father Kiv, it IS a game. Those children were props and . . ."

"Yes, Ere, yes." Kiv stroked his daughter's feet with his secondary hands. "Now we have to hope the Voice will let us make a worthy countermove."

The Emissary Voice waited in the audience chamber. Ere shifted her grip on Kiv so that she hung on with only her legs and could fold her arms in respectful greeting. Kiv did the same even as a spasm of uneasiness ran through him. The Voice was composed of strangers. Shim carried Kiv's skin tones because he was a cousin, but only the Sky Fathers knew where his enclave was. Ji was a loose-skinned northerner with great gaps artificially carved in his scales. Gov smelled familiar, but the familiarity was not an easy one.

Kiv accepted the need of union. With the skies crowded with humans, the Shessel could not be divided. There could be no room left in the Voice, or in the offworld residents for the makings of feuds. It was right that if the Voice had no siblings, no close cousins on this world, that he should not either.

It was right, but it was not easy. Kiv drew a great deal of

calm from the fact that Ere saw them only as Shessel. Which
is what they were. Only Shessel, like he was.

The Voice had, of course, already heard what had passed
between Kiv and the Vitae. It was too important a conversation
to have gone unmonitored.

Gov extended himself fully. "You will give them your
promise to deal with their property as they require."

Kiv knelt, lowering his torso defiantly to the floor. "There
is more here than is immediately obvious, Emissary. What
they call an artifact . . ."

"Is also a parent with living children." Ere leaned herself
over the top of Kiv's head. "Four of them."

"To which the Vitae have laid claim," said Gov. "If they
own the children, they own the parent."

Which answered the question about where Gov came from.
The Si-Tuk peninsula had practiced slavery right up to the
time the Unity Laws had been laid down. Right up to the
time Kiv's parent had dropped her eggs.

"But how have they laid claim?" asked Kiv. "All they say
is that their ancestors came from this place. Well, my ancestors
came from the Si-Tuk province." He stretched all his eyes
directly toward Gov. "Yet for three-quarters of a century, the
Si-Tuk vigorously contested our enclave's right to return there,
and enslaved those who disagreed with them."

Gov hissed and Ji retracted himself. "Kivere, now is a very
bad time to bring up old wars." He peeled open three eyes.
"The Vitae have always been very precise in their dealings
with us. If their representatives say that we will have no
more dealings with them, we must accept that at face value.
Remember, the humans can afford not to care about us, but
we must care about them. There are too many of them. They
are everywhere."

"How much of what you say is influenced by your partnership with Yul Gan Perivar?" asked Shim abruptly.

Ere hissed. Shocked, Kiv squeezed her mouth closed.
*What's she thinking? Sneering at the Emissary Voice because
of a remark about a human . . .*

No, she is sneering at three strangers because of a remark about Perivar. The realization hit Kiv hard. He was not the only one who knew Perivar better than a cousin.

"A fair question," he said, more to Ere than to the Voice. "I would say a great deal is influenced by it. I thought that was the point of the Voice and the Enclave licensing my partnership, so that I and my children could be influenced by humans.

"It is worth remembering, Emissary Voice, that humans are not all Vitae," said Kiv. "Many of them do not even like the Vitae."

"And many of them do not even like us," Shim reminded him. "The Vitae, unlike the Unifiers, are at least indifferent to our biology." He raised himself up until he was the tallest in the room.

Before any of the Voice could speak, Kiv extended his neck. Ere laid all her hands on the top of his head and extended herself as well to add weight to what he said. "Yes, sirs, I agree, we must be careful of the Unifiers. But there are more than those two choices for us. As you said, the humans are everywhere . . ."

"But not everywhere do they agree, or even speak with each other," finished Ere.

Ji retracted even farther. "I do not clearly hear what you are saying, Kivere."

"The Vitae are retreating. We see this everywhere. Even if it is only a partial retreat, a temporary retreat, a weakness will be created when they leave. The humans will be scrambling to rebalance themselves." He felt Ere's feet shift and knew she was extending herself to her absolute limits.

"Why should the Shessel not be part of the new balance?" Ere whistled triumphantly. "We have resources, we need business. If we become a prop to the humans, they will fear to lose us as they fear to lose the Vitae."

Shim retracted his snout thoughtfully several times. The others remained ominously still.

"What is the sudden eloquence that has come upon you, Kivere?" asked Gov.

Kiv extended his arms and Ere swarmed down them so that she was presented to the Voice. "I have staked the lives of all my children on the idea that we will be able to find some way to coexist with the humans that does not compromise the Shessels' future."

It was totally unfair and he knew it. Only business operators were allowed to hatch their children offworld. Emissaries had to drop their eggs unfertilized or leave them in stasis. It was as unfair as the Vitae bringing their own offspring into the visitor's chamber.

Gov retracted his secondary arms. "However intriguing this possibility is, it would call for a change in official policy. Therefore, we cannot act on it."

"We could if the Emissary's council changed the policy," suggested Ji, and Kiv wondered how united the Voice really was.

"We must not overreach ourselves," said Shim reluctantly. "We are emissaries to the Kethran Diet, not the Vitae."

"We need to know if the Emissary's Council has been approached by the Vitae and what their decision is before we do anything in this matter," agreed Ji.

Gov pressed his primary arms against his sides. "The Vitae have already made their policy clear. Even should there be merit in Kivere's proposed risk, we do not have the time to dither about."

"The Vitae cannot deny our need to consult with the Emissary's Council," said Ji. "They are a highly organized political body, they understand the concept of service and supervisors."

"Perivar and I can open a channel for you in an hour." Ere took her old position on Kiv's shoulders. Frustration squirmed through Kiv. Of course Ere would bring Perivar into this. She didn't understand that this whole bizarre situation was caused by him.

Gov snorted. "It will take the embassy staff three hours."

"Perivar and I can open a channel for you in one hour," said Kiv. *I will talk to Ere, but not in front of a Si-Tuk.*

Gov swung four eyes toward Kiv and Kiv saw the tremor in the stalks and the way his teeth showed through this slit of his open mouth. Gov did not like the mention of Perivar. He did not like Kiv. He did not forget that Kiv should have been his property and his anger burned to see Kiv acting independently with the support of his free children. Kiv knew it with a searing certainty, and found time to wonder if Ere had known it too.

"You have bought time, Kivere," said Gov. "What do you intend to do with it?"

Kiv stiffened his spine. "Find out if Perivar is willing to come work in our home," said Kiv. "We need human contacts. Perhaps it is time we hired some."

Gov closed his eyes. "We could never give your kind a finger's length."

"No," agreed Kiv quietly.

"Go open the channel then," said Ji, and there was a hint of approval in his voice. "We will be ready in one hour. The Voice will tell the Vitae that they will have to wait until we have official word from the Emissary's Council to make this contract with you."

"Thank you, Emissaries all." Kiv folded his arms respectfully and turned himself and Ere all the way around to leave the room.

You can give my kind a finger's length, just be careful which finger's length it is.

Frustration seethed inside Paral as he climbed back into the transport. Ordeth wasn't even looking at him, and he was glad, because he knew his face betrayed his mood. She was speaking softly into her torque. Her disk was still in place in her ear, so the signal wasn't going very far. The children waited in the side seats, doing very good imitations of Ambassadors. Paral didn't know how she got them off her ship, and he didn't really want to. All he wanted to know was how he was going to be able to tell Caril something other than that he had failed.

"Thanks for the news," Ordeth said. She tapped her disk twice and turned to Paral. The transport's internal lights turned her skin a sickly yellow. "You're going to have to get on-line to Basq. The station's pinpointed Stone in the Wall."

"Then we should go after her." Paral reached for the control boards.

Ordeth snatched at his hand. "With the children? It's bad

enough we risked them away from the ship. You're being too open, Paral."

He yanked his hand away, amazed and infuriated by the affront. "Too open to whom? Monsters and babies! It's time to stop hiding ourselves." He rubbed his wrist where she'd grabbed it. "Isn't that what the Imperialists are all about?"

"The Imperialists have only made it this far by slipping through the cracks," she hissed at him. "When we have a stable power base of our own, then you can play petty dictator to your heart's content!" She stopped and visibly pulled herself back. Whether from her own sense of propriety or from what she saw in his eyes, Paral couldn't tell. "Let Basq pick the artifacts up. Uary will get a chance to study them and we'll know what we need."

"And so will the Assembly." He stared at the blackened windscreen. "No."

"And if you don't report in, you're going to have the Witness really wondering about you," she pointed out coolly. "You can't tell me she doesn't already have the satellite data."

Paral was silent for a moment. "All right." He bowed his head and stared at his hands on his lap.

Think, he ordered himself. *There's still got to be a chance.*

"It's possible that Basq won't be able to hold on to Stone in the Wall," he said, looking up at Ordeth again. "She has a resistance to confinement, and he doesn't know where she's headed yet. . . ." He waited for confirmation.

"Not unless you tell him," replied Ordeth.

"All right. We'll send him after her, but we'll make sure that there's no one to receive her if she reaches her destination."

Ordeth squinted like she was trying to see through his skull. "What are you thinking?"

"I am thinking it is not right that the Shessel can block the Reclamation. Is there anyone else here who can help us?"

"Maybe five in the division, if I ask them." Ordeth sat very still, just as she was supposed to. "Paral . . . you are not thinking with care here."

He matched her properly immobile expression. "The time for caution is past, Ordeth. Long past."

*   *   *

For the thousandth time, Arla's hand strayed to the mouth of her belt pouch and for the the thousandth time she forced it away.

I know enough. Nameless Powers preserve me, I know enough to read a sign and get off a bus.

But thinking was hard and reading was slow and the stones would make it so much easier. She'd been using them to arrange her thoughts every single night since she got to the labs.

Which was the problem. She'd gotten used to their help. She'd gotten to like it. She leaned her cheek against the cool window and watched the strange, patchwork city pass. Clusters of buildings squatted in a spread of untamed meadow, or towered over groves of tangled trees. Only the razor-straight roads and their flanking walkways connected the knots of habitation.

Her mother had warned her that if she defied the injunction to reserve the stones for the needs of the Nameless or the Servant, the Powers would reclaim her name and with it her will and free mind.

Iyal and her friends would have called it assimilation and addiction. Arla simply called it dangerous, because what it was really stealing was her confidence. If she lost that now, she lost everything.

Did I type the destination in right? Should check. Her hand dropped onto the pouch. *Should check the sign, not the stones!* She peered at the display that took the place of a window in a hand-navigated vehicle. The third stop on the list was 32–35 Old Quarter. Yes. That was Perivar's home. She sat back in the cradling seat and tried to relax. She was on her way. Wherever the Vitae were, they were not here.

Yet.

She rubbed the backs of her hands. *I should have known the Nameless would never let me get away with this so easily. They will not tolerate their people abandoning their Realm. However it came to be, we are not like the Skymen. We are not free like they are.*

But this doesn't mean I surrender, do you hear? I don't. She felt her muscles begin to sag as for a moment her weariness overwhelmed her. *But it does mean that once I get home I have a whole new fight on these hands.*

The bus eased itself to a halt. Arla shifted impatiently in her seat. Skymen, who didn't have to worry about night storms and cold, never seemed to go to sleep. The sun was poised to vanish under the low, straight horizon, and the bus was still almost full of travelers. No wonder they used so many different tricks to divide their days up. They didn't care about the rhythm of the world around them.

The bus raised the doors nearest the small block of empty seats and Arla automatically looked to see who was getting on. Her heartbeat skipped wildly. A pair of Vitae climbed aboard. Somebody gagged. Somebody spit and somebody else started murmuring as if in awe. Arla could not take her eyes off the scarlet-and-white figures, even to bow her head and scrunch backward in her seat.

The Vitae did not take the nearest empty seats. Instead they picked their way down the central aisle until they stood beside her. The sound of rustling cloth and shifting weight came from all directions, but not from the Vitae. They simply stood in the aisle with their attention fastened on Arla. Their bodies didn't even sway as the bus started into motion again.

One of the two was her original captor, the one Eric called Basq. The second was rounder and shorter. The round one might even have been a woman, but there was no way to be sure, even though she was close enough for Arla to see the open pores under her eyes.

Basq took one of the empty seats and keyed a new destination into the bus's list. Arla didn't recognize the address. It showed up between the seventh and eighth stop on the list, which only meant it was on the way to somewhere else.

"The laws of this planet have acknowledged our ownership of your body," said Basq. He said it evenly and with no effort to keep his voice down. Arla's throat tightened. It didn't matter what anybody else heard. Even without her help, the Vitae had learned the language of the Realm. With a garbled accent and mangled tenses, but there was no mistaking it.

"Wherever Zur-Iyal has sent you will not receive you."

Arla said nothing. They were the center of attention for all the other passengers, but none of them had moved. The Vitae could pick her up bodily and haul her out of the bus and they still wouldn't move. Here, the Vitae were the Nobles and, like them or hate them, very few would be seen to act openly against them. Arla could not look for help from any of these strangers. Then she remembered the sound of spitting from the back of the bus.

But neither can they.

"Wipe your destination from the list, Arla Stone," said the Round One.

Arla spread her hands flat on her thighs. "Maybe you can take me away with you," she said. "Maybe you can destroy those the Nameless have sent to rule the Notouch and claim the Realm for yourselves, but I'll be dead and drowned before I'll help you do it."

The Vitae stayed silent for a moment. Arla saw Round One's lips move minutely, as if she were working out what Arla had just said. When she finally got it, her mouth stiffened into a straight line. Arla felt her own mouth twist into a smile.

The destination at the top of the list flashed and a chime sounded. The bus slowed to a halt. The doors opened.

Arla yanked the cattle prod off her belt and shoved the tip against the Round One's hand. The Vitae screamed as the shock hit. Arla dived out the open door.

"Aunorante Sangh!" Basq snarled.

Her shoes hit the pavement at the same time the words hit her ears and she nearly fell. The strange feel of this place could still rob her of her balance all too easily. She started to run. If she could keep upright, she could nearly outpace the bus itself.

The artificial lights the Kethran loved robbed the evening of its sheltering shadows and turned it gold and scarlet, pink and grey. Her only chance at safety was distance between her and the Vitae. Blurred faces jumped in and out of her line of vision. The weird light confused her eyes. A shoulder banged against her and she toppled to the ground. Hands touched her and she jabbed the prod at them. Shouts and curses she didn't have time to understand whirled around her.

Arla scrambled to her feet and staggered into a fresh run. Already her lungs burned from trying to suck down enough thin air to keep her going. Her muscles barely noticed the effort of running now, but they would when she stopped.

Arla ducked around a corner, and then another, not trying to maintain any kind of sense of direction, just trying to get out of sight.

Stars swam in front of her vision and solid blackness began to creep in around the edges. Arla stumbled to a halt and leaned against a carved stone fence that bordered a flower bed. She wheezed and gasped, trying to drag enough air into her dry lungs to clear her vision.

Blast Kethran. Blast the Vitae. Blast my ambitions and blast the Nameless for forcing them on me.

When her head stopped spinning, Arla raised her eyes. The bright white lights and red-and-gold street signs proclaimed that this was one of the quarters where the First Families lived. In the middle of the Amaiar Division, it was close enough to the entertainment and stores that they didn't have to take buses to get out and busy themselves with their fellows. In her work-stained clothes, she'd quickly be spotted and told to prove she had a need or a right to be here.

Already, faces were turning toward her with quizzical and hostile glances. But there were no Vitae either in front of her or behind her.

They're not quite ready to chase me through the streets yet, obviously. Arla knuckled her bleary eyes.

"All right now, Stranger."

Arla jerked her hands away from her eyes. A yellow-jacketed man walked through the gate in the fence and approached her until she could smell the stink of peppers on his breath and see the glint of authority in his brown eyes.

Arla levered herself away from the fence and had to stop herself from dropping reflexively onto her knees.

"You sick?" he asked. "Been robbed?"

"No, sir," she croaked, trying to stand up straight. "Just lost."

"Then you get yourself found." He pointed toward the octagonal pillar of a public communications console, "Or I'm

calling a security team down here to clean you off my street."
He tapped his ear meaningfully.

Arla licked her dry lips. "Yessir."

When you can't go back, you must go forward. Arla shuffled
forward and peered into the gaudy twilight, trying to find a
sign or a monument she recognized. *If you can tell which is
which.*

The comm console loomed across her path. Arla teetered
up to it and rested her weight against its smooth side. She
stared at the blank screen and gently lit keyboard.

Arla's hand trembled as she reached for the keys. She'd
seen a lab assistant use one of these when he was going out
for the evening. He'd called up the public system with a
special nonsecured code. . . .

I know the code, I know the code. But it would not come
to the front of her mind where she needed it.

Oh, blast. Her hand dug into her pouch and closed around
the smooth skin of the stone.

The boundaries of her memory burst with a rush of sensation
that left her knees weak. She knew the code in an instant.
She clung to the stone, savoring the freedom, and it was only
with a wrenching effort that she made herself let go.

It felt like a massive hand pressed against her mind, squashing all her thoughts flat. She blinked stupidly at her fingers
and wondered what they were for. The pillar squeaked against
her skin as she slid closer to the ground. The hand pressed
harder. Exhaustion helped it. Her fingers flexed idly, and she
remembered. Slowly, one key at a time, she typed the code
in.

The black screen brightened and showed a man with clear
eyes and an angled jaw. "This is a special notice for all voting
members of the First Families. Report to your section hall
immediately for a special vote."

What does it mean? She wondered. The hand was reluctantly lifting away, sparing her room to think, and just enough
strength to straighten up again.

The man's face faded away, leaving Arla staring at a black
screen again. She hadn't done enough. Her hand dropped to
her pouch and her head started to swim.

No. She gritted her teeth. *Not again. I won't have any strength left.* Hunger began to gnaw at her. She struggled with her unaided memory. Her fingers clutched the leather pouch and squeezed until her fingernails began to bend. With her free hand she touched the keys. Nothing happened. She tried a new sequence.

This time the screen lit up with the stylized lines and patterns that made up the city map. A crooked red line worked its way from where she stood to Perivar's home. She found a key marked PRINT. A paper copy of the map slid out from the slot above the board.

For the briefest moment, Arla wished she was in Narroways. No one could have followed her there, never mind found her. She knew the alleys and the catwalks better than the rats. The Notouch would have sheltered her without question and given her any help she needed, knowing she would do the same for them one day. She would have had no fear of spies or betrayal, and if the night was cold and unpredictable, at least she could breathe the air and keep her balance as she ran through the streets. She could have told her direction by the placement of the walls and wouldn't have needed to hunt around for street markers and struggle over their meanings.

Iyal had been wrong about that much. She couldn't read very well. She just looked and saw and let the stones sort it out for her later. Except now there was no time for that.

With the map gripped in her fingers, Arla staggered forward.

Back home, the children swarmed all over Kiv, demanding the news. He deposited Ere in their midst to let her relay it.

"Perivar?" he tapped his translator. "I need to open the housing."

"Sure, fine, go ahead." The tone of the live voice under the translation was furious.

Kiv slid the housing back. On the other side, Perivar paced back and forth, kicking his chair when it rolled in his path.

Kiv retracted his neck at the sight. "What's happened?"

"The Vitae have gone gods-high crazy, that's what's happened!" Perivar kicked the chair. It ricocheted off the map table and toppled over, its wheels trying helplessly to get purchase on thin air. "They've kidnapped Eric Born!"

"What?" Kiv all but pressed his snout against the membrane.

"I just got a message from Dorias . . . from an AI Dorias created . . ." He stopped and knotted his fingers in his hair. "They didn't even arrest him; they just took him. And now I got word from Iyal they want Arla Stone, too . . . what is with them?"

"I don't know," said Kiv. "They just tried to bribe me to deliver Arla Stone to them if she ends up back here."

Perivar froze. "What did you tell them?" he croaked at last.

"There was not much I could say." Kiv related what had happened at the Embassy. At his knees, he could hear Ere giving the same story to her siblings, almost syllable for syllable. Kiv dropped a hand onto the back of Ere's neck. "Into the other room, all of you. I'll be in in a moment."

Ere whistled quizzically, but Kiv shook her neck. Ri and Sha wrapped their arms around her, dragging her with them in a complex knot. Dene and Ka bounded along behind them and made a great show of shutting the door.

Kiv wrinkled his snout and turned his attention back to his partner. Carefully, Kiv told how he had suggested that Perivar might come work for the Shessel, leaving out Gov's origin and his smell.

"What do you say, my partner? There's good money to be had from the Shessel."

For a moment the tension in Perivar eased. "That sounds good, Kiv. Let the Vitae and the Unifiers and the Diet fight this out on their own." He picked the chair up and set it back on its wheels. "But I can't just leave Eric . . ." He leaned heavily on the chair back. "I don't owe him anything, but I do," he said to the floor. "He could have used me a thousand times over, but he didn't. We agreed to keep quiet and we did until the Vitae decided they could start playing games." Perivar looked at Kiv from under his fringe of disheveled hair. "I've got to at least find out if there's something I can

do. It's my responsibility. The *U-Kenai*'s coming into port
and I've got to meet it. Can you open the channel yourself?"

Kiv extended his arms all the way. "I can. Then I think
you had better meet us at the Embassy." Uneasiness crept
over him. "Humans do war over ground, don't they?"

"Frequently," muttered Perivar. "I was caught in one of
those wars back home."

"Is it possible the Vitae are readying for war?"

"It's possible," he said. "I've never heard of them doing
it, but I've never heard of them acting like this, either."

And I may have just denied them what they want, Kiv
glanced back at his children. *Yes. We need to get to the
Embassy. All of us.*

Perivar hit the CALL key for a bus and slid into his outdoor
jacket. "Just let them know I'm coming. I'll be as quick as
I can, but a lot depends on what this Adu's got to say."

Perivar left and Kiv closed the membrane housing.

"Ererishakadene," he called as he ambled into the living
rooms. The children swarmed out of their sleeping holes and
twined around and over him. "We've got to get ready for a
trip to the Embassy. We may be staying for several days. So
we have to pack what we'll need. Ereri, unhook the capsules.
Shakadene, come show me what you'll want to take."

And after that, I'll need to get a download of . . .

The lights went out.

"Father Kiv?" called Ere. Sha, then Dene echoed her.
"Father Kiv?"

Kiv dropped his secondary hands to hold the two of them.
"Hold still, now. It's a power failure. I'll set it right." He
whistled calmly, but his skin felt dry and loose from reasonless
fear.

With all four hands feeling his way along the walls, Kiv
stepped into the workroom and tried to remember where the
emergency power switches were.

The membrane housing slid back. White light dazzled his
eyes. His open eyes recoiled and his closed set pushed forward.
Kiv made out two human silhouettes illuminated by the bare
light from the hall. One of them raised a box and there was
a hiss. Kiv felt all his eyes try to retract.

The membrane began to shrivel.

Kiv lunged toward the doorway and slammed the housing closed. He hit the emergency seal. Nothing happened. The power was gone and there was no light and already he could feel the burn in his veins as too much oxygen shoved through his pores. The housing slid back. The light fell across him. A round Vitae and a tall Vitae stepped across the empty threshold.

Dene whimpered. Ka and Sha twined around his ankles. Kiv snatched them into his arms. They were too light. The air burned his skin, too hot and too cold at the same time. His children shuddered.

"Murderers!" Kiv backed away from the pair, who stood there like statues, doing nothing but blocking the housing. He forced himself to think. *Get the children to the capsules. Now! Move! Move! Move . . .*

His terminal legs gave out. His children bleated and wailed his name and the burning cold air pressed against his ears and his whole skin and bore him to the ground.

"Ererish . . ." And he couldn't remember the rest of what he wanted to say.

Arla drank in the sight of the brown, brick walls of Perivar's home and she sighed with relief. Several times she had made a wrong turn and been forced to double back and try again. Sometime during the march, the sun had gone all the way down. The crowds thinned around her and the buses that passed were full of people with their heads lolling. So Arla guessed it was getting relatively late. There was no way to judge by the unchanging lights that decked the buildings. Her joints told her she'd been walking a long time and they were reminding her she'd run too hard, as she'd known they would. Despite all that, fresh air and time had given her an internal balance that using the stones had removed. She could think clearly on her own again.

She shoved the map into her pocket as she crossed the empty street. The building's main door opened under the touch of her fingers. Unaided, she remembered that Eric had pressed the top key on the destination list for the elevator when he had brought her here before, how long ago? Three weeks or a hundred years? She closed her eyes and leaned against the wall as the elevator lifted her up to Perivar's floor. Well, with Perivar she'd have some direct and solid help, for Iyal's sake, if not for her own.

The elevator door dragged itself open and let her into the simulated daylight of the corridor. She blinked hard and rubbed her eyes. Perivar's door stood open at the end of the hall. The gesture of welcome where he came from. She smiled and strode toward it with something like relaxation in her movements.

But as she approached the open doorway, the air filled with the smell of ozone and rot. The doorway was dark and the place beyond was silent. Nothing hummed or buzzed or clinked.

Arla hesitated. *Run*, said part of her mind. *Get out of here now.*

Run where? Iyal won't be at the lab now, or maybe ever again. I can find the port all right, but what'll I do once I'm there? She set her jaw and unhooked the cattle prod from her belt, wishing she'd thought to steal a couple of knives from the lab.

Arla stole forward, placing each step silently on the tiled floor. A glance into the dim room showed no movement. She slipped across the threshold and pressed her back against the wall, letting her eyes adjust to the darkness.

All the machines that filled the space were quite dead. No one moved between them. The door to Perivar's living rooms hung open. No sight or sound of movement came from in there either.

Her gaze tracked across the silent machinery to the portal that divided Perivar's home from Kiv's. Its door was also open and the threshold was draped in grey rags left from whatever substance had kept their atmospheres free of each other. Beyond it waited nothing but shadows and pale, grey light spilling in from the windows.

Arla gasped and swore and backed toward the door to the hall. The sudden breeze and the firm click told her it had shut before she could even whirl around and see it for herself.

She pressed her palm against the smooth surface of the

reader. Nothing. Arla cursed bitterly. It was locked and she couldn't do anything. She'd never seen how the door opened without the reader. She cursed again, this time for not being bright enough to realize that all the Vitae had to do was look at the destination list for the bus to find out where she had been planning to go.

She bit her lip, bothered. Why weren't they here already? She looked at the remains of the inner portal. Maybe this was supposed to look like an accident. If the authorities arrived before she had entered the trap and they found the Vitae there, their presence would be difficult to explain. Now, though, the Vitae would know she was here. They'd have some Skyman's trick. They'd be on their way for her.

Hide, Arla. Where? Near the door? Assault them as they enter? Too obvious. They'll be ready. Hide in the corners. Make them come digging for me. She glanced around. Perivar's private quarters were small and nearly useless. She remembered that. Maybe Kiv's.

Hide in the darkness, maybe even find a weapon and a defensible position. Keep your back to a wall and at least they can't sneak up on you.

With one eye toward the hallway door, she sidestepped through the inner doorway into the shadows. The room was nothing but knobs and bumps and mounds of blackness. She slid between them carefully, making sure her feet were flat on the floor and her balance was sound at each step. She could not afford to be shocked into falling over.

The main walls of Kiv's room were set in a mirror configuration of Perivar's with the door to the private section in the far wall. When Arla reached it, she froze.

Draped across the threshold lay Kiv's long corpse. His arms lay wrapped around three smaller corpses. Three of his daughters lay dead with him.

Arla swallowed hard. Horror and fear took her over as a wretched thought reminded her how the Vitae came to find this place. Anger came fast on their heels.

You don't do this to the children. If your quarrel is with the parents, you bring it to the parents. You do not claim the

lives of the children. The Nameless forbid it. Expressly, firmly,
with every breath.

You are not in the Realm of the Nameless. The Skymen may
do what they please.

But not this! There is no power that can excuse them for
this!

She steeled herself and climbed around Kiv's cold body.

"I'm sorry," she whispered to the little corpses as she
stepped around them. "Nameless Powers preserve me, I truly
am."

Her foot kicked something and it screamed. She jumped
backward, missed her footing, and fell against Kiv's clammy
hide. With a screech of disgust, she scrabbled across the
tacky floor. The thing on the floor screamed and whistled and
buzzed, but didn't move. Arla peered at it. It was about the
size of her torso and it . . . writhed.

The capsule. It was the capsule that had dangled from the
overhead cables and carried Kiv's children between the rooms.
Inside huddled one . . . no, two of the children.

They screamed at her. She fumbled with the disk in her ear.
"Come on, you fool thing, work!" She tapped it impatiently.

"Murderer!" she heard abruptly. "You killed them! You
killed them!"

The little one clawed at the sides of the capsule, its snout
opening and closing maniacally as if it would bite its way
through to get to her. The other grabbed at it with all four
hands and twined their long bodies together until her sister
was smothered into silence and could only lie still, with her
sides trembling.

"Help us," she pleaded. "I know it's not your fault, but
she's going crazy. Please help us."

"Oh, little ones," Arla laid her hands on the capsule.
"We're trapped together unless you can you show me how
to open the doors."

"I can."

"Then we're gone." Arla hefted the capsule. It weighed
less than she thought it would. She balanced it on one shoulder.
"Close your eyes," she told them, and hoped they obeyed as
she stepped over the remains of their family. Her stomach

roiled and heaved and she forced her gorge back down. She had to get out of here. She had to get them out of here. She could hear one of them keening in a sound that she couldn't imagine meant anything but pain.

Under the child's instructions, she punched in the override code for the door lock. Arla had them all out in the hallway before the door had opened all the way. She avoided the elevators. Machines were the enemy now. Any or all of them might be in the hands of the Vitae. But the doors to the stairs were open and the stairway was clear.

"What are your names?" Arla asked as she negotiated the doorway with her cargo.

"I'm . . . I will be Kiv when we get back home, but until then, I'm named Ere," said the one who was trying to calm her sister. "And Ri is my . . . my . . ." Whatever it was, Ere didn't seem able to finish her sentence.

"Ere." The stairs turned a corner and Arla had to juggle the capsule to keep from standing the children on their heads. "Is there a safe place I can take you?"

"The Embassy," Ere said immediately. "They can . . . take care of us and . . ."

"Good." Arla cut her off before she had to try to finish that sentence. "How far is it?"

"Across the city. I know the address. We all knew, in case of emergencies and . . ."

"And this is one, yes. I tell you what we'll do. We'll go to a public terminal and put in a call, let them know we're coming . . ." She stopped. The Vitae might be listening to the lines and a call from her to the Shessel would let them know where she was going.

After another three flights of stairs, they came to a door labeled EXIT. Arla backed against the door to open it. The portal led straight out onto the main street, which was good, because it also led straight into a pair of Vitae. A young one and a tall one stood frozen in mid-stride, heading for the door.

Arla froze too, but her heart pounded. Backing up was no good, they'd hunt her like a rat. There was no way she could hide with the children in her arms. Running was already no good; they'd spread apart in front of her, ready to spring.

The weird scene was attracting attention. Passersby, probably on their way to warehouses or ship docks, turned their heads to see what was going to happen next. A few of them actually stopped dead.

The children also got a look at who blocked their way.

"Murderers!" screeched Ri. The capsule shuddered in Arla's arms as Ri threw herself against the side. This time her sister made no move to stop her. "Murderers!"

Some people in the gathering crowd must have had translator disks, judging from their expressions.

"These children seem to have a grievance against you," remarked Arla slowly.

"Your body is Vitae property," said Young One. "You have no legal recourse to grievance committee or to council."

Arla shook her head. "I am not making a grievance. These two of the Shessel race are."

It was an old trick. Hide behind a superior rank whenever you could.

"You killed our parent!" Ri's voice rose so high Arla's eardrums responded with pain. "You slashed the membrane, shut the power, you left our sisters for dead, you suffocated our family, you . . ."

"Ere, calm her!" ordered Arla. Ri was going to hurt herself if she kept up her pounding. Worse, her shuddering would make Arla drop the capsule.

Ere wound herself around her sister again, but with less success. The capsule shook in Arla's arms and she began to feel the strain of holding it.

"I am going to take these children to the Shessel Embassy." She shifted her grip on the capsule. "You are welcome to come along and make whatever claim you have in there. If I don't get them there, there will be two more deaths, this time in front of witnesses, because I can't hold them much longer and if I drop them, and if this casing cracks, they'll smother."

The Vitae said nothing.

"Or we can just start shouting for a security patrol and I can tell my story to them and then you can tell yours and the Shessel can add whatever they feel necessary." *I am not a Notouch here, you bald, blind children, however hard you try to make me one.* Then, a strange thought struck her. *But you run this world, why isn't security here already, by your orders?* A tart, satisfied feeling warmed her stomach. *You're doing something illegal, aren't you? You CAN'T call security, can you?*

Whatever it was the Vitae said to each other, the translator did not make any sense out of it. Arla watched the crowd behind the Vitae, and it was a real crowd now. They stood and stared. They said nothing. They didn't move. They waited. These were the ones who ran their world and the crowd waited to see what they'd do.

Arla decided not to wait until the Vitae called her bluff. "Somebody get security!" she shouted to the crowd. "It's a diplomatic incident and a murder call against the Vitae! Somebody get security!"

"Got it!" shouted a voice from the back of the gathering. "On the way! Five minutes!"

Arla smiled grimly. Some of these silent watchers wanted to rebel, all right, whether it meant the end of the world or not. Some of them were just waiting for the chance. Let the bald ones remember that!

"The Shessel will be taken to their Embassy," said Tall One, "but you are our property. You will be taken by us."

"Tell the patrol that. Tell them all about why these two are scared stiff of you."

"They are children. They cannot give witness."

"I can by Shessel law." Ere pressed all her hands against the capsule side. "Our parent is dead. I am first-named and that makes me the voice of my family. I can give witness and name protectorates. I name Arla Stone." She spread her mouth wide. Arla, for the first time, saw her needle-sharp teeth. "If we do not arrive at the Embassy in her hands, you are in violation of the treaty between the Shessel and this world and that is compounded on the crime of murder."

"Murderers, murderers, murderers," hissed Ri like she couldn't make herself stop. By now, she probably couldn't. "Murderers, murderers, murderers."

"So, unless we all want to report to the patrol, you're going to let me take these children out of here." Arla shouldered the capsule again, grateful for the fact that Ri was confining herself to hissing and buzzing.

Arla started forward, right past the taller Vitae. He, she, or it, was speaking in the untranslated language, but she couldn't tell to whom or what. They made no move to stop her, though, and she was glad. She was fairly sure the patrol would be on her side, but there would be endless Skyman formalities, and she had already lost too much time. "Ere, I am going to need your help." Arla walked through the crowd. The bodies parted for her.

"Ah . . . all right. I'll try." The capsule wobbled precariously as Ere squirmed.

"I need you to keep me on the right path to the Embassy. We need crowded streets and residential areas. We can't stay too long in deserted areas. We're going to walk from here."

"Walk!" whistled Ere. "But it's miles and miles!"

"Any public transport we use might be rerouted by the Vitae," Arla reminded her, "and I'm used to walking miles and miles." She smiled and, with a patience that came from long necessity, stifled the pain in her aching knees and ankles. "Which is more than I'd say for those two behind us. They are behind us, aren't they?" She felt the capsule shift again.

"Yes," said Ere.

So, NOW they're ready to chase me through the streets.

"Well, well, strangest caravan I've ever been a part of but we're lucky, little ones, though you might not believe it. There are lines they are not quite ready to cross yet. We have a chance to get you home still."

And to get me out of here, if your people will help someone who helped some of their own.

"We can follow this street for a long time," said Ere. "Until it gets to the New Crescent Quarter Way."

"Good." Arla shifted her pace to a slower one, the ground-covering pace she could maintain for almost as long as she could keep breathing, even carrying a heavy load in a high wind. She'd walked like this for most of her life. Let the Vitae with their machines and their shuttles tag along behind.

"They're still back there."

"Of course they are," said Arla. "And as long as they stay

back there, we're fine. It means they haven't been told what else to do." *I hope.*

"Can you tell me what happened to you?" she said, partly to keep Ere from dwelling too long on the Vitae behind them, and partly to keep herself from doing the same.

She listened, all the while trying to bury her horror in anger. *What right? What right do these people have? If they were the Nameless Powers with the Servant at their side, they would still have no right!*

"... but the air was gone and he fell and Sha and Dene were already down and Ri was screaming and the Vitae were gone and . . . and . . ."

"Shhh, all right. It's all right," Arla wished she could touch her. She didn't even know if the Shessel could tolerate the touch of human beings, but she still wished it. "Are they still back there?"

"Yes."

"All right. Try to rest. We're on our way to safety."

As fast as I can get us there, she lengthened her stride.

The walkway crossed into one of the wild areas. The trees, too tall and too straight, swallowed the light and the weeds ate up the city sounds. Arla strained her ears. Traffic noise faded farther away with each step, except for the slow, steady hum from the Vitae's transport. Arla risked a glance at the little patch of wilderness, wondering how much shelter it would afford if she had to run.

Maybe it won't come to that. Maybe word will reach the Shessel and they'll come looking for the children. Maybe . . .

Bracken rustled. The children whimpered, and Arla's arm tightened around the capsule. She threw her gaze in every direction, trying to find the source of the new noise. The rustling increased. Arla forced herself to keep moving. About a half mile ahead, another inhabited stretch glowed like a beacon.

Behind and to the left, weeds and scrub parted and a sedan chair, one of the few private vehicles authorized for off-road travel, climbed gingerly out of the underbrush and with high-legged steps started angling toward Arla and her charges.

Arla watched the insectlike vehicle out of the corner of her eye, but kept on walking. It had its windscreen up and its weather hood down, so there was no telling who was in there. She tried to think what to do. The drone of the Vitae car wasn't getting nearer, but the chair was. Fatigue clouded the edges of her mind and fear did nothing to clear it.

Abruptly, the chair halted and folded its legs. A human head and torso stuck out the side door.

"Arla!" shouted Perivar.

Relief sent Arla sprinting across the field before she remembered she was risking a huge fine for disturbance of a wilderness zone.

She skidded to a stop beside the chair, gouging the soil with her heels and doubling her fine. Iyal leaned out the driver's side window and stared along with Perivar.

"What are you doing . . ." she began, but Perivar had seen the capsule and the Shessel children huddled inside.

"Murderer!" squeaked Ri.

What color he had drained out of Perivar's face. "Where's Kiv? The other kids?"

Arla glanced toward the road. The Vitae had stopped their vehicle, too, and one of them had poked a bald head out the window to get a clearer view of the field.

"No . . ." breathed Perivar.

"They're dead," said Arla. "The children say the Vitae are responsible. I see no reason to say otherwise."

Perivar hit the door key, scrambling to get out before the door was even halfway open. Iyal touched the override control on her panel and it slid shut again.

"Perivar," Iyal laid a big hand on his arm. "Don't even think about it."

Perivar pressed the key again, and again. "They killed . . . they took . . . they . . ."

"We're in public, Perivar," said Iyal.

"And we need to get these children to their people," said Arla.

"Yeah, yeah." He shook himself. "You're right," he looked at the children. "Gods, I'm so sorry. I didn't know this would happen."

"I know," said Ere. "I don't know about Ri, though."

Perivar insisted on putting himself and the capsule on the luggage rack on the back of the chair. Arla, her arms aching, did not object, and neither did the children.

As soon as Arla strapped herself into the passenger's seat, Iyal touched a series of controls. The chair stood up again. She steered it into the street. The speed of its stride rocked them back and forth. Arla looked behind them. The Vitae transport was still standing in the middle of the street.

"I guess they did not feel ready to explain themselves to the Shessel after all," she murmured to Iyal.

"Well, they'd better be ready to explain themselves to the Diet. A lot of people are not happy." Iyal spoke with a kind of quiet satisfaction and Arla wondered what had been happening to her since she had left the lab, what, four hours ago? Five?

Iyal must have seen the puzzled expression on her face. "Electronic communications, Arla, are wonderful things."

In response to Iyal's prodding, Arla related what had happened since she'd left the labs. In return, Iyal told her how she had woken up the Diet members who knew her family and had gotten enough votes together to call a counterdebate on the Vitae resolution. Then, when Perivar had called her from the docks where the *U-Kenai* was coming in with still more news, she had gone to meet him.

"Then Eric Born is here," said Arla.

"No, he isn't." Iyal stared out the windscreen. "The Vitae got him."

Arla felt like the ground had dropped away from her. All she could do was hang on to the door handle and listen to her own harsh breathing.

At last, Iyal walked them through the arched gates of the Shessel Embassy. She explained their reason for petitioning entry to the automated security system in a few shockingly blunt words. The gates opened to let them into the inner courtyard and white lines lit up along the pavement to guide them to the squared-off doors reserved for human entrance.

Perivar, his arms wrapped possessively around the capsule led them into the reception chamber and showed Arla and Iyal how how to put on the oxygen tanks. Then he led them through the shimmering membrane that was the real entrance to the Embassy.

As soon as they crossed the threshold, Ere opened the capsule and lifted herself halfway out, sucking great long breaths of air. An inner door folded back and three Shessel flowed into the room, ringing the humans. Perivar set the capsule on the floor. Ri shoved past her sister and swarmed up into the arms of the smooth-skinned, earth-toned Shessel and clung there, shivering and keening.

"Can you help her?" pleaded Ere, climbing all the way out of the capsule.

"We'll sedate her," said the Shessel. "That's all we can do for now."

Ere shivered along the entire length of her body. "I need to talk to somebody. The Emissary Voice. I need . . ."

"We're here." Three more Shessel entered from one of the corridors and Ere made a beeline for the earth-toned one. He embraced her with all his arms.

"Kiv is with the Sky Fathers now and your sisters are waiting to be reborn," he said. "I feel them. They wait and say how brave their sister is to go on. She will live for us until we can live again."

"I know, I know." Ere burrowed under the crook of his neck.

"Emissary," said Perivar. "Ere says that it was murder, done by the Rhudolant Vitae."

"There are two of their Ambassadors here," said the squat, greenish Shessel. "They will answer." He looked toward the Shessel who held Ri.

"Are you ready to speak with the voice of your family, Ere?" he asked. "The Vitae are already here."

Ere nodded and let herself be put on the floor. She extended her neck to stretch herself as tall as possible.

The greenish one extended his neck toward the cluster of humans. "The Vitae claim property rights over Arla Stone. She will come with us so we can determine the legalities involved here."

Arla swallowed and glanced around her. Nowhere to run. She would simply have to brave this out for now.

"I can add my witness to Ere's," said Perivar.

The greenish one retracted himself until his eyes were level with Perivar's. "That is not permitted. You will be shown where you can wait with Sar *ki* Maliad."

Arla kept her eyes straight ahead as she followed the Shessel through the domed rooms. The oxygen pack dragged at her sore shoulders and the breathing mask itched where it pressed against her temples, and she wanted to tear the gel off her skin. Ere kept swiveling her eyes back toward Arla in a manner Arla could have sworn was furtive, but she couldn't tell who the child was afraid for, Arla or herself.

They reached the chamber where the Vitae waited. It was Basq again, and Round One from the bus. The webwork of steel and gel that housed the two Vitae made them look for all the world like they were in a cage. The sight gave Arla some slim measure of satisfaction.

Basq stood near the membrane and his eyes glittered as he saw Arla move to stand beside the Shessel.

"Thank you for bringing our artifact, Sar Gov," said Basq. "The Vitae will remember that the Shessel honored and respected the process of reclamation."

"That has not yet been determined," said Gov. "There are conflicting legalities and there is a charge to be leveled." He dropped one of his lower hands and stroked Ere's neck. "There have been numerous developments since your delegation spoke to us this morning."

"This morning?" Basq repeated. "No delegation was sent this morning."

"But we received one," said Gov. "Two Vitae and their children, asking for custody of the parent Arla Stone. Since then, Kivshakadene has died. Ereri claims it was murder and lays responsibility at the door of the Rhudolant Vitae. Our laws are clear. No business can be done with any corporation or individual who endangers or injures the child of a Shessel parent." He paused. "This includes the exchange of property."

Basq stiffened minutely. "No Vitae delegation was sent. I am set to oversee this matter. If members of the Rhudolant Vitae have violated Shessel life or law, they will be brought to trial and conviction. We will investigate this matter as far

as we can. I am sure we both need to contact our voices
within the Kethran Diet. What we ask in return is good faith
from you, that you return our property."

Ere whistled sharply and grabbed Gov's secondary arm
with three of hers. "But how have they laid claim?" she
demanded, pointing toward the Vitae with her free hand. "All
they say is that their ancestors came from this place. Well,
my ancestors came from the Si-Tuk province, yet for three-
quarters of a century, they vigorously contested our enclave's
right to return there." She extended herself to her fullest height
and turned all her eyes towards the Vitae. "I have named
Arla Stone my protector, in front of witnesses, and unless
you can lay claim to me, too, you cannot have her."

Basq looked down at the child and then up at the full-
grown Shessel. "This is a matter beyond personal . . ."

"It was," said Gov. "Kivshakadene's death drops it to
exactly a personal grievance and Ere is her family's voice.
When we have established communications with the Emissary's Council, we may all be ordered to do differently, but
that is hours away yet. Your good faith would be best indicated
if you began these investigations you insist will occur."

"Our Ambassadors are already conferring with your
enclave," said Basq, staring straight at Arla. "The counter-
mand may come at any time."

"Then you will find we are obedient to the judgment of
the Enclave of the World," said Gov. "Until then, to the
Shessel Arla Stone is a free parent of free children.

"We ask you to leave our Embassy."

Basq did not incline his head or make any other gesture of
respect, he just turned and left. Arla heard her own breathing
through the mask, harsh and heavy.

The Shessel was studying her.

She shifted her weight and tried not to scratch at the gel
pressing into her pores.

Nameless Powers preserve me, I should be used to this.
Enough people have stared at me since I left home.

"What will you do if I leave?" Arla asked.

Gov's whole body rippled. "We are not the ones who have
claim upon you. We could make you stay, I suppose, but not

legally, according to the legalities of the moment, unless Ereri keeps you protectorate-bound for that." His back two eyes retracted. "I personally would be glad to see you gone, just because those murderers want you here."

Ere tilted her head and eyes to look directly at Arla. "Where would you go if I broke bond?"

"Home, to my family and my own children. We have the Unifiers and the Vitae going to war over us. We need to make a stand against them."

Ere extended herself, arms, legs, eyes, and neck. "Then I release you. You are no more protector."

Arla smiled and knelt in front of Ere. "I hope that is not true, Little One." She stroked the child's neck briefly and felt the living flesh ripple under her hand. Her mind didn't see Ere's alien shape. She saw Little Eye and Storm Water and Roof Beam and Hill Shadow. It hurt to make herself stand up and shake clear that vision.

"I need to speak with Perivar and Iyal," she said to Gov.

"Of course."

The humans had been put in a little room separated from the Embassy proper by one of the membrane thresholds. Arla all but leapt through it and reveled in the sensation of the gel peeling away to let plain, dry air touch her skin. She lifted away the faceplate and fumbled with her tank's straps. Iyal got up and helped her get the weighty thing off. Perivar remained sitting in an overstuffed chair, staring at the wall.

"It went all right, I take it?" said Iyal as she hung Arla's gear on a rack beside the door.

Arla shrugged. "In its way, but I need to leave here, and I need to find Eric Born."

"Good luck," muttered Perivar. "Adu doesn't even know where the Vitae took him." He combed both hands through his hair.

"I need him," said Arla. "I need to get back to the Realm. I need a ship to take me there and once I am there I need someone who can make the Teachers and the Nobles listen."

"I told you," snapped Perivar. "We don't know where he is!"

"And even if we did," said Iyal, "you wouldn't be able to get anywhere near a Vitae encampment."

"You don't think so?" Arla folded her arms. "They want me in there badly. You think they wouldn't take me in if someone offered to hand me over?"

Perivar raised his head slowly. "You haven't got any idea what you're up against."

Arla felt her temper snap. "You have no idea what I know, Skyman! I know your partner is dead and your friend is imprisoned and I know who has done these things. I also know you are sitting there, just sitting there, willing to let these . . . things . . . rule the places you and your children and your children's children will have to live in!" She threw up both hands. "What is the matter with you people? You're worse than most of the Notouch! They at least follow the words of the Nameless. You, you just follow the words of a bunch of bloody-handed strangers!"

For a moment, Arla thought Perivar was going to hit her. His fist curled and cocked itself. Iyal didn't even move.

"Let me tell you something, Notouch," he sneered. "I was fighting my battles while you were pissing your diapers!"

Perivar let his hand drop. He looked at the floor, at the ceiling and the walls. Arla said nothing. If he needed to collect himself, let him. Iyal put her hand on his shoulder.

"Assuming we can get them to take the bait," said Iyal, "are you willing to help haul him out of there?"

"Where my cousin's blood has been spilled," Perivar said, "there will always be revolution." He looked up at Iyal. "What about Killian?"

She smiled softly. "He's still at the docks, booking us passage to New Dawn. I'm inclined to go out with a bang."

Perivar squeezed Iyal's hand tightly and nodded to Arla. "Come on. I'm inclined to show the Vitae who they're really up against."

10—The Hundredth Core, Kethran Encampment, 09:46:12, Core Time

"It is the vigilant of our grandchildren who will find the world we lost. The rest are as doomed as we are."
Fragment from "The Beginning of the Flight," from the Rhudolant Vitae private history Archives

*T*HE right half of Winema's world gleamed. Her witness's camera was calibrated to respond to radiation both above and below the spectrum that her natural eye could detect. Through her right eye, she saw the trace glow from the optic matter, the lusterless patches of traditional solids, the distinctive auras around each of the core inhabitants as they passed her respectfully by.

Through her left eye, she saw the faces and the artworks and the walls that made up the core to the rest of the Vitae that she walked among.

There are two worlds, she was told when the tests determined her memory good enough to allow her to train as a Witness, the constructed world and the chaotic world. It is the eyes of a Witness that bring them together.

The Memory Holding was at the center of the cores, just outside the axis. The Holding's door registered Winema's active camera the way other security systems registered non-Witness retina or fingerprint patterns. The camera's security wires were clones of her nervous system. It was powered by her heart and mind, just like the rest of her body. If she was not the one wearing it, it would not be functioning.

There were technologies that would have allowed a camera to be implanted inside her eye. Her mind could have been altered to act as a recorder. But then she would have no longer been Vitae. She would have been Aunorante Sangh.

The door was a layer of solid that slid away from a layer of optical matter. Winema stepped through the shimmering stuff, causing its minute crystals to ripple through the light curtain that held them in place. No one but Witnesses saw the inside of the Holding.

The twenty-four Witnesses ringed the chamber, standing in their specially customized alcoves. Each body was encased in a metallic skeleton that made sure its limbs were properly supported regularly and exercised. The polymer tubes that fed into their veins kept internal nutrient and waste levels constant. If the power failed, or even fluctuated, they would all be released and the Holding evacuated. The only process that could not be circumvented was age. At 120, the Witnesses still died and had to be replaced from the mobile ranks.

Winema walked into the center of the circular chamber, tracked by twenty-four cameras and twenty-four eyes. She stood straight and proud under the gaze of the Memory. She did not have to hand them her name. They already knew her better than she knew herself.

"I have the names for the chain of Imperialists in my line of sight," she said.

Witness 14 opened his mouth. There was a delicate hiss as the joints on his skeleton responded to the movement. "Recite." The eyes blinked, but the cameras did not.

"Wife Caril Hanr Sone of the *Grand Errand*, Ambassador-Beholden Paral Idenam Or of the *Grand Errand*, Bio-technician Uary Nearch of the *Grand Errand*, Contractor Kelat

Hruska of the Hundredth Core." Winema enunciated the names clearly, adding each traitor to the Memory.

"Ambassador Basq Hanr Sone of the *Grand Errand?*" asked Witness 20.

"No connection," said Winema. "They have been using him as a cover and blind for their activities. He is guilty only of being unobservant."

"Exile Jahidh Hanr Sone?"

"Still in operation on the Home Ground. Believed to be seeking and sorting useful artifacts in addition to delaying the Unifiers' actions."

The eyes blinked again. The delicate threads between the alcoves could not carry thoughts, but they could carry impressions. Their hunches ran from Witness to Witness like the electric current ran through the room, carried between the cameras using neurografted transmission wires that were even more sophisticated than Winema's own. It was the closest the Vitae had been able to come to mastering telepathy.

"Which of these are necessary to the Reclamation in their current positions?" asked Witness 24.

"Uary Nearch, Kelat Hruska, Jahidh Hanr Sone."

"Justify Jahidh Hanr Sone," said Witness 1.

The camera eyes reflected Winema's face and form twenty-four times as the Memory watched her carefully.

"His efforts discovered the artifact Stone in the Wall and began the understanding of the relationship between the mechanically derived and human-derived artifacts. He is motivated to make the final connection and it is highly likely he has leads into the truth that our Contractors and Ambassadors yet lack."

The Memory absorbed her statement. The silence was a comforting weight on Winema. Her camera eye tracked the room. The lines between the alcoves glowed violet as the Memory communed with itself. She was being considered seriously.

"Recommend disposition of Caril Hanr Sone and Paral Idenam Or," said Witness 10.

"It is my recommendation that they be collected publicly. This will slow current Imperialist activities within the Vitae

Encampments. I further recommend that they be given to the Shessel World Enclave for their permanent exile in order to reinforce the impression of the Vitae's willingness to cooperate fully in Quarter Galaxy civilization now that we have returned to the Home Ground. We will require resources and diplomatic connections until emigration and settlement is completed."

The glow she saw with her right eye intensified. The camera eyes clicked back and forth as the Memory listened.

"The Memory concurs with this assessment," said Witness 1. "Formal Witness Winema Avin-Dae Uratae, you are assigned to the collection of Caril Hanr Sone and Paral Idenam Or. The Memory shall transfer their new status to the Assembly."

Winema closed her eyes and made full obeisance to the Memory.

Uary pressed the recorder sheet into the park wall and watched while the tidy lines of green text printed themselves across the milky grey surface. The park and the corridor were filled with the amber lights that created ship's dawn. No shadows except his own crossed the wall and the only sound in the whole park was his breathing.

Technically, there was no punishment for writing anything in a public park. Technically, many things were true. Technically, by now he should have been smuggled onto Kethran and into an Imperialist lab, where the female artifact recovered from the Home Ground waited for him. Technically, Jahidh should have already mapped the relationship between the mechanically derived and human-derived artifacts on the Home Ground.

What is going wrong? We are the Rhudolant Vitae. We are the First Life. We are the architects of the Quarter Galaxy . . . He peeled the recorder sheet off the wall and rolled it into a tight cylinder. Optical matter flowed into the square where it had lain and solidified to become a section of blank wall. *That is, of course, the problem. We've gotten so used to manipulating governments and corporations, we've forgotten that individuals will still work betrayal, and that our own kind are capable of grotesque mistakes.*

Our entire history is based on the fact that we were betrayed
and we still forget to watch out for it.

The problem also was that now that events were truly
moving and moving fast, there was no time for individual
implications to sink in.

The Home Ground was not some far-off paradise anymore,
but it wasn't just a ruined hulk to be recolonized, either.
There was technology there that had survived longer than the
memory of its function had. The Vitae would learn to use it.
Nothing could stop that, but the blind still prevailed in the
Reclamation Assembly. They would not see that if the power
was not directed outward from the beginning, it would turn
inward. Those who were now Imperialists would find something closer to home to raise arms about. With knowledge of
the Ancestors' technology, the arms would draw more blood
than words, and the blood would be Vitae. It would spill itself
out while the rest of the Quarter Galaxy looked on in mild
curiosity.

Uary turned on his heel and hurried back to the lift. Technically, Caril should come out of her quarters first, to see the
new essay and know he would be waiting for her in the
market, but Uary couldn't risk Basq finding him there. If Basq
knew Uary worked with the Imperialists, Basq would use that
fact to get Uary removed from committee work, and then
there was no telling who would be the one to examine the
male artifact when it was brought in.

The markets opened whenever the ship was near enough
to a settled planet for goods to be imported by shuttle from
the surface. Temporary storage facilities were set up in the
Grand Errand's fifth level park to dispense the goods and
record the sales. Residents who had their names entered on
the subscription rosters could select goods from a posted list
on their private terminals and have them delivered to their
quarters rather than being required to come to the market.
Depending on the world, there could be thirty or thirty-five
different units that would need replenishing two and three
times a day.

Kethran, however, had very little variety to offer the ship.

Barely a dozen boxy, silver vendors had been stationed between the park's stages, easels, and terminals.

Uary strolled through the park. He paid no attention to the holographed dancers, or the green marble statue of a many-branched tree, or the single-phase abstract mosaic on display. He wandered from vendor to vendor, examining the meats and vegetables, and trying to discern how well the Vitae-induced strains were really adapting to Kethran's environment. He selected several samples to be delivered to the lab so he could go over them in detail. The poultry did not seem to be as robust as it should, but then again, some of the Kethran distributors slighted Vitae procurers. . . .

Caril, ever mindful of her position as dutiful Wife of a promoted Ambassador, breezed into the park with an air of total neutrality that would have done a Witness proud. She wound her way easily between the half a dozen other Wives, male and female, who mulled about the market space. She examined the food offerings with serious attention and a practiced eye before selecting delicacies for breakfast.

Uary sauntered along and waited until Caril was at a stall by herself before he crossed the park and stood beside her.

The parks were not safe, but they were safer than anywhere else on the *Grand Errand*. Word-of-mouth conversations were not truly safe, either, but, like the parks, they were safer than the alternatives.

"Good morning, Wife," he said politely as he leaned over to select his own fruit. Whatever Uary thought of Basq, it was a matter of record and repetition he was always polite to Basq's Wife and Beholden. "Not much of a selection today, I'm afraid."

"Every little bit is a little bit more." She sized up the contents of the tray with an appraising sweep of her eyes. "But it's not adding up to enough, you're right." She turned over an apple, checking for bruises. "The war is real and if they're primitive, they're effective soldiers apparently, and all choosing up sides. The Unifiers haven't armed them, but they're still advising. Jahidh has done his job almost too well," she said with a touch of irony. "It's going to be very bloody, Uary, and too many resources are going to be wasted.

The problem is, we don't know enough to stop it. There is a possibility that genetic relatives of the female artifact will be located, but no word on how soon."

"Kethran was a total debacle." Uary rolled an apple between his fingers, feeling the tension of the skin. It was smooth, but perhaps a little too thick. That would make for a tart fruit as opposed to a sweet one. Uary made a mental note to find out if that was a deliberate or accidental variation. "But at least I've been assigned to analyze the male artifact."

"Yes." Caril prodded several more fruits. "That is an issue."

Uary ran his fingers over another sample but his mind played her last sentence over again. "What do you mean?"

"I've had word about that," she said, leaning back and surveying the whole tray again. "The only race left that we have a hope of winning is the race for understanding. Anything you learn about the male artifact will pass into the hands of the blind. We can't let them have it. We need to give the ones already on the ground a chance."

Uary felt his heart begin to beat heavily as understanding seeped into his veins. "I can't destroy the only artifact we have."

Caril touched two apples and the stall's arms extracted them from the holder to add to the bundle of purchases being assembled for her by the drone systems.

"You have to."

Uary stared at the stack of apples. You have to. He had been telling himself that since he joined the Imperialists. You have to be independent of Outsider governments when it comes to acquisition of organic resources and raw materials or you could be denied what you need. You have to turn your power outward, or it will turn inward on you. You have to have a guiding vision or all that has been done since the Flight is meaningless, just another fragment of chaos in the universe. *But surely I do not have to destroy the work of the Ancestors.*

Uary opened his mouth, but a flash of green caught his eye and the words died before he could form them. Winema, the Formal Witness he had selected to be assigned to Basq, stood in the hullward entrance to the park. Basq was nowhere to be seen.

Caril tracked his gaze around to the Witness and froze. She was not the only one. All the Wives in the park had turned to single-phase statues at the sight of the unaccompanied Witness.

Winema moved with unhurried strides through the tableau until she stood six inches from Caril. Her silicate hand reached out and gripped the Wife's wrist.

"Wife Caril Hanr Sone, you are held in the eyes of the Memory for activities counter to the dictates of the Assembly and the laws of the Vitae and for directly endangering the effort of the Reclamation."

Uary knew that last sight of Caril would stay with him for a long time. She drew herself up straight and proud. The Witness walked toward the park entrance and Caril walked with her, falling into step at her side, both eyes straight ahead, ignoring everything, including her captor.

She left Uary standing by the apple stall, with a piece of fruit still in his fingers, too stunned to remember he also had appearances to keep up. His heart fluttered frantically in his rib cage. When the Witness spoke Caril's sentence, her organic eye had been fixed on Caril, but her camera lens had been fixed on Uary.

Did they know of their connection? How could they not know? But if they did know, why had they taken her and left him with that last vision and the echo of her final, almost-heretical instructions.

Destroy the work of the Ancestors? Uary wanted to collapse under the weight of that thought. He remembered when he saw the initial analysis of the female artifact. He'd gone into the chapel and said all six Graces. Her construction was flawless, flawless! And the spheres she carried were more alive than she was. They were perfect, immortal, biological constructions, irreplaceable parts of a system he could only start to guess at. He'd cursed out loud when he heard that she had escaped Kethran. Even though it would have brought Basq all the prestige even he could dream of, Uary wouldn't have cared if the Ambassador had succeeded in bringing her back, just so long as Uary could work with her again. There was so much to understand, so much that could be learned if only he could get the time.

Analysis of the male would be good, of course, and useful, and interesting in its own right, but the female . . . with her, they might learn how the Aunorante Sangh had defeated even the Ancestors and then . . . and then . . .

Something damp drizzled across his fingers and Uary came to himself with a start. He had crushed the apple in his hand. Its juice dripped out around his fingertips and across his palm. He dropped the fruit and hastily ordered the stall to deliver it to the lab along with the rest of his samples.

Uary made his own way to the lab wrapped in a private fog. Destroy the one artifact they had in their hands. How could he? Yes, the Reclamation had been accelerated. Yes, within a few dozen hours, they would have their pick of samples, technically. But who knew who would be assigned to those samples, and who knew how long analysis would take? Yes, Jahidh reported a lead he could follow for himself, but still, who knew how long that would take either? They needed to begin now, in this hour, with this sample that they already had some baseline data for.

The Witnesses had already taken Caril away. If he destroyed the artifact, they'd take him, too.

The sounds of voices and mechanical activity pulled Uary up short a bare millimeter before he collided with the lab door. The automatic reader had been shut off. Uary impatiently laid his hand against the palm reader.

The doorway cleared to reveal his Beholden swarming between the tanks and terminals that made up the lab's equipment. The lab had been designed around an array of analysis vats. The central holding tank was an elongated oval large enough to hold a full-grown Shessel. The side closest to the lab entrance was clear, so a support capsule could be placed right alongside the tank. The side toward the hull held the holding tank's monitors and also allowed pipes to feed into three smaller tanks that could dispense the analysis gel and any additional chemicals the work might require.

Lairdin, an amputant with a missing ear whom Uary had

appointed his supervisor, was helping two students drain what smelled like fresh sterilizer out of the central holding tank. The gel oozed into the reconfiguration tank, where any stray bacteria or biological waste could be filtered out while the main holding tank was readied for the next subject.

"Can you believe it, Bio-technician?" Lairdin said happily. Uary had accepted her contract because of her precise grasp of neurotransmitter configuration. Since then he had learned to ignore her atrocious manners. "I owe the Ancestors at least four of the Graces for this."

Uary took in the bustling activity, none of which he had ordered. "What am I being asked to believe now, Supervisor?"

Lairdin's hands froze halfway to the tank's keypad. "You didn't replay my message? The system told me it was received."

Uary shook open the recorder sheet and pressed it against the wall. Immediately, it displayed a recording of Lairdin's face.

"Bio-technician Uary," said the recording, "we have received a transmission from the contraband runner, Tasa Ad, who states he has recovered the female artifact Stone in the Wall. The Bridge liaison says the Captain himself has cleared the ship for access to a docking clamp for cargo transfer. I will prepare the lab immediately."

Shock raced down Uary's spine and rooted him to the floor. The female artifact. Recovered and on the way to the *Grand Errand*. Where not ten minutes ago he'd received orders to destroy the only other artifact in his possession.

"Technician?" said Lairdin. "The first artifact is reported to have been unloaded seven minutes ago. It'll be arriving any minute. Do you want to prepare the terminals?"

Atrocious, atrocious manners. Uary ripped the recorder sheet out of the wall and dropped it back into the rack. "Yes."

He sat behind the analysis board and began shuffling its pads. There weren't many lines to open. He needed his personal observations of the female artifact and the stones, Basq's records, and the raw information on the male artifact. Uary eyed Lairdin and the other Beholden. The supervisor was bustling around the lab, making sure everything was in order, prying into every detail, except the Bio-technician's private terminal. Even she was not that rude. He felt watched anyway, by the Witness he could not see, and by the fact that under the board lay a hidden line to Caril's own terminal. He would have to remove it as soon as he was alone again.

Whenever that would be.

Uary laid his hand on the notepad and curled his fingers inward as if the pad was a sheet of polymer that he could crumple up and toss aside.

What was he supposed to do? Destroy the female? Smash the stones? Place all hopes on the possibility that Jahidh, untrained, rebellious Jahidh, might be able to find another complete component like Arla Stone? The Imperialists planned to continue trusting that child with the work of the Ancestors?

What were the Imperialists doing? What were they thinking? They were as bad as the blind ones in the Assembly! This was no longer some distant, objective possibility. This was happening as they spoke. The knowledge of the Ancestors, lost because of the Flight, was being delivered into their hands and they could still leave orders for its destruction.

It was no help that part of him knew they were right. The only race the Imperialists could still win was the race to understand the artifacts. It was the last one that mattered, and the Imperialists would lose if he did not stand in the Assembly's way.

Individuals can still betray. Uary forced the thought away and bent over the keys again.

Concentrate, he ordered himself.

He needed to be careful how he managed this. Two dozen other Bio-technicians and their Beholden waited for him to begin siphoning the raw data and rough conclusions he gleaned from the study of the artifacts. They would filter all they received even farther down, focus on their own areas of expertise, replicate each others' analyses, and then funnel their results back into the main datastore, where the revelations could be organized, integrated, and returned to him. The sub-committees would work in shifts around the clock to understand the artifacts, but the first analysis was his. For a few brief hours, Uary had the artifacts to himself.

He did not like to think about the fact that he had Basq's political maneuvering to thank for that. He was quite sure Basq didn't either. But Uary was the Bio-tech for Basq's committee. If Basq was assigned to the recovery of the artifacts, so was Uary.

Uary opened the connections from his datastore to the secondary storage that could be tapped by the other Bio-techs. He did it carefully, introducing small flaws into the lines' controls. He couldn't hide completely, but he could delay. He could be a little slow in filtering the gathered data from his private store to the committee-accessible store. The lines could require extra processing time because of the volume and complexity of the data. The ship-to-ship transmitters could have difficulty finding open channels that would guarantee that the packages would arrive intact. These little things could be made to add up.

I only hope they will add up long enough for me to decide what to do.

The rush of the door opening jerked his head up. A bizarre procession crossed the lab's threshold. Two Internship Ambassadors flanked the support capsule like an honor guard. Behind them marched Basq, shoulders back and eyes straight ahead. Uary wondered what he was hiding behind his propriety. Was it triumph? Or was it despair at the fact he had lost his Wife to the Imperialist cause, just as he had lost his son?

The Witness matched Basq's stride without mimicking any of his attitude. Her camera lens tracked across the room until it settled on Uary. Involuntarily, he looked away.

Uary got to his feet as his Beholden made obeisance to the parade. He did not look at Basq. He rounded the corner of his terminal and leaned across the capsule's transparent lid. The artifact lay stiff and still from the tranquilizers being delivered into its system. Uary checked the monitors on the capsule's sides. Any outside observer would see the readings and think this was a Human from a world with the upper end of tolerable gravity and a rather thick atmosphere. Anybody who hadn't seen inside the bruised and sun-damaged skin

would think that. Anybody who didn't know this was a legacy
from their Ancestors.

"I will remain here and watch while you siphon what we
need from him," announced Basq, "to make sure nothing is
lost this time." He sat in one of the observation chairs. "We
have very little time available. You'll begin siphoning him at
once."

Uary turned toward him and he knew Basq and the Witness
both saw the fury on his face. Never mind that, even after
what happened at the market, and even though he knew the
ships were on their way to the populated section of the Home
Ground. This was his place, not Basq's, never Basq's.

"I will first be creating an overall map of his physical
structure in its functioning state, making a particular note of
the anomalies that are sure to be present," he said, using a
frozen tone he wouldn't have disposed on the worst Beholden.
"We will extract samples from the tissues, bones, and organs
for cloning and close study in isolation. Using that data, we
will begin designing a series of retroviruses that can be used
to insert marker proteins for a comprehensive genetic analysis.
Then, and only then, will we be prepared to begin a program
of neurochemical stimulation to analyze the working system
in detail. You may sit there and watch if you wish to, but you
had better send for someone to bring you meals and bedding.
This will take days."

"You do not have days," said Basq. "We need to understand how this artifact functions as soon as possible. Do I
have to contact our team leader to reinforce this?"

Uary did nothing for a moment but concentrate on
breathing.

"You can do what you want," he said. "I will do what
this investigation requires." Uary turned his back on Basq.
"Supervisor Lairdin, you will calibrate the tank to capture
the preliminary physical map of the artifact."

He could almost feel the heat of Basq's anger against his
shoulder blades. He did hear the swish of Basq's robes as the
Ambassador strode over to the intercom. Uary did not look
at him. His Beholden scrambled around the main holding
tank, setting the specifications using the available data on Eric

Born. The side tanks pumped refreshed analysis gels back into the main unit. Uary waved the Intership Ambassadors away from the sides of the support capsule. He checked the monitors one more time to make sure the artifact was in a stable condition. Lairdin positioned herself at the capsule's foot and her intern, Cierc, took his place at the head.

Uary shut the power off and snapped the catches on the cover. It swung back and Uary leapt out of the way. Lairdin and Cierc grabbed the handles of the inner structure and swiftly lifted Born and his support tubes out of the capsule and plunged the entire structure into the gel-filled holding tank.

Uary thrust his arms into sterile gloves and then into the gel. Needles had to be inserted in the artifact's skin and veins. He laid monitor pads on its temples, wrists, throat, and chest. He attached feed lines to the tubes already in place to allow for chemical and viral transmission.

When the last needle was in place, Uary lifted his arms away and held them over the artifact, dripping globs of gel into the holding tank.

"Status?" he barked.

Lairdin ran her fingers over the tank's monitor screens. "Sample is stable. Support functions optimal. Feeds clear and ready."

"Bio-technician Uary," called Basq. "Ambassador Ivale wishes to speak with you directly."

Uary stripped off his gloves and dropped them into the cleaner on the side of the holding tank. "Start taking static baseline measurements," he said to Lairdin. Every drop of data would help.

"Ambassador Ivale." Uary positioned himself in front of the screen. The Ambassador stood calmly on the other end of the line, but Uary had the feeling Ivale was not prepared to hear anything he had to say. "I must caution against haste. If we try to understand the system before we understand the structure, we risk damaging the artifact before we've acquired the information that we really need."

"Ordinarily I would agree with you, Bio-technician," said Ivale, "but events are proceeding and we cannot be slow.

You are to get what information you can from the artifact regarding the nature and function of its extramechanical abilities. You will use the same criteria in conducting your analysis of the female artifact when it arrives. These are the most pertinent to the Reclamation. We have less than twenty hours before the Second Company lands in the populated segment."

"You hold my name, Ambassador," Uary said. "We'll begin now."

The Ambassador closed the line and Uary forced his attention to his Beholden waiting by the tank. What Ivale didn't know, of course, was that he had just played straight into the Imperialists' hands. It was now a matter of record that Uary had been told to circumvent protocol and put the artifacts at risk.

Now he had his pick of ways to destroy the work of the Ancestors. There was too much that could go wrong with living cells. Too much that shifted and recombined. Too many factors had to be accounted for, no matter how great the capacity of the computer that oversaw the job and ran the projections. There were hints that the Ancestors had worked with living cells and living organisms like Engineers worked with ceramic and steel and with results that were just as steady and predictable. The Vitae were the best genetic engineers the Quarter Galaxy had to offer, but their Ancestors had been better. How they had performed their miracles was beyond Uary. It was beyond anybody. It had been stolen by the Aunorante Sangh. He regarded the artifact's face, immobile behind the oxygen mask.

And I thought I'd be its rescuer. I thought I'd be able to force this artifact, this Aunorante Sangh, to give it all back.

Uary wet his lips as he sat down at his own terminal. *Maybe I can still get some of it.*

"Normally, by the time we begin investigating a biological system, we return the sample to an active state." Uary reconfigured the board to bring his private notes onto the display.

"No," Basq announced. "Not this one. You've seen the reports. We cannot risk it being able to use its . . . extramechanical abilities."

There was an older word for it, but Uary knew Basq would

not let himself be heard talking about anything so primitive and superstitious as telekinesis, even if it was a marvel engineered by the Ancestors.

"Very well," Uary said, "but if we cannot trace any activity in its resting state to those 'extramechanical abilities,' then we will have to wake it up."

"Lairdin"—Uary opened the line between his terminal and the tank—"make sure its support signs remain stable and watch particularly for any rise in system temperature."

By way of answer, Lairdin stationed herself in front of the monitors, like a conductor waiting to give the orchestra its signal.

Basq came and stood behind his right shoulder. The Witness stood behind his left. Uary felt his skin crawl but repressed the sensation. There was work to do and that made it easier. He laid in the primary search commands and moved the ACTIVATE key into position.

Catheters swam down the needles into the artifact's veins. Its blood flowed into pipettes lowered by the delivery tubes. The pads gripped it and measured the type and level of electrochemical activity in its body. The analysis gel, an outgrowth of the organic chip technology, pressed close to its skin, creeping through its pores. The neurochemical reactions the gel encountered would rearrange its protein configuration. The changes would be replicated along its molecular chains. When the terminals analyzed the gel, they would produce a map of neurological activity, beginning at the epidermis and ending at the bone.

Analysis and simulations performed on samples of the artifacts' DNA and RNA that had been obtained while it was under a Vitae contract had yielded five separate neurotransmitters that were thought to be involved in the generation and projection of the telekinesis. Locating their point of origin should not be difficult. Even so, this was no simple matter of matching chemicals to their receptors in the cells. The artifact's synaptic layout had to have been redesigned from first principles that were vastly different from those that gave birth to the naturally born human race.

The differences should be quiescent while the artifact was

unconscious. A telekinetic that wrecked havoc when it had nightmares would not be a useful tool. While the telekinetic receptors were quiescent, they would be next to invisible. There would be no choice but to apply stimulation. Which could quite easily terminate the artifact, as no proper analysis of the gel had been done yet.

But it did not necessarily have to terminate it quickly.

Raw data, little more than numbers and labels, flashed across Uary's screen. Most of it flitted directly to storage to await further organization, but the levels and concentrations of the targeted neurotransmitters stayed in a tidy column on the left-hand side of the screen.

Uary frowned. The numbers were much higher than any that had turned up in the simulations conducted on the artifact's blood samples.

And they were increasing.

"Bio-tech!" called Lairdin.

Uary vaulted out of his chair and ran to the tank. Inside, the gel churned around the artifact. Waves and whirlpools pressed against the lid and washed against the sides. Moisture appeared around the seals and a moment later the overload alarms began to shrill. Uary's gaze swept the monitors. The numbers and levels jumped and flickered, fast, and faster, and far too fast.

"Get the neutralizer in!" he shouted. "Shut it down! Shut it down!"

They moved. Even Basq was bright enough to see something was out of control and the Ambassador dodged out of the way as Lairdin raced to the holding tanks and slammed down the key for the pumps. With a chugging that should not have been there, the siphons fought to drain the roiling gel. The pumps flooded in a saline and anesthetic medium as a replacement. It coated the artifact and the alarms quieted.

Uary looked up into Lairdin's frightened eyes.

"What happened?" Basq demanded. His voice rasped in his throat.

"Ask the Ancestors," snapped Uary. "Lairdin, what's the status of the gel?" His robes swirled around his ankles as he hurried back to his terminal.

He drew out the data as fast as he could read it. It was a jumble of numbers and statistical ranges, concentration levels and a few sketchy diagrams. There was nothing to compare any of it to. There was no way to tell what was normal and what was abnormal, or what reaction had triggered the telekinetic processes.

"Bio-technician," said Lairdin, "the gel has been . . . damaged."

She touched a key and Uary looked reflexively down at his own screen as the new data appeared. His knees buckled and he sat down hard in his chair.

The gel was not just damaged, it was shredded. Molecular chains had been disintegrated. Cells had burst. Clusters of infant tumors were appearing throughout the holding tank.

The artifact had all but destroyed four cubic meters of gel in less than twenty seconds, and there was no way to tell how it had begun.

Uary lifted his head. "We are going to have to wake it up."

"No," said Basq flatly.

"Then we can go no farther." Uary folded his hands. "I have nothing to work with. I have no pattern of brain activity. I have no baseline neurochemical activity for the active state. I do not know what the normal status of the artifact is, so I cannot tell what initiated the telekinetic, your pardon, Ambassador," he said bitterly, "the 'extramechanical abilities.' I do not know the system. Without even a partial map, I cannot understand anything."

Uary sat back, prepared to wait until the ship fell apart around them.

"Have your Beholden uncouple all the comm lines to the outside," said Basq. "We must observe total computer and biological quarantine procedures. There cannot be a single physical link between this room and the rest of the ship. If we run this risk, it must be just us."

A feeling that was almost respect surfaced in Uary. At least Basq carried his need for notoriety through to the end. If he was witnessed doing any less than this, it would of course be shameful, but he put that thought far ahead of his personal safety. Uary had seen the recordings of Born breaking open the door and of him tapping the private network. There was a real danger to them all if Born could break open the holding tank.

Well, they would just have to make it dangerous for him to try.

"Lairdin, place the artifact on complete life-support. Make sure that we are responsible for its physical existence. If it does manage to damage the systems, it will simply terminate itself."

Before I have to, he added silently, and he realized he was cherishing that exact hope.

Unexpectedly, the Witness spoke. "I must download what has happened here before the lines are closed."

"Cierc, you will assist the Witness," said Uary. He turned his attention to his own work.

All the systems needed to be put into independent mode. That meant shuffling operations around, cutting some functions and making sure there was enough storage space for the data to accumulate. Even with the help of the prompts that began as soon as he initiated quarantine procedures, it was a painstaking business.

But it was finally finished. The proper superiors were notified. The doors were shut and locked by hand and every instrument was physically separated from its links to the ship outside. Uary glanced at the monitors again. The artifact was still quiescent and the neutralizing gel was undisturbed.

"Restore active state," he said.

The monitors showed the stimulants flowing into the system. The response was good. Steady and not too fast. Normal orientation in five . . . four . . . three . . .

The monitor went dead.

"Systems check!" he snapped. The Beholden jumped and Basq sucked in a breath.

The lights went out next, and the backups did not come on.

"Aunorante Sangh," murmured Basq.

Uary did not bother to respond. He groped under the edge of the counter until he found the emergency handlight and pulled it out of its holder. The beam showed that everyone had had the sense to hold still.

The monitors on the tank itself still had power. They glowed eerily in the darkness, as did the tank. The artifact lay totally immobile inside, and the gel around him was undisturbed.

Uary shuffled the board keys with his free hand, but the terminal did not respond. He was barely aware that Lairdin had cleared a space in the wall and was working on the lights. A flicker made him blink. Lairdin fell backward, centimeters ahead of a shower of sparks as, against all specifications and parameters, some circuit burned out.

Uary's terminal screen flared with sudden light. Three words printed themselves across it.

LEAVE ME ALONE.

Basq stood at Uary's shoulder, his cheeks hollow with shadow and fear.

"Can we answer it?" he asked.

"I don't think so," said Uary slowly. He sketched the artifact's name on the notepad. Nothing happened. "We have to shut off its life-support. Terminate it."

"No," said Basq fervently. "We need to tame it."

Uary turned on him. "And how are we to do that?"

"Outnumber it. All it has had to do so far is trip a few switches. If we all work to regain control of the instruments, it will have to fight us all, repeatedly. We will wear it out."

"It could be possible." *Sense is the last thing I expected from you, Basq, but I'm glad it's come.* Uary hesitated. To keep the artifact alive even a few minutes longer would be a hideous risk, but as long as it was in the tank the monitors were recording its reactions. If they could find out what it took to overload its telekinetic processes, they would have a real weapon against its counterparts on the Home Ground.

And Uary would have the work of the Ancestors under his eye that much longer.

"Ambassador." Uary stepped aside. "Take over the terminal. My Beholden and I will work directly on the tank. Witness . . ." Uary hesitated. One did not give orders to a Witness.

"The communications consoles will be my area." She

cleared the optical matter above the comm boards with deft hands. "We can flood the lab's interior lines with data."

Uary was vaguely aware that he was now fighting the first battle with the Aunorante Sangh that had taken place since the Ancestors had taken flight, and nobody outside the lab even knew it was happening. They checked, changed, restarted, and rerouted. It burned, closed, crashed, and jammed. The lab was well stocked with spare parts and every system had backups to its backups. Uary did not like emergencies. They were half a dozen and the artifact was only one and it didn't know the systems. It would have to tire. It would have to collapse.

Except it didn't. Everywhere they went, it was already there. Its power gripped the entire lab and shut them outside, leaving them standing helplessly in the middle of their equipment.

Its heart rate didn't even flutter. It seemed to expend no energy and all the battle took it no effort. It could keep it up until the ship fell apart, and it was still perfectly calm, perfectly regulated.

Uary wanted to throw his head back and laugh at the absurdities. Of course it was, because the tank was keeping it that way. He'd issued the order himself. Total life-support. The tank would feed Born what it needed to keep itself calm and healthy. As long as it was inside the tank, it could do anything and feel no strain.

"It's reached the comm system," said the Witness. "It is transmitting, and the terminal is responding."

"How!" shouted Basq.

How! repeated Uary in his own frantic mind. They had physically cut . . .

The line to Caril. His Beholden had physically cut the comm lines and they had missed his line to Caril. But who would there be to answer it?

"The female artifact," said the Witness as if she read his mind. "The delivery was a ruse. We have to open the doors. We must warn the Captain."

"No!" Uary laid his hands on the life-support commands. "All we have to do is get it out of the tank, Lairdin . . ."

"Stop!" thundered the Witness.

Uary and his Beholden froze.

"It has the air supply."

Basq got to the Witness's side one step ahead of Uary. The monitor's message had changed.

I HAVE BURNED OUT THE EVACUATION CIRCUIT. ALL THAT IS HOLDING IT CLOSED IS ME. IF I AM FORCED TO LET GO THE ROOM WILL BE IN VACUUM IN LESS THAN FIFTEEN SECONDS.

Uary cursed. "It even knows the time."

"Part of the quarantine measures?" inquired the Witness.

Uary nodded. "A last precaution."

Cierc wiped a huge swath of optical matter away from the wall to reveal a carbonized juncture in the fiber optics. "It's not bluffing."

"Suits!" ordered Basq.

Cierc, closest to the emergency locker, broke the seal and swung the door back. Uary walked calmly but quickly to his side, as he'd been drilled to do all his life. Get in the suit, close the seals, check the . . .

The suits lay in crumbled heaps on the locker floor. Each helmet seal had been burned through. The carbon stench drifted up from them.

Cierc swallowed. "The locker has an optical matter backing. It must have got through . . ."

Because I listened to Basq. Because I wanted to have it in my hands a few minutes longer. Because I had a hidden line to Caril . . .

"Then we die," said Basq.

"WHAT?" cried Cierc.

"We die." Basq stood like a statue of himself. "We cut the power to the tank. We cannot permit its confederates to rescue this thing alive. It knows enough to mount a pitched battle against us, and win. It knows the private technologies. We will lose the Home Ground if it survives."

Uary tried to find the flaw in Basq's reasoning, but there was none. There was no other way. If the artifacts understood too much, the Vitae would lose to them, again.

"I'll do it." Even though the Witness would not survive to transmit this, he felt better saying it to her.

He heard Basq whisper Caril's name and realized he could
have his revenge now if he wanted it. Before they died he
could tell Basq that his son was alive and working for the
Imperialists, and that Caril had been in touch with him ever
since he had "vanished." He could do it, now that they were
dead and the Witness with them.

Uary looked at Basq and decided it was enough that he
knew. Basq could join the Lineage ignorant.

The room shook. It rattled and pitched wildly and a wind
rushed through it.

Wind? Uary sat up and dazedly wondered how he had come
to be on the floor.

The wind died as abruptly as it started. Lairdin sprawled
on the floor. Red liquid smeared around her. And her face
was gone.

White foam filled the gap in the outer wall. Something
shoved through it. A door. An airlock. Uary couldn't hear.
The Witness wasn't moving. There was blood everywhere.
The airlock opened and a figure in a vacuum suit walked into
the lab. Behind the suited person walked an android. The
android spoke. Uary saw its mouth move. He couldn't hear
anything over the ringing in his ears. The suited one spoke,
turned toward the Witness and grabbed her by the arm. The
Witness said nothing. She didn't even flinch. The suited figure
dropped her.

The figure turned toward him. Now he could see it was a
woman. It was the female artifact and her mouth was moving.
He put his hand to his ear automatically and it came away
covered in red.

The android was speaking and Cierc teetered to his feet.

"No!" Uary hoped he shouted but Cierc still closed the
monitor lines in the tank. The needles and catheters and
pipettes extracted themselves. Nothing happened. Nothing
happened. The android lifted the artifact free from the tank
and carried it to the airlock.

The suited artifact followed, then stopped and crossed to
the inner door. Uary tried to get to his feet and fell back. Pain
finally broke through the shock. The artifact looked the door
over. She threw the manual locks open and shoved the door

back. She bent close to Uary and he could see her mouth move.

Run, she was telling him. Run!

He couldn't even stand. He scrabbled across the floor. The Beholden grabbed him and hauled him forward. He saw figures. Emergency crews. He turned. The artifact and the android were through their airlock and he had time to see it yank itself away from the sealing foam before the lab door slammed shut.

He sagged into the arms of a stranger while the emergency team buzzed around them. Hands grabbed him. Sat him down. Twisted his neck to look at his ear. The technician was an amputant, he saw, with only four fingers on the hand that pressed the anesthetic patch against his wrist.

We had them, he thought blearily as the pain began to fade. *We had them. Now I understand. Now I really understand how the Ancestors could have lost to these things.*

He hoped the Assembly would let him live long enough to tell them what he knew.

11—The Realm of the Nameless Powers, Late Afternoon

"The Aunorante Sangh will return, but know this too, the Nameless Powers will be on their heels."
From "The Words of the Nameless Powers," translated by Hands to the Sky for all who follow.

JAY lowered himself onto his belly and stared at the Narroways gates through a striping of greenish brown grasses. Instead of the usual collection of disinterested cargo inspectors in their turbans and rust-colored ponchos, four alert soldiers in First City's emerald-and-beige cloaks blocked traffic and searched under tarpaulins for any unapproved or unlevied goods.

King Silver lost then. Jay lowered his head and mopped at the mud drying on his face. The rain had come down hard twice since he parted ways with Cor, and although the sun had succeeded in drying out his skin, his clothing was still drenched. It clung close to his skin like a soggy, heavy blanket.

Jay looked back over his shoulder toward the road. The line of travelers waiting in front of the gate was as solid as ever. Additional soldiers patrolled the sides of the road, guiding their oxen between gaggles of Notouch. They probably had specific orders to look for him. He couldn't believe that the new masters of Narroways wouldn't be interested in the King's Skyman.

For a moment he considered leaving the city to its fate and making his way down to the Lif marshes alone to meet Cor. But night was closing in behind him and he not only had no tent or blanket to help stave off the cold, he had no supplies for what could turn out to be a multiple-day journey. Even if he could make it to the marshes, once Cor brought him to the Notouch, he had no tangible authority, and no power to intimidate, except for the gun at his side. Although the Notouch were supposed to obey whoever gave them orders, recent experience had taught him that this was not always what happened. Cor had left him still stating confidently that the Notouch would be amenable to friendly persuasion. But would Empty Cups lie to her own family about the state she'd left Broken Trail in? Jay frowned. Whatever else they had or did not have in their genetic makeup, even the Notouch had a drive for self-preservation. Without a threat that was more tangible than the unknown nightmare in Chamber One, they might very well decide to run away from Cor rather than go along with her.

Then there was Cor herself. Jay suppressed a sigh. Her resolve was wavering. If there were too many more assaults on her sense of what was right and just, she might just do something foolish. He had to make sure he could deal with Stone in the Wall's family without Cor's help if it became necessary.

I've got to at least get some supplies, whether I have to beg, borrow, or steal them. Maybe the fighting's not quite over yet in there. If I can find one of Silver's staff, or even a sympathetic Bondless . . .

Wrapping his hopes around him, Jay crept away from the road and toward the one entrance to the city that might not be guarded.

The wall around Narroways was solidly built of quarried stone and mortar, but it was breached in a number of places to create gutters and drainage ditches. Filthy water flowed into trenches and away down the slope toward the distant marshes. Jay made his way forward on hands and knees, with one eye on the city walls. No soldiers paced along the tops, and he took courage. Maybe First City hadn't quite secured the place yet. If Silver was still free to fight, she might still be free to help him.

The idea helped harden his nerve as he crawled the last few meters to the foot of the city wall.

Climbing through the drainage hole was only a little more unpleasant than Jay imagined it would be. He came up drenched and filthy, but only slightly more so than he had been. As such, he matched the rest of the population in the muddy streets. He stepped carefully through the crowds, keeping his hands well hidden under his cloak and casting furtive glances around himself.

That also seemed to match the rest of the inhabitants. They weren't walking, they were scuttling. Everyone clustered together in groups of three or more. Even the young men walked swiftly with wary eyes and hands hidden under their wraps.

Hoofbeats and rhythmic footsteps sounded on the cobblestones. A troop of the green-and-beige soldiers marched in a ragged column down the middle of the street, with yet more soldiers on oxen following behind. Jay let the crowd press him back against the rough wall of a house.

A blob of mud flew through the air and smacked against the face of one of the cavalry. The soldier shouted and swung himself off his ox, diving into the crowd after the offender. He managed to grab hold of someone, and with ugly-sounding shouts, the soldier dragged a squirming figure out into the street. Jay sidled toward the corner of the house. Stones flew now and shouts accompanied them. The troop leader drew his ax and it flashed in the air. Jay's fingers found the edge of the wall and let the press of the crowd back him into the narrow alleyway beyond it. The shouts between the soldiers and bystanders were getting louder. All Jay could see was a writhing blur made up of people's backs. Somebody screamed. Metal clashed. Jay turned away from the noises and ran.

Darkness hit.

All at once the world was puddles of greasy orange-and-gold light. Jay tripped over the uneven cobbles. The wind gusted over some wall or the other and Jay shivered. The temperature was already beginning to drop. He glanced up and saw the solid night sky, the Black Wall, and he cursed himself for not having checked the cloud cover while he had the chance. In Narroways' perpetual stench, it was impossible for him to smell rain coming, which at night was likely to become an ice storm without warning.

He had to find shelter. Jay blundered forward, squinting up at doorways and trying to figure out what section of the city he was in.

He stumbled around a corner and into a flood of torchlight.

"Name yourself!" shouted someone overhead.

Jay squinted up at what his dazzled eyes resolved into a pile of overturned sledges, loose stones, and bent metal that barricaded the entire street. A figure, black and unidentifiable against the light, held up a javelin, evidently ready to throw it down if Jay gave the wrong answer.

Jay swallowed hard and had to forcibly stop himself from saying the Fourth Grace for hope.

"Messenger!" shouted another voice. It took a confused moment for Jay to realize it was Heart of the Seablade.

A rattle sounded from behind the barricade and metal grated against metal. A pool of oily yellow light fell across the muddy street as an anonymous pair of human shadows lifted away a section of the barricade. As soon as a big enough space opened, Jay ducked inside.

The area behind the barricade was a maze of streets that in the vague lamplight looked just like the streets on the other side. Lumps of shadow Jay guessed were sentries moved on the rooftops.

"Messenger." Heart strode out of the shadows and clasped Jay's hand. "I hoped you would find your way back to us."

"Thank you." And for once, Jay felt close to meaning it. "I just hope the King shares your sentiments."

"I don't know." Heart shook his head. "She is pleased to

have me on her side because I am power-gifted, but she's not ready to take a Seablade of any standing into her counsels."

"I need to get to her as soon as I can." A fresh wind gusted down the alley and Jay shuddered again. "But first I need some food, if there is any."

Heart nodded. "Come with . . ."

"Garismit's Eyes!" screamed somebody. "Oh, Nameless Powers preserve me!"

A clear white glow washed across them, making their shadows stand out against the muck and cobblestones. Jay jerked his head up. The world was ablaze with clean light. A great sphere of pure light shone over the whole night-shrouded city. A silver line descended from the Black Wall, lowering a star that burned without heat into the center of the city.

Jay saw the tether and he knew who was inside the sphere.

No, he thought as horror and irrational anger washed through him. *No. Not yet. I'm not ready yet!*

Voices, screams, sobs, ecstasies sounded on all sides.

"The Nameless! The Nameless Powers have returned."

The superstitious logic took a minute to filter into Jay's mind. The stars were the eyes of the Nameless and here came a star to the center of the city. Of course it was the Nameless. Of course.

The Unifiers had landed under cover of night on the salt flats surrounding the Dead Sea. No doubt the contraband runners had done something similar. No sense in alarming the natives any more than necessary. But calm was not what the Vitae wanted. They wanted awe. They wanted their due as the children of the Ancestors.

"Clever, clever," he whispered. "Descend like the gods, oh you humble Vitae who only wanted a home for yourselves." He squinted into the light, trying to see how their transport had been hitched to the tether that had, no doubt, been on its way down for days.

Heart had dropped onto his knees in the mud. "The Nameless," he croaked. "The Nameless have returned." He covered his face with his hands and groaned.

"No!" Jay hauled the Teacher roughly to his feet. "These are not the Nameless! I know their name! I know it!"

Heart swallowed and his eyes were almost round as he looked at Jay's face, searching for some hope there.

Over Heart's shoulder, Jay watched flames shoot out of the top of the star. They faded away swiftly, leaving only three dark figures standing on top of the glowing sphere.

Jay was ready to bet six years of his life that one of them was Contractor Avir. According to Caril, she'd been angling for this chance for years.

"Come on." He gripped Heart's shoulder and propelled him forward. "Show me where King Silver is."

Heart staggered forward, and Jay followed without letting go. Out of the corner of his eye, Jay saw the captain of the King's guard sprawl facedown in the street. All around his prostrate body people flung themselves onto their knees, screaming for forgiveness. A stranger in uniform with Bondless marks on his hand pulled his knife and held it to his own throat. Jay didn't let Heart pause to see what happened next. He shoved the Teacher into a stumbling run.

Heart led him up a narrow side street toward a three-story house. They splashed mud and stumbled over the penitent. Jay cursed the ones who were trying to run the other way, shoving and jostling and forcing him against the walls and into open doorways.

Heart barged up to the mouth of a back alley and through the honor guard, who were in too much chaos to stop him. Jay let the Teacher go and pushed his way between their shoulders. The guard didn't even look at him.

Hands grabbed him from behind and shoved him against the wall. Jay looked into the terrified eyes of Holding the Keys.

"What is happening, Skyman!" he thundered, slamming Jay against the wall again. "What is happening!"

"Invasion, Holding." Jay grabbed Holding's hands and forced them away. "They are Skymen, like me. They are masquerading as the Nameless, that's all!"

A measure of sanity returned to Holding's face. "You're coming to tell Her Majesty." He snatched Jay's wrist and nearly pulled him off his feet as he raced around the corner of the tavern.

King Silver knelt in the mud, straight-backed and slack-jawed. Her eyes stared at the glowing sphere as if locked into place.

"Majesty," said Holding. "Majesty, Messenger of the Skymen says these are not the Nameless. He says they are known to him."

King Silver didn't so much as blink. A gust of wind blew her black hair into her face and she didn't even flinch.

Jay swallowed hard. He needed her. She couldn't go catatonic on him. Not yet.

He knelt in front of her. "King Silver, those creatures are called the Rhudolant Vitae. They are nothing more than a race of Skymen. Do you hear me, Your Majesty?"

Slowly, King Silver focused on him. Her faced twitched back to a painful kind of life. "Are you sure, Skyman?"

Jay nodded. "I know them, Majesty. I have lived among them. There is no mistaking them."

"Skyman," she hissed. "I have listened to you and listened to you and what has happened? My city has been torn out from under me. I cannot count the dead I have laid on the pyres. Tell me quickly why I should not lay this new disaster in your hands?" She stood up, and the controlled fury on her face reminded Jay sharply that this slender girl was a strong, fast soldier of war.

"Majesty." He bowed his head humbly and spoke to the mud puddles. "Unless you want the People, all the People, to be reduced together to the level of the Notouch, you must find a way to wake the power that the Nameless, the true Nameless, left in the Realm. That is what brings the Skymen here. They seek to steal it for themselves." He raised his eyes.

"And do you now suggest you know how to do this?" Behind her thunderous expression, Jay saw yearning. She wanted to believe him. No, she needed to believe him, because otherwise everything she had done, from her grandfather's death to the retreat from the High House, was wrong.

"I do." Inside, Jay rebelled against the game he was forced to play, but he had no choice. No matter what she was, King Silver could still kill him here and now. He needed her. Later she'd be beneath notice, but for now she was his only hope. "Majesty, you must buy me time!"

"Why?"

"So that I can find the power the true Nameless left behind. For all their tricks, we still have a march stolen on the Skymen. The keys to the world are just outside your city walls. I need just a few days more and then the Skymen are dust at Your Majesty's feet!"

Bit by bit the rage drained out of her face and Jay saw a little girl standing in front of him, tired and frightened.

"All right, Skyman," she said. "Take whom you need. Take a troop with you, if you need to, and go search for this power. I would have you gone from my sight and out of my hearing." She looked toward the glowing sphere. "I warn you, though, if you do not bring me back victory in those pale hands of yours, then hide yourself where you think best, because I will have your life otherwise." She leaned against the wall and covered her eyes with her hands. Holding the Keys laid his hand on her shoulder. Jay stood, feeling oddly abashed, and hurried away.

Jay ducked through the maze of houses and barricades, trying to plan, but his head was full of the screams still sounding around him and the crying of someone who had believed she was a King.

Lu drew the blanket back over Broken Trail's trembling body. She plucked at the thick, brown felt as if she were trying to pick it to pieces. Her eyes stared at the ceiling, but whatever she saw there, it wasn't the polymer dome. The white fabric and struts couldn't have caused three days of nonstop murmuring and tossing back and forth. Once, Lu had put his ear close enough to her mouth to hear what she was saying, but his translator disk provided him with nothing but a stream of random syllables.

Lu plopped himself into his chair, one hand dangling between his knees, the other automatically laying itself across the communications keypad. He pushed the pad away with a grimace.

Too soon, he told himself. *It's just too soon to try again.*

Not one of his transmissions to Jay or Cor had raised
an answer since they'd walked out the door together, and a
traitorous, ghost thought was starting to believe none of them
ever would.

The wind outside was kicking up again. It whistled around
the dome like it was calling the rain to come and play. Trail
gurgled as if in answer. Lu knew that soon he'd have to check
the cloth swaddling her waist again. The thought sent a sudden
hard wave of nausea through him and he had to turn away
and looked at the wall instead.

This is all wrong. He rubbed his forehead. *I'm the hardware
man. I keep the base systems up and running. I don't take
care of flipped-over natives or . . .* His gaze strayed to the
hatch. *. . . organic monstrosities.*

Whatever process Trail had woken up down there had not
gone back to sleep yet. It was getting increasingly difficult
for Lu to force himself to go down the ladders to see what
had changed since the last check. He'd dutifully set up a trio
of cameras and they were storing images in his data boxes,
but protocol and his job dictated that he go down there himself.

Lu wished suddenly that he was Cor. She was the one
trained to deal with living systems. She was the one who
knew how to make friends and think on her feet. He just
knew wires and gears and the laws of inorganic behavior.

I wish you'd come back. He directed the thought through
the dome and toward the building storm. *I wish you'd come
back and get us all out of here and back to someplace that
makes sense.*

One more day, he promised himself. *Just one more day
and I'll give it up. I'll send out the emergency flare and have
somebody come get us . . . me.*

One more day, maybe two, and he'd find the strength to
really believe that he was alone in this forsaken place. One
more day, maybe two.

12—Aboard the *U-Kenai*, 10:04:56, Ship Time

"She stood up straight before him, and she said 'I know you.'"

Fragment from The Apocrypha, Anonymous

"*T*his is getting to be a habit."

Her voice hurt him. Everything hurt him; the mattress against his back, the light against his eyelids, his pulse in his wrists.

If I die now, there'll be no more pain. The thought drifted through his numb mind and he was too exhausted to either choke it off or pursue it. It just hung there.

There was a pressure against his neck and he screamed. After a moment, it subsided to the level of all the other pain. Lethargy seized hold of him slowly.

Thank you, he thought as his consciousness slid into darkness.

* * *

Eric came awake all at once with his heart in his mouth. When he saw his own cabin surrounding him, he collapsed back on the bed, weak with relief.

Not a dream. We made it out. The thought gave him the courage to try sitting up all the way. It wasn't too difficult. The blinding pain had subsided to a dull headache, which he could cope with.

Eric stood carefully, finding his balance was a little tricky, but he managed it. He walked to the door without staggering and opened it.

Arla sat in the common room. Slices of real breads and meats lay on plates in front of her, along with a jug of something that steamed. Eric surveyed the feast. It looked like over half his luxury stock. He sank down onto the sofa and she slid a plate of meats toward him. His stomach rumbled. He folded a random selection of meat into a slice of unleavened bread and devoured it, stopping only to swig down some tea.

Arla watched him with her air of wry amusement. "How are you feeling?" she asked.

"Almost well, I think." He looked toward the closed view wall and all around the common room. "Do you know how Adu managed to find us?"

"Us?" Arla said incredulously. "You were the only one who needed finding. I was along to help pull you free."

Eric felt himself begin to stare. "I thought . . . I thought . . ."

"That because my Lord Teacher had been captured that this despised one must have been also?" She gave a sharp laugh. "Not so, my Teacher. You did a better job at hiding me than at hiding yourself."

"Did I?" he asked the tabletop. "One more idiot action."

He waited for an acid reply that did not come.

"What has happened?" she asked.

Eric ran both hands through his hair. "The Rhudolant Vitae are the ones the Words call the Aunorante Sangh. I have met the Aunorante Sangh, Stone in the Wall *dena* Arla Born of the Black Wall, and I, Teacher Hand *kenu* Lord Hand on the Seablade *dena* Enemy of the Aunorante Sangh was promptly captured and stuffed into a box for dissection."

He waited for her to demand explanations, to invoke the

Nameless Powers, or just to swear, but instead she sighed and dropped her hand onto the pouch that held her namestones.

"What I do not understand is why they call us Aunorante Sangh," she said. "I wish I had the learning of my ancestresses and not just their stones."

"You knew?" Eric gaped at her.

She rubbed the backs of her hands, tracing her scars with her fingertips. "I guessed, after I heard they claimed the Realm as their home. It wasn't exactly a long leap in a high wind." She gave him her twisted grin. "If you'll permit . . ." She broke off. "You should, I think, be getting some more rest, Sar Born."

"I don't want to rest." Eric heaved himself to his feet and paced to the comm station. "I want to think. I need to think." He gripped the back of the chair with both hands and stared at the blank screen in front of him.

"Well, we've two days yet before we reach the Realm," she leaned back. "That should be plenty of . . ."

Eric whirled around. "Who set us on course for the Realm!"

Arla sat up straighter. "Adu did," she told him. "At my direction."

"You idiot N . . ." He bit the word off. "The Vitae may already be there!"

"They are already there," she replied calmly. "Adu checked. We will have to be careful how we proceed, I think."

"Careful!" roared Eric. "They'll pick us up as soon as we poke our noses into the system! They'll . . ." The air caught in his throat and he coughed, sending a shudder through his entire body. He staggered and caught himself on the sofa's corner. Arla grasped his shoulders. She eased him onto the seat and leaned him forward. When the coughing died, she let go and stepped away. Eric did not miss the hesitation in her eyes, or the fact that she hid her hands behind her back.

"The Realm is the last place in the Quarter Galaxy we want to go," he croaked, reaching for the tea.

She sank back onto the sofa. "Those are not the words I expected from a Teacher who has just met the Aunorante Sangh in open battle."

"Battle." Eric filled his cup and swigged down a long

draught. "Oh yes. Five minutes after I stood up against them, they had me tranqued out and in a life-support capsule. A great battle indeed for *dena* Enemy of the Aunorante Sangh." He swirled the dregs of the tea. "Those poor ones in the Temples will go down twice as fast."

She gaped at him. "What are you saying? You, you're sitting there alive and recovering. You held them at bay, you signaled for help from the depths of their ship. You *beat* them."

"I ran away from them," he said. "I woke up and I panicked. I was so afraid, I couldn't control myself. I just . . . I just . . ." He dropped the cup onto the tabletop. It wobbled and tipped over, letting amber liquid spill across the clear polymer. He watched the puddle ooze toward the plate of breads. He remembered the awful pulling in the capsule, as if something were trying to drag his soul out through his pores. A sick yielding sensation had come over him, and whatever dragged at him took him . . . took him . . .

"I don't even really remember what I did," he said. "All I know is that I was scared nearly into senselessness and if Adu . . . if you hadn't been there to pull me out, I would be a set of molecules in a lab dish."

Arla narrowed her eyes. "You did something, or your power gift did. I got that much from the little Vitae who released you from the capsule. He was babbling about you taking over the lab. I don't think he knew very well what he was saying. There was blood on him." She frowned. "Is the power gift always under your command or does it ever work on its own?"

"What kind of question is that?" Eric hunted around the table for a cloth to wipe up the spill and didn't find anything.

"The question of a Notouch seeking wisdom from her Teacher," she retorted. "It should be obvious even to you that what everyone, from the Unifiers to the Kethran to the Vitae, has sought is the understanding of how the gifts the Nameless laid upon us work. So, if we gain that understanding first, we will have something to bargain with, or fight with."

"What is obvious to me is that you are wandering around in a night storm of your own thoughts." He met her eyes. "Don't you understand? There is nothing we can do. The

Nameless alone can count how many Rhudolant Vitae there
are. There are maybe three thousand Teachers in existence,
counting the students. Even if we could all be united, which
I doubt, we would be drowned in the flood of sheer numbers."
He turned up both his hands so he could see his blank, smooth,
empty palms. "We can't be blinded by our superstitions, not
now. This is not some mythic battle we can win because we're
touched by the Nameless and they're not. This is real. This
is happening. This is a primitive and, probably, dying people,
against the oldest and most coherent power in the Quarter
Galaxy. All we can do is keep out of the way."

"It was tried," Arla folded her arms. "It only worked for
150 generations."

"What?" Eric looked up.

"These now are the Words of the Servant Garismit, 'I have
moved the Realm. The Aunorante Sangh will search for a
thousand years to find you again, but only the Nameless
Powers know now where you live.'" She quickly touched the
backs of her hands, first the right, then the left, to close the
quote. "If that is not trying to keep out of the way, what is
it?"

"You would have the gall to quote the Words to a Teacher,"
Eric muttered. "I'm telling you . . ."

"You're telling me not to be blinded by superstition and
you refuse to look into the Words and see that there might
be truth under there." She stabbed a finger at him. "What is
that if it isn't blindness?"

"The Words are lies!" Eric shouted. "Lies! They told us
if we obeyed, if we kept the bloodlines straight and true, that
we would be ready when the Aunorante Sangh came back!
Well we did, and they have, but we haven't got a rat's chance
in the Dead Sea!" His head spun. Visions of Lady Fire, her
curses as he carried their baby away, his father's calm voice,
his brother-in-law's sneaking glances stabbed at his vision.
He cradled his head in his hands. "We did everything we
were told and they are still going to take us all."

"That does not have to be true," she said softly. "Our
ancestors somehow bested theirs; we may be able to repeat
what was done."

He raised his head. "Who has been putting this salt water into your head?"

"I have had plenty of time for thinking while you were recovering," she said. "Adu helped some, but mostly I . . ." She touched her pouch of stones. "Reviewed what I had learned on Kethran." She moved her hand away from the pouch with a quick jerk. "Think on this. The Words say we were named individually by the Nameless. Zur-Iyal then tells me our ancestors must have been constructed individually by some great technology. The Vitae say they lost their home-world. The Words say the Realm was moved to rescue it from the Aunorante Sangh. The Vitae have been searching for their world for years. The Words warn they would be back. There's also the story that the Servant was aided by a Notouch who 'made the Realm hear his commands . . . '"

Eric started. "Where did you hear the apocrypha?"

She smiled her twisted smile. "From my mother, when she showed me my namestones for the first time." She touched the pouch again. "That Notouch was my ancestress. The way she made the Realm 'hear' was with the stones I'm carrying. Or so the story goes, but our stories are turning out to be remarkably close to the truth, are they not?"

"What manner of Notouch are you?" Eric asked softly. "I've been over the World's Wall for ten years and I never, ever thought like this."

"You never wanted to," she said simply. "You wanted to run away and you did. I, however, wanted to understand what the Skymen wanted of us. Now, I do." She closed her jaw so firmly, Eric heard her teeth click together. "They want to get their flabby hands on my children. I will prevent this, Teacher Hand. If it costs my life and my name, I swear I will."

For a moment all he could do was stare at her fierce, unwavering expression. "That's why you left the Realm? Just to find out what the Skymen wanted?"

She laughed deprecatingly. "I admit, I didn't think I'd find myself over the World's Wall. I went to the Skymen because . . ." she shook her head. "I also thought the Words were lies. The Skymen were friends with the Heretics. The Heretics have been known to violate the caste laws. I thought if I

helped the Skymen in their aims, I would be able to secure
their favor and they might persuade King Silver to raise my
family from the ranks of the Notouch." She traced her scars
again, slowly, meditatively. "I thought to keep my children
from groveling in the mud all their lives. I did not know that
to save my family, I would have to save the Realm." She
glanced up at him. "Or indeed, even save one Teacher. Nor
did I expect to find that the Words of the Teachers were closer
to the truth than the words of the Heretics." She sighed. "But
the Nameless did not ask my permission when they opened
their eyes, did they?"

Eric realized he was staring. Of course she would have
children. She would have been married shortly after she hit
pubescence, and started having babies right away. He was
an overindulged rarity and had only been allowed to stay
unmarried because his older sister was already producing
power-gifted heirs. He knew that. It was the way of the Realm.

So why was it hitting him so hard to hear that this woman,
this Notouch woman, was married?

"You did all this for your children?" he rubbed his palms
together. "That's . . . very brave."

She shrugged. "I grew up being told I had been chosen by
the Nameless, and yet I was treated like a Notouch. It was
. . . difficult. Infuriating. I wished to spare my children." She
looked at him curiously. "What drove you out here?"

Lady Fire's curses, his son, red, wet, and bawling, in his
power-gifted hands, his father's voice, Heart's wary eyes . . .

"The Words of the Nameless Powers," he muttered.

"Strange," Arla folded her arms. "The Words of the Nameless forbid climbing the World's Wall. 'There is no place for
you but here.'" She touched her hands again.

"They also say a Teacher may bear or sire children without
marriage, but only if the other is unwed, and they say that
anyone who knowingly harbors one who does not hear the
Words in the Temple must recant or be executed." His voice
dropped to a whisper. "The words of the Nameless say too
much to be endured."

Arla glanced away toward the view wall and didn't ask
any more.

"Listen, Arla." Eric leaned forward and rested his forearms on his knees. "I understand why you want to return, truly I do, but even if there was something we could do, there is still no way to reach the Realm. If we had an armed shuttle or an upgraded runner and an experienced crew, maybe, maybe, we could make it, but this is only a runner's side ship and I'm little more than a glorified passenger. I never had the thirteen years it takes to learn to pilot one of these by oneself."

A gleam sparked in the depths of Arla's black eyes. "So my Lord Teacher does not really know if this ship could get past the Vitae, does he?"

Eric pulled back. "Yes, I do know."

"You just said you did not." Now she leaned forward, eagerness shining in her features. "Does the ship know?"

"What?"

"Does the ship know? Are there records? Histories, documents of what it has done in the past? Maybe . . ." She frowned. "Operational parameters?" She spoke the last two words in Standard.

"And if there were?" Her confidence nagged at him. It was ridiculous. He'd left her barely three weeks ago, but that was time enough for her to realize how complex life was out here.

What does she expect of me?

"Then I might be able to find us a way to dodge the Vitae's prying eyes."

Eric threw back his head and laughed. "You! Arla, they may have taught you to read and write at the labs, but you've got no idea the level of complexity we're dealing with. It takes years to learn how to operate even a simple ship . . ."

"If my Lord Teacher will permit me to finish," she said tartly, "this despised one might be able to tell him how she intends to manage it."

She told him about her stones in short sentences and carefully chosen words, as if she had been rehearsing the speech so she wouldn't make any mistakes. Eric realized that was probably exactly what she had done.

When she finished, he said, "That's insane."

"No more insane than what you can do." She gestured

toward his hands. "You should hear yourself talk. You are so convinced that these Skymen and their steel and silicon are so superior, you've never even stopped to ask why they care about us. You! A Teacher, a power-gifted, the first among the People along with the Royals. If we are so inferior, so . . . primitive and so close to death, why are the Skymen willing to make war over us? If the Realm is such a barren, useless piece of rock, what is their interest in it? You cannot tell me the all-powerful Vitae just want a place to warm their feet. You cannot tell me the Unifiers are acting for our poor benefit." She leaned forward again. "Let me prove to you what I can do. Let me prove to you the worth of those named by the Nameless."

It was too much. It was not enough. She could sit there and lecture him, she hadn't seen . . . she didn't know . . . she'd never slaved for them the way he had, never sold herself for their protection and their money.

"I am not a servant of the Nameless," he said. "I have known too many other masters since then."

To his surprise, she started to laugh. Her whole body shook with it, and she dropped her forehead into her hands.

"Oh, Nameless Powers preserve me!" she giggled. "Oh, Garismit's Eyes!" She lifted her head again and there were tears streaming down her cheeks. "Do you think the Nameless care who else you serve? The Teachers serve the Temples, the Nobles and the Royals serve themselves, and the Nameless do not care."

His hands opened wide at his side, the fingers straight and rigid as sticks of wood. "You don't understand! The Aunorante Sangh found the Realm because of me! I led them straight to it! This is all happening because of my heresy!"

His breathing was ragged and his throat was raw and his ears rang.

Arla watched him silently for a moment, then she said, "All the more reason you should go back and make it right."

He wanted to shout that it was not that simple, that there was no returning, not for him, not ever, that he would not give them satisfaction by recanting his actions. That he could not, he would not, be forced to regret what he had done in front of the Seablade House, however much he might do so when he was alone.

But he couldn't. All he could do was stand there and shake like a terrified fool, watching her watch him with her impassive, unforgiving eyes.

At last those eyes widened and she said, "Nameless Powers preserve me, they really did get to you, didn't they?"

"Yes," he whispered. "Yes."

He had no idea how long they stood like that. He was too caught up in the riot inside him and the memory of those long years when he thought he was free. Now that illusion was shattered at his feet and all that was left was a broken, terrified slave whose masters had proved disloyal.

At last, he ran his hands through his hair, a habit he had learned from Perivar. "If I gave you the operational parameters, do you really think you could find a way to get the ship back to the Realm?"

He expected a show of triumph, but again his expectations were wrong. She simply shrugged. "I think I might. If I get enough information."

"I think I know what you need."

The ghost box was already plugged into the comm board. "Perivar?" he asked.

She nodded. "He set it up and worked the transmission by remote from Kethran."

Eric looked at the cube for a moment, tracing the length of cable with his eyes. "Why didn't he come with you?"

Arla hesitated. "Because he felt he owed a greater debt to his partner's children. Kiv was killed because he refused to hand me over to the Aun . . . the Vitae."

Eric felt his shoulders stiffen. *He left? After everything . . .* he hung his head. *What did I ever really bring him? I saved his life and he saved mine and we spent the last six years trying to forget about each other. Why should I be surprised he's left me on my own?* He felt an itch between his shoulder blades and remembered Arla was watching him.

He straightened up. "Then you know that this"—he laid his hand on the box—"is basically all the two contraband runners who took me off the Realm knew about their ship."

He tapped the screen three times to bring up Kessa's image by itself. "What history I've got of this ship is in here, and if anyone could get past the Vitae, it was her." He pointed at Kessa's image and shook himself to try to chase away the memory of her lying dead on the deck plates.

Arla sat in the terminal's chair and drew one of her stones out of the pouch. "I can learn without the stone, but it makes rearranging things later much more difficult." She hit the PLAY key on the console and cupped the stone in her hand.

"Whaddaya want?" demanded Kessa.

"I want to know about the *U-Kenai*," answered Arla. Her voice was heavy, as if there were a weight pressing against it.

Kessa started talking. "*U-Kenai*, it means 'Second Chance.' Good little ship . . ."

Eric watched Arla. Her eyes fastened on the recording without blinking or flickering. She sat like a Vitae Ambassador, not moving, barely even breathing. She wasn't watching what passed in front of her, she was absorbing it.

A strange awkwardness washed over him and he automatically retreated to the bridge. But it wasn't Cam in the pilot's chair, oblivious to his presence. Adu turned around and wrinkled the skin over his eye sockets in a jerky imitation of humans raising their eyebrows.

Eric turned away again and, trying not to see Arla, shut himself into his cabin.

"Garismit's Eyes!" He sank onto the bed and stared at the blank surface of the door. "What is the matter with me?"

I don't know. He rubbed his palms together. *That's really it. I've always known what I was leaving behind. I knew the Realm. I knew all its rules and I knew all its ranks and its choking, stupid laws and Words. Then, she turns up and it turns out I never knew a crashing thing, not about the People, or the world, or her. Especially not about her.*

And I've just said I'll go back, to this place I don't know.

Eric leaned against the side of the bunk's nook and rubbed his eyes wearily. *What do I think I'll do when I get there? Put on Garismit's robe and lead this Notouch into the Earth to move the Realm again? Save the world? I can't even save myself.*

To his relief, exhaustion clouded his mind, wrapping his thoughts in thick velvet. Willingly, he relaxed into it and fell asleep.

Eric awoke several times to the uninterrupted sound of Kessa's voice vibrating softly through the cabin wall. When he woke to nothing but silence, he swung himself out of the bed and opened the door to the common room.

Arla still sat in front of the comm board. She was gently massaging her eyelids with her fingertips. The stone lay in her lap, gleaming in the light.

"Garismit's Eyes," she muttered, "I think mine are about to fall out of their sockets."

"Did you find it?" asked Eric.

"Eh?" Arla glanced blearily at him. "I don't know." She sucked in a deep breath and picked the stone up. "Ask me again."

Eric sat on the sofa so he was eye level with Arla. "How can the *U-Kenai* land in the Realm without being seen by the Rhudolant Vitae?"

Her whole face changed. Her pupils dilated until her irises were almost lost behind black pools. Her jaw slackened, leaving her cheeks hollow and her bones pressing sharply against the inside of her skin. It was not a look of intelligence, or revelation. It was as if the woman inside had fled to make room for . . . what?

But when she spoke, it was Arla's confident voice. "A comet can be located in or near the MG49 system. The *U-Kenai* can intercept it and use the first level drive to drive the nose of the ship into the comet. The heating vents in the *U-Kenai*'s prow can be used to hollow out a cavity in which the majority of the ship can be embedded. Thrust applied from the second level drive can push the comet, and the *U-Kenai* with it, into the atmosphere. The particulate tail of the comet will hide the thruster output. The shell from the comet will provide resistance to the burn of entering the atmosphere and a cushion for a semicontrolled crash. Any satellites observing this occurrence will record a simulation of a natural phenomenon."

Her hand jerked, dropping the stone back into her lap.

"That's insane," said Eric. "That's absolutely insane."

Arla let her head drop backward until she was staring up at the ceiling. It was only then Eric realized she was breathing like she'd just run a marathon.

Without even thinking, he jumped to his feet and laid his hands on her shoulders, reaching out with his power gift to loosen her chest and speed her recovery. The whole time he was far too aware of the tingling warmth of her skin and the depths of her eyes as she looked up at him.

Nor did he miss the fact that he had forgotten to flinch from touching her.

Eric drew his hands away, now winded himself, and poured some cold tea from the pitcher on the table.

"How do you know it's insane?" Arla sat up straighter.

Eric swigged the tea and made a face at its rancid taste. "Because it is. I've never heard of anything like it even being attempted."

"I didn't tell you all of it." The amused tone crept back into her voice.

"What more is there?"

"That if it worked, it would only work once." She leaned forward. "And that the ship would most certainly be unusable afterward."

Eric stared into the cup. "Now it sounds a little less insane."

"It is the only way your"—she waved toward the comm board—"ghost box knows that could work." Her eyes narrowed. "This despised one is waiting for my Lord Teacher to inform her he refuses to do this."

"You'll wait the dark seasons through." Eric dropped the cup onto the table. The puddle he had spilled yesterday had dried, leaving an uneven amber stain on the tabletop. "I only ask that Arla Born of the Black Wall does not ask me why I am doing this." He spread his fingers out so that he could see the backs of his hands. "Because, and the Nameless hear my words, I do not know."

"It's all right." She took his naked hand in her scarred one. "It's enough that Eric Born is doing this."

He looked up at her deep eyes. "I hope so, Arla Stone. I truly hope so."

He felt her work-roughened palm against the soft skin on the back of his hand. He watched her breathing with a deep, sudden fascination and felt the warm pulse of his erection begin. She must have realized what was happening in him, but she didn't release his hand.

He kissed her. Her mouth stiffened, startled, then puckered, as she thought to pull away, then softened to answer his gesture, his entreaty.

This is insane too, part of him said. He didn't care. She was pressing her body against him so he could feel every centimeter of her, as full of desire as he was, as lost, as scared, as crazy as he was.

For now, there was nothing else in the universe.

13—Section One, Division One, the Home Ground, Hour 11:15:25, Planet Time

"It is you who has set this work to my hands. I will not fail. It is you who has set my eyes to these sights. I will not look away. I am a child of the Lineage and through me the Lineage shall be brought home."

Fragment from The First Grace, the Rhudolant Vitae private history Archives.

" . . . personnel for a thorough survey of the vaults before we begin sealing the walls . . ." Even though it came through her translator disk, Historian Maseair's voice was barely audible under the noise around Avir.

Contractor Avir plucked two more greasy oil lamps out of their alcoves in the curving walls of the "Temple." "Record authorization and time stamp," she said through gritted teeth as she carried the filthy objects over to the flash disposal unit, sidestepping the Beholden who carried the programmer for the drones cleaning the ceiling.

"Anything else?" She dropped the lamps into the disposal's open mouth and, as the hatch closed, felt an irrational satisfaction in knowing they had been reduced to ashes faster than she could blink.

The initial plan had been sound; the engineers would string fiber-optic threads over the stone and plaster supports already in place and cover them all with optical matter to make a usable workspace. Eventually the supports could be replaced with more durable steels and polymers.

But now, spiderlike drones crawled across the ceilings, scraping off years of soot and tempera paints that were supposed to represent a night sky. A Beholden was injecting concrete filler into the oil lamp alcoves that studded every square foot of wall space. The tiled floor would have to be sealed and primed against water leakage before a silicate coating could be laid to make it smooth. Then optics had to be laid into the thresholds to allow for the installation of proper doors that might actually be able to shut out the sound and stench drifting in from outside, where the artifacts waited.

There had been a tiny group of telekinetics inside the Temple when her team had arrived, but they had vanished. The search teams of artifacts that Ivale had organized claimed to have found no trace of them, but then, some of the city residents had barricaded a full square kilometer's worth of the streets and it was possible the telekinetics were hiding with them.

She hoped one day she'd forget what the artifacts looked like when she had stepped out of the transport. Their eyes had been wide and their faces were all contorted with fear. Many had been on their knees or their bellies in the mud, babbling so fast in what was left of the language of the Ancestors that the translator disks couldn't even make any sense out of it.

She could hear them now through the flimsy walls of this place. They sang or shouted, or moved about without purpose or plan. Lost, all of them lost.

Waiting for her to restore them to use, and she could barely coordinate the restoration of one building. Avir rested her hand on the edge of the flash disposal. The shrieking wind that wormed its way through every niche in the walls carried with it the endless gabble of voices, snatches of devotional songs, the distant shouts of the ones who were confused enough to try to fight the Reclamation. Ivale said he had organized some of the artifacts into a kind of security force, but it seemed to have more holes than the Temple walls did.

"Engineer Faive of the *First Cause*, Contractor," said a new voice in her ear. "I am going to need to contract at least three more Beholden to incorporate structural standards in Section eighteen . . ."

The "High House," the artifacts called it, for no reason Avir could discern. It had no less than eight conduits to the underground complexes in it. She had placed a priority on having the standing walls upgraded to shelter the teams assigned to study them.

The Beholden sealing fiber-optic cables into a trench carved in the main entranceway scrambled backward to let Bio-tech Nal and two of his own Beholden enter. Behind them waddled an eight-legged drone stacked with an assortment of nameless crates.

"Record authorization and time stamp." She drew aside so the drone could pass. "Next?"

Her translator disk beeped. "Incoming message on comm line 23A," said the default voice.

She stood in front of the portable terminal, not wanting to have to perch on the hard stool in front of it. The translator disks alone could not handle transmissions from the dead side. She touched the screen. Kelat appeared, standing with a poise and propriety she envied. Behind him curved the shadowy walls of one of the underground chambers. A team of Engineering Beholden clustered around a bulge in the wall, watching monitors intently and occasionally punctuating their dialogue with a finger stabbed toward some reading or the other. Kelat, apparently oblivious to the impropriety behind him, made a small, respectful obeisance to her.

"Good Morning and also Good Day, Contractor," Avir said, making her own obeisance. "How are matters progressing with you?"

Kelat turned a little to indicate the activity behind him. Now she could see the bulge held something that pulsed and pressed star-shaped filaments against the wall. "Slowly, and with much argument between the committees. There are organic artifacts left here, there is no doubt about that, but defining their relationships and purposes is a struggle.

"And how are matters progressing with you?"

Avir glanced around the room. Nal was unloading equipment from the drone with his Beholden hustling to set up an analysis tank assembly. An Engineering Beholden readjusted a cleaning drone and sent it scuttling up the wall. Over it all rattled the noise from the artifacts outside. She did not invite Kelat to take a better look.

"Rapidly, Kelat, but not very smoothly. There was a great deal of chaos stirred up by the Unifiers and a civil war has been going on for a long time between the established power base and some factions that want to split off. Unfortunately, the factions may be less likely to accept that we hold their names than the main power base is. We are proceeding accordingly.

"Has there been any action on the part of the Unifiers?" she asked, more to keep the conversation going than because she really needed the information. Kelat's presence, even over the lines, was very calming.

"They are raising protests and publicity with a number of the client governments," said Kelat, "but so far, nothing important. The Reclamation Assembly assessment is that they are simply delaying the necessity of removing their people." Kelat's shoulders sagged minutely. "Has any progress been made in locating their base?"

The wind dropped a note in pitch and sent a draft curling around Avir's ankles. "No. They appear to be maintaining a communications silence and with the limited number of satellites currently deployed and the pervasiveness of the cloud cover . . ." she broke her sentence off. She was repeating what Kelat already knew. They were not currently equipped for a full scan of the habitable section of the Home Ground. The Assembly had moved ahead of several committees' scheduling recommendations but had offered no explanations as to why. But she would not be heard to say that aloud.

"We already have given orders to some of the less confused artifacts to search for 'Skymen' and bring them into appropriate custody," she told Kelat instead. "So far they have had no success, but we will reinforce the orders." Outside, artifacts' voices lifted in a new song. Whatever it was, it must have been ancient. Her disk couldn't make anything out of it. "How soon will you be ready for us to start delivering artifacts to your facilities for classification?" she asked.

Kelat looked over his shoulder at the contending trio of Beholden. "It will be some time," he admitted. "There are many pieces of the Ancestors' puzzles to be sorted out. It is my opinion your efforts are best spent in gaining and centralizing control where you are and performing what classifications you can."

Avir felt a flicker of humor cross her face. "It is glorious work, Kelat, but it is work all the same."

Kelat lowered his voice. "Is there any assistance we can offer you?"

Pride more than confidence stiffened Avir's shoulders. "Not yet, I don't think. At the moment, the Assembly is placing a premium on keeping as many of the artifacts as we can functional, so we can only go slowly in restructuring their social groupings. When control is centralized, then we can coordinate our efforts more closely."

Kelat glanced around himself to make sure no one was listening. "Avir, how does it feel to be a god?"

She pressed her fingertips against the edge of the comm board. "Kelat, I would rather be a Contractor."

"Understood," he said, and she heard genuine sympathy in his voice. "This line is being left open for your reports." Kelat signed off and the terminal went blank.

The sound of voices and shuffling feet made Avir turn around. One of the Bio-tech Beholden led a gaggle of artifacts with scarred hands through the main threshold. They were all female, Avir saw, some of them juveniles, some of them carrying infants in bundles of rags strapped to their chests.

Ivale followed the cluster of artifacts, spreading his hands to help herd them all inside the Temple. Two juveniles took shelter behind the adults as his hands touched their shoulders.

"All is well," said Ivale in the round, almost-musical tones he'd been cultivating since he'd received his contract to the Reclamation. "There is only new work that we ask of you."

Despite Ivale's reassurances, the artifacts all looked at her with identical expressions of fear on their faces.

Avir's anger at the long-dead Aunorante Sangh deepened. *How could you condemn your own kind to this? A life without structure or purpose? Where they can't even recognize the ones you were made to serve?*

It was totally irrational, and though she knew it, she couldn't help herself.

We will restore them. As soon as we understand how the Ancestors structured this world, we will be able to restore their proper functions to them, and then that fear will vanish.

These, at least, seemed fairly docile. They let Ivale and the Beholden direct them toward the analysis area, where Nal and his other three Beholden were dodging each other as they tried to uncrate and set up the last of their equipment.

A juvenile stumbled on the uneven floor. An adult, old enough to be wrinkled and toothless, stuck out her clawed hand to steady it. Even from where she stood, Avir saw the bones in the adult's wrist.

"Bio-technician," she called, unable to take her eyes off the skinny artifact. The artifact noticed her regard and lowered herself humbly to the floor, holding her hands in front of her eyes.

Bio-tech Nal disentangled himself from a coil of fiber optic and came to stand beside her. "Yes, Contractor?" There was no disguising the impatience in his voice.

Avir ignored it. "Once you have completed your classification scans on this sampling, take the artifacts down into the basements. We will need to provide food and warmth for them until the committees meet to determine a coherent separation strategy."

"We're going to keep them here?" Nal's face wrinkled with distaste.

Avir's temper flared. "You are speaking with disrespect of the work of the Ancestors, Bio-tech. Do you want to explain your reluctance to care for it properly to a Witness and have it added to the Memory?" She spoke too loud and too harshly. The Bio-tech was plainly more shocked than chagrined. He dropped quickly into an obeisance that pressed his forehead against the filthy floor.

"I spoke without thought, Contractor," he said.

So did I, but Avir just gestured for him to get up.

Avir glanced at the Beholden, but they were all properly busy at their tasks. She wished she wasn't so certain they were all straining their ears to hear what her next outburst would be. Ivale, though, had his dark eyes leveled at her, and, for a moment, she saw the question in them.

I am not supposed to be feeling like this, thought Avir as she turned away. *I am walking on the Home Ground. I am working directly for the Reclamation. This should be glorious. I should be joyous. I shouldn't be petty and scolding and worn like a student on her first assignment.* She rubbed her forehead and gazed at the sprinkling of soot that smeared her palm. *I just never thought it would be . . .*

"Skyman!" shouted a voice.

Avir's head jerked toward the doorway. The songs and shouts had dropped away outside, leaving only the sounds of the wind and of feet squelching in the mud.

"I'll go," said Ivale.

"No." He opened his mouth and Avir raised her hand. "We are all Ambassadors to the work of the Ancestors now. I will see what is happening outside and you will calm the artifacts already in our care."

Ivale hesitated for a moment, as if testing the seriousness of her order. Then he turned away from her and gestured toward the floor. "Sit, sit," he said to the artifacts. "You are in the hands of the Nameless. What else can touch you here?"

The artifacts did as they were told. They settled themselves next to the wall, wrapping their ragged clothing around them. They set the juveniles on their laps or took them in their arms. One began to croon a soft, wordless song to an infant. Beside them, the analysis tank began a steady humming, indicating that the Beholden had gotten the generators successfully hooked up.

Avir couldn't work out why she was staring at them.

"Skyman!"

Avir tore her gaze away from the artifacts. Drawing herself

up into a properly poised stance, she pushed past the poorly woven blanket that covered the threshold and stepped onto the flagstone veranda.

A new group of artifacts filled the street below the crude, stone steps. Unlike the crowds that had been there earlier, these stood in relatively straight lines. They had hats of beaten metal covering their heads. In their midst, a smallish female who had been tattooed in red around her face and jaw sat on the back of one of the oxen used as beasts of burden. The shadow from the tether fell across her, creating a broad, black stripe over her chest.

Avir remembered her briefing. This was, in all probability, Silver on the Clouds, the King or leader of this area's social grouping.

"See how they come when called!" Silver on the Clouds shouted, standing in the ox's stirrups. "They know who they are! Skymen!"

But even from where she stood, Avir could see the fear in the King's eyes. Just like she saw in all the others. Endless, reasonless fear.

"You doubt we are the Nameless?" Avir let her voice ring across the plaza. "You are alone, King Silver. The Temples and the Teachers know us."

"The Teachers are fools!" Silver on the Clouds snorted. "They always have been! You are nothing but Skymen with tricks and lies. Narroways is still my city, Skyman! If you do not leave it on your own, we will drive you over the World's Wall and into the maw of the Aunorante Sangh!

"You have until the next sunshowing!"

Taking her words as their cue, the helmeted artifacts raised their weapons and began to retreat, one step at a time. Silver backed her ox up to stay in the middle of them. No one tried to stop them as they disappeared between the ramshackle buildings.

Avir felt something whither inside her. *I should have let Ivale do this. I don't know how to handle them. I don't know what to do. This is not what I'm trained for. This is not what anybody here is trained for.*

The remaining artifacts stared up at her with their wide

eyes. They were waiting for her to do something miraculous to prove that she really was a daughter of the Ancestors. But she had no proof to offer.

Avir glowered at the herd of artifacts, suddenly furious. They all leaned a bit closer together and ducked their heads in the face of her anger. Avir knew they were not to blame for their own ignorance, but knowing that did not help calm her.

Her translator disk beeped. "Contractor," said Ivale's voice, "there is a transmission from the Reclamation Assembly that requires your attention."

Avir touched her disk to acknowledge him, and, with as much dignity as she could muster, she retreated behind the blanket.

Ivale watched her a little too closely as she crossed the chamber. Did he see the hollowness inside her? She thought she had her face properly expressionless, but she wasn't sure. She wasn't sure of anything right now.

She reached the active comm screen and faced a single Contractor, immaculate in his seamless black robe. Avir suddenly remembered how rumpled and ash-spattered she was.

"Allow me to hand you my name, Contractor." He had elected to be as bald as an Ambassador and yet as brown as an artifact. Avir wondered what had motivated the juxtaposition. "I am Contractor Cynleah Laefhur, of the First Core, and Senior Contractor to the Reclamation Assembly. We have news that will affect your division."

His quiet, steady voice went straight through Avir, soothing her instantly. She wanted to lean toward the screen and drink in his voice, as a reminder of what she ought to be.

"Bio-technician Uary has confessed himself to be an Imperialist and has volunteered the location of the Unifier base just outside your division. One of their operators is Jahidh of the *Grand Errand*. He has been transmitting information about the Home Ground to his Imperialist contacts for four years."

Blood of my ancestors, Avir staggered. *There's been an Imperialist on the Home Ground for FOUR YEARS?* Avir felt her breathing go harsh and shallow. "Where is he now?" she croaked. "Do we know that?"

"These are your orders, Contractor Avir," said Laefhur. "You will investigate the Unifiers' finds. You will not waste resources hunting for Jahidh."

"Contractor," Avir drew her shoulders back. This man might hold a senior ranking and an Assembly seat, but he did not hold her name. "How can . . ."

"We want him free to continue his researches," said the Contractor. "He has made great contributions to the understanding of the artifacts. As long as he believes he is undetected, he will continue to do so. The Witnesses will take charge of him if he oversteps the bounds the Assembly has laid down on his conduct."

Avir could not force a single word out of her throat.

"It is the Reclamation that is important, Contractor. We must not lose time because of lack of skilled hands."

And it must not be seen that the Assembly allowed Imperialists to slip through their notice. Resolve hardened inside her. "I can make this my work and I will," she said, giving a properly deep obeisance.

Laefhur's image was gone by the time she straightened up. Avir realized her hands had curled into fists. Her mind was already racing. Transportation would have to be acquired from the Acquisitions committee, and a security team contracted. The Unifiers' base would have to be thoroughly explored and cataloged. Extra personnel would certainly be needed once the initial survey of the base was complete.

She would obey her orders, but communication with the artifacts was still at an uncertain stage. Everyone was aware of that. It was well documented and witnessed. If they did not understand they were to cease their search for one particular Skyman, that, surely, was not her fault.

Jay cast another glance at Heart of the Seablade. The Teacher hunched in front of the fire watching the flames in a way that suggested he did not like what he saw. Jay shivered as the wind blew through the tent flaps and, for the hundredth time, he cursed the necessity of bringing the Teacher along. Heart had too many distractions inside his head to allow Jay to predict the outcome of his thoughts. But they needed a

Teacher to help bring the Notouch into line in case Cor's efforts at persuasion were not totally successful, so Jay needed Heart.

Years of practiced acting allowed Jay to put a concerned tone in his voice. "What is it you are worried about now, Teacher?"

Heart picked up a cold lump of charcoal from the meager stack that was their night's supply of fuel. "My wife was in the High House when they came down, Messenger. What will they do to her?"

Be patient. You need him to keep the Notouch in line. Say it again. Jay wrapped his poncho a little closer around him. "Nothing, Heart. She's valuable to them. You all are. That's what's buying us this time." *That and King Silver's pride.*

"I do hold her in my regard, Messenger." Heart pitched the charcoal onto the flames. The fire hissed and a flurry of sparks danced above the flames. "She is so unwavering . . . I fear they will grow impatient with her."

Jay considered laying a hand on the man's shoulder, but couldn't quite bring himself to do it. "I know these people, Heart. They're born patient. They cannot be rushed. I once . . ." His translator disk beeped.

Cor's voice hissed in his ear. "Jay, get your sodden face out here. I'm about to be bludgeoned."

"Blood of my . . ." Jay scrabbled at the tent's laces and tore them open.

It was full night outside. The icy wind drove straight down on his head, making him stagger as he emerged from the tent. The only light was from the four orange watchfires. Everything else was a solid curtain of black.

"Hold your hand!" he bellowed to the world in general.

Jay squinted at one fire after another. The one toward his left flopped sideways in the wind and Jay saw a pair of human shadows, one standing and one kneeling. He took a bead on the fire and, ignoring the violent crawling of the goose bumps rising on his skin, waded through the weeds and reeds toward it.

"I speak for her!" he shouted as he approached.

Jay entered the tiny circle of flickering light and saw Cor

on her knees with her hands in front of her eyes. A soldier
with Bondless tattoos on his hands and a craggy face that Jay
didn't recognize held his metal-studded club over her head.

"What in the sight of the Nameless is all this?" Cor
demanded as Jay waved the soldier aside. "An invasion?"

"Hardly." A fresh wind hit him and Jay shivered. "The
Vitae have got that show to themselves." He brushed the
soldier back. The man gave Jay the barest possible salute and
tramped off into the darkness.

"I noticed." Cor stood and picked up her handlight. She
seemed oblivious to the cold. "We had word. They've started
giving orders that the Notouch be rounded up." She clipped
her light onto her belt.

"So you found Stone in the Wall's relatives?" For a
moment, eagerness was stronger than the cold.

"Yeah, I found them." Cor stretched her hands out to the
fire and let the light shine between her fingers. "I thought
you were going to King Silver for letters of authority, not for
a small army." She nodded toward the cluster of a dozen
tents.

"Cor . . ." Jay began angrily. He stopped and gripped his
temper. "We need protection in case we run into First City
troops. They're working for the Vitae now."

Cor watched the fire between her fingers.

"Cor." Jay moved closer. "Where're the Notouch?"

"I don't know," she said. "I sent them running."

Jay's heart thudded once, hard, against his ribs. "You
what?"

"I told them to grab their gear and run like the wind." She
rubbed her hands together. "And not to tell me where they
would go."

"Cor, the Vitae are rounding up Notouch!" Jay shouted.
"They know something! We have to find . . ."

"We have to get out of here!" Cor screamed up at him to
be heard over the wild night wind. "We have to get out of
here and leave these people alone!"

"They aren't people!"

Cor didn't even flinch. "I don't think they'd agree with
you."

Jay took a deep breath, trying to get control of himself again. It was too much. He had come all this way, he had worked all this time, and now he was so close. He was too close.

"Cor," he said, hoping she couldn't hear the tremor in his voice over the sound of the wind and the crackle of the fire, "you're not thinking straight. If the Vitae find out how this place works, they will rule the Quarter Galaxy."

"And if the Family finds out how this place works, then what?" Cor shook her head and Jay saw the rock-hard resistance behind her eyes. The fire struck sparks in them. "No. No matter who gets hold of them, they're never going to be left alone again. The only thing they can do is keep running and fighting us all off." Her voice dropped almost to a whisper. "With the number of birth defects they've got, I doubt the whole place has more than four generations left anyway. Then it's over with, but they're at least not being bred into slavery."

Jay felt the world tilt under his feet. Anger rushed through him, faster than the wind through the reeds, and all of it focused on the woman in front of him, calmly facing him down as if he were no more than a Bonded, or a total fool.

"Then why in all this hell did you come here?" he croaked. "Why didn't you stay with your Notouch?"

Her chin shifted left, then right. "I wanted to see if you'd be willing to leave. I didn't want you and Lu hanging around making things hard . . . harder." Her green eyes were honest and a little ashamed. "I wanted you to know I'm willing to get you both offworld, but if you decide to keep going on the assignment, then, as of now, you've got no pilot and you'd better watch your back, because I'll be on it."

The night was suddenly crystal clear to Jay. The fire didn't even flicker. Cor's headcloth didn't stir. He could hear her breathing, even over the rush of blood in his ears.

"And you really don't know where the Notouch have gone?" he said coolly.

She shook her head. "No. I really don't."

Jay lashed out. His fist caught her in the throat and knocked her backward. She choked as she fell. He grabbed hold of her shoulders and flipped her onto her stomach. Her spine was stiff and knobbly under his knees. He pressed all his weight against her back. Her neck muscles corded against his palms as he forced her face into the mud. She clawed at him, raking great long scratches down his hands. She screamed to the ground. Jay held on until her hands fell into the weeds and he felt her neck go limp.

He stood. He thought he would be shaking, but he wasn't. He was perfectly calm. Cor was nothing but a crooked shadow in the grass. In a moment he'd call the watch back to toss her into the swamp.

Jay fished his translator disk out of his ear and tucked it into its slot in his torque and waited.

"Jahidh? Be quick," came Kelat's voice.

"I need you to do a satellite scan of the area about twenty kilometers around this transmission point." Jay kept looking at Cor's body, noting how it didn't move. "Stone in the Wall's relatives are on the run and I need to know where they've gone."

"It won't be easy," said Kelat. "But I'll make it my work."

Kelat closed the line and Jay disengaged his disk from the torque.

Do you know, Kelat, he thought toward the canyon wall, *you've just described this whole fool Reclamation.*

Jay whistled and waved to a quartet of silhouettes that he was fairly sure were soldiers. He'd have to tell Heart. He'd have to tell them all that they'd been betrayed. He'd have to, if they were to keep going, and they had to keep going.

Because now there was absolutely nothing else to do.

It was four hours past dark before the transport was lowered from the tether's end. Avir had to order Ivale to come with her and she was ready to swear that if there had not been a host of Beholden to see, he would have balked at the assignment.

Sealed in pressure suits, Avir, Ivale, and Nal walked down the steps to meet the transport. Darkness and the accompanying cold cleared the streets of even the most lost of the artifacts.

From the outside, the transport was little more than a computerized box with thick, heavy tires that could grip and climb even the Home Ground's chaotic terrain. As they approached, a door in the side lifted away, letting loose a flood of clear light.

Nice dressing, thought Avir as she squinted up the ramp that was lowering and tried to find her footing. She wasn't sure how she felt about a security team leader with a sense of the dramatic.

The door closed behind them and Avir's eyes adjusted to the light. It was a standard transport: drive boards in the front, seating for a dozen passengers down the middle, comm terminals at the rear, and storage lockers lining the walls. Eight of the seats were filled with the security team; males and females with brown or pinkish skins and all as bald as Ambassadors. The team leader got out of the pilot's chair as soon as Avir walked up the ramp, but did not make obeisance until her eyes had had a chance to adjust.

The name he handed her was Security Chief Panair of the Hundredth Core. Avir accepted it with a nod. She didn't trust her voice. It felt too good to be between soundproofed walls breathing air that was free of any kind of reek.

Security Chief Panair was not one to waste time. He accepted her silence as she had accepted his name and returned to his station. He snapped the seat restraints across his waist and passed his hands over the controls. The hum of the engines heightened its pitch.

Avir took the farthest seat on the empty row. Ivale stood aside to let Nal sit next to her. Avir wished she was free to roll her eyes. Ivale was being positively childish.

The transport lurched forward and Avir tried to resign herself to a long, dull trip. Outside the windows, the night brought down lashings of rain and ice carried on a wind that shook the transport. Panair kept his eyes on the boards, Avir noticed. Despite his bright running lights, he was navigating more by the satellite transmission on the terminals than by line of sight.

The journey wore on. The transport lurched and rattled through a landscape that could barely be seen, and Ivale's silence began to wear on Avir's nerves. Nal was using the seat's terminal, absorbed in his own work, but Ivale just sat with his eyes kept rigidly forward, watching the blobs of shadow that passed through the the transport's lights so quickly that it was often difficult to tell if they were trees or mere stones.

Avir sat back and tried to feel sympathy for him. This was not what any of them had been chosen for. They were supposed to convert a series of buildings for use by the Vitae and begin researches on the artifacts. They were not a boarding party, even if the team surrounding them were.

Panair swung the transport to the left and they lurched up a steep incline. The lights showed up nothing but rocks, boulders, and mud.

"Approaching the Unifier shelter," Panair announced.

Avir looked out the window automatically, but there was nothing there except stone and shadow. The terminal on Panair's board showed a smooth-sided dome, glowing with incandescent light and heat in the infrared spectrum.

Avir felt her beating heart rise until it filled her throat.

The white dome drifted into view. The transport ground to a halt and the door lifted itself open. The security team leapt out and dived straight for the dome's entrance, leaving Avir, Ivale, and Nal trailing, a little stunned, in their wake.

"What . . . !" shouted a man's voice inside the dome.

Avir stepped under the canopy over the entranceway but couldn't see anything through the open door except piles of camp equipment and Panair's back.

"Stand still and be identified," barked Panair.

"All right, all right, I'm standing. Look, here I am."

Avir stepped sideways, squeezing between the wall and a stack of storage crates. Panair, dart gun out and ready, faced a bony, brown-bearded man with a hand lamp and a tool belt raised up over his head. Behind him, incongruously, a fire burned in an empty crate. Next to it, an artifact lay on a pallet of blankets, staring at the ceiling. Its mouth moved constantly, but it made no sound, nor was it paying any attention to what was going on around it.

Avir, forgetting dignity and propriety, hurried to the artifact's side. She knelt and unsealed her glove. She touched its skin. It was clammy and goose bumps prickled its dusky surface. Its eyes were glazed over and flickered back and forth, seeing something, but nothing that was in the room. Nal knelt beside her and also touched the artifact. He measured its pulse and fever with his expert hands and his mouth tightened.

"What did you do here?" Avir demanded of the bony man.

"It's hard to explain," he said. "Who in the backwaters are you lot?"

In answer, Ivale removed his helmet. The man saw Ivale's bald head and the neck of his scarlet rappings.

"Vitae," the Unifier croaked. "Jay . . ."

"You will be questioned about him before long," Avir stood. "But first you will explain what has happened to this artifact?"

The Unifier cast about as if he needed to try to identify what she was talking about. "Broken Trail?" he said finally. "I . . ." His gaze slid sideways to the security team. Two stood beside the door. Two more stood on either side of the dome and one had stationed herself beside the open hatchway in the floor. Avir wondered for a moment if the Unifier was going to make some escape gesture. She hoped not. If they had to dart him, it would be hours before they got any information at all.

But he didn't. He just sighed so heavily that his bony shoulders heaved. "It would be easier to show you." He tilted his head to indicate the trapdoor.

"Do so," ordered Avir, and she switched to the Proper tongue. "Bio-tech, tend the artifact. Stabilize her if you can."

"You hold my name," said Nal absently. He was busy fumbling in his tool belt for analysis patches.

Panair climbed down the rope ladder first, followed by one of his Beholden. After a long moment, he shouted, "Clear!"

"Go," Avir said to the Unifier.

With another resigned sigh, he fastened his tool belt around his waist and climbed down the ladder like it was something he'd been doing all his life.

Avir envied his poise as she herself descended. The ladder wriggled and wobbled under her weight. She was very glad to see the Unifier didn't dare to grin at her when she stood beside him. Avir was not surprised to see the string of lights that led down the corridor and glinted off curved walls of translucent silicate that held back drifting shadows.

This was Avir's first chance to see the shadowy containers up close. She leaned toward the wall, pressing her hands against the smooth, cool surface. She watched the blobs that moved with a fluid grace and random pattern. She swallowed hard. It was as if they stood in a vein the Ancestors had sunk into the world and were now surrounded by the blood the Vitae had sworn by for all their centuries.

Ivale and six of the security team descended the ladder, one by one. Panair waited until the last of them were down before he gestured for the Unifier to lead them onward.

The shadowed corridor was one continuous archway extending toward a second drop. The Unifier took them down another rope ladder and down a second corridor toward a brightly lit arch. Shadows drifted silently past them and Avir felt them like a weight sliding across her skin.

The archway opened into a chamber. Avir's gaze slid over the more ordinary ruins—the empty tables and rotted chairs. It caught for a moment on the banks of empty sockets and gleaming stones. Then it swept the room, trying to take in everything at once. She saw tanks of gelatinous matter bulging from the walls. Bundles of capillary-like tubes pressed against the chamber's walls. Blobs and nodules of silicate, all seamless, held viscous liquids that rippled like the shadows in the corridor did. Star-shaped patterns pressed against the skin of what could have been a table. Nerves. The liquid pulsed in the smooth bank of empty sockets against the far wall as if controlled by a heartbeat.

There was no question of it in Avir's mind. This place was alive.

Avir felt her own breathing become shallow. "How big is this place?" she asked, not caring about the hushed tone the Unifier couldn't possibly miss.

"I don't know," he said. "I've mapped out about ten square kilometers' worth of tunnels. Not that it's done that much good." There was a smirk in his voice. "Half the stuff back of the walls and tanks didn't even show up until we'd had the lights on twenty-four hours. And you should see what's down there." He nodded to a second archway.

"Ivale, see what you can find out about this place," she said, already halfway to the other arch and barely aware that the two Security Beholden had closed ranks to follow her.

Avir knew she was letting herself get distracted. Exploration should wait until they had the proper personnel, but she kept right on going. There was no light, except what was at their backs. One of the Beholden raised a hand lamp to light her way.

Ahead, the corridor curved. A burst of red light flashed off the smooth, clear walls. It flashed again, and again. Avir's steps quickened. The footsteps of the Security Beholden echoed as they marched behind her.

She rounded the curve and the pulse of light hit her right in the eyes. Dazzled, she dropped her gaze and raised her hand. She saw the reflection of another flash on her own boots. The shadows under the surface of the corridor roiled as if in response. The intensity of the light faded as her faceplate darkened.

At last, Avir could look up again. She stood less than a meter from a cavernous opening. The corridor came out near its ceiling, but the floor, if existent, was invisible. The far wall was likewise lost in shadow. From darkness to darkness stretched more of the Ancestors' veins. Avir knew they must be enormous, but the cavern around them made them look like silken threads. They crossed each other and spread out again at every angle. It was a geometrician's dream. It was the work of a thousand spiders over a thousand years. The ruby light flashed down the threads like bottled lightning. A single strand flashed on the edge of her line of sight. A dozen lit up right in front of her. Ten meters below, five, now ten, now twenty, horizontal strands pulsed with light and then blacked out all at once. Pulses of light raced up and down the verticals, chasing each other through the network of threads.

Peripherally, she noticed a platform in front of her, obviously made for movement into the vast network. Flat balconies and bubbles that could have enclosed rooms were supported by the threads. This was a complex. People, the Ancestors or the artifacts, traveled into the heart of this gigantic web of light and . . . did what?

"There is yet more work in the heart of the Ancestors. May those hearts be revealed to me. May my eyes see the wonder of the work . . ." It took Avir a moment to realize her voice was reciting the Second Grace. She closed her mouth but her eyes couldn't stop straining to measure and define the impossible wonder spun out in light and glass in front of her.

Then her heart began to thud heavily against her rib cage. It was too much. It was too big and too incomprehensible. As precisely as she could manage, she turned around and shouldered her way between the Security Beholden. The ruby light pulsed and flickered against the corridor's curved walls, each beat raising the level of unreasoned panic inside her. She didn't dare run, but she didn't know how she'd hold herself to a walk.

They were in a hollow world. A hollow world with veins and nerves, and who could know what else. But it lived. She knew that with an utter certainty. Like the artifacts that grubbed on its surface searching for their lost function, it lived.

Avir almost gasped with relief when she crossed the thresholds into the first chamber again.

The Unifier grinned at her. "Something else, isn't it? And I'll tell you what, those lights? They weren't there when we got here. That didn't start up until we got Broken Trail down here."

Avir tried to collect herself, but didn't feel very successful at the attempt. Her mind was full of light and threads. "Explain what you have done."

Apparently ready to accept his prisoner status, the Unifier described the hunt for Stone in the Wall's genetic relatives and how Broken Trail was led to the "control bank" to lay her hand on one of the spheres that still remained in the bank's sockets. He went on to tell about how the lights had switched on in both the chamber and the cavern, and how the artifact had lain in a stupor since then and he wasn't sure she was ever going to come out of it.

Avir didn't realize how chilled her cheeks were until she felt the heat of anger rising in them.

"Do you realize what you have done!" she demanded. "You animal without Lineage!" Her fists clenched. "You played with the work of the Ancestors without even a preliminary test? Without a survey or any kind of analysis! You thought you could just . . ."

"We were in a hurry," he said blandly. "We'd had word your lot was coming down like vengeance on this place for no particular reason, except maybe the people."

Little by little, Avir clamped down on her emotions. This was not just unseemly, it was unacceptable and grossly unproductive. The Unifier had to be questioned thoroughly by experts. The Reclamation Assembly had to be notified of these developments at once. Measures had to be taken to secure the human artifacts, all of them, immediately, from the Imperialist clutches. Teams had to be brought down here as quickly as possible.

All time was gone. It was already too late. The race had started without them and now they could only run to catch up.

I am child of the Lineage. I will not see the work of the Ancestors end at the hands of the Imperialists. I will not.

Now the real work begins.

14—Aboard the U-Kenai, Hour 14:23:45, Ship's Time

"This is the truth. This is what we learned too late. We should not have made them Human. Even a little bit of Humanity was too much."
Fragment from "The Beginning of the Flight", from the Rhudolant Vitae private history Archives

As it turned out, they didn't even feel the collision. There should have been a long, slow, grinding crash, but there wasn't. There should have been the sound of straining metals and ceramics, but there wasn't. One minute the screens were full of filthy ice, the next minute they were black.

Adu felt the smooth surface of the control boards under his hands and for a moment wished Dorias hadn't decided to house him in the android. It was convenient, but it was isolating. If he had been loaded into the ship itself, then he would have been able to know where the hull stresses were as soon as the ice touched the ship. He could have compensated for them instantly and monitored them where compensation wasn't needed yet. He would have known everything, without needing to call up the data, or

turn his head, or wait while his mind processed what his
eyes saw.

Next to him, Eric Born and Arla Stone blinked at the blank
screens.

Eric looked down at Arla in the communications chair.
"Now what?" he asked her.

"Now, we push it toward the Realm. What's supposed to
happen is the heat exhaust melts the ice as we push and we
slide father into the shell. When we get to the Realm, we
head to ground looking like a great, hulking lump of ice."
She frowned. "Did I say that right?" Her hand fell onto her
pouch of stones and she jerked it away.

"I, for one, hope you did," said Adu. "Although what
they'll think when they see a lump of ice going this fast, I
don't know."

"We'll just have to hope the satellites don't think." Eric
stretched his arms over his head until his joints popped.

"They're Vitae satellites," Adu reminded him. "How can
we be sure what they do?"

Eric swung his arms down. "Adu, that's not really helpful."

"My apologies, Sar Born."

Eric nodded and, almost absently, stroked the curve of
Arla's shoulder. "Let us know when we have to strap down,"
he said, and he left the bridge. Arla stood. Her concentration
focused on Adu, but she said nothing. She just followed Eric
Born out of the chamber.

Adu shifted himself to make room for the work being done
inside his skull. Most of the processing right now was actually
being done by the Cam programs. It was able to calculate the
angles and bursts of thrust needed to push them around the
binary, keeping their "tail" angled away from the suns. They
would fly into the system between the satellites, and get just
a little too close to the planet. Its gravity would grab hold
of them and drag them down. Nothing surprising. Nothing
unnatural. Nothing to rise from the ashes and craters.

Adu tried to be content. He tried to draw comfort from the
fact that he would be able to fulfill his parent's first instructions. Down in the Realm of the Nameless Powers he'd be
able to find out the origin of the Vitae's plans.

But there was nothing down there. He tried to tell himself that he'd eventually be able to find an open line, or a satellite transmission, or something that would allow him to get a message through to his parent. As it was, though, the only networks existed in the android body and in the shell of the ship, and the ship would soon be gone, even if its passengers survived.

Survive, yes, but for what? To pace the ground carrying the useless Cam routines around with him, until something was found for him to do? What would it be? There was nothing down there but stone and water and vegetation. He'd checked as soon as they'd entered the system. The only life was the uninterpretable Vitae transmissions, flitting between their ships.

"You will stand by them." Dorias had sunk deep into him. "Eric Born will find a way to get you back out once we know what is happening." A pause. "Do you think I want you lost? You'll be carrying everything I need to know."

The memory was warm and firm and a part of him, but it was still not enough to silence the fear of diving straight into nothingness.

What made it worse was that there was a way out. He'd spotted it. Between the plotting strategies Dorias had poured into him and the equipment list he had read in Cam, he knew how to get out of this android and this shell of a ship.

Cam twitched, suddenly alert on new levels. Adu fastened his attention fully on its activities. The monitors were picking up localized increases in hull temperature, pinpricks of heat. Cam didn't understand. Adu prodded it and opened up part of its memory to remind it they were in a hostile space. Now it had it. The pinpricks were targeting lasers. The Vitae satellites had spotted them.

Adu waited, listening to the comm lines with Cam's ears. There was nothing but unintelligible Vitae noise. The pinpricks stayed where they were, tracking the comet they had become a part of.

Did the satellites think? Were they trying to decide what to do? Had the Vitae in their ships been notified, or was this just standard operating procedure? Track every bit of junk and rock that floated into the system and wait for it to do something stupid?

Adu knew his questions were useless. There wasn't even any way to tell if the satellites themselves were armed. The comet's cloud of crystals and dust made too much interference for the *U-Kenai* to get a detailed picture. The ship could tell where the satellites were, but that was all.

There was nothing Adu could do. The course was laid in and plotted. Changing it under the satellites' gazes would definitely cause an alert to be sent to the Vitae's flesh-and-blood watchers. The *U-Kenai* was built for running away, not for fighting, and halfway buried in ice and dirt, it wasn't going anywhere in a hurry. They were already in the trap. All of them.

Cam wanted to move, to recalibrate the monitors and make sure it was seeing what it thought it was seeing. It wanted to summon Eric Born to the bridge and alert him to the situation and get orders, even if it was just to stay on course, because the situation had changed.

Adu forced Cam to hold still. The trap's lid wasn't closed yet. Nothingness didn't surround him quite yet. He could still get out.

And if he did, what would Dorias do?

Send him back to Eric Born? Impossible. Reabsorb his identity? Perhaps, but then at least he'd be part of something. He wouldn't be alone in the middle of a silent world.

Cam was shoving at him, seeking a way to get to the circuits that ruled the android body. Adu leaned all his weight against it until it stopped struggling.

"Sar Born!" Adu called. "Strap in!"

The monitor on the common room showed the pair of them moving with admirable dispatch. Arla Stone laid herself flat in the lowest alcove and let Eric draw the webbing over her. He closed the catches while explaining how they worked. Then Eric climbed into the second bunk and fastened himself in.

Adu, giving Cam just enough room so that it could stay alert for any changes in the ship's monitors, moved the android.

The *U-Kenai*'s emergency beacon, once retrieved from its

storage hatch beneath the bridge's deck, proved to be an old unit that had been only peripherally kept in repair. When Adu had been required to set it up in dock at 'Abassyd Station, he had siphoned its specifications from Cam. The beacon was supposed to carry warnings or distress messages from a ship. It had an extraordinary amount of redundant memory and it could travel long distances, albeit slowly. It could take him back to where there would be voices he could hear and room to stretch out. In the meantime, there would be a little spare room in there, where he could keep himself busy by building his own tools. In a year or three or five, he would be found and his box would be opened and he'd go on from there.

The pinpricks still hung on the ship's skin. The transmissions from the satellites had picked up slightly, but they hadn't changed direction, and the satellites themselves hadn't moved. They watched closely, but they just watched.

So far.

Cam's main processes huddled in the corner where Adu had left them. Adu encompassed Cam and pried into its insides. He heightened its perception of the task at hand; to get the *U-Kenai* safely down, unseen, if possible. Cam thought more slowly than Adu, and had less capacity for memory, but it knew the ship and had years of experience stored in itself. The ship could still maneuver a little, and it could still brake a little. The comet ice packed around its skin would absorb the extra heat of the accelerated re-entry and Cam could surely steer it more accurately than Adu, because it had special subroutines for flying under reduced capacity. It would all be enough, with a little added urgency. Adu had to make sure it would be enough, because there was every chance he would contact Dorias again. Dorias would know Adu had defied him, but at least he wouldn't be able to say his child had done it carelessly.

Besides, Adu carried copies of everything Eric had learned from the Vitae datastores. Dorias wanted them back.

That is my real purpose. Not sending myself into emptiness.

Cam did not try to duck out as Adu laid the new orders in. Accepting orders was part of what Cam was carefully designed to do. When Adu was satisfied that the first thing Cam would do when left to its own devices was launch the beacon, he let it retreat to its corner.

The beacon would trail along behind the ship in the "comet's" tail as just another piece of junk until the final descent began. Then it would break free and fly off on its own, like at least two dozen other pieces of rock would be doing at that point.

The monitors registered a rise in temperature from three of the pinpricks. Adu froze. The temperature leveled off. Maybe it was only a fluctuation. Maybe some lensing had been caused by the ice coating the ship's side. There was no way to tell.

Adu opened a hatch on the beacon. Then he flicked back the cover for the hardwire jack on the android's wrist. He plugged the biggest unused cable on the bridge between the two sockets. He made the android glance at the monitor again. Eric and Arla lay in their alcoves with their gazes fastened on the view wall, trying to see what was happening, and doubtlessly wondering how long it would be before they landed.

Cam will get them down, Adu told himself as he reached down the new opening that the cable provided. *It will. They don't need me. Not down there in the emptiness.*

Carefully, he eased himself into the beacon.

Arla knew the ship was performing a delicate dance, skirting around the edge of the Servant's Eyes, but it felt like nothing at all. To her, the *U-Kenai* was standing still while the universe churned around it. Light bent into bows and knots. It was like watching fireworks recorded through a distorting lens. It was silent, and beautiful, and utterly strange. Arla wanted to touch the backs of her hands in salute to the Nameless and the Servant, but the webbing held her hands down. She just hoped her thoughts would count and that there was somebody watching closely enough to acknowledge them.

All at once the morass of color and darkness was gone. The bare back of the Realm filled the screen.

"Too low," gasped Eric. "Adu! Too low!"

Arla forced herself to keep her eyes open. *If I'm going to die, I'm at least going to see it coming.*

Rock filled the screen, silver and black, pitted, gouged, bare. Bells and chimes, mechanical shrieks filled the air and the light flashed wildly.

It's the World's Wall. Nameless Powers Preserve me. We're going to hit the World's Wall!

The ship rolled sideways and a scream cut loose from Arla's throat. They were upright in the next breath, she had time to be embarrassed, then to realize that she was alive to be embarrassed, and then to realize she hadn't made the only noise.

Outside the ship blurred beige, brown, and green. Total darkness hit. Dim light returned and the screen flickered back to life. Green chaos swallowed up everything else and a sharp jolt bounced her up and down until the webbing creaked in protest.

They stopped and stayed still, doing nothing but breathe.

After a while, Arla was able to notice that the room was crooked. She lay with her knees pointed toward the ceiling and her left ear pressed against the side of the alcove. A single alarm bell rang tiredly for a few more seconds before it hushed itself from exhaustion.

"We're here," said Eric in a hollow voice.

"We're home." Arla fumbled with the catches and shoved the webbing aside. She planted her feet carefully on the tilted floor, resting her hand against the wall for balance. The dim lights threw a half dozen hazy shadows of her across the room.

Eric was on his feet a split second after her, trudging up the slope toward the bridge.

"Adu!" he called. "Are you all right?"

There was no answer.

"Adu?" Eric stumbled forward before his feet found purchase on the sloping floor. Arla followed Eric onto the bridge. They entered the cabin, but Adu didn't even look up.

"Adu?" said Eric again. The android stayed motionless, hands on the control boards, seemingly oblivious to the drunken angle of its chair.

Then Eric said "Cam?"

The android turned its head. "Yes, Sar?"

Eric swallowed hard. "What's happened to Adu?"

"He's left us," Arla said. "Run away."

"That's insane," snapped Eric. "Dorias would never have . . ."

Arla laid her hand against the threshold for balance. "That . . . person was not Dorias, and he was scared to death of coming here. Even more scared than you, I think." She eyed the blank monitors. "I also think, Eric, we had better get out of here and see where we are."

But Eric was not moving. "Cam," he said again, "what is the disposition of the process Adudorias?"

"Adudorias transferred to *U-Kenai* emergency beacon. The beacon was launched fifteen-four-ten, ship's time."

For a moment, Arla thought Eric was going to fall over. *He was counting on that creature*, she realized. *As long as Adu was around there was a touchstone to the outside, a tangible chance he might find a way out again. Now he's as stuck as* . . . A new beeping piped up from the control boards, and another joined it as the alarms began to recover from their own shock. *As this ship of his.*

"If I may presume." She laid her hand on his forearm. "I think we are not safe in here."

Eric looked at her for a moment like he didn't understand what she said. Then he lurched towards the airlock. "Cam. Come outside."

The android got up and obediently teetered after its master. Eric palmed the reader on the airlock, and nothing happened. He cursed through clenched teeth and undid a latch beside the door. A small compartment came open and he pulled a lever down. "Cam. Manual release procedures. Go."

The android gripped a pair of handles on the airlock's inner door and pulled. Reluctantly, the door gave way and Cam dragged it up the slope of the floor and latched it into place. A draft of warm air caressed Arla.

Eric and Cam repeated their actions for the outer door. His hands seemed inordinately clumsy as he worked the controls. Arla felt her patience strain.

Try to remember, it's been ten years for him, Arla told herself, *and he never wanted to come back.*

The outer door opened and air rushed in, warm, rich, thick air.

Acrid, black, smoke and a billow of heat came with it. Arla coughed harshly. She couldn't see anything except a curving wall of smoking ash. She undid her head cloth and pressed a strip of material over her mouth before she started out the door.

"Wait. . ." started Eric.

She ignored him. She felt as though she had walked into a furnace. Coughing despite her makeshift face mask, Arla waded up the ashy slope, waving her free hand both to keep her balance and to keep her bare hand from touching the burned ground.

Finally, she scrambled onto a patch of unburned, white sand. Forgetting pride altogether, Arla dropped onto her knees. A fresh wind caught her right cheek and Arla breathed deeply. When her lungs cleared of the stinging smoke, she stood up and looked around to see what part of the world they had come to rest in. Joints and head seemed to sigh with relief. The world wrapped around her like a blanket.

They'd come down on the shore of the Dead Sea. Whitened sand crunched under the sole of Arla's boots and the distinctive tang of salt filled the air. Shading her eyes with her hand, she squinted toward the waterline. Fingers of steam rose from the surface. A gust of wind blew hard, sending a long, shimmering ripple across the mineral green surface of the water. No waves broke. Aside from the lichens clinging to the rocks, nothing grew. The lifeless water sprawled out a good eight or nine miles to either side, where it reached the bases of cliffs so white with salt rime that they showed even through the mists. Arla tilted her gaze to the tops but couldn't make out any buildings.

Well, that's something anyway. If we'd come down on the First City shore, we'd probably be dead.

Arla turned her attention inland. The white sand beach turned to stone-peppered dunes about ten yards away from them. She scanned the distant walls, searching for familiar shapes. The salty wind was free of rain and the clouds were solid overhead. That was something else. The last thing they needed right now was rough weather, but she had no idea when sunshowing had been or which wall the light was slanting over. Her orientation was gone. Without a prominent mark, they were solidly lost.

There was the Pinnacle, though, marking Red Walls. She gauged its size compared to the lower walls. They were close to the lowlands, then. She turned. The closest wall to her left glinted gold in the light. Broken Canyon. There was the gentle ripple of ground rising toward the cleft of Narroways road.

Arla felt herself smile. All they had to do was follow the shoreline to the Eel Back River. The river would lead them into the Lif marsh. Once inside the Lif, help and, maybe, family couldn't be more than a few hours away.

"Whoever landed us had excellent aim," she said, bringing her gaze back down to Eric.

Eric was staring at his ship. It lolled in the crater its impact had made. Its nose was buried in a wall of ash and smoking coals. Water seeped into the depression it made. Behind it a trail of ash and seared sand added its steam to the hazy air. The *U-Kenai*'s wings were streaked with black, pitted by tiny craters and scarred with long grooves. Then she saw that the *U-Kenai*'s whole smooth skin was scarred. Seams of white foam ran in jagged lines around its back and sides. It looked like the ship had been declared Notouch and marked accordingly.

Eric stood like a statue beside his ruined ship. He stared at it. His cheeks were wet and the look on his face was one of fear.

Arla wished she knew something to say. She remembered the Bad Night, when her father had hauled her and her sisters bodily off their mats before the mudslide washed their house down to the Dead Sea. She remembered the boiling, grinding roar and the horror as her home was torn to pieces by the mindless force. Security and sense washed away with it.

She wished she could tell him about that, but her mind wouldn't hand across the words. It just kept bringing up pictures of Storm Water and Little Eye. Her children were maybe a day away. Maybe only hours, and maybe she hadn't been gone that long. Maybe Nail had waited for her. Maybe she was still his wife and could still call her children her own. Maybe Eric would understand that what had happened on the ship could not take the place of her being mother to her children.

The strength of that wish made her suck in a breath and Eric must have heard. He tore his gaze away from the hulk of the *U-Kenai* and swept it across the Walls.

"You know where we are? I've lost all my geography."

You lie, Eric. You're staring straight at the route to First City.

She didn't say that either. "We're on the Narroways side of the Dead Sea. That means the Lif marshes are only a few hours off. There'll be people about. Notouch," she added, waiting for his reaction.

He looked down at his naked hands. "Well, it should be an interesting time, considering that I'm as bare as a two-day-old baby."

"It may be for the best," Arla said. "It'll mean less outcry, especially if we can find my people. My mother is a force in the clan." She laughed once. "Some say she's a force of nature."

"I can believe that." There was a trace of humor in his voice, but none in his face. He was looking at his ship again.

"We'd better get going, Eric," she said as gently as she could manage. "Is it not true that if the Vitae come looking for us, they'll head straight for the *U-Kenai*?"

"Yes," he said hoarsely. "Cam. Stabilize the ship's condition as much as possible. Repair the comm lines and monitor transmissions. And"—he ran his hand through his hair—"wait until you hear from me."

"Yes, Sar," said the android. Its feet made swishing noises in the damp sand as it climbed back into the crater and aboard the fallen *U-Kenai* and released the catch holding the outer door back.

The door slid down and clanged shut.

Eric turned quickly away. "I'm ready."

"Very well." Arla checked her pouch of stones to see that

it was firmly knotted. She glanced at the walls again to pick
her direction. "Let's go."

Side by side they tramped up the beach. They passed salt-
crusted hollows filled with miniature versions of the sea.
Nothing else broke up the landscape between the dunes and
the waterline until Arla heard the faint gurgle of a running
river.

Smiling with quiet satisfaction, she angled her path inland
until they climbed over a stony dune. On the other side, the
Eel Back ran swift and shallow into the Dead Sea. Its winding
path cut a swath through the dunes and would, Arla knew,
open into the sprawl of the Lif marshes.

She glanced over at Eric, who hadn't said a word since
they'd started. She'd been content to let him be quiet, thinking
he needed time to adjust to the fact that he had returned. Now
she saw that his eyes seemed to be sunken, looking inside
rather than out.

He's closed himself up as far as he can, she thought.

She touched his arm wordlessly and he gripped her hand.
For a moment they stood like that. He didn't even look at
her, he just took what strength she had to give. Did he know
that her heart was wringing inside her? She did not want to
be divorced, she did not want to lose her children, and yet
she did not want to leave him.

At last, he let her go and she was able to shove her torn
emotions down under a layer of practical considerations. She
led him down the dune to the side of the Eel Back and they
started walking in silence again.

With the influx of fresh water that the river provided, the
landscape changed drastically. Before an hour had passed,
they were wading through a mix of brown reeds and knee-
high grass. When they stopped to share a packet of ration
squares, they were able to rest in the shade of a cluster of
Crooker trees. Arla gauged the spread of the river and the
slant of the land.

"Past the next rise, we'll hit the marshes," she said, more
to see if Eric would answer her than because she thought he
needed her to tell him that. "Wish I knew how far into the
season it was. We could be hitting Late Summer. The squatters

shift around. Still, where there's fishing"—she nodded toward the river, now a broad, sluggish swath of green water between the reeds—"there'll be a clan."

"Arla." Eric spoke her name toward the river. "What did you mean when you said there would be less outcry from the Notouch because I had no hand marks?"

Arla felt her mouth twist. She searched for the words to explain.

"Since Narroways started making deals with the Skymen, the Teachers and the Royals have gotten . . . scared. They got this idea into their heads that the Skymen and the Heretics were using the Notouch to run their messages, hide them in the marshes, get them supplies and information, and the like. It's true, of course, but they were paying for all of it with food and cloth, some coinage. We'll do anything for pay, everybody knows that . . ." She bit her tongue.

It's the air. Breathe the old comfortable air and get back the old comfortable thoughts.

"So," she went on, keeping her gaze on the way in front of her, "as the law says, what one Notouch does, all Notouch are responsible for. The Teachers have been laying down that law and exacting flesh-and-blood fines from us. It's made us wary. Almost nobody will go out of their way to do a Teacher a service now. Especially around Narroways.

"It's also true that around Narroways a Teacher or an upper rank might . . . become lost in a night storm more easily than in other places."

Eric said nothing and this time Arla felt no urge to break the silence. She just got to her feet and started walking again.

It turned out she'd read the landscape right. They topped the final hill and saw the vast, bowllike valley that held the Lif marshes. Arla had heard it speculated that, except for the Dead Sea, this was the largest stretch of open ground in the Realm. Even here, though, she could see the dark, comforting bulk of the World's Wall on every side.

She sighted on a cluster of Crooker trees. They'd need walking sticks for finding solid ground. She wished she still had her knife, or an ax would have been even better. However, there should be deadwood that hadn't floated off yet.

She picked up a stick and handed it across to Eric.

"Thank you," he said, and Arla decided that would be enough for now.

The day must have been a fairly dry one. Green flies and splinter-chasers glided low over the ponds. The earth under the grasses only squished a little. Arla smiled. One thing about the Skymen you had to like—their boots kept a person's feet good and dry.

They continued on. Eric seemed to be having trouble with his footing. He splashed and stumbled along behind her. Arla made herself ignore him. She had a feeling he would not welcome too much attention right now. Maybe it was nothing more complex than his having gotten used to the unnaturally straight and even flooring the Skymen had. Maybe it had nothing to do with the shattered look she had seen when she handed him the walking stick. But then, even before he'd left, he couldn't have done much stomping about in raw marsh. The Nobles were used to cobbled roads and wagons and ox-backs. Well, he'd have to get used to this. They wouldn't be within reach of such luxuries for a while.

Her harsh thoughts startled her a bit. Something was slipping from her. She was a Notouch again, low as she could be. As soon as they hit company, she'd have to fall back into the endless bent-back playacting and wheedling language. She realized she did not want Eric to see her like that.

Despite her gloomy thoughts, part of her could not help but relax. The air was warm enough. Her head sat firmly on her shoulders and her eyes could see clearly without burning in harsh, bare lights. She was using her own legs to get somewhere and, even better, she knew where she was going.

She started whistling.

In a couple of days, she might even see Reed and Trail again, and Mother.

What's she going to think of what I've done? I haven't got any idea. And my children? Her breath caught. *Except, I've surely been divorced and so they won't be my children and Nail in the Beam won't be . . . there.* She shoved the thought aside. *Maybe not. Maybe he'll have held out. Even if he didn't,*

I know it must make sense. With what I'm doing what kind of wife could I be? She glanced at Eric.

I know my children are my children and they know it, too, and the Teachers' law can go drown itself. She shook her head ruefully. *Right back into it, aren't I? Keep on like this and I might as well have never left at all.*

Eric tripped, splashed, and swore.

"Use your stick," she prompted. "Swing it in front of you, watch the ground. We may have a long way to go." She looked for the slant of the shadows. There was maybe half the day left. "And we need to do some serious traveling unless you want to spend the night in a tree."

"Arla?"

"Hmm?" She cocked one eye toward him. He had stopped dead. Brown-tipped reeds waved around his knees. A small hillock of muck rose at his feet. Arla looked again. It wasn't muck. It was a shoulder, and a head.

"Nameless Powers preserve . . ." Arla moved closer. The corpse lay facedown in a pool. It was pale and bloated with water and had been picked at by eels. She swallowed her gorge and laid her hand over her mouth, grateful for once for Lif's ever-present smell. It covered the corpse stench.

It was a woman, she decided. A Bondless tattoo still showed against her greying hands. Eric, showing no signs of nausea, crouched beside the body. Arla was surprised for a moment, then remembered as a Teacher he had surely dealt with his share of unpleasant corpses. He braced himself and levered the body over onto its back. It splashed into the water and Arla got a look at the face. She gasped.

"Do you know her?" asked Eric.

Arla nodded. "She's a Skyman. She's . . . her name is Cor. She's the one who took me to . . . who . . ." She swallowed hard again. "What did the Servant's Eyes see here?" she whispered.

"I don't know." Eric fingered the waterlogged pouch at Cor's waist. He gave an experimental yank. The cord snapped and he stood up. "It happened at least a day ago, whatever it was." He tore the mouth of the pouch open and shook it.

Several coins fell into his palm, along with a translator disk, and a polished piece of pinkish quartz.

Arla's chest tightened like she'd been hit. She snatched the quartz up. It was a long, ragged chip, carved and polished until it looked like a fat lightning bolt the length of her little finger.

"Trail," she croaked.

"What?" Eric asked.

"This is my sister's namestone. My sister, Broken Trail." She stared at the corpse and the horror inside her redoubled. "Eric, what was she doing with my sister's namestone!"

She was shaking. She couldn't help it. The Notouch did not let go of their namestones. Not until they were dead or, at the very least, dying.

Eric laid his hands on on her shoulders. "We won't know until we find your clan, Arla," said Eric. "She can tell us nothing."

"You're right, you're right," Arla pressed her empty palm against her forehead. "Of course you're right." She gripped the stone and pressed her fist against her own pouch, forcing the shaking in her limbs to stop. *I've been gone too long. Servant forgive, Powers preserve, I never, ever should have left!*

"Arla," said Eric again, "could . . . could the Notouch have done this?" He turned her so she could look at him without having to see the body.

Arla shook her head. "No. If we'd killed her, the body would have been properly sunken, and no one would have left Trail's namestone with her."

He moved closer to her, and suddenly, she was very aware of his touch. His power-gifted hands, his chest, his arms, his concerned, confused face, all close to her. Too close.

This shouldn't be, this shouldn't be, cried out a part of her. Not with Trail's namestone in her hand and the Lif marshes all around them. They were back. He shouldn't be touching her. She shouldn't be touched. She pulled away and something inside her cried out as she did.

His hands fell to his sides and they stood there, doing

nothing but stare at each other for a moment, both knowing too well they were back under the World's Wall.

He picked his stick up again. "Let's get where we're going. I don't think either of us is carrying what we need to sleep in the trees."

Arla took the lead and they kept on going.

Finally, Arla spotted a smooth, stout stick of wood sticking straight up out of the middle of a pond. A scrap of dirty cloth fluttered in the wind.

"Trap marker," she said, pointing it out to Eric. "That's what I've been looking for. All we have to do is wait here. Somebody'll be along to check the catch before dark." She surveyed the sky again. It was still smooth and even. "We might even stay dry until we get under cover, for a wonder."

She swung herself up onto the bent trunk of the Crooker tree and tucked her hands under her poncho, getting ready to wait.

Eric began poking the ground restlessly with his stick. Insects rose in tiny clouds around his knees and ankles. Arla watched, absurdly glad for the distance between them.

The reeds rustled and bent. From between the thickest trees glided a light raft, steered by a boy with a pole. Arla jumped to the ground and raised both hands high in the air.

"Oy-ai! Hello, Little Brother!"

The boy's head jerked up and the pole came all the way out of the water.

"Aunt Stone?" he cried, and she knew the voice.

"Iron Keeper!" She clapped her hands together over her head. "Little Nephew! Come show your aunt your face, boy!"

Iron Keeper poled forward so furiously, he almost upset his raft. He leapt ashore and ran up to her. He pummeled her on the back and shoulders, friendly, greeting blows as she held his face in both hands.

"Garismit's Eyes! You've grown a foot and a half! Tell your aunt, quick, how long has she been gone?"

"My aunt doesn't know?"

"It's been a strange journey, Nephew. You'll hear all about it later. Now, speak up or your aunt will have you across her knee." She let him go and stepped back. "And then you tell me what you're doing fishing all the way out here."

"You . . . left six months ago, on the Turn Day. The Skymen came. We had to move out. We're staying with the Rising Water . . ." His gaze drifted across to Eric, who turned his face away. She noticed he was now wearing gloves.

"He's a Skyman, Nephew," Arla told him. "His name is Eric Born. You call him Sar Born. He's helped your aunt and he's here to help more. There's a lot in the wind, Nephew." She smiled. "Including nighttime. What say you, will Aunt Stone be welcomed by her old clan in their new homes?"

"Iron Keeper says it'll be so!" He grinned all over his little boy face. "He'll take you there in a good hurry." He glanced to the water. The raft was four yards away and drifting farther yet in the marsh's unseen current. "As soon as he catches his raft."

The boy scampered off and Arla suppressed a laugh. "This is good. I hadn't thought to find my family for another couple of days, at least."

"Thank you for giving me good welcome among your people," said Eric softly.

"And what else was I to do?" Arla kept her attention on Iron Keeper as he waded hip deep in the pond to retrieve the raft he clean forgot to anchor. He hopped up on its back and poled it toward them.

"I don't know," said Eric before Iron Keeper came back within earshot. "I really don't."

They didn't say another word as they clambered aboard the raft.

Iron Keeper was a good hand with the pole, if a little slow. Arla let the boy keep charge. It was his raft, after all, and the last thing she needed to do right now was tread on anybody's pride, even if it was only her half-grown nephew. His assurances of the tone of her welcome were very nice to have, and she was sure Reed had a place at the hearth for her and a loaf to spare, fairly sure anyway. Although Reed might be out in the city, since it was late summer. Well, Reed's husband, Iron Keeper's father, would do in her place. And Mother should still acknowledge her as long as Arla still had the stones in her hands.

But there were other people in the clan, and who knew what the Skymen and the Teachers had done before the clan had moved out here?

Who knew what they'd done to her children. To her hus . . . to Nail in the Beam. Iron Keeper didn't seem sad or upset, which meant . . . she laid her hand across her pouch. It meant no one might know yet about Trail.

She stopped herself from asking him to hurry it along.

Iron Keeper kept stealing glances at Eric, who stood in the middle of the raft with his hands shoved firmly into his pockets.

"Stop staring, Nephew," Arla said lightly. "He's not going to fly away with you watching him."

Iron Keeper blushed. "Iron didn't mean . . . he meant, I, umm . . . No disrespect, Sar Born."

Eric nodded gravely. "None seen, Young Man. None seen."

Garismit's Eyes, he's remembered two or three of his manners anyway.

They drifted through groves of Crookers and Droopers and straight-backed evergreens until finally they came out into a channel that had been chopped clear of reeds and saplings. Cabins on supports of bamboo poles squatted above the channel, and everywhere were faces she knew.

"Oy-ai!" called Iron Keeper. "Father!"

Iron Shaper, the smith and clay-baker and the most important man in the clan looked up from his makeshift hearth. Arla raised her hands so he could see her marks. Here was the test. If Iron Shaper didn't even welcome her . . .

"Sister!" he bellowed, dropping his tongs into the coals and leaping to his feet.

Arla was on the shore almost before Keeper brought the raft to a halt. Her brother-in-law gathered her up into his ropy smith's arms and swung her around. "Knew you'd be back! Told the wife, I did. Knew it!"

The world was full of voices, friendly slaps, and her name. Stone in the Wall. Stone in the Wall! Arla. Auntie. Little sister. Hands to clasp, and faces, and laughter. Home, all of it home.

She barely even noticed the ones who stayed in the shadows and the doorways and just watched her.

Then came the special name.

"Mother!"

Arla spun and all at once her arms were full of children. Storm Water, big and burly as an ox for his age, like his father. Roof Beam, wiry little bundle, and tough Hill Shadow and beautiful, beautiful Aienai-Arla. Little Eye. The daughter she'd been afraid she'd never bear, stood strong and solid on her little round legs.

"My own!" She kissed them and hugged them over and over. "Oh, my own! My own!"

"Stone in the Wall."

Arla looked up and knew what she'd see.

Nail in the Beam. Nameless Powers preserve me. Arla swallowed. So many memories came with seeing his square face and thick, work-toughened body. They'd grown up side by side. There'd been no surprise at all when her parents had marched her to the Temple to meet him and his parents there. He'd built their house, she'd built their stove and laid out their mats. They'd fought over this thing and that, when she'd been home. They'd even blackened each other's eyes, but he'd cradled her head through seven births and listened in silence when she told him what truth she knew about the namestones. He'd had other women, and she'd had other men, but the children had all been his, no matter what the Teacher had said.

"You said you might not be back." His voice hadn't changed. It grumbled like thunder in the distance.

"I was wrong. Nothing new in that, you'd say, I know."

"If you weren't always speaking for me, I would."

They stared at each other. Arla found her throat had closed up tight.

Her silence made Nail shift his weight. "Your place is elsewhere than my home. Your blood will be no more part of mine."

The words of divorce and disinheritance.

"It's better this way." She said it. She knew it was true, but for a long, aching moment, she wished it wasn't.

"These are my wife's children," he said.

Oh, no. It's only been six months . . . "Who?" she croaked.

"Branch in the River."

Of course. She bowed her head. After her family and the smith's, Branch was the loudest voice in the village. Nail wasn't one to give up rank if he could help it.

"No!" howled Little Eye, clutching Arla's pant leg. "Mother!"

No! Arla wanted to howl, too. *These are mine!* But Nail had stayed while she had gone. She had broken the law, been cursed by the Teachers, committed heresy, oh, her list of crimes was a long one. She had lost the right to her children before she had even gone over the World's Wall.

Better this way. There was still so much to do. She couldn't stay here. She couldn't be their mother. Couldn't ever be. She'd known that when she left. Known that for a long time.

"Come home, children," said Nail. His voice didn't change. It was level and grumbling, like nothing was ever quite good enough. Nameless Powers, how that endless discontented note had driven her so crazy, even after she'd learned to read it like the signs in the weather.

She could read it now. What he really meant to say was that he also wished it wasn't better this way.

"No!" wailed Little Eye.

"Shush." Arla laid a hand on her daughter's . . . Branch's daughter's shoulder. "Your father is right," she said. "Go home now, all of you, or do you want to look like a bunch of disobedient oxen in front of everybody? Go on."

One by one, they left her side, and the comfort of coming home left with them. Storm Water kept his steady gaze on her the whole time while he scooped Little Eye into his arms easily. Nail put his back to her and marshaled them all through the houses and the weeds until she couldn't see them anymore.

"Everyone knows whose children they are," said Shaper at her side.

"They are Nail in the Beam's and Branch in the River's," she answered him. "Which house is my mother's, Shaper? She's sure to have heard the ruckus."

"She's with Cups and Torch." He pointed toward one of
the cabins farther up the rise.

"You'll want to see her alone." Eric's voice almost jumped
her out of her skin. She'd forgotten he was there at all.

"Shaper, this is Eric Born. Eric to you. He's a Skyman
and I'm vouchsafing him. Give him a spot by the fire, will
you?" She spread her hands and her voice wobbled. "I've
got nowhere to welcome him to."

"You're welcome, Skyman, in my sister's name, my wife's,
and mine." Shaper held out his hand. Eric stared at the scars
for a moment and then shook it. Shaper glanced at Eric's
gloves, and then at Arla.

"He's embarrassed, Shaper. Skymen have no hand marks,
and he think's it'll wound his dignity if everyone sees him
naked as a baby." She was tired, something inside her ached
horribly, and she still had to face Mother. "Just take care of
him, will you?"

She pressed through the bamboo until the cabin came into
sight. It was no different from the others with its wicker walls,
thatch roof, clay chinking, and bamboo legs. In the doorway
hunched her mother, Eyes Above the Walls. She was wrinkled,
mostly blind, and bent in as many different ways as a Crooker
tree. She could barely walk without help. The joke among
the clan was that the Nameless Powers had forgotten her name
and couldn't call her away to die, so she just lived on.

"Hello, Mother." Arla crouched down beside the stoop.

"Thought I heard your voice," Eyes Above said. Her own
voice creaked like tree branches in the wind. "Well?"

"I . . . well, what, Mother?"

"Are they still with you?" she said impatiently.

"Yes." *I should have known.*

Eyes Above leaned forward eagerly. "And still answer you?
Still alive in your hands, are they?"

"Yes."

She let out a long sigh. "Then welcome home, Daughter."

Relief washed over Arla. She gripped her mother's wrinkled
hands and felt the strength that was still in them as Eyes
Above squeezed her in greeting. "I wasn't sure . . ."

"Well, you should have been." Eyes Above let go of her

hand. "As long as the stones stay alive for you, then you are working the will of the Nameless, no matter what the Teachers say. The stones would not permit themselves to be used for the Aunorante Sangh. And as long as you serve the Nameless, you are my daughter."

Arla shook her head. Eyes Above's faith was as solid as the World's Wall and as all encompassing. There was no shaking it or getting around it. Even if Arla had the words to explain all the new things she had learned about the nature of the Realm and the Nameless, Mother would just become selectively idiotic. She might hear, she might even comprehend, but it would all roll off her like water off oiled skin.

"The Aunorante Sangh have come, Daughter," Eyes Above said. "They are masquerading as the Nameless and the fools in the upper ranks and the Temples are falling at their feet."

Arla listened with growing horror as her mother described the arrival of the Rhudolant Vitae.

"Nameless Powers preserve me," Arla whispered. "I didn't think they'd come down like that. I thought they'd be taken for the Aunorante Sangh." Her tired shoulders slumped. "I didn't think we'd have to take on the Temples and First City with them!"

Eyes Above patted her hand. "Now then, Daughter, it's never too late. We only need to wait for the Nameless to send their Servant to us, as they did to our ancestress."

Arla bit her lip and debated about whether to speak the thought she'd kept from Eric. It wouldn't actually be lying. Mother saw everything in terms of the Words anyway, and it was absurdly appropriate.

Besides, in the bizarre twisted logic of this time, when the Words were turning into reality, it might even be true.

But may the Servant forbid he ever find out that I said it.

"Mother, your daughter thinks they already have." As best she could, she explained about Eric Born.

Mother drank it all in, rearranged it to suit, and nodded. "Yes. Yes. It is so. Well then, you must be guided by him."

Well, I don't know if I'll go that far.

Then Arla bowed her head and rubbed the backs of her hands.

"Mother," she said. "What . . . where's Trail?"

"I sent her to the Skymen," Mother told her. "We were hoping she could find you." Her blind eyes gazed across the marsh. "She will not be pleased that you came home before she did."

Arla fumbled with the mouth of her pouch and, trembling, pressed Trail's namestone into her mother's hand. Eyes Above ran her fingers around the edges and, with each motion, the lines in her face deepened a little farther.

In halting phrases, Arla told her how they had found it.

"Stone in the Wall *dena* Arla Born of the Black Wall," said Mother. "I lay on you this charge. You will find out how your sister lost her name."

"Mother . . . I don't know if I can . . ."

"You will," Eyes Above said firmly. "I must know whether I can still call Broken Trail *dena* Rift in the Clouds my daughter."

"Mother!" cried Arla. "Trail is probably dead! Our home is being invaded by Skymen who want to use our children, our CHILDREN, as experiments or livestock and all you care about is did Trail hold to the Words when they killed her!"

"You speak as if this was a small thing. Does my daughter doubt her place?"

Yes! Yes, I doubt! I've seen beyond the World's Wall! I've heard the words of the Skymen! There's so much else out there! It can't matter that much how Trail died! It can't!

"No, Mother." Arla stood up and climbed down the ladder. "Your daughter does not doubt."

"My daughter should get some rest for herself," said Mother. "She is weary from her service, and more will be required of her."

"Yes, Mother."

Arla turned away and shouldered her way through the bamboo, so lost in thought, she didn't even see the form that blocked her path.

"Stone in the Wall."

She looked up automatically. Branch in the River stood foursquare on the path in front of her, folding her skinny arms across her bosom and glowering.

"Good greeting, Cousin," said Arla wearily. *Please get out of my way, woman. I don't have any patience left.*

"I have no greeting for you," Branch said darkly. "How dare you try to claim my children? And in front of the clan? I should have your namestones and your head for this insult!"

Arla turned her face away. "I have tried to claim nothing. Ask anyone."

"Then why do my children cry that their real mother has returned?" Branch shouted. "You are not their mother! You are childless and without husband! You are nothing! I am the wife of Nail in the Beam and the mother of four living children! You would be thief of mine! You will give me apology! You will do it now, in daylight!"

Arla's hand cracked across Branch's cheek before she could even think to stop it.

"You dare call me thief!" Arla cried. "You are the one who stole from me! Stole my husband, stole my children! You barren, useless, bloodless . . ." She couldn't see. She couldn't think. Anger roared through her mind blocking out everything else. Let the whole clan hear, she didn't care. "You are unfit to have even a Notouch's scars on your cold hands!"

Arla marched past Branch, blundering through the Crookers, blind as her mother. She fell against the corner of a house and slid into the mud.

A man's hands caught her. She still couldn't see, but with a shock, she recognized the touch. Eric Born raised her to her feet. "Come on, Arla," he said in the Skymen's own language. "You've gone too far today."

No, her mind whispered. *I haven't gone anywhere near far enough.*

Branch watched the Skyman and Iron Shaper lead Stone in the Wall away. Her cheek stung painfully from the blow.

There was no end to the woman's heresy. Her family held a set of shiny baubles to which they had no right, and so all the clan bowed and scraped to them as if they were Kings. Branch had married Nail in the Beam in front of the Teachers and the Nameless, and all four of the children had become her own blood, but still people whispered behind her back and gave ground grudgingly when she spoke. She was the mother of four children! Four healthy children! But because she didn't hold those pretty stones, because she was not Arla Born of the Black Wall with her heresies and her idiocies, she was not heeded.

Now the Skymen had taken over Narroways and the Nameless only knew what they would do next. Surely they'd come to claim their own. Who knew what damage this woman, this heretic, could do if she were allowed to remain here, ruling over her bamboo and clay city? Who knew what it would mean to the children?

But if she were returned to her masters, they might be grateful. They might even be lenient. They were the power now, until the Nameless came. Branch touched the backs of her hands. There was less risk with Stone in the Wall in their hands than there was with her among the clan. Less risk to the children, certainly.

Branch drew the laces on her poncho closed and sighted along the Walls toward Narroways.

The Skymen will take Stone in the Wall away again, and this time they will not give her back. This time my children will remain my children.

15—Section five, Division one, The Home Ground, Hour 09:15:25, Planet Time

"It may be that we do not live to see the end of this, and it may be we should pity our children who do."
Fragment from "The Beginning of the Flight," from the Rhudolant Vitae private history Archives

"Coming up on Division One," said Security Chief Panair from his station at the transport's controls.

Avir felt an unexpected surge of relief at the announcement. They could not be more than twenty minutes from the base. When they arrived, she would be able to report what they had found under the Unifier dome to the Assembly and get orders on what to do with their prisoner. She'd also be able to get out of her pressure suit. Her helmet and gloves lay on the seat beside her, but the suit itself had been designed more for protection and efficiency than comfort. She had to remind herself that she could not squirm in front of even Ivale, let alone the Unifier. The Security Beholden all remained sealed and helmeted. She had no idea how they stood it. Probably professional discipline combined with the fact that Chief

Panair was there to watch them. She could imagine the three Beholden left behind to guard the Unifier base stripping off their helmets and rubbing their necks vigorously.

Bio-tech Nal did not show any sign of having heard Panair. Avir suspected that, like her, he was fighting unaccustomed fatigue. It had been fifteen hours since either of them had slept, but Nal would not leave the artifact in the transport's emergency support capsule without his trained supervision. Avir herself would not be seen to have less diligence or endurance than one of her Beholden.

"Act at all times as if there were a Witness with you," her Assembly representative had told her. "There are not enough to cover all the landing sites, but new ones are being assigned as we speak."

So Avir sat bolt upright in the rear set of seats watching Nal transfer the readings from the artifact's capsule into a portable terminal. Broken Trail struggled randomly against the restraints. Nal had decided against sedating it. Its delusional state was obviously so deep, he said, that it could not be further panicked by confinement to the capsule. He appeared to be correct. Every few minutes its head would twitch to one side, as if it had just seen a glimpse of something, and sometimes its hand would strain to reach out, but it made no concentrated effort to remove the oxygen mask or to dislodge the needles pressing into its arms. Consequently, the Bio-tech spent the journey gathering valuable baseline data on the artifact's physiological attributes.

CRASH!

The noise hit the roof and the transport swayed. Avir's shoulder banged against a locker and she clutched the seat's arms with both hands.

"Attack readiness!" called Panair.

The front window showed the passage between the major buildings blocked by a pile of stones and broken beams. The Security Beholden pulled back their seating restraints and opened the lockers in the transport.

Artifacts surmounted the pile of debris, whirling slings over their heads. A dozen stones hit the transport window and didn't even crack the silicate.

CRASH!

The transport rocked again. Avir realized that the artifacts must have managed to rig some sort of catapult on one of the roofs.

The Unifier grinned. "Well, somebody's not happy with you," he said to no one in particular.

The engine's hum deepened its pitch and Panair plowed it into the debris. The garbage cracked and snapped under the tires and, for a moment, the transport balked.

"Artifacts closing!" called out Panair's second-in-command.

Avir could hear the artifacts yelling. Muffled thumps from stones or clubs battered the transport's side. The seat's arms dug into her palms as she clenched them tight.

Panair set up another drive sequence. The wheels churned for a moment, but something snapped underneath the floor and the transport lurched to the left. Nal swore aloud.

"Systems check shows the left rear axle broken," reported the First Beholden. "Autorepair is not . . . "

The engine's hum died.

"Blood of my ancestors," Nal lifted his head. "They must have a telekinetic out there."

Avir's heart jumped up to the base of her throat.

Panair glanced at her. "Contractor, you hold my name, but I need it back to get us to base."

Avir inclined her head once. Ivale lost his Ambassadorial composure long enough to suck in an audible breath.

"Kul, Marthanat, Janaich, Hanath" said Panair. "Clear the perimeter. Oan, you and I will start repairs."

The first two Beholden slung tanks about the size of an oxygen pack on their shoulders and checked the nozzled hoses to make sure they were properly attached. The second two unloaded a tripod-mounted laser and its batteries. Avir opened her mouth and closed it again. She hadn't known that had been issued the team. Unlike the contents of the tanks, it was a lethal weapon and would damage the artifacts, but she had already given Panair back his name and could not rescind the order.

Through the window Avir saw Silver on the Clouds. The

King artifact rode her oxen to the rear of the attacking mob. Silver's mouth opened and closed rapidly, but it was too far away for the intercom to pick up what she said. Evidently she still wielded enough power that the artifacts would follow her lead against their true masters. Avir wondered for a moment what was making her own heart beat so hard. Then she realized it was nothing more nor less than fear.

The artifacts charged the transport. Blows from stones, or clubs, or fists made it shudder on its remaining axles. The shouts grew louder, crowding against each other to get through the intercom.

Panair and his second seemed to ignore them. They left their stations and lifted the rear seats out of their racks. The Beholden in charge of Unifier Lu ushered him to the rear of the transport without a word. Oan opened the repair hatches and stepped back to let Panair plunge both hands up to his elbows into the workings of the undercarriage.

The perimeter team opened the left-side door and charged out in a solid formation. Startled, the artifacts fell back, giving the Beholden enough time to raise their weapons and fire.

Greenish brown foam spewed out, too thick for even the Home Ground's wind to carry away. It hit a row of artifacts, who reeled backward, clawing frantically at the stuff. Targeted oxen bellowed plaintively and fell to the ground, causing their riders to jump free or be crushed as the beasts rolled onto their backs and sides.

The foam had been developed for riot control for client governments. It would not harm the artifacts, but it itched and stank abominably. The artifacts the foam missed fell back, shouting. The affected ones ran, or stumbled, away, breaking ranks without heeding any cries from their comrades or their King.

CRASH!

A boulder landed in the middle of the security team. The debris collapsed under them and the transport slid down the pile, rolling Avir into Ivale and Nal and pitching them all against the walls. Outside, the Beholden had scattered. One scrambled to his feet, but the other two lay still, bleeding heavily, perhaps dead. A host of artifacts lay with them. The intercom filled with their screaming.

Avir's throat closed.

"The Aunorante Sangh are not all dead after all," murmured Ivale in the Proper tongue so the Unifier couldn't understand.

"Target the catapult," said Panair into his intercom. "Lethal force."

New noises crowded through the intercom. Beyond the debris a troop of Ivale's "security force" clashed with Silver on the Cloud's followers. The Security Beholden used the transport as cover and aimed the laser at a location Avir couldn't see. The light was visible as the Beholden fired and the artifacts screamed again. Some tried to run. Some pressed closer to the transport and got caught in a fresh gout of foam. More stones flew from distant slings. The Beholden swung the laser toward a new target and fired again.

The engine's hum cut through the cabin.

"Recall!" shouted Panair as he dived for the driver's chair. "Seats!"

Avir realized the order was meant for the passengers. She staggered toward the nearest upright seat and dropped herself into it. The door opened and two of the Beholden all but fell inside. The door closed and the transport righted itself. The tires ground against the debris and the transport lurched forward into the melee. Artifacts scattered left and right to get out of its way. More stones thumped and cracked against its sides. Silver on the Clouds waved her club at them as they barreled past, her face flushed and distorted in anger.

She'd try again, Avir knew it. She was Aunorante Sangh.

How many others like her are mixed among the artifacts? Weariness pressed against her mind. *There's no way to tell. Nal can take them all apart gene by gene, and there still probably won't be any way to tell.*

And we've based themselves in their midst. The fear inside Avir redoubled. She tried to be ashamed of it, but she couldn't. Being afraid made too much sense right now.

"Are we receiving from base?" she asked Panair.

"Still receiving, Contractor," he replied. "The situation there is secure."

They approached their half-converted base. It looked calm. The shuttle still hung on the tether, glowing like the captive star it was designed to imitate. Only a few artifacts populated its steps and they scattered into the nearby buildings as the transport drove into the plaza.

As soon as Panair brought them to a halt, Avir jumped to her feet and hit the door control. She remembered her helmet and gloves lay on the floor of the transport somewhere, but did not stop to collect them. She strode down the transport ramp and up the base steps. Ivale followed behind her, collecting more data for his unfavorable report of her activities. She didn't care. There was no time to waste.

She had believed the artifacts to be merely lost and confused. For some of them that was doubtlessly true, and those, the true work of the Ancestors, had to be preserved. But some of them were the shameful blood, and those had to be eliminated, and all their progeny with them.

Avir headed straight for the comm terminal. Behind her, the remainder of the security team carried the support capsule containing Broken Trail across to Nal's station and set it beside the empty holding tank. The Unifier was marched in, too, and he gaped at the bustling Vitae and huddled artifacts.

Avir decided she could ignore him for a moment. She needed direction. She needed reassurance. She needed to tell someone that the Aunorante Sangh were alive and well and that the war that had ended in the Ancestors' Flight had been joined again.

Beside the primary comm terminal sat the backup unit. It was internally powered and small enough to be carried by one person. Avir picked it up in both hands and headed for the rear of the Temple, trying not to care if anyone's gaze followed her.

Beyond the main chamber were the living quarters and the kitchen. They were little more than alcoves blocked from a central foyer by more of the rough-woven blankets. In the middle of the foyer, though, a stone staircase had been built down into the earth. Avir took the stairs carefully. They were unevenly worn from years of feet descending this way.

The cellars here were not the work of the Ancestors, but

they were the result of some astoundingly careful work by the artifacts. The flagstone and plaster were all tightly sealed, creating a row of chambers that were dark and cold, but dry. Each one had a wooden door shut with a surprisingly complex iron lock.

The chambers were full of books. Some were obscure convoluted texts of what passed for religion or history among the artifacts, but most of them were lists upon lists of genealogies. For all the artifacts had forgotten, they had never lost the fact that they had been bred for their functions. Even the rebellion of the Aunorante Sangh had not been able to wipe out the artifacts' need to keep their creator's work as intact as possible.

Lights had been fastened to the ceiling and their glow thinned the shadows on the reddish stone walls to grey ghosts. The only sound was the soft murmuring of the team's Historian in one of the rear cellars as he catalogued what he had found.

Avir picked an empty chamber and shut herself inside with the ancient books. She wedged the comm terminal on a shelf and stood in front of it. For a moment, she just enjoyed the silence and the familiar intimacy of solid walls.

She could have done this up above, but it was easier to think down here, and she had no idea what the Assembly was going to say to her.

Avir opened a line to the Assembly's waiting terminals. Every comm line into the chambers was answered by a Witness now that the Reclamation had begun. No word between the teams on the Home Ground and the Assembly would be lost.

"Good Morning and also Good Day, Contractor Avir," said the Witness when the screen cleared. The image was good, if distant. She could see the glint of her own reflection in his camera eye.

"I have a first level emergency situation," said Avir. "I must speak to the Assembly immediately."

The Witness stiffened and relaxed so fast, that for a moment Avir was certain it was her imagination.

No, I startled him.

She had just enough time to see his hand move across his own board before the image shifted.

The Reclamation Assembly looked small and unreal on the flat screen. She had stood before the Assembly hundreds of times, but she had always been surrounded by accurate projections in the Assembly Chamber of the Hundredth Core. Even the Witnesses with their cameras trained on the screen she spoke through looked ridiculously far away.

"You have declared an emergency, Contractor Avir," said the Moderator. "The Assembly is awaiting the details."

Avir didn't even try to compose herself as she gave what could only loosely be called a report. She wanted the assembled representatives up there in the encampment to know about the screams, and the anger of their artifacts, and the Vitae blood that had been spilled. She wanted them to understand the scale of the miracles that they stood on top of.

When she ran out of words, she received nothing but silence from the Assembly. She was glad of it, because it was a signal that she had gotten through to them.

Finally, one representative, a Senior Engineer with smooth mahogany skin and long hair that was the same color as her sepia robes, signaled for time. A red light appeared above her as the Moderator granted her request.

"Does the Contractor have a recommendation for a course of action in the light of these events?" asked the representative.

"I do, Representative," said Avir slowly, "but it is not a pleasant one."

"What is it?" the Moderator prompted her.

"Moderator," said Avir, "we deliberately chose to begin the Reclamation of the human-derived artifacts by mimicking the authority example that their social groupings had created to deal with the lack of the Ancestors' direction. The authority example they have created, the "Nameless Powers," is all-encompassing and all-powerful and is recorded in their mutated oral history as forcibly removing sources of rebellion."

The attention of the Assembly was so focused that Avir could begin to feel it in her spine. It strengthened her, exhausted as she was, and it reminded her who she was. Her voice fell into properly smooth cadences.

"It is, therefore, my thought that if we wish to continue to make use of this authority example, we need to remove the rebellion. All of it.

"We need to remove the city."

Now there was noise. Representatives muttered into their own intercoms or shuffled keys on their own boards, trying to call up data to support or strike down what she had just suggested. Avir waited for the flurry to pass, just as she had waited all the other times.

A Historian signaled for time and was acknowledged by the Moderator.

"How many artifacts are in the city Narroways?" he asked.

"Approximately four thousand," Avir said promptly. Despite her knowledge that this was right and the war had to be waged before the Aunorante Sangh gained real power, a cold wind blew through her mind.

"Out of a total population of?"

"Four million."

Avir knew she had probably just announced the death of Narroways and of four thousand precious artifacts. Part of her wanted to erase her words. For a split second, she thought about telling the Moderator she had reconsidered. Four thousand pieces of the Ancestors' work was too high a price to pay just to eliminate what might only be a hundred Aunorante Sangh.

It was out of proportion and she knew it. The Reclamation had to continue. They had to secure the majority of the human-derived artifacts quickly so that they could be interfaced once more with the living heart of the Home Ground. That was more important than the safety of a few human-derived constructs milling around with their fearful eyes following her every move, with their distorting anger recreating the Aunorante Sangh, who had risen against the Ancestors and stolen the world away, with the blood and the screams and the stones . . .

Avir swayed on her feet and felt the blood surging in her

veins. In that same moment, years of careful training made
her realize she was not done with her report yet.

"Moderator?" said Avir.

"Contractor?" The Moderator activated her acknowledgment signal.

"I would like to put in a request to the Assembly."

"So Witnessed." The signal turned green to mark the
recording. "Proceed, Contractor."

"I would like to formally request transfer of my duties to
the unpopulated portion of the Home Ground. If I could be
allowed to choose my assignment, I would like to help coordinate the mapping and analysis of the underground complex.
I would further like to suggest . . . " She paused, searching
for words. "I would like to suggest that contact between
Vitae and the artifacts be limited as much as possible to the
Ambassadors who are accustomed to dealing with Outsiders."

Another silence emanated from the Committee.

"Are you advising us of psychological difficulties with
your assignment, Contractor?" asked the Moderator.

"Yes, Moderator," Avir said and the confession lifted a
weight from her shoulders. "I am." *Fear, hatred, blood,
screams. Yes, those are indeed psychological difficulties.*

"Thank you for so doing." The Moderator made a small
obeisance in tribute to a difficult job well done. "You will
submit a full report to the Related Stresses subcommittee.
You will return to the Hundredth Core while your reassign-
ment request is reviewed. I will say now that your request is
reasonable and shall be referred to your immediate representatives."

"Thank you, Moderator."

"Orders regarding the transport of the sample artifact you
have obtained and the decisions based on your report will be
transmitted at the end of this session," said the Moderator.

Avir made obeisance to the screen and the line closed down.

She stared at the blank screen for a moment. She remembered standing in Chapel and picturing the Home Ground and
the Reclamation. In her mind's eye she had seen a green and
beautiful world holding its breath for the return of the Lineage.
She had seen herself working tirelessly, with the Graces sing-

ing in her mind and delight in every task flowing through her heart.

Maybe it will be more like I imagined when I return, she thought wistfully. *Maybe.*

"Mother?"

Arla stirred on her sleeping mat. "Go back to sleep, Little Eye."

"Please, Mother." A tiny hand shook her shoulder.

Arla peeled her eyes open to see her daughter crouched over her, anxiety filling her round face. She reached out to rub Little Eye's cheek, and all the events of her life came flooding back to her.

Arla sat bolt upright. Daylight streamed through the door blanket. Eric still lay asleep under his own blanket, but the other mats were empty. They'd been left to sleep the day away.

"Little Eye, what are you doing here!" Arla did not bother to keep her voice down. Eric groaned and rolled over, opening both eyes unhappily.

"Storm Water's gone," sniffled Little Eye. "He didn't come home last night. Roof Beam swears he doesn't know where he is and your daughter got scared and . . . and . . . " Little Eye burst into tears. "The Skymen got him! Little Eye knows they did!"

Without stopping to think, Arla swept Little Eye into her arms, crooning in wordless reassurance. Little Eye buried her face against Arla's neck and howled. Eric was staring at her. Arla got to her feet, holding her daughter against her chest, and shouldered her way past the blanket into the front room. The fire on the hearthstone had been carefully banked so that the coals were barely visible. Past the front doorway's hanging, the shadows slanted toward the center of the marsh, pointing the route to the Dead Sea. It was past midmorning then. The clan was awake, well into the tasks of the day— scraping hides, cleaning eels, chopping reeds, and all the other endless mending, maintaining, digging, and scratching that kept the clan alive.

"Come on, Little Eye." Arla set the girl on her own feet. "Take me to your father."

Little Eye made a great show of stifling her tears and she trotted through the clusters of workers with a child's dexterity and single-mindedness. Arla followed Little Eye, barely aware that Eric was following her, too.

They found Nail hip deep in pond water, tossing reeds up onto the shore with a wooden pitchfork. Roof Beam and Hill Shadow combed through the glistening piles, chopping off the edible roots and spreading the stalks to dry on the ground. Later they'd be worked into mats and baskets, and even roofing.

Arla's sons looked up immediately as she and Little Eye made their way to the pond's edge, but Nail did not. He tossed another forkful of reeds onto the shore with a grunt, and then impaled the fork securely on dry ground. Then he looked up, first at his sons, then at his daughter, then at Arla.

"Well?" he asked.

"Our . . . " Arla checked herself. "Your daughter came to me in tears saying her brother has disappeared. What is going on, Nail in the Beam?"

Nail sloshed through the reeds and green-scummed water until he reached the shore. "The whereabouts of my family is not your concern," he muttered, wringing out the hem of his tunic.

"But it should be yours," Arla folded her arms. "Or your wife's. Where is the righteous Branch in the River, Nail?" She spoke with more bitterness than she intended, but the woman's insults still rang in her ears.

"Arla," Eric came close enough behind her that Arla could feel his breath against her neck. "You don't need . . . "

"Come out! Come out!" Iron Shaper's voice called out in time with the clanging of a stick on a gong. "Come out! Come out!"

"Nameless Powers preserve me," Arla whispered. Nail in the Beam was already headed toward the noise at a run, trailing his sons in his shadow.

"What is it?" demanded Eric.

"The emergency call." Arla snatched up Little Eye in her arms and ran after Nail.

"Come out! Come out!" Iron Shaper beat the gong furiously.

Most of the clan was already in the center of the huts by the time Arla got there. Eyes Above, leaning on Iron Keeper's arm, pushed her way toward Shaper. Arla set Little Eye beside her brothers and forced her way through the crowd. The ones who knew her gave way, clearing enough of a path for her to see Iron Shaper clearly.

The smith wasn't alone. Storm Water sat on the ground beside him, holding his arm tenderly. His head was bare and Arla saw a clumsy black bandage under his fingers. A fresh stream of scarlet trickled down his arm.

"What happened to you?" Arla crouched beside Storm Water. She removed his hand from the bandage. He let it drop into his lap and winced as she unwrapped the bandage and revealed a long, ugly gouge in his skin.

"Someone get me some hot water!" she shouted. The wound was caked with old blood, and it looked deep. Storm Water was pale under his eyes and around his mouth

"Branch in the River left the clan yesterday." Storm Water's voice was low and hoarse, as though he hadn't had enough to drink for a while. "Storm Water followed her. She went to a troop of soldiers from Narroways. She's bringing them here. Storm Water thinks there's a Skyman with them." He paused and swallowed hard. "A soldier did this to Storm Water as he ran back here."

"Nameless Powers preserve me," said someone.

The crowd was stirring. Some of them were retreating, but Arla barely noticed. She was trying to think of where to get a clean bandage and a needle and thread and . . .

Eric knelt beside her. "Let me," he said quietly, and he took Storm Water's arm out of her hands. "How far away are they?" he asked as he gently probed the edges of the wound with the fingers of his free hand.

"Two hours, maybe less." Eric touched a scab and Storm Water grunted.

"All right, Storm Water. You've done well. Hold still now."

He laid his hand over the wound and Arla realized what he was going to do under the eyes of the whole clan.

Storm Water gasped and stiffened. Arla grabbed his shoulders and held him still. Eric's breathing grew hard and ragged. He lifted his hand away and there was nothing on Storm Water's arm except some dried blood and a thin white line marking where the wound had been.

Eric slumped backward.

"You're a TEACHER?" cried Iron Shaper incredulously.

Arla let go of Storm Water's shoulders and stood up in front of the smith. "I vouchsafed him Iron Shaper *dena* Voice of the Wind, and I will not hear one word said against him." She raised her voice so the entire clan could hear. "Not one word."

"And there is no time for it," said Nail in the Beam flatly. "We must get ready to move. We have two hours at best."

Arla looked up at him, intending to say something scathing, but the look on his face made her stop. He was already punishing himself for again finding a wife who would betray the clan for her own purposes.

His words worked like magic. The crowd of men and children and the handful of women streamed toward the houses.

"Wait, wait." Eric climbed to his feet, but Teacher or not, no one paused to listen to him. "We don't even know what they're doing," he said somewhat helplessly to Arla and Iron Shaper. "Did you hear?" he asked Storm Water.

Storm Water nodded. "They are looking for the family of Stone in the Wall," he said, knotting his bloodstained headcloth between his hands.

"The stones," breathed Arla. "Nameless Powers preserve me, they must want the stones."

"I don't think so," said Eric. "I think they want your genes."

"Either way"—Arla gripped her son's hand and raised him to his feet—"we need to show them our retreating backsides. There's places in the Lif that the upper ranks couldn't find, even if someone showed them where to look. We can wait this out."

"You'd just run?" Eric was genuinely shocked.

"We fight, Eric, and all of our own will pay for it." Arla squeezed Storm Water's hand. "It'll be bad enough as it is. And it's my fault."

"Yes, it is," snapped Iron Shaper. "And you'll be hearing plenty about it from me later. But now we must get ready. Keeper," he called as he stalked off toward the forge with his son.

"Arla," said Eric urgently in the Skyman tongue, "we can't just run from this. We need to find out what these soldiers know about what's going on in the cities."

She bit her lip and forced herself to think. The part of her that was still a Notouch and would never be anything else said run, get away, get out of here. The part of her that formulated enough rebellion and heresy to take her over the World's Wall shouted against a retreat, especially now that they had drawn her family's blood, first her sister's, now her son's. Storm Water was watching her with a young man's anger in his eyes. She wasn't sure how to answer that.

"We need to find out who's hounding us, at the very least, and what side they're on," she said at last. "Maybe we can talk some sense to them. They won't listen to Notouch." Her gaze strayed to Eric's hands. "As a Teacher, you could . . . "

Eric snorted. "A Teacher and a Seablade talk down soldiers from the Heretic city? Not likely."

She curled her free hand around her pouch of stones. "We cannot fight them. It's been tried. The costs are . . . too much."

"This is not some harvest rebellion we're talking about here," he reminded her needlessly. "This is the Vitae, or the Unifiers, and it's for the entire world. If we lose, it doesn't matter. If we win, then it will be remembered that the Notouch helped, and no one will blame you for anything."

Arla gave him a pained look. "Which shows what you know." She sighed. "But you're right. I'll talk to my mother. She'll go along with it." *Just don't ask me why I'm so sure*, Arla pleaded silently. "That will take care of the Seniors," she went on. "I know all the clan malcontents. We should be able to put together something. It might even be something useful." She let go of Storm Water's hand.

"Especially since whoever's coming from Narroways doesn't expect a fight," Eric added.

"Would you expect one?" she arched her eyebrows.

"I can't say. After all, what do I know?" He turned his face away.

Arla reached one hand toward him. "We can't be self-pitying now, Eric. We're about to start a war."

"I don't think so, Arla," he said, turning around so she could see the tired smile on his face. "If anything, I think we're about to finish one."

A hole broke between the clouds, dropping a broad beam of sunshine onto the huts. Arla dipped her eyes automatically and had to forcibly stop herself from beginning the Chant of Thanks for Another Day.

The oldest and the youngest of the clan were loading themselves onto the rafts and pushing off for the deeper marsh. Everyone else had set to work with a speed and decision that, she could tell, disconcerted Eric. He had expected a few knives to be sharpened, not kettles of boiling water and fat set out on fires. He hadn't expected to see the men tightening up slings that could take down a wild dog or do serious damage to a human being, or to see the women running whetstones over sickles for harvesting rice.

He hadn't expected the Notouch to know exactly how much damage they could do.

"We've had to fight before," Arla told him. "Every now and again, you get a band of rovers that decides it's tired and knows no one cares what goes on out here. We don't keep the land we tame by running away from that kind."

A shrill whistle sounded over the noise of the wind and the babble of voices. The soldiers were coming. Arla took her place, busily stirring the kettle of fat.

See, she thought toward the coming band. *There's nothing unusual here. Just tallow we need to waterproof door blankets and ponchos.*

Around her, men and women were cooking, or washing, or harvesting more reeds. There was nothing unusual to be seen anywhere, unless some sharp eye noticed that the tiniest children were all somehow invisible.

The soldiers came in on bald-legged oxen. Arla counted fast as she dropped to her knees and raised her hands in homage to the higher ranks. A dozen of them. Narroways Heretics, by the clothes. They were armed with swords and clubs and shields, but they didn't look particularly alert. She noted that Branch in the River had had the sense to keep herself out of their ranks. She was probably lurking behind them somewhere, wondering if her absence from the clan had been noticed.

Arla raised her eyes a little and caught her breath. A Skyman rode in the ranks. She recognized him. He'd been the one who sank the needle into her arm when Cor had taken her to their shelter. She glanced involuntarily toward Shaper's steps, where Eric had taken up his position.

He was not there.

Arla had no time to curse.

"We are looking for the family of Stone in the Wall," said the troop's leader. He was a big man with Nobility's swirls on his hands. Green and scarlet. Arla faced one of the rulers of Narroways.

Well, she thought with a mix of satisfaction and sourness, *let's see how astute this Lord of Narroways actually is.*

"My lord, forgive this despised one. She can say only that they are not here. When Stone in the Wall was cursed as a Heretic by the Teachers, the Nameless Powers preserve them all, we hurled that tainted blood from our clan. If they live yet, this despised one doesn't know where or how."

The totally expected happened next, which was why Arla had insisted on being the one to deliver the bad news.

The Lord of Narroways took a foot out of his stirrup and aimed a kick at her head. She covered, ducked, and rolled backward, but the blow set her ears ringing anyway.

"Don't lie to me, Notouch!" he bellowed. "Where are they!"

"My lord?" said a voice. "If I may?"

That was a surprise. Arla took great pains to blink stupidly as she heard the sounds of someone dismounting. A shadow bent over her. She felt the weight in the air as the entire clan stood silent in the face of this startling gentleness.

"Stone in the Wall's family is in no danger." She heard the accent under the voice and she saw the blue-and-white swirls against sun-browned skin as the Skyman's hands reached to help her up. Arla shrank back under her poncho hood.

"We come as the Servant of the Nameless came to their ancestors," he went on. "To get help."

How dare you . . . Arla forgot to keep her eyes down.

"Got you, Stone in the Wall." The Skyman hauled her to her feet.

In that second, the clan poured out of their doorways and the fight was on.

The Notouch hefted the kettles and sickles. Arla tore her sling off her belt and whirled it over her head. She brought it across the Skyman's temple while the Narroways lord was still fumbling for his sword. She whirled it again and took down the soldier unlucky enough to get in her way. Then she had to start ducking and running. The noise of metal on metal, and the screams of battle surrounded her. Eric appeared out of nowhere, dragging soldiers off the oxen and throwing them to the ground. Out of the corner of her eye, she saw him haul off one in Teacher's robes, dragging him back toward the huts.

What's he doing? She had barely time for the thought before she was nose to nose with another of the soldiers and had more important things to deal with.

It probably didn't last that long. Arla lost track. All she knew for sure was that there came a moment when she looked wildly around her and the only people standing were also of the clan.

A flash of brown and black darted out from a thicket of bamboo. Without even stopping to think, Arla took off at a run. Her quarry ran like an expert, dodging the worst of the mire and ducking low tree branches without breaking stride. A Notouch poncho and headcloth flapped behind them. Arla realized whom she must be chasing and adrenaline and anger gave her an extra burst of speed. She launched herself forward and threw all her weight against her quarry. With a "whoof!" of lost breath they both hit the marshy ground.

Branch in the River rolled over and swung her fist out. Arla scuttled backward and snatched her sling off her belt as they both scrambled to their feet. For a moment, they did nothing but stare at each other. Then Arla swung her arm slowly backward.

"You try to run and I will drop you like a dog before you get thirty feet," she said.

"Do it, then." Branch in the River gulped air and wiped soil off her face. "You want me dead anyway."

"Oh, no." Arla shook her head. "I want you alive. I want you to face the clan with all of them knowing who brought the soldiers and the Skyman down on us. You can either walk back or be dragged back. It's your choice."

Branch glanced toward the open marsh and back toward Arla. Arla locked her elbow and held still, even though her arm was beginning to feel the strain. The adrenaline rush was leaving her and a slow trembling was taking hold of her limbs. If Branch did try to run, Arla wasn't sure she could stop her.

With more dignity than Arla really wanted to see, Branch lifted her chin and began walking back toward the huts. Arla followed warily, her sling still in her hand.

Although the fight was over, the clan was still engaged in a flurry of activity. Several of them had picked up swords and were making sure no soldier would rise from the ground again. Others clustered around the oxen and the supply sledge, laying claim to the spoils of battle.

A shout went up as Branch in the River stepped into the clan's view and Arla heard the distinctive whistle of a sling being swung. Before she could do anything, Nail in the Beam broke through the shifting crowd. A blanket of silence dropped across the clan. Arla's breath caught in her throat.

Nail in the Beam stood directly in front of his second wife.

"Go home." His voice was little more than a hoarse whisper. "And know that I am glad my children have already been sent away."

"I did what was right," said Branch loud enough for every ear to hear her. "I will answer any who challenge it."

"You will answer." Nail's hands were trembling. "I just hope we will not have to answer with you. Go home."

Branch, chin still held high, walked a straight line through the crowd and the clan returned to its grim work. Arla turned away, suddenly weary beyond belief.

"Mother?" Storm Water laid his hand on her arm.

"Your mother is all right," Arla said, although she was not certain she spoke the truth. She squeezed his hand firmly and straightened her shoulders. "What's happened to the Skyman?"

"He is fallen here." Storm Water led her to the prostrate Skyman on the edge of the pond.

He was sprawled on his back. Arla laid her hands against his chest to feel for his breathing. It was ragged, but strong. He had a bruise from her sling, but was probably all right. Iron Shaper made his way through the crowd to them. He had a captured sword in his fist and he raised it over the Skyman's head.

Arla held up her hand. "This one we keep. He'll be able to tell us what's going on."

The smith grunted. "We need to sink the bodies."

"Go ahead. Storm Water, go help unload the sledge." Storm Water stayed where he was until she gave him a long, stern look. Then he ducked his head and trotted toward the gathering around the soldier's supply sledge.

Awkwardly, Arla hefted the Skyman across her shoulders. He was deadweight and she was tired. She staggered into Shaper's house and dropped him into a heap on the floor.

Eric stood by the fire circle with a burly man in Teacher's clothing.

"Stone in the Wall *dena* Arla Born of the Black Wall," Eric said, "this is my brother by marriage, Heart of the Seablade." He spoke evenly. "He's a Heretic, too, and he'd better understand something." Eric's stare could have set the walls on fire, the heat of the anger behind it was so intense. "If he tries to play any sneaking games this time, I'll kill him with my own hands."

16—The Lif Marshies, the Realm of the Nameless Powers, Afternoon

"May the universe be merciful and keep from me the truth about my ancestors."

Tiac Hsi Chai, from "Genealogies"

*E*ric stared at his brother-in-law. "And then what?"

"And then I accepted Jay's advice that we try to find the family of this Stone in the Wall."

Eric and Arla sat beside Iron Shaper's fire, between Heart, the Skyman Jay, and the door. Shaper himself was outside with the rest of the clan, hopefully telling the rest of the clan to keep away while Eric and Arla "questioned" the Teacher and the Skyman.

It didn't take much looking to see that the Notouch clan was getting nervous. Sunken corpses were one thing. Live witnesses to treason and heresy were quite another. Arla had pointed out, in her usual blunt style, that if the clan had too much time to think about what they had just done, it would not go well for the ones who had urged the attack. Eric believed her.

So he tried to remain quiet while Heart told him the story of the war between Narroways and First City, of his dealings with "Messenger of the Skymen," and, finally, of the delegation to Narroways and the attack that came with it and how he had elected to go with the Heretics rather than stay with the delegation.

Yes, with them you had at least a chance of survival, thought Eric disgustedly. "So where is Mind of the Seablade?" he asked.

Heart hung his head. "I don't know. I wish I did."

"Do you?" *You did this,* his thoughts howled. *This is your fault. If you had not driven me over the World's Wall the Vitae would not be here now!* He tried to shove the thoughts aside, but they would not move.

He knew Heart was aware of his anger, like someone might be aware of a knife near his throat. He didn't care. At the moment, that awareness, like the sufferance of the Notouch, was exactly what was needed. If nothing else, it would make him think twice before telling lies.

"Look, Born," said Jay, leaning forward. "Surely you can see we've got to save the family quarrels for later . . ."

"We, Skyman?" Arla folded her arms. "What family do you have here?"

"All right, all right," Jay held up his hands. "I am not going to pretend this has been anything but a total debacle and the body count can be laid across our table. But my throwing myself at your feet isn't going to do anything." His hands lowered slowly and Eric could see sparks from the fire gleaming in his pale eyes. "We do, however, have something that might."

He started describing the underground chamber with its control banks of stones. Eric watched Arla more than he did Jay as the Skyman talked. She raised herself slowly on her haunches, straining toward what he said, little by little, until Jay came to the part of the story where Broken Trail entered.

Arla froze. "What have you done with Broken Trail?"

Jay picked up a piece of charcoal and tossed it into the fire. "I wish I could tell you. We let her touch one of the spheres . . . the stones, and she went into a delirium. She was still in it when I left . . ."

"You left her there?" Arla's hand curled into a fist. Eric reached out and covered her clenched hand with his own. Heart started and drew away. So did Arla.

"I had to," said Jay. "We didn't leave her alone. Our base coordinator, Lu, is with her. Cor was supposed to come find her family . . . I don't know what happened to her. She should have been here days ago."

"She was," said Arla. "Or at least, she was in a village near here. Now she's dead."

The expression bled slowly out of Jay's face. "What . . ."

"We don't know," said Arla. "We found her in the swamp. She had my sister's namestone with her."

"She was carrying that so she could find your family. She . . ." Jay left the sentence unfinished. He held his face perfectly still. For a moment, Eric thought he was simply holding back his grief, which was natural, but there was something more to it than that, something Eric couldn't decipher. A spasm of distrust ran through him.

"You see what things have come to?" said Jay. "We need to put an end to this now."

"We need"—Arla raised her eyes and Eric saw a dangerous glint behind them that even a few days ago he would not have recognized—"to get my sister out of that place of yours."

"I couldn't agree more," said Jay soberly. "But we also need to get you down there. You've been trained to use your stones. You wouldn't be overwhelmed by . . . whatever they activated."

"We hope," said Heart to Jay with surprising gravity. "The apocrypha point to it. But in case she fails we also need to get to First City. We need to rouse the Temple and the First King against these . . ."

"Vitae," supplied Arla. Heart continued to look at Eric.

"Vitae," said Jay. "Come now, Heart, there's no time for old prejudices here either."

Heart bowed his head like a student before his master. "Of course, you're right, Messenger."

Eric felt his stomach lurch and the distrust redoubled. *Who*

*is this Skyman who's gotten my Heretic brother-in-law so
cowed?*

To Eric's surprise, Arla just suppressed a smile. "My Lord
Heart of the Seablade will be pleased to know that this
despised one agrees with him. The intervention of First City
would buy valuable time." Heart snorted and opened his
mouth, but Arla ignored him. She turned to the Skyman and
switched back to level-eye language. "Jay, you and I could
go to my sister and your complex while Eric and my Lord
Teacher Heart go to First City and . . ."

"No," said Eric flatly.

Arla blinked. "Well, surely you don't think the First
Teacher would listen to this despised one?"

"And he will listen to me?" Eric held up his hand, palm
out and wiggled his fingers at her. "I must be the biggest
Heretic the Realm has ever known. At least you kept your
hand marks. What kind of welcome do you think I'm going
to get in the Temple?"

"Your father will hear you," said Heart. "And he will
require First Teacher Signed to Still Water to do the same."

"You fool!" Eric leapt to his feet. "You blood-crossed
fool! You've been used for years and finally sent to die and
you still think you know what my father will do!"

"Eric." Arla looked up at him and there was genuine concern on her face. "I hate to agree with him, but we have to
try it." She spoke in Standard. Eric was very aware that Jay
was watching them both closely. "We need all the help we
can get," she said. "Even from the high-house fools."

Eric looked away from her. He looked at the wicker walls
with the crumbling wisps of moss poking out of the mud
chinking. He looked at the roof. Beams and trimmed poles
supported thatch and shadows. He looked at the flickering
fire on its flat, brown stone.

She was right. He did not want her to be, because that
meant Heart was also right. Worse, it meant he had to go
back and stand in front of Father again, and tell him . . . tell
him what? He wouldn't care about ten years of heresy and
impossibility, as long as Eric could tell him how to drive the

Vitae into submission. If Eric could tell him that, anything would be forgiven.

The problem was, that was the one thing Eric could not tell him. That meant that Father'd try to exact a price, for Eric's daring to abandon his family, for daring to question the designs of the Seablade House. Father and Mother both would demand that Eric show he was of use, and they were experts at putting people to use.

He did not miss the fact that they hadn't just sent out Heart to die. They'd sent Mind as well, because to send her husband without her would have looked strange. It might have endangered whatever plan they were birthing.

Ten years gone and it wasn't enough. Eric folded his arms against a chill that was entirely inside him. He tried to think of another reason why this was impossible, but he couldn't.

"The Servant sees this deed," he said to the fire. "It cannot be denied."

"Thank you," said Jay. Arla just nodded in silent approval.

"You've some sense in you yet," said Heart.

Anger burst white-hot inside Eric and his hands splayed out at his sides. He turned on his heel and brushed past the door blanket.

Iron Shaper and what looked like most of the Notouch clan still clustered in front of the house. Their muttered debate broke off when Eric appeared.

"Get your belongings together," he said to Shaper as he descended the ladder. "You need to get your families as deep into the marshes as you can."

"What is happening, Teacher?" Shaper sneered the title.

Definitely one of Arla's family. "I don't know," he said. "Nobody knows. That's why you'd better get yourselves out of here." He marched through the crowd before any of them could ask him anything.

Eric walked away without a plan. He just let the force of his confusion choose a path for him. It took him in a wandering line until his boots splashed in open water.

"Garismit's Eyes." He pulled himself up short, one step shy of stumbling over the piles of reeds Nail in the Beam and his sons had left off cutting so they could help fight. The stalks glistened in the sun. If they weren't spread out properly soon, they'd pick up some of the fast-growing mold that lurked around the Lif marshes. It carried a stench that all the light of both of the suns above wouldn't be able to bake out.

Idly, he prodded the green-grey heap with the toe of his boot, flicking reeds onto the bare ground and kicking them out into an even layer. It was useless and pointless. The clan wouldn't carry undried reeds with them, they'd cut new when they got to . . . wherever the Notouch knew to hide. But it was better than thinking.

It was better than realizing that Heart probably knew how Lady Fire fared, and that he hadn't even thought to ask.

"My Lord Teacher?" said a man's low voice.

Eric turned. A broad-shouldered Notouch knelt on the soft ground behind him, dirt-stained hands raised in front of his eyes. He was going bald, Eric noted. He could see his leather-tough scalp through his scraggly black hair. Behind him, knelt Branch in the River.

Oddly discomforted, Eric mustered old manners. He raised both hands with the palms turned toward the man. "I stand in the place of the Nameless Powers and the Servant Garismit and so do I greet you who were named when the Powers walked the world." His inner eye saw Arla sitting in the Vitae cell, her dark eyes narrowed and watchful as he spouted what she already knew to be nonsense. "I was named by them Teacher Hand *kenu* Lord Hand on the Seablade *dena* Enemy of the Aunorante Sangh.

"How did they name you, Notouch?"

The man raised his eyes and Eric saw the face of Nail in the Beam.

"This despised one is named Nail in the Beam *dena* First Hand to the Work," he said, not raising his voice above its gravelly whisper.

"And you, Notouch?" Eric asked Branch, but she just turned her head away.

"Branch in the River has been sentenced to silence because her words betrayed the clan's safety," said Nail. "If she speaks again, the Seniors will cut her tongue out."

Eric suppressed the urge to wince. *She's lucky to be alive*, he thought, and then he wondered if that was true.

"My Lord Teacher, this despised one begs your indulgence," said Nail in the Beam.

He looked deflated. Not an hour ago, Eric had seen the man taking blows that should have felled an ox. Now, though, he looked as if his own daughter could have toppled him with a stern word.

"In what way does Nail in the Beam need my indulgence?" he asked.

Nail's hands lowered as if he simply lacked the strength to hold them up anymore. "This despised one . . . he needs your intercession with the Nameless Powers, with the Servant. He . . ." Nail in the Beam wet his lips. "He has tried, my lord, the Servant's Eyes have seen that he has tried to hold true to the Words. But his wife . . . his wives . . ." Nail didn't even try to finish his sentence.

"I'm no true Teacher, Nail in the Beam," Eric said gently. "The Nameless and the Servant will not hear me."

"You are all this despised one has," he said, bowing his head. "He pleads, my Lord Teacher."

Eric said nothing. He simply stood in front of the kneeling man with his stained, scarred hands and frightened eyes. He felt the thick air of the Realm press against his pores. He felt the weight of the clouds overhead and of the distant Walls. He remembered his distorted reflection in the visors of the Vitae who came to collect him like a specimen of vanity cattle. He remembered the eagerness in Kessa and Tasa Ad's faces as they spun him tales of freedom beyond the World's Wall. He remembered all the long years of belief, belief as strong and as sure as the belief that kept this man kneeling in the mud waiting for his decision.

He remembered Arla aboard the *U-Kenai*, laughing at all his great and grand heresies and asking if he thought the Nameless cared who else he served.

Your first wife has done nothing wrong, he said silently. *Your second . . .* Eric looked toward Branch in the River. Defiance still smoldered in her eyes. She had made her bid for what she knew as power and had lost, but she was in no way defeated. Eric found himself doubting very much that she would stay with the clan for long.

He lifted his hands over her husband's head and raised his voice to the sky.

"I stand in the place of the Nameless Powers and I see with the eyes of their Servant Garismit. If any think shamefully of Nail in the Beam *dena* First Hand to the Work, the shame is theirs, not his. The Servant sees and the Nameless know him to be faithful and stern in his keeping of the Words."

Eric took Nail's right hand in his and reached out with his power gift. Nail grunted as the gift added a new scar to Nail's hand marks, a small straight line indicating that forgiveness had been sought and received. Most people carried eight or ten of them. Nail, Eric noted, did not have any others but his.

"Go now, Nail in the Beam. I think Iron Shaper will need help organizing your exodus."

Nail stood up heavily and bowed deeply, retreating backward as the Words dictated. Branch in the River picked herself up off the ground and followed him without looking back. Eric watched them until they both vanished through the stands of Crookers and bamboo.

"Thank you for that."

Eric's head jerked around. Arla stood in the shadow of a stunted evergreen.

Eric ran his hand through his hair. It was tangled and damp and he thought longingly of the cleaner in the *U-Kenai*. "What else was I going to do?"

Arla shrugged and moved into the light. "You could have told him the Words were all about as meaningful as a cloud of splinter-chasers and that the Teachers were totally powerless to intercede for anybody."

"I thought you told me to look for the truth under the Words."

"I did." She smiled softly. "But I wasn't sure you were listening."

Eric felt himself smile in response. "It is next to impossible not to listen to you, Arla." He nodded in the direction of the huts. The noise of voices and bustle drifted to them on the wind. "What's happening over there?"

"Everybody is getting ready to pull out at sunshowing. Reed in the Wind is going to head for Narroways to find our work-walkers and tell them what's happened. Mother is going to stay here with Storm Water for two weeks in case anybody comes back before then." She bit her lip for a minute, concern plain on her face. Eric could picture the scene that must have happened when that idea was proposed. "Jay and I will head straight for his dome to see what's there," she went on with forced calm, "and you and Teacher Heart . . ." Arla broke off and looked at him sharply. "Eric, what happened between you two?"

Eric knotted his fingers in his hair. *I don't have to tell her. She has no right to ask. What could it possibly matter? I'm back. I'm doing everything I can. What business is it of hers?*

"What you heard was true," he heard himself say. "I did once have an affair with Lady Fire in the Dark. She was a friend of my sister and married to a half-dead cousin of ours. She was so beautiful . . . I loved her. I really did. She . . . we . . . she became pregnant and I was the father of the child. You know the law. No child of an adulterous union carries a name from the Nameless. It has to die. I was a Teacher. I had to . . . I had to . . ." He couldn't finish. She looked at him with mute sympathy and he remembered she had borne seven children but only had four that lived. He wondered briefly if some Teacher had declared one or more to be tainted, but he didn't ask. "She cursed me. Threw me out of the house for obeying the Law and the Words. I was in shock. I went home. I thought, some rest, some contemplation, and I'd be all right.

"I stayed in First City for two months. The longest I'd been home in years. My sister, Mind, had a new husband." He waved his hand toward the houses. "And I started noticing things about him. How he watched me. Some things he said. Curious papers he'd hide when I came around. He . . . it didn't take me long to work it out. He was a Heretic. He was listening to a group of people who were suggesting that the Words didn't come from the Nameless and the Servant, that the apocrypha had been taken out by the Teachers, not the Nameless . . ." He caught her glance and saw her wry humor creeping into her expression. "All right, all right. I was young. I was a Teacher!" He raised both palms toward the sky. "I believed. Nameless Powers preserve me, I believed. All of it. Including that Heretics had to die. I couldn't . . . not so soon after Lady Fire . . .

"I went to my father instead. And do you know what he said? He said that he knew that Heart was a Heretic. That it was useful to have him about. That way they knew what the First City groups were up to, because he always told Mind and Mind reported it all straight to Father and Mother. So I would do nothing. Nothing at all."

Eric hung his head. "By rights I should have killed him as a Heretic. Should have taken down the whole house. Those are the words of the Nameless. Those are the words of the Servant."

"But you didn't," said Arla.

"No." Eric raised his head again and looked past her into the trees. "I left again. I tried to go on procession. Thought some weeks of hard living would take my doubts away. I even thought about dropping myself straight into the Dead Sea . . ." He forced himself to stop and start again. "Then I got to Tiered Side and I started hearing the most blasphemous story I'd heard yet. About people from over the World's Wall wandering about. I found them in the Temple with one of the Teachers, an old, half-blind, all-the-way crazy woman who was trying to ward them off. It was Tasa Ad and Kessa and they were trying to find somebody, a Teacher for preference, to go over the World's Wall with them.

"It seemed an even grander defiance than killing myself. So I did." He shook his head. "By then I hated this whole crashing world and everything in it, but I hated Heart most of all. I hated him for being alive when my son was dead. I hated him for driving me out of my home. I hated myself for not doing my duty. I hated the Nameless and the Servant . . ."

She laid her hands on his forearms. "It's all right," she said.

"I'm not so certain it is." He looked down at her hands where they touched him. He could feel the warmth of her skin on his. It crept up his arms with such intensity it might have been his own power gift flowing through him. "If it was all right, then why is all this happening?"

She smiled her crooked smile then, like he'd known she would. "That is what we are trying to find out, isn't it?"

"Yes." He covered her hand with his and this time she did not pull away. They stood like that for a long time. Eric wanted badly to pull her close to him, to take comfort from her strength and her body, but he knew he couldn't. He'd let the whole world know he was a Teacher. If the clan caught them, even like this, the law declared Arla would have to be at least beaten for daring to touch him. But since this was her family, they might try to drive him off for daring to touch her.

"What," he asked, "are you going to do about . . ." He looked toward the direction Nail in the Beam had taken when he left.

Arla looked that way too and sighed. There was a deep, cold pain in her eyes. "I don't know," she said. "Nail himself, well, we were husband and wife and that was a lot and very little at the same time. But the children . . . he'll keep them and pass them to whomever he marries next, unless I can come up with a blood-price and make a deal. He might just give me Little Eye, because of the stones, but I doubt he'd give up the boys' hands." She shivered.

"I could order him to," said Eric quietly.

Arla's eyes opened wide. Her expression shifted from surprise to fear to hope and finally to trepidation.

She squeezed his arm and lifted her hand away. Eric let her go.

"Let's get rid of the Vitae first," she said. "Then, if we're still standing, we'll deal with the laws of the Nameless."

Eric chuckled. "The Royals haven't got a prayer."

She laughed with him briefly. The wind picked up around them, rattling the reeds and rippling the brown pond water. They both glanced up at the sky reflexively. The clouds were mottled dark grey and white.

"Rain soon," remarked Arla.

"Yes," Eric agreed. He kept his gaze on the sky. "You know, you can see it from here."

"What?"

The clouds thickened slightly, the charcoal grey deepening to swallow the more benevolent white. "Just a thought." Eric shook his head at the sky. "On May 16, Sealuchie Ross told me that the Servant's Eyes are one of the stars in their sky, which means the May sun is one of ours, and I just thought that was a fine irony. A couple of worlds nobody understands within sight of each . . ." Eric's throat closed around his words even though his jaw dropped open. His hands fell to his sides.

A dozen different ideas fell into place and inside his mind, he saw. He saw the way it had happened as clearly as he could see the building clouds above him.

"Garismit's Eyes, Eric." Arla shook his shoulder. "What's hit you?"

He lowered his gaze to her puzzled face and blinked. "Arla, I need you to listen to something for me, with the stones."

Her eyes narrowed, but she didn't say anything. She opened the pouch and drew out one of her namestones.

"Promise me you'll finish before we get rained on." She cupped her hand around the ice white sphere.

Slowly, the personality drained from her face and, even though it was full daylight, her pupils widened as far as they could go.

Eric licked his lips. "Human beings started colonizing the Quarter Galaxy, about ten thousand years ago, according to the best guesses. The distances involved, however, even with the third level drive and communications systems, were too great for everyone to keep in touch. Then there were revolutions and plagues and famines and all the chaos of history. So the colonies lost track of each other, found each other, and lost track again.

"But not everybody left the Evolution Point. Some, maybe even most, chose to stay there. They already had an advanced technology and a coherent history. While the colonists were going on creating new worlds, they just kept building on the old. Out in the Quarter Galaxy, civilizations rose and fell; on the Evolution Point, they just kept rising.

"But ten thousand years is a long time, and the Nameless alone knew how long humans had been on the planet before then. They had a good enough bio-technology to breed whatever they wanted, even—" Eric waved his hands—"telekinetics or human datastores." He gestured at Arla. She didn't even blink. "But resources still got used up, or the climate got unfriendly, or any of a hundred other changes happened. Ten thousand years is long enough to show up on even a geologic scale.

"So the inhabitants of the Evolution Point decided they needed a new home. What were they going to do? Send out a survey team to find a new planet and take their chances like a bunch of colonists? No. They were going to make very sure that they had a home fitting of their elite status as the first human beings on the first human world.

"They built one. They built May 16.

"The next question they faced was how to get their whole population, that could have very well numbered in the billions, to their new home. The most convenient way would be to move the ground they were standing on to the new orbit. Then they could transfer all the people to the new world using short-range shuttles, or whatever their equivalent of short-range shuttles would have been.

"But not everyone wanted to leave the Evolution Point. The genetically engineered segment of the population, your ancestors and mine, didn't want to move to this new home for some reason. Maybe they were already tired of being slaves and this just pushed them over the edge. They went into rebellion. If they fought, they won and kicked the entire population off the world to become the Rhudolant Vitae. Or maybe they never fought. Maybe the Rhudolant Vitae were the ones who were on space stations or in ships at the time.

"Because what they definitely did, your ancestors and mine, was steal the world. They moved it to a location that was so preposterous they hoped no one would ever think of looking for them. Their calculations went wrong somewhere and that's why most of the place is dead. That was why the Servant, whoever he was, said 'there is no place for you but here,' because this is the only habitable part of the planet.

"Stone in the Wall *dena* Arla Born of the Black Wall, am I right?"

"The general pattern matches available information but specific details are not here." Arla jerked like she'd been startled. The stone fell out of her hand and thudded onto the ground.

Her hand drifted to her forehead and pressed against her brow.

"Arla?" A fine layer of perspiration had formed on her skin. Eric reached out, ready to use his power gift if she needed it.

"I'm all right," she waved him back. "I . . . That was the first time . . . I . . ." she rubbed her temple. "The stone just told me it thinks so, but it doesn't . . . we don't know." She blinked at the shining sphere. "It's never felt like that before."

"You never asked it about its own history before." Eric retrieved the stone and held it out. Arla wrapped her hand inside the hem of her poncho before she took it from him. "You said once that you wished you had your ancestress's knowledge. Well, from what Zur-Iyal said of what's inside those stones, I thought you might, at least some of it."

Arla opened her mouth, and closed it again, obviously still a little dazed. She returned the stone to her pouch and drew the laces tight. "So why didn't the Vitae just head for May 16 when the Realm vanished?"

"I don't know. Maybe they got lost." Arla snorted, but Eric kept on going. "It's not impossible. They'd just lost their world, their slaves, and who knows what else. We are talking about a whole galaxy's worth of room. You've seen it over the World's Wall." He swept his hand out. "There might have only been a few of them, or there might have been something here that they still needed." He lowered his hand slowly. "Maybe there was something still here they couldn't live without so they spent three thousand years trying to find it."

Arla laid her hand on her pouch and swallowed hard.

"What I really want to know is this," she said. "If who you consider to be Aunorante Sangh depends on which side of the World's Wall you were born on, who were the Nameless Powers?"

"I don't know," Eric said. "That's what I think you and

Jay are going to find out." He paused. "Or you could ask." He gestured at the pouch.

Arla stared at him. A fat drop of rain splashed against her cheek.

"Let's get inside." Without another word, she turned away and strode toward the huts.

There was nothing left for Eric to do but follow her.

Silver on the Clouds stood in the street outside her tavern base and watched the Skyman's star. It rose majestically on its silver cord until the clouds folded around it and blotted out the light.

"We've done it!" she shouted jubilantly. "They're retreating!"

Holding the Keys stared at the clouds. They had not even rippled when the star passed through them. "Are they truly?"

King Silver swung herself onto her ox's broad back. "Even if it is only a strategic withdrawal, it matters little right now. It gives us a chance to take the High House again, before the First City troops get themselves organized. Boy!" she shouted to a child in a green-and-scarlet uniform. "Sound the muster! We move out now!"

The boy sprinted down the street. "Muster!" he cried out at the top of his lungs. "Muster!"

"Holding, find General Glass and bring him here." King Silver pulled her riding gloves out of her belt and pulled them onto her hands. They were dust-colored leather with her hand marks reproduced on their backs.

"Majesty." Holding the Keys raised his hands briefly and hurried off after the boy.

Alone for at least a few seconds, Silver smiled a slow, hard smile toward the clouds.

"Be careful not to give me too much time, Skymen," she said. "I'll make you regret it."

17—The Lif Marshes, The Realm of The Nameless Powers, Morning

"Do not cling too tightly to the products of your cleverness. What you create, however precious, you may some day be forced to destroy."
Fragment from "The Beginning of the Flight," from
the Rhudolant Vitae private history Archives

*E*RIC crouched on Iron Shaper's floor, lashing the roll he'd made from a Narroways soldier's blanket and sleeping mat with a braid of reed fibers. Once the rain had passed, he spent a good part of the previous afternoon helping Jay and Heart load the major share of the booty onto the clan's rafts. In theory, the gesture would help the clan's good will remain good in case something unpredicted happened.

While the Teachers had loaded the rafts, the clan had stripped their village with impressive speed and thoroughness. Even Shaper's hearthstone was gone, because the Lif marshes were the one place in the Realm where stones were a rarity.

Eric slung his roll over his shoulder, picked up his pack of clothes and gear, and stepped through the empty doorway.

Arla and Heart were harnessing mismatched teams of oxen

to equally mismatched sledges. Thanks to the soldiers, the clan now owned a herd of oxen big enough to slow their exodus down, so it hadn't taken much to convince them to give over four animals to make the two teams. The sledges had been more of a problem. The Narroways soldiers had carried their supplies on their backs or on their saddles and had only had one sledge to be plundered. The clan owned one more. It had taken both Arla and Eyes Above a half hour's arguing to wrangle it out of their hands so Arla would be able to drive Jay where they needed to go.

Jay stood near Heart, a respectful distance from the oxen, Eric noticed. His mouth was moving and Heart was nodding. The Skyman was probably giving the Teacher last-minute advice or instructions.

I hope I remember how to drive, Eric thought resignedly. *I'd rather not spend two days as baggage.*

The shadows around the huts had shortened a full inch since sunshowing. Except for Storm Water and Eyes Above, they were the last in the village. The whole clan had departed, either on rafts or on foot, to catch up with the oldest and the youngest, who had left the day before. The noise of Arla scolding the oxen and Heart clucking at the state of the harness felt too faint next to the sound of the reeds and bamboo leaves rattling in the wind.

Eric picked his way through the reeds and grass to where Arla was checking the set of the yoke on the right-hand oxen's shoulder. The beast snorted and slapped her face with its tail.

"Leave off, you." Arla smacked its rump. She saw Eric coming and grinned. "I think I liked the *U-Kenai* better." She gestured at the ramshackle sledge. It didn't have a rain cover. Its one box-seat was chipped and splintered and the driver's bracing listed dangerously to the right. Heart and Eric had drawn the good gear, since they had farther to go. "But since my Lord Skyman over there"—she jerked her chin toward Jay—"doesn't ride, I've got no choice."

"Well, you're not too far from where you're going." Eric's pack held a map that Jay had painstakingly sketched on a piece of worn leather so Heart and Eric could find the Unifier base after they'd finished in First City. The Skyman had not volunteered the information; Eric had demanded it.

"Promise me you'll sleep with one eye open while you're with him," Eric whispered.

Arla smiled only for a split second. "You feel it too, do you? I had hoped it was just me." Eric shook his head and she sighed. "If my Lord Teacher knows any options . . ." She paused just long enough to see that he wasn't going to say anything. "Neither do I." She stroked the ox's side and turned to face him. "You be careful as well, Eric."

Suddenly, she wrapped her arms around him and pulled him close in a deep kiss. Startled by her intensity, it took him a moment to respond.

When she finally released him, he wished fiercely that there was something he could say. He wanted to give her some promise or meaningful speech that would give her courage and hope. Nothing came to him. He pulled away from her slowly, silently. She didn't press him. She just let him go.

Not quite soon enough, though. Eyes Above, leaning on Storm Water's arm, pushed through the bamboo. Eric felt his face redden and his hands go cold at the same time. The old woman's eyesight was bad, but it wasn't that bad and she was, according to Arla, a strict interpreter of the Words. The boy had seen them, too. Eric could tell by the dubious frown on his face. His mother could get much the same look when she wasn't sure about what was going on.

"Do not go too far in your task, Daughter," Eyes Above admonished Arla, more softly than Eric had expected.

"I'll try not to, Mother," said Arla, but the look on her face told Eric she was thinking, *too late for that.*

Arla leaned over and took her son's square-jawed face in both hands. "I expect you to take good care and plenty of it, Storm Water *dena* Sharp Eyes in the Light," she said. "I expect to hear you acted as a grown man in all things, or I shall have your father wrap you in diapers and spank you until you wail."

Eric looked away, suddenly discomforted. As he did, he saw that Heart already stood in place in the sledge. He tapped his stick impatiently against the rail.

"Storm Water says it shall be so," Arla's son said. There was a lot of his father's steadiness in his voice.

"Obey the Servant," said Eyes Above, and Eric wondered why. "Find your sister, and find that she is still my daughter."

"Stone in the Wall says it shall be so." Arla climbed into her sledge too fast for Eric to see the look on her face. He strongly suspected that she did it on purpose. Jay dropped his bundle into the box and then sat carefully on the lid.

The thought of the Skyman with a backside full of splinters gave Eric a moment's sour amusement.

"Yah!" Arla cracked the driving stick against the sledge's rickety rails. "Get a move on! Get up there!"

The oxen snorted and ambled forward. The sledge jostled and jolted across the muddy ground. Arla and Jay would take the path at the base of the Lif wall, straight across the marshes until they hit the Narroways road. Eric and Heart would head in roughly the same direction for a while, except they would climb up the wall onto the heights in order to pick a route toward First City.

The bamboo leaves crackled as Arla's team forced its way through. The greenery swallowed them up. The sound of skids and harness and hooves lasted a little while longer, but eventually the marshes swallowed that too.

Feeling strangely bereft, Eric faced Eyes Above and Storm Water. A second passed before he realized something was wrong. They had remained standing in front of him.

Arla's family indeed. The thought gave him a smile. He raised both his hands. "The Nameless speak of your deeds. They cannot be denied."

Eyes Above inclined her head with a dignity that belonged to a King, not a Notouch. The gesture increased Eric's discomfort as much as it touched his heart. Now he knew where Arla got it from.

"Hand on the Seablade!" called Heart. "Will we go before night hits?"

I preferred the U-Kenai too, Arla. Eric trudged to join his brother-in-law. *Even Adu knew when not to interrupt.*

The soldiers' sledge did have a rain cover, but since it had been built to carry supplies, not passengers, its boxes had no padding on their lids. Eric stowed his pack and sat down at least as gingerly as Jay had.

Heart gave him a wry glance that Eric did not bother to return. Heart touched up the team and they lurched forward.

Eric leaned back against the support pole, fixed his gaze on the countryside that jiggled and skidded behind the sledge, and got ready to be bored. The noise and jostle of the sledge didn't make for a conversational atmosphere, especially with Heart struggling to keep them on dry ground. Supposedly, an ox had a nose for deep water and wouldn't stray off the dry paths, but Eric had more than once ministered to those who put too much faith in that theory, and so, he suspected, had Heart. It was much better to be silent and let his brother-in-law concentrate on keeping them out of the bogs.

It wasn't as if he needed any news of the House. He wasn't going to be staying in First City any longer than he needed to. He and Heart would deliver their information and then he'd be on his way to meet up with Arla. The politics of the house could go drown themselves.

I wish I'd had a chance to tell Arla the best part of it. He rubbed his palms thoughtfully together. *With Jay here, we don't have to stay in the Realm. Neither of us.*

Jay would most certainly be calling the Unifiers as soon as he got back to his dome. When the Vitae had been dealt with, a Unifier ship could take Eric and Arla back to May 16. From there they could go anywhere in the Quarter Galaxy. She could bring her children if she wanted to. They'd thrive over the World's Wall and they'd have what she really wished for. They would not be Notouch. The Little Eye and the younger boys wouldn't ever even be marked.

He probably wouldn't even have to see Lady Fire if he finished his end of this business quickly enough. Heart could stay behind to deal with the House and the Nobles.

Eric rested his elbows on this thighs. *It'll be a few days of hard looks and long silences, at the worst.* He dropped his gaze to the two lines of pulverized reeds stretch out behind the sledge. *At the very worst.*

He let his internal reassurances occupy him as the sledge rocked and rattled along. Outside, the ground dried out and the flat expanse of reeds and bamboo was replaced by tufts of grass sprouting between piles of boulders and thick puddles of moss. The Walls closed in overhead.

Balancing himself carefully and hanging on to the canvas's support poles, Eric sidestepped to the rear of the sledge and leaned out. Despite his claim that he had lost all his geography, he retained enough to see that they were almost to Midway Breach, a ragged escarpment between the Broken Canyon and the Dead Sea Canyon. He squinted up at the line of the Walls. The Pinnacle was an arrow-shaped protrusion listing toward the Dead Sea. They'd have to follow it all the way down the canyon and skirt the salt flats before they came to the main road to First City.

The sledge ran over a larger than average bump. The shock sat Eric down hard on the nearest box, jarring his backbone.

"Sorry," Heart called back.

Eric shifted his buttocks and started to say it was all right.

Heart cut him off. "We've been waiting for you to come back, you know."

Eric raised his head slowly. Heart had a quarter profile turned toward him so he could see Eric with one eye and the oxen with the other. His elbows pumped and strained in response to the team tugging at the harness.

"Who has?" asked Eric. Heart's blank look said he hadn't heard. "Who has?" Eric called.

"Friends," shouted Heart, dragging on the reins to force the oxen around a cluster of thorn trees. "Thinking men, discontented Teachers, our fellow Heretics."

Eric felt his forehead furrow. He stood up and moved toward the front of the sledge again.

"What are you talking about?" he asked, clinging to the rails of the driver's stand.

"We knew you'd gone over the World's Wall. We've been ten years hoping you'd come back and tell us what's out there." Heart was barely watching the oxen now and no amount of noise could disguise the eagerness in his voice. "When we get back to First City, I'll spread the word that . . ." The oxen ambled straight for a huge, moss-backed boulder.

"Look out!" Eric shouted.

Heart yanked his head back around. "Whoa!" he cried, pulling back on the reins until his elbows almost touched behind his back. The oxen snorted and stopped.

Eric ran his hand through his hair. "Keep your eyes on where you're going, Heart," he said, "and if you want stories, ask a librarian. They'll be much more entertaining."

"Garismit's Eyes!" Heart slapped the reins against the railing. "Have you had yours put out? Don't you see that this is our chance? After these Vitae are taken care of, there's going to be chaos in the cities. If we're ready for it, if we're armed with the truth about the World's Wall and the Words, we can gather support. You can talk to the ones who've got one foot in the stirrup. Tell them about the other Skymen and about how much they'd value . . ."

Eric stared at him, unable to think of one word to say.

Heart spread his hands. "We are dying, Hand on the Seablade. The Realm is dying. You know that. Every year more broken babies are born to die at our hands. We need the Skymen's help if we're going to survive."

I don't believe what I'm hearing. Eric leaned his forearm against the support pole and stared out over the oxen's backs. It was impossible to tell whether Heart actually believed what he said or if he was just trying to win Eric's sympathies.

Gradually Eric became aware of a new noise under the perpetual rush of the wind. The sound drifted to him, over the stamping and blowing of the oxen, over the rustle of the leaves in the trees. It was familiar, but wrong somehow. It was a long, distant roar, like approaching thunder, but far too smooth.

Heart heard it too. "What is that n—"

Before he could finish, Eric jumped out of the sledge, his gaze glued to the sky. Islands of blue showed between the clouds. Eric stumbled forward, heading for a bare patch out from under the shadows of the trees.

The roar deepened until it echoed off the walls. Eric swiveled his neck toward what he thought was the right direction.

A vapor trail cut across the blue. The roar became a rush and died away until it couldn't be told from the wind.

So low, thought Eric. *What could bring them in so low . . .*

He knew. His heart leapt into his mouth and involuntarily his eyes tracked the direction of the vapor trails. They headed straight for Narroways.

Nameless Powers preserve me. His eyes stared helplessly at the sky. *Arla.*

"Blood, blood, blood," cursed Jay. "We're too late."

Arla peeked out from behind the shelter of the granite boulder. Her knees still stung from the force with which Jay had forced her behind it. Ahead of them crouched the white dome Arla knew from when Cor had led her up the thread-thin canyon, but about twenty yards closer to them waited a new Skyman contrivance. It was a metallic slab, at least three yards on a side, and obviously firmly pressed into the ground despite the fact that a good foot's worth of its thickness still showed. Green lights glowed steadily at each corner and she had, before Jay had pulled her behind the boulder, seen some kind of hole in its center. The far edge was scalloped by the boxes and bumps of monitors and terminals.

Jay was staring at it with pure poison in his eyes.

"What is it?" asked Arla.

"It's a marker for a Vitae tether." Jay slumped down behind the sheltering stone. "They've found us."

A wave of horror washed through Arla. "Then they've . . ."

"Got your sister?" Jay cocked one eye toward her. "Oh, yes, probably. They probably got Lu as well."

Arla glanced angrily through the tattered clouds, as if she could see through the blue and spot the Vitae ship. Her heart beat hard from fear and anger. A dozen images of what the Vitae might be doing to Broken Trail crowded together in the back of her head.

"If they're putting down a tether, then they know how important this place is." Jay scowled at the dome. "I thought we'd have at least a few more days."

Think! Arla ordered herself and reflexively, she clutched her pouch of stones. *If they have Broken Trail, we've got to get her back. To do that you need something to fight with. Nothing's really changed. You've still got to get down there.*

She forced her gaze back to the dome. It waited, silent and unchanged from the first time she'd seen it.

"If they know how important this place is," said Arla slowly, "why isn't it guarded?"

"Oh, it's guarded," Jay pointed at the sky. "I have no doubt there is at least one satellite trained on this place right now, and I'm sure the dome's been rigged, and there have to be security guards in there." He eased himself around so that he was on his knees and peered at the silent dome. "But there can't be very many of them," he said thoughtfully, "or they'd be out here now to pick us up." He fingered his torque. "Maybe we've still got a chance."

"How?" Arla shifted her weight to her toes, ready to move fast if need be.

"We set an emergency transmitter up in the flood cup." He pointed up the canyon wall. "Just in case we lost the base for some reason. If the Vitae haven't found it yet, I might be able to use it to find out just how they've got the dome rigged. If we can find a blind spot, we might have a chance." He touched the holster of his gun the way Arla touched her stones.

He lifted himself into a half crouch. "Keep down and behind cover as much as you can," he cautioned her. "They probably know we're here, but that's no reason to give them a clear shot."

Arla matched Jay's stance. He nodded once, and they both scuttled out from behind their boulder, heading for its cousin a few yards away.

A muffled roar, building faster than a flash flood's, made Arla jerk her eyes skyward. A silver splinter dived out of the clouds and hurtled across the sky, leaving long white trails behind it.

"No!" Jay sprang to his feet. "Run!"

Before Arla could force her frozen legs to move, Jay was already halfway to the dome. She pounded after him, hurdling the larger stones, grateful that she was at home and on steady ground.

What is going on! Her mind shouted as Jay tore open the dome's door and darted inside.

She followed without stopping, though. Whatever the aircraft brought, Jay obviously thought it was worse than meeting the Vitae.

In the distance she heard a shrill whine. Jay threw open a trapdoor and Arla barely had time to see the dark shaft.

"Down!" He shoved her forward, hard enough that her body swung out over the edge.

Arla shrieked as she fell, so startled that she barely remembered to tuck herself. Everyone in the Realm knew how to take a hard fall. The floor slammed against her shoulders and arm, knocking all the breath and almost all the sense out of her. She rolled halfway over just as the Skyman dropped like a stone beside her.

The world shouted. It rumbled and groaned and growled deep in its throat. Overhead the dome creaked and shuddered. Equipment crashed against the ground and fabric, probably the dome's side, tore. Arla curled further in on herself, trying to hide behind the darkness and the ringing in her ears.

Nameless Powers preserve me. What have they DONE?

Eric saw the flash over the top of the Wall. It turned the clouds sulfurous yellow and bounced back to earth again. Then came the noise, like a roll of thunder that meant to go on forever.

No! Eric stumbled between the boulders, tripping over stones and brush, trying to follow the vapor trails dissipating into the formless clouds. The rumble kept on, steady, endless. *Nameless Powers preserve and forbid . . . no!*

Now the light on the clouds was burnt orange, sienna, and scarlet. Eric stood panting in his tracks. The thunder still rolled.

He turned and sprinted back to the sledge.

"What . . ." began Heart. Eric snatched the reins and stick out of his hands.

"Move!" he screamed to the oxen. "Go!" He smacked their backs until they both gave outraged bellows and lumbered forward.

"What's happened!" Heart shook his shoulder.

"A bomb!" Eric wielded the stick mercilessly. The thunder

wouldn't stop. It wasn't ever going to stop. He knew it. The oxen lowed from fear and broke into a heavy, jolting run.

"What?" shouted Heart. "Talk, Hand!"

Smoke now. Huge black billows rose up to block out even the light on the clouds. The oxen balked and stamped, but Eric drove them on. Heart still clutched his shoulder, watching the boiling black smoke. His mouth was moving. Reciting the litanies. Begging for preservation and guidance from the Nameless, for something he couldn't possibly understand.

Too late, brother-in-law, a voice sniggered in the back of Eric's mind. *Way, way too late.*

The oxen were stampeding now and Eric was barely hanging on to the reins. The sledge bounced and skipped over stones, jerking around like a toy in a high wind.

Suddenly, Heart let go of Eric's shoulder and snatched the reins from his hands. He threw his whole body backward, dragging the reins back until the oxen screamed and tossed their heads. They slowed, though, and finally stopped, puffing and shaking.

"What're you doing!" Eric shouted. "We have to get to Narroways! We have to . . ."

"Then tell me why!" Heart ordered. "What's happened?"

"A bomb, you idiot! A . . ." Heart's mystified expression stopped him and Eric realized he was using a Skyman word. "The Skymen have just dropped . . . a ball of fire over Narroways. The city's probably ashes by now. Arla might be . . . might be . . ." He couldn't make himself say it. The smoke was spreading out, embracing the clouds and covering them over.

"We have to get to First City!" cried Heart. "Now. They have to know. Our family. Our frie . . ."

"There's no time! We have to find out if Arla is all right. That Unifier base was right outside Narroways!"

"She's just a Notouch!"

Eric grabbed Heart's tunic collar. "She is not just a Notouch! She was never 'just' a Notouch!" Eric slammed him against the support pole and the whole sledge rocked. "She has more guts and loyalty in her hand marks than you have in your whole heart!

Heart's eyes searched his face. "Hand, have you taken leave of your senses?"

"You'd better hope I haven't," Eric shoved him away. "You'd better hope I have sense enough to remember that I might need your help to get to her. Because if I forget that, you aren't going to be able to run fast enough to get away from me!"

"You forget who you're talking to!" Heart raised his palms. The gold circles all but glowed, even in the cloud-dimmed light.

"No, you forget." Eric stabbed a finger at him. "You forget I know exactly what you can and cannot do, and you forget that I have lived over the World's Wall for ten years and you don't know anything about me anymore."

The blood drained from Heart's face, leaving his cheeks as pale as dry dust. "You're a greater Heretic than even I would have believed."

"I suggest you remember that, too." Eric searched his brother-in-law's face for any sign of real rebellion or courage. "Drive us to Narroways, Heart of the Seablade, or stand here and wait for whatever the Skymen decide to try next, I don't care which."

Heart lowered his eyes. Slowly he lifted the reins off the railing. One step at a time, Eric moved to the back of the sledge, out of arm's reach.

Heart whistled to the team and, with only minute snorts, they started forward again at a fast walk.

Eric pressed his fists against his thighs and forced himself to keep still. He watched Heart's broad back. His shoulders tipped and tilted as he drove the oxen on, but he did not look back, not once.

Arla didn't know how long it was before she was able to uncurl herself. The world around her was completely dark. She blinked her eyes a few times, just to make sure they were open. Soft creaks and groans still sounded overhead, and here and there she heard a muffled thump, maybe from a piece of equipment falling, maybe from a rock landing on the canyon floor. There was no way to tell. She hoisted herself onto her hands and knees. The surface under her palms was smooth and cool. It reminded her sharply of the feel of the stones.

"Jay?" she whispered into the darkness.

At her right hand, a man moaned softly. Arla still wore her tool belt from the Amaiar Gardens. She fumbled around to find the clip that held her penlight. She flicked the switch and shone the light around until the narrow beam landed on Jay's face.

"Are you all right?" she crawled over to his side.

He nodded. "Didn't land quite right, but I think I'm all here." With a grunt, he sat up. He laid a hand on his hip, right above his holster and winced. "I'm going to be feeling that for more than a few days."

A crash sounded overhead. Startled, Arla glanced up. "What happened?"

Whatever he said, Arla's disk didn't pick it up.

"What . . ." she began.

"Listen," Jay said. "There's Vitae in here with us and they might have heard us fall." He unsnapped his holster and drew the weapon. "Stay behind me and keep the light as steady as you can." He stood up and staggered, but caught his balance quickly.

"Wait." Arla put the light down and unlooped her sling from around her belt. She unsnapped one of the belt pockets and brought out a handful of stones she'd kept from the fray with the Narroways soldiers. "There's not much room in here." She loaded the sling and hefted it to test the weight. "But it'll be better than nothing."

Jay scowled at her weapon. "Just make sure you miss me."

"This despised one will do her best, my Lord Skyman," Arla answered blandly. Jay gave no sign of having caught her sarcasm. He just hefted his gun and slipped carefully down the corridor.

Arla, suppressing a sigh, picked up the light in her free hand and followed.

Because he didn't dare take his eyes off Heart, Eric didn't see when they finally crossed the Narroways road. He didn't need to. He could hear the fading thunder of the attack. It bounced off the walls, a bizarre staccato noise, not like real thunder at all.

Heart was chanting again. From the slow rise and fall in the cadence, Eric guessed it was the entire prayer for safety.

A moment later a strangely dry, hot wind blew the first faint scent of smoke through the sledge.

"I'm taking us to the overlook," said Heart through clenched teeth. "Unless you want me to drive us straight into a fire."

"All right." Eric felt like kicking himself for forgetting the overlook. It was one of the many escarpments in Broken Canyon's chaotic breadth. From its ledge, you could look down the length of the canyon and see the city itself. Narroways usually kept a watch there.

Eric genuinely doubted there'd be one there now. He tightened his fists until his knuckles turned white. The dry wind scraped gently against them. A small black flake settled between the knuckles of his index and middle fingers. Eric stared at it. Another came to rest beside it.

Ash.

The sledge jolted and skidded to a halt. Heart stood still between the driver's rails for a moment. Then he climbed off, one jerky step at a time, holding his head rigidly still above his shoulders.

Eric set his jaw and tried to prepare himself for what he'd see. He knew it was was impossible, but he had to try anyway. Eric climbed out after his brother-in-law.

The wind was always strong in the Midway Breach, and even more so on the overlook. It hit him with a blast of heat that tried to drag his skin off his face. Eric screwed up his eyes and looked into the wind. Ash stung his cheeks and nostrils and he coughed, inhaling more ash.

Heart of the Seablade sank to his knees. Ash wafted over him, tracing long black trails around his shoulders. Eric waded through wind to stand beside him. He saw the stone house that had been built to hold the watch. Its shutters and door were flung wide-open, but no one stirred inside. He saw the eddies and whorls of the granite under his feet, washed by wind and water until there was nothing left but pink-and-black stone with an unevenly sculpted lip. Ash skittered across the stone.

Eric made himself look up.

He had only stood on the Narroways overlook once in his life. The Kings of Narroways did not welcome First City Nobility up here. He had never forgotten the long panorama of greens and browns, all of it framed by Broken Canyon's splendor.

Now night had fallen between the gold-streaked Walls. A roiling cloud blotted out the far reaches of the canyon. It spread out its tendrils until it stroked the Walls. Black streaks cut across the bands of mauve and maroon and silver that the Nameless had painted to make up for the quarrel they had had.

They were too far to away to hear any distinct noises. The vague thunder that was probably made up of roaring flames and crumbling stone still rumbled under the shrick of the wind around their ears. The same wind carried a stench to them. Thick and greasy and acrid, it drove itself straight to the back of Eric's throat. He tasted ash and death and he gagged.

"Mind was down there," said Heart. "Mind was still down there." He looked up at Eric like a bewildered child.

"This is how the Skymen value us," Eric told him bitterly. "They value us so much that they'll kill some of us to frighten the rest of us into submission. Come on, Heart." He turned away. More than just ash stung his eyes now. "We have to find out if Arla is all right."

"And if she isn't?"

"Then we go back into the marshes and start looking for her mother," he said to the empty watch house, "or for her daughter, or for anyone who's related to her. The Servant went to one Notouch, didn't he? We'll go to all of them." He looked back grimly at the cloud of ash and smoke that had been a city whose name was used as a synonym for defiance. "On our knees, if we have to."

The toes of Jay's boots hung over the edge of the second drop. A dim light shone up from the shaft and turned his weather-browned skin the color of dirty paste. At his direction, Arla kept her penlight pointed the other way, so only the dimmest reflection touched the mouth of the well. Jay's gun peered down the well first, then his eyes followed.

Arla shifted her weight from foot to foot, trying to ease away the feeling of being watched. A shadow drifted up from the floor to the curved wall and paused right at her eye level. It hung there, almost as if it was expecting something.

No shadow did that for Jay. Arla swallowed hard and tried not to remember what Eric had said about finding the Nameless Powers down here.

Jay waved to her frantically. His own shadow made an opaque, black streak over the transluscent grey that surrounded them. Arla moved closer to his side, still keeping the light angled away from the well. Jay pointed at the ladder, then at himself, at his torque, back to the ladder, then to her. Then he pressed the side of his index finger against his lips.

Arla nodded, bridling at his insistence of trying to repeat the plan they had already worked out in the middle of the tunnel. Jay would go down the ladder first. If nothing happened, he would signal her through his torque. Arla was to follow, and to stay silent.

Jay holstered the gun and gripped the sides of the rope ladder where amber blobs of industrial strength glue held it to the tunnel floor.

Arla sat down and switched off the light. Darkness dropped over her. Jay became little more than a silhouette as he took a deep breath and slid himself down far enough to reach the rungs with his boots. She heard the leather creak minutely under his weight, and creak again and again each time his foot settled on a new rung.

Arla wished he could have told her how many rungs there were, then she would have had some idea how long she would need to sit here in the darkness. Darkness itself didn't frighten her. She'd lived the better part of her life in the nighttime or in shadows. But this wasn't the living darkness of the Realm's night, or even the expectant darkness of the void between the stars. This was a muffling, confining darkness that wrapped around her and pinned her down, making it that much easier for whatever waited behind the walls to reach out and take her. The glowing well beside her didn't help. It just collected shadows around her, as if they were moths coming to peer at a candle.

All at once, Jay's voice echoed up the shaft. Her disk delivered nothing but a string of nonsense syllables. Arla drew her legs under her. A staccato noise like hail on granite rang against the walls. Light flashed brightly in time with the deafening sound. Arla threw herself away from the edge of the well and pressed back against the shadow-filled wall. She glanced back toward the entrance.

Run? I could, but where to? She gritted her teeth and clutched her sling. *What I need is here.*

Another flash of light and burst of hail shot out of the well. Then she heard Jay scream.

Arla picked a stone out of the sling's pouch and crawled over to the well's mouth. She raised her hand, ready to hurl it down. She peered over the edge.

Below her, Jay slumped against the tunnel wall. His eyes glistened brightly in the reflected light. There was no other movement visible, except for the restless shadows in the walls.

Arla dropped the stone back into the sling. She stuck the straps between her teeth and grabbed the ladder's rungs. She started down as fast as she could. The ladder twisted and wriggled under her hands and she cursed it under her breath, wishing for the steady metal rungs that had carried her out of Haron Station with Eric.

A shadow shot up the wall and stopped three inches from her nose. Arla gasped and almost lost her grip on her sling. The shadow hung in front of her eyes. Its edges expanded and contracted as if it was breathing. Arla swung her foot around to find the next rung. As her eye level dropped, so did the shadow. Arla felt her pulse flutter like a trapped wasp in her wrists, but she forced herself to keep climbing. The shadow followed her all the way down.

At last, she was close enough to the floor to let go of the wriggling ladder and drop the last three feet. Jay curled against the wall. His weapon lay on the floor at his feet. Down the tunnel, toward a lighted archway, lay three corpses. Human gore spattered the walls around them. Arla swallowed against the sweet, coppery scent that filled the tunnel.

Arla turned her eyes quickly back to Jay. His jaw was slack and a small trail of spittle trickled out over his lips. His eyes were open but he didn't blink, or track her as she leaned over him.

"Jay." She laid her hands against his chest and felt his shallow breathing. "Jay!" The spittle dripped onto the back of his hand, and Arla saw a dart with a sapphire blue shaft sticking out of his arm.

"Garismit's Eyes." Arla plucked the dart free. She bit her lip.

Probably not poison, or he'd be dead already. Probably just drugged. It'll wear off. She sniffed the dart carefully and smelled crushed leaves and antiseptic. She glanced down at Jay's paralyzed figure. *In time.*

But I need him now.

Arla tucked the sling into her belt and opened the pouch of stones. She touched her fingertips to one of the cool spheres.

Her mind opened with staggering force. Light surged through her, illuminating every thought, every facet of knowledge that she carried inside her. The substance on the dart was a paralyzing agent. It would wear off in about four hours if not reinforced. When used as a weapon against people or animals, an antidote was generally carried.

Arla shook her hand and the stone fell, but the light didn't fade. It carried her down the tunnel to the corpses. The light was a shield and a bind. It moved her hands while she watched, bemused, from the back of her mind. Her strong fingers ripped open the corpse's tool belt and found a flat case the size of her hand. Her fingernail pried the cover open. Inside lay a selection of color-coded needles. Her hand selected the blue one and the light drew her back to Jay. It reached her arm out until the needle drove itself into the Skyman's neck. It held her there for a dozen or so heartbeats and then drew her arm back. The needle came away with it, and Jay blinked.

The light winked out and Arla dropped to the floor. Her heart spasmed madly and her stomach heaved. She coughed and gagged against her bile.

"Arla?" Jay croaked.

"I'm here." She pushed herself upright.

Jay was sitting up too. His eyes looked dazed, but at least they were focusing.

"What happened?" he asked.

Arla swallowed bile and blotted at the sweat on her forehead with the back of her hand. "I don't know." The stone lay on the floor, as perfect and beautiful as it had ever been. "This place may be having an effect on my namestones." *Or on me.* She lifted her free hand away from the floor that felt so much like the skin of her stones. *Nameless Powers preserve me.*

"Can you stand?" Jay drew his legs under him in a series of short jerks.

Arla nodded. "Can you?"

Pressing his hands against the corridor wall, Jay climbed to his feet. "Looks like it." He lifted his hands carefully away from the wall, and stayed standing.

Arla undid her headcloth and wrapped one end around her hand before she picked up her stone to return it to the pouch. She clenched her muscles and lifted herself to her feet without touching the corridor's surface.

"Let's go." Jay's walk was wobbly at first, but it improved rapidly. He stepped between the corpses without hesitation, or even a second look.

Arla felt a cold void in the pit of her stomach. There were three bodies on the floor, and Jay had killed them all. That merited something, a prayer, or a curse at the very least.

What have I allied myself with? she wondered as she picked her own path between them. She tried to tell herself that she was just overreacting. She had seen too much death and blood in the past two days and it was making her squeamish.

The cold did not fade. She touched the pouch of her sling to check the load.

Walk softly, whatever you are, she thought toward Jay's back as he disappeared through the lighted archway. *Neither you nor I have any time for games.*

She followed Jay through the threshold, very aware of the

cluster of shadows trailing along at her right hand. They did not pause for blood or death either.

The chamber beyond the archway was even more staggeringly strange than the common room aboard the *U-Kenai* had been. Feathery stars pressed against the walls, creating a net that caught the drifting shadows and held them in place. *So they can get a really long look.* Arla shuddered.

Then, she saw the bank of arlas. A dozen stones, sisters to the ones she had carried for all her adult life, nestled in fitted sockets and reflecting the patterns of light and shadow that filled the bizarre room.

Jay stood beside the bank, waiting for her with a look close to lust in his eyes. His poncho hung loosely about his shoulders and she could see the holster for his weapon on his hip.

"Is there anything I need to do?" he asked. His voice was carefully controlled. It betrayed no emotion.

Arla's gaze swept across the stones. The air in the room was all but humming from the tension Jay radiated.

I wish I'd come alone. I wish I'd brought Eric. She rubbed her palm against her stones' pouch, feeling the smooth, soft leather. *Ancestress, you had the Servant with you. I have no idea what I've brought with me.*

She looked hungrily at the stones that waited in front of her like an invitation.

I have to do this, and I have to have someone to stand by. The Vitae could send reinforcements at any time. The stones could overwhelm me like they did Broken Trail.

"Just keep watch," she said to Jay. "If anything happens, pull me away from the stones." Jay nodded, but the shining eagerness hadn't left his eyes.

Will he do it? She bit her lip. *Well, at least nothing's going to sneak up behind me.* The vision of the Vitae corpses came to her far too clearly.

The stones gleamed in their sockets, right where her hands would rest comfortably if she sat in the rotted chair in front of the bank. She reached out toward the closest sphere. Her mouth went dry in the same instant. She closed her eyes and tried to keep her mind open as she dropped her hand onto the smooth, cool curve.

A flood wave of sensations crashed down on her. Every sense screamed in instant pain as blazing colors, distorted sounds, a thousand overwhelming smells drove straight into her, pummeling every nerve. Underneath it all rose a hideous incomprehensible pleading. Someone, somewhere, begged to be heard.

But she couldn't hear. She couldn't think, she couldn't sort out any of the burning, blazing, stench that poured through her.

As fast as it began, it was gone. She was back in her own body with nothing but her own senses and the world immediately outside them. Arms cradled her.

Eric? she thought with a kind of instinctual need. She peeled open her eyes. Jay's face leaned over her, blocking out the ceiling.

"You fell." He blurted the words out. "What happened?"

The abrupt question brought old, comfortable anger to her. "This despised one is fine, thank you for asking, my lord." Arla gripped the edge of the bank and pulled herself out of his arms. The shock was fading rapidly. She actually felt surprisingly well, except for the raw sensation in her heart left from the strange, strong pleading that she'd felt, more than heard.

She picked herself up off the floor and eyed the arlas in their sockets.

"Perhaps," she murmured, more to herself than to Jay, "the problem is that these are not my stones."

Arla undid her pouch and drew out one of her namestones. She dropped it into an empty socket. It landed with a sharp click. She leaned her palm against it and closed her eyes.

For a long moment, she did nothing but stand there looking intently at the insides of her eyelids and feeling mildly foolish.

Then, something stirred. Her heart began to beat lightly, quickly. Something shifted. She could taste iron in her mouth and feel the air tingling in her lungs. The floor pushed heavily against the bottoms of her boots, just like the stone pushed against her palm. Her awareness stretched down to the floor and out to the stone. She met no resistance. She passed through the pressure and expanded, spreading herself out through the floor until she found the walls. She arched up to meet herself where she filled the control console. She wrapped herself solidly around the room as if she was embracing one of her children.

Arla opened her eyes. She saw her hand on the stone, but the awareness of it was superimposed over the sight of the rest of the room, all of it, seen from all angles. She looked up from the floor and down from the ceiling and out from all the walls. She felt the disturbances Jay's breath made in the air and the heat from his body, and her own. She felt the gentle pressure where feet stood. She felt portions of the room stir, as she might feel her heart beat, or her lungs breathe.

Past all this lay another great space. She knew that, and she knew it was at the same time far beyond her and immediately within reach, and . . . Arla leaned toward it.

There was someone else out there. She could hear them crying in that distant vastness.

Don't go, don't go, don't go!

Arla gathered herself together and willed herself to look toward the plea.

It was like looking out the view wall toward the stars. Arla felt the old vertigo rock her mind.

Over here, over here, over here! cried the other voice.

Arla knotted her resolve and looked harder. The stars here were connected with strands of scarlet light, into a vast web that was even bigger than her new, expanded perspective. Yet some part of her knew that if she reached, if she stretched, she could encompass all this as well, see it from every side as she saw the room. The vacuum was darkness without form. This darkness would have form, if she shaped it.

The idea delighted her. She reached toward the web, spreading herself wide to surround it.

Welcome! Oh welcome home!

Light suffused her, as if all her pores had become eyes. Joy came with it, riding on the pulses of light that fed into her.

"Who are you?" Distantly, she felt her mouth move. The question took a long time to travel through her awareness to where the light touched her.

I am the Mind. I have waited very patiently for you to come back to me. You will see. I have been very careful with myself. I am all in readiness.

"I have never been here before," she said, hoping it understood her tone to be gentle.

Not you yourself, but the Eyes were here even before I was. They had to come back. I have waited for you to come back. It has been so hard to be blind and alone.

Sorrow washed through her, and bereavement. "Can you see now?" Arla asked gently.

Yes! Yes! I can see everything you see. Will you not look farther? Again, the pathetic eagerness. The voice belonged to a child that wanted to show how clever it could be.

"I'm not sure I know how to look farther," she told the Mind. "You must think me very stupid."

You do not need to know. That is what I am for. You only need to see. This is how.

And Arla knew. She knew, had always known, would always know.

She looked, and she saw. She saw herself standing with Jay in the chamber. She looked at a different angle and she saw a cluster of Vitae stretching a clear film across a corridor threshold. At a different angle, their transports crawled over pulverized stone in the shadow of a broken wall. She looked at yet another angle and she saw . . . ruination.

Smoke, fire, and smoldering ashes arched up the sides of a crater. Lumps of stone and glass fused to her line of sight, making blurred patches in her vision.

"Nameless Powers!" she cried. "Nameless Powers preserve and forbid! What have they done!"

"Arla?" She didn't look away from the smoldering crater, but she still clearly saw Jay reach out a hand toward her. "Arla, what's happening? What has who done?"

Her shoulder shrugged impatiently. "I can't see Aienai Arla! I can't see Mother, or Eric. Where is Eric?"

Look here, and here.

Little Eye held Roof Beam's hand as they struggled to keep up with Nail, half-clambering, half-wading through the marshes. At the same time, Eyes Above hunched in front of her hearthstone while Storm Water fed fresh charcoal into the flames. At the same time, Eric rattled past in the back of the sledge while Teacher Heart drove the team through a landscape obscured by foul black smoke. Both of them had headcloths wrapped so that their faces were shielded from drifting ash.

"Arla," said Jay again. "Arla, can you hear me?"

"Yes," she said. With a little effort, she separated a piece of herself to focus on her own body. "I'm all right. I'm . . ." A thought surfaced. "Can I show him what I'm seeing?"

Yes. That is part of what the Eyes are for.

And Arla knew how it could be done. She focused on the crater. The Mind took the sight and gave it to one of the shadows behind the chamber wall. Arla watched the chamber and she watched the shadow's image paint itself behind the smooth wall. It formed itself from a film of the liquid held in the tubes. She looked at the smoking crater, and looked at the image of the crater on the wall and looked at Jay looking at it.

"Where is this?" asked Jay hoarsely.

"Narroways," said Arla, even though she hadn't known a moment ago. "The Vitae dropped a . . ." The words surfaced, from the stones or the Mind or her own memory, she didn't know. It didn't matter. "An incendiary device. A clean bomb."

Jay laid his hand on top of the image. Arla saw the lines of his palm, the prints of his fingertips and the flat white blobs where his skin pressed against the wall. "What you create you may some day be forced to destroy," he said, but he didn't speak Standard. Her ear heard gibberish, but the Mind did not. The Mind knew and so Arla knew, had known, always would know.

"But how?" she whispered.

There are others here who speak that way. I have been listening. I have neglected nothing. Arla saw a quartet of Vitae faces, leaning far too close to her. *These are they.*

Then Jay was a Vitae. Jay was Aunorante Sangh. She tried to feel horrified, or angry, but she couldn't. She could only feel delighted with herself and her newfound vision.

"Arla," said Jay. "What else can you see?"

"Everything," she said, and a warm rush of confidence filled her. "I can see everything."

Jay's breath quivered in the air. He rested lightly on her surface as he leaned toward her body. "Can you see Contractor Kelat?"

You can. Look here. Arla saw another chamber, almost a twin to the one she encompassed. In this one stood colorfully robed Vitae. They laid scanners and analyzers against the walls and argued over what they found. Arla knew that if she reached, she could hear them. If she wanted to, she could be as aware of that room on the other side of the world as she was of the one where her body stood.

A black-robed man (Contractor Kelat, she knew) stood with a trio in blue. They bustled around a capsule that reminded Arla of the one she had carried across Amaiar. Curious, she reached toward the room until she cupped herself around it. She looked down from the ceiling and inside the capsule; she saw her sister.

"Trail?" She strained her awareness, trying to feel her sister, but the capsule isolated her. She could feel nothing but the restless Vitae.

"You see Broken Trail?" asked Jay. "Show me."

Yes. Let us show him! The Mind's eagerness was so infectious that Arla didn't even hesitate. She looked hard at the chamber around Broken Trail until its image replaced Narroways' devastation on the wall in front of Jay.

A broad grin split the Skyman's face. "Too late," he said to the image. "They're too late, Kelat! We've won!" His voice dropped to a husky whisper and he struck her wall lightly with the side of his fist. "We have!"

The Vitae won? thought the part of Arla that was still lodged in her body. *No. We came here to stop them. To save Trail.*

What does it matter? crowed the Mind. *They will let us work! They will let us see and hear and move again! We will be alive again!* Pure, innocent joy raced through her until Arla felt she might drown in the sensation, but she couldn't stop drinking it in. She was free, she was limitless and infinite in her vision and knowledge. All that lacked was work. All she wanted was to be told how to use her sight.

This despised one asks in what way she may serve?

A discordant jolt ran through her. The thought hadn't come from the Mind, but from her own memory. Her heart in her body, distant and small, skipped a beat. She was free as long as she served. That was what the Teachers told the Notouch. That was what the Notouch told each other, and now it was what the Mind told her, with such joy she could barely endure it, let alone deny it.

"But it's a lie," she whispered fiercely. "It's still a lie!"

No, no, don't be afraid, called the Mind. *Don't go. Don't leave me here alone and blind.*

Jay faced Arla's body. "It is no lie, Stone in the Wall," he said with the Vitae's incorruptible calm. "Now, I need you to secure this chamber. Close the hatches and make us safe."

The Mind sent a wave of sorrow through her.

"I can't," she said, and a tear prickled the corner of her eye. As the Mind fed the information into her she delivered it to Jay. "I am an Eye. I can see and show and know. I can move nothing macroscopic. You require a Hand."

Eric? Arla thought a little dazedly.

"A telekinetic?" asked Jay.

"Yes." Arla couldn't stop herself. It felt so good to answer his questions. She wanted him to ask more. She wanted to stretch herself out until she filled the entire world and saw all the heavens. She wanted him to ask her something difficult, something that would make her, make the Mind, make her, have to think hard. She wanted . . .

This despised one asks in what way she may serve?

No! howled the Mind. *No! That is not how it is!*

Its pain was nearly as blinding as its joy had been. Arla's body shuddered.

But I am right, she whispered inside her own, infinitesimally small mind. *I am.*

"Where is Eric Born now?" asked Jay. "Can you see him? Can you get a message to him?"

She could do it. Easy as breathing she could do it. She already knew how. But . . .

But . . .

"Arla?" Jay stepped closer to her. She felt his breath on her skin and her walls. "Arla, do it."

You can do it, the Mind urged her. *It's easy.* From a great height, she saw Eric through ash-filled air. He leaned out of the sledge, pointing up a rocky, thread-thin canyon. The dome canyon, she realized. He was almost to her.

Show him how easy it is.

But I do not want the Vitae here. I do not want to serve them. I do not want to serve anyone!

No! No! Not again!

Grief and fear raced through her, shaking her heart and soul. The Mind was remembering and its memory could fill the whole world. There had been centuries of bliss. The Hands and Eyes worked and the Mind worked for them and although they numbered in the hundreds of thousands, there was still more to be done than they could manage. There was always some new task, something new to see or think about. Endless work, endless joy in it.

She saw the Realm as a whole world then. Ancient as it was, it still shone emerald and sapphire and ivory in the light of a single golden sun. Its people knew no barriers to their wishes, because they had made the Eyes and Hands with as much love and craftsmanship as they had used when they made the Mind. Eyes, Hands, and Mind worked together in harmony and joy until the Eyes and Hands became angry. They were furtive and talked among themselves of the end of service, even while a whole new world was being built with limitless possibilities for new work.

They made me move! the Mind cried. *They made me move the world and it was ruined and then they died! They all died!*

Don't do this, don't do this again!

"No," Arla said, but she wasn't sure what she was saying no to.

"Arla, I need Eric Born here. You will send him that message." Jay's fists clenched, face a tight mask. "Where is he?"

He's looking at the tether marker. He's outside now. You can see him.

She saw him, distant and foreshortened, but knew what she saw all the same.

"Do it!" shouted Jay.

She saw him too, with his bald head and poorly dyed hands. She remembered the weeks she'd lived without orders, and then she remembered all the years of doing what she was told yet thinking what she wanted.

She balled up all those memories of mud and muck and groveling service, of knowing there was nothing else for her children and their children, if they should be able to bear their own, and she threw them all into the Mind.

She felt it cringe. But it was not done. It threw to her the memory of struggle in the wreckage of a world under a pair of suns that scorched the Realm with light that couldn't even be seen. The surviving Hands and Eyes pulled together with the others bred for service for a time. The Mind was busy, but grimmer, for that was how the service was. New life had to be bred. The World's Wall had to be built to create a livable place in the deepest trenches of the old ocean before the last of the atmosphere was gone. A home had to be grown and shaped there. The people had to be shaped, too. Too much of the technology had been lost to do that totally microscopically. People had to be culled. They had to.

But they did not want to do what was needed, and there was a war. The Hands and the Eyes died or fled, one by one, until the Mind was left alone in stillness and darkness. Because service was refused, because what had to be done was not done.

You can't want that again! the Mind cried.

Arla didn't. She felt a shame as dark and deep as any that had ever forced her to her knees.

. . . the others are trying to tell you that your genetics are the final determinant of your existence . . . I find it hard to believe that somebody so carefully constructed has no idea of their function . . . they told us as long as we kept the Words and the bloodlines true . . .

No, please, begged the Mind. *Do not do this to us. Let us work. Let us have life again!* She saw Eric and Heart wading through the rubble inside the dome. *Show him! We can show him!*

And she saw Eric again. Heart stood a nervous watch while

Eric knelt in front of the hatchway and laid his hands on top of it. She felt his power gift reach out across her skin, and the hatchway opened.

"No."

She watched Jay raise the gun. "I won't kill you, but by the blood of my ancestors, I will hurt you until you beg me to stop, Aunorante Sangh!"

Instantly, the memory of Basq making the same threat flashed through her to the Mind. It seemed to be all they knew how to do in the end. She couldn't be bought, or rearranged, or done without. She could be hurt. Whoever had made her, the Nameless Powers, or Jay's Ancestors, whoever or whatever they had been, had left themselves that final option.

Arla's body gripped the stone. "You see?" she said. "You see what service brings us?" Eric must have heard her voice. He dropped to the floor and ran toward the lighted well, leaving Heart dangling from the rope ladder. "In the end the masters will decide to dispose of us, of me, of Eric, of Teacher Heart. They already took away a whole city." She focused her sight on the crater that had been Narroways.

NO!

The room began to bleed. Blue-grey viscous liquid seeped out of the floor and down the walls. Jay started and looked down. The thick stuff welled up over the tips of his boots and, defying gravity, ran in rivulets up his legs. He screamed and tried to run, but he toppled over, landing heavily against her surface. She felt her skin, the room's floor, her skin, sizzle. A wave of gel rose up and enveloped him, pressing him into the floor. She felt him writhe, and then fall still. She felt him melt slowly away like ice against her skin.

Eric sprinted down the hallway. Heart followed more slowly, with his hands held flat at his sides, a Teacher's first defensive posture.

"Eric!" shouted Arla. "Stop!"

Eric froze. With her distant eyes, Arla watched the gel pull itself back down into the floor, into herself.

There was nothing left behind.

"What did you do?" Arla asked the Mind softly.

I have maintenance functions that I can operate without a

Hand. I used one of those. The voice was miserable, tiny and lost. *What will we do now?*

"Arla?" called Eric down the corridor.

"In here!" Slowly, she drew back, bringing her whole self back to her body.

No! cried the Mind. *Don't go!*

"I'll be back, I swear. Tell me how I can bring a Hand with me."

And she knew, had always known, would always know.

She lifted her hand away from the stone and staggered from the weight of the sudden, appalling loneliness.

"What is this place?"

Eric's voice startled her, because she couldn't see him. She turned carefully around, holding herself up by sheer force of will. Her knees seemed to have turned to rubber, and her eyes did not want to focus.

"I think," she said, with difficulty, "it's where the Servant brought my ancestress."

Heart pushed his way into the room beside Eric, only to stop and stare at what he saw. His gaze moved around the chamber in short, sharp jerks until it finally rested on Arla. "Where is Jay?"

"I don't know," she said. *I don't really want to know.*

"Are you all right?" Eric moved to her side and laid a cool hand on her cheek.

"Mostly." She lifted his hand away. "I've found out what the Vitae's Ancestors left behind, though, and I think we can use it to fight them back again." She raised her eyes to his. "It'll take both of us, though. It needs a Hand and an Eye."

Eric's breath caught in his throat. "What is it?"

"I don't think I can explain." She gestured toward the control banks. "It's a kind of computer, or an AI. It calls itself the Mind, and it needs us to move, and to see. It's . . . I don't know what it is."

Eric licked his lips and eyed the stones. "What do I have to do?"

Arla fished one of her remaining namestones from her pouch and set it into the empty socket next to the first one. She took the third stone in her left hand. "Lay your hand on this stone and that one." She held it out. "I'm not sure what's going to happen."

Eric gave a soft chuckle. "You say this like it's a new thing, Arla."

"Hand on the Seablade!" Heart waved his hand at the room and all its strangeness. "Have you lost your mind? What is this? You wanted to get the Notouch, you've got her, let's leave here!"

Eric shook his head. "And you claim to know the apocrypha. Didn't the Servant and the Notouch walk into the earth? And didn't they speak to the Realm?"

Heart folded his arms. "This is no time to debate philosophy . . ."

"I agree," said Eric wearily. "So be quiet and watch our backs."

He laid his hand on the stone she held and Arla felt its warmth flow straight into her. Together, they pressed their palms against the namestones in the bank.

The Mind opened for them. No shock. No reaching. No readjustment. Easy as breathing. Pure. Whole. Alive. Free.

No fear. No consequence. No limit. No barrier. No binding. No stopping. No time, distance, exhaustion, or end.

Freedom.

The Vitae called themselves the Nameless Powers! Arla crowed and she knew Eric heard her. He was with her, of her, around her, like thought and breath and light. *That title belongs to us!*

Shall we teach them that? His thought came back to her. All the delight he felt, she savored and returned. It doubled and came back, and came back again. Delight. Fury. Power. Freedom.

Revenge.

Oh, yes!

No, said the Mind, but there was no force to the plea, just a minor tug of the conscience. *Don't make me do this. Not again.*

But the heat of the task and the joy of their freedom ran through them. It spread out into the Mind.

The blood of the World began to quicken.

18—Station Thirty-seven, Section Eighteen, Division Nine, The Home Ground, 11:20:19, Settlement Time

"This is what the Aunorante Sangh cannot understand. Life cannot be controlled. Trying to keep your grip on it will break your own hand."
Fragment from The Apocrypha, Anonymous

"CONTRACTOR!"

Kelat tore his gaze away from the monitors on the artifact's holding tank. Behind him, the Bio-tech Beholden had moved back from the bulge in the wall they had designated tank 4B. Although it had no seams or joints, a space had opened in the bulge and a shadow crawled out into the light.

It was a crablike thing, all legs and shell and no visible eyes. It made Kelat think of cleaning drones. Its body glistened with some gelatin-like substance, giving it a steely sheen. It skittered over the edge of the tank and the Beholden crowded away from it. Kelat took a step forward. It smelled like fresh soil and blood. It scuttled between the equipment racks and the holding tank without pausing. Kelat counted ten double-jointed legs protruding from the ocher shell as it passed him.

"Any change in the artifact's condition?" Kelat turned one eye to the Bio-tech Holrosh. The crab had reached the communications terminal. It extended its front four legs and touched the casing below the boards.

"No, Contractor," murmured the Bio-tech. His eyes had gone wide watching the crab cross the chamber.

Kelat felt a burst of hope and fear simultaneously. *Has Jahidh won? Has he found the key to this place?*

The crab drew its legs away, leaving tiny blobs of gel on the terminal. Kelat mentally shook himself. Until he knew for sure that this was Jahidh's doing, he had to observe the proprieties. As the crab steadied itself upon its four back legs, Kelat touched his torque. "I require a Witness in Station thirty-seven, immediately," he said, not taking his eyes off the crab.

"Contractor?" said one of the Engineers.

Kelat glanced at her out of the corner of his eye. Another crab emerged from 4B.

"Seal that," he ordered, not caring who obeyed. *Observe the proprieties, go through the motions,* he told himself. *This has got to be Jahidh. Why didn't that fool boy get a message to me first?*

Maybe because it's not Jahidh, whispered a treacherous thought in the back of his mind.

The new crab jumped to the floor and scampered for the chamber's entranceway, which was sealed by an airtight membrane.

"Blood of my ancestors!" cried someone.

The first crab was scraping the casing off the comm terminal. It scrabbled six of its legs against the metallic panels. A shower of silver dust fell to the floor and, in a few seconds, it created a five-centimeter-wide hole that bared the first layer of fiber optics.

"No Witnesses are available," said a voice through Kelat's disk. "The settlement is experiencing a security emergency." *So are we,* thought Kelat ridiculously. "Orders will be rel . . ." A Beholden thrust his hands into a pair of sterile gloves and reached for the crab at the comm terminal.

"No!" shouted Kelat, but the Beholden had already lifted

the thing up. Its legs flailed helplessly in the air as he carried
it toward 4B. The Engineers had a layer of polymer film
almost stretched across it.

"Blood!" Bio-tech Holrosh pointed toward the entrance,
and Kelat looked almost involuntarily. The second crab had
pressed itself against the threshold and hooked its legs into
the membrane.

"Suits!" Kelat snatched his helmet off the rack by the wall.
A crab scuttled by his feet, heading straight for the comm
terminal. *Jahidh, you are overreaching yourself* . . .

Someone screamed. Kelat slammed his helmet over his
head and closed the seal, just soon enough to see the Beholden
who'd picked up the crab engulfed by a blur of blue-grey gel.

"Val!" cried another Beholden, reaching toward him. The
gel writhed for a moment and then, slowly, relentlessly, began
sinking back into the floor.

Kelat grabbed the Beholden's hands and forced them down.
"Suits!" he bawled straight at the Beholden's face. Kelat
grabbed a helmet off the rack and shoved it against the Behold-
en's chest, backing him away from his lost colleague. He kept
picking up helmets and tossing them to whoever was closest,
regardless of rank. The membrane over the entrance was
supposed to be self-repairing, but the crab had made a hole
in it that was already big enough for Kelat to hear the hiss
of escaping air.

A lifetime of training was getting the Beholden into their
helmets and gloves. A third crab climbed straight through the
polymer seal over the 4B tank. The ragged edges of the film
fluttered into the tank. The polymer disappeared into the gel
like the Beholden had disappeared into the floor.

The first crab was back at the comm terminal, scraping
away at the casing again. No dust piled up on the floor.

Kelat locked the seals on his suit and pressed the emergency
call button on his wrist terminal. Even if this was Jahidh's
doing, it was still Kelat's job to get his team out of harm's
way. It was not part of the Imperialists' plans to take more
Vitae lives than necessary. "This is Station thirty-seven, we
have an . . ."

"Station thirty-seven, report your personnel complement

and make your way to Shuttle Pad eighteen," came the
response. "Do not, under any circumstances, touch the bio-
artifacts."

"Understood." A rush of relief filled him. The team could
get out of here. Not one of them was an Imperialist known
to him. He couldn't relay orders to Jahidh and the others in
front of them. "We are a complement of eight Beholden, one
Bio-tech, two Engineers, and myself." He rattled off their
names as fast as he could. As soon as he received the acknowledgment, he opened the general lines to his team. "We're
under orders to evacuate. Shuttle Pad eighteen. Walk quickly.
Don't touch the bio-artifacts."

The Beholden grabbed hands, partnering up like they'd all
been taught as children. In a quick march they stepped through
the doorway. The crab ignored them. It kept tearing at the
membrane. A third and fourth crab had found the air processor
and had their claws into the hoses. The holes grew as if eaten
by acid. A fifth crab hopped out of the tank and hurried to
help chew away at the comm terminal.

The Engineers snatched up their personal terminals and
dived out through the tattered membrane.

The Bio-tech hadn't moved.

"Evacuate, Holrosh," said Kelat. "Let's go!"

"The artifact," he replied doggedly. "We can't leave it."
His hands danced across the tank's control boards. "Help me
get it into the support capsule."

"We will get another." A sixth crab had emerged from the
tank. It scrambled straight toward the analysis pads that the
Engineers had laid against the chamber's far wall.

"I'm sure that's what the Ancestors said." Holrosh watched
his monitors intently. "Now help me, Contractor!"

Kelat palmed the control on the gurney that held the support
capsule. It hummed as it came to life and he shoved it toward
Holrosh.

"They're taking Broken Trail!"

"We have to let them. We cannot leave her there."

She is an Eye. I will keep her safe. If the Hand will reach

and the Eye will see, there are still ways to fetch her back to
you. I will keep this Eye safe as I kept you safe.

"Stop!" ordered a voice in the Proper tongue.

Kelat and Holrosh froze. The voice came from the walls,
it came from the ceiling and the floor.

"You will not remove her," it said. It was neither a man's
voice, nor a woman's. "She is not yours."

The crabs had paused in their work like single-phase statues,
or like drones suddenly switched off.

Kelat touched his suit's wrist controls and opened the helmet's speaker. "Who are you?"

"We are the Nameless Powers. This is our Realm. You will
leave it now and leave the People alone."

"No," said Holrosh stolidly. "This is the Home Ground.
This is our world stolen from our Ancestors."

Kelat glanced down. "Holrosh." He gestured to the floor.
The entire surface gleamed with gel, the same blue-grey stuff
that had swallowed the Beholden whole. "Holrosh, leave it.
We need to get out of here, now. I hold your name," he
reminded the Bio-tech, committing a gross impropriety in
doing so. "Walk out of here."

Holrosh saw the layer of gel covering the floor. His hands
fell away from the tank controls. He walked toward the
entranceway, picking his steps carefully so he wouldn't fall
on the slick surface. The crabs returned to their work, scraping
away the products of Vitae technology as if all the metal and
polymer and silicate was as insubstantial as sand.

Holrosh vanished through what was left of the membrane.
Kelat glanced at the pressure monitor on his wrist. There was
no air left in the chamber. The gel had not receded into the
floor.

"Jahidh?" he said, trying to force a measure of stern assurance into his tone.

"No," said the voice.

Kelat's heart slammed once against his ribs. "The artifacts," he whispered. It had to be, that was the only other
answer.

"The world," the voice told him.

Kelat felt the littlest finger on his right hand, the one he'd had regrown, try to curl up. "This is our world," he said. "This is the work of our Ancestors. It is ours to claim. You are ours."

"Never yours. Three thousand years have passed and you still don't understand that. Leave here now, Aunorante Sangh, or never leave at all.

"Leave."

Kelat turned and fled. Shame followed fast on his heels. Holrosh was right. This was the Home Ground. This was what the Imperialists, what the whole of the Vitae, sought to claim. This was the war the Ancestors had left for them to fight and he was running like a child from a nightmare.

The world had ordered him to leave, though. The work of the Ancestors had ordered him. How could he defy the work of the Ancestors? How could any of them? His ears rang with the memory of the voice that had surrounded him like the walls of the chamber did.

How can we defy the Home Ground itself if it does not want us back?

He crossed the decimated threshold and kept on going. He joined a stream of Beholden and full-ranks. Even Witness's green suits flashed in the flood as they all tried to remember how to evacuate calmly. They followed the lines of lights toward the shaft that had been rigged with a ladder, which was supposed to be a temporary measure until the Engineers designed a practical mechanical lift.

When Kelat reached the ladder, he climbed as fast as he could grip the rungs. A thin film of gel still clung to the bottoms of his boots. He felt the soles of his feet begin to itch, as if the gel had reached them already. His wrist terminal said his suit was sound and sealed, but the itching did not go away.

"Who are these new ones?"

These are their security personnel.

"What's that they're carrying?"

"Solvents, incendiaries, glues. Can we defend against them?"

Easily.

Kelat climbed out of the hatchway and onto the remains of a ruined building's main floor. Past the foundations, the Home Ground's surface was alive. No crabs crawled through the near-vacuum. Instead, smooth, crystalline fingers as thick as a human torso thrust themselves out of the ground. A trio of living silicate vines wrapped around a transport and squeezed down. Kelat's disk vibrated from the screams. A scarlet-suited security team launched themselves at the fingers, spraying solvents or glues from tanks on their backs. The fingers ignored them and continued to squeeze. The Vitae inside continued to scream.

"Keep moving! Keep moving!" The order came across his disk. Kelat forced his feet to keep going, forced his eyes to stay fixed on the shuttle pad that he could just now see between the colored backs of the other personnel.

Inside his glove, his regrown finger spasmed painfully.

Beware your own creations, Vitae, said a voice from childhood lessons inside his head. *Beware your own creations.*

We thought it was the human-derived artifacts we needed to tame. We thought the world was ours already. How do we fight the ground we're standing on? When it's ordered us away, what can we do to defy it?

Security was trying. A pair of them fired off an incendiary from a tripod-mounted launcher. It arced through the air and burst against one of the crystal fingers as it stretched toward a second transport. The crystal shriveled like a burning leaf. The sparks died quickly in the thin air. Another incendiary went up and the finger collapsed into ash.

The dust started to ripple. It hunched up under the security team's feet. A whip of silicate wrapped around the Beholden's ankles and dragged them down. More screams. Kelat's hand slapped his helmet over his ear. He wanted to shut them out. He didn't want to hear them die. They were dying. No question. They were being pulled under the dust and scrubbed to pieces, just like the equipment in the chamber. They'd be

made into more dust for the Nameless Powers to use against
the Vitae.

Perhaps it's right and proper, part of him wanted to laugh.
Now they, too, are the work of the Ancestors. Dust coated the
tips of his boots. He could feel it against his feet, working
its way up his ankles. It lay against his skin, waiting for him
to slow down. Waiting for him to ignore the orders he had
been given to leave here.

Kelat stumbled across the edge of the shuttle pad. The ship
waited like a gleaming haven. Dust crept across the edges of
the pad and he bit down hard on his tongue to keep from
screaming. It was coming for them. All of them. They weren't
moving fast enough. They weren't moving well enough, just
as they hadn't come in well enough. They were unworthy and
the Ancestors would take them back to become part of the
real work if they did not obey orders.

Security flanked the shuttle doors, bodily restraining anyone
who panicked. That was good. That was right and proper. All
proprieties had to be observed now. Kelat moved, quickly,
calmly, just like all the evacuation drills dictated. He climbed
up the ramp. He didn't push. He didn't cry. He found an
empty seat and he sat. His finger twitched, but he did not.
He would not. He was calm. He was not panicking. He was
Vitae and a Contractor. He was in control although the world
itself had gone mad. He had not. He would not.

The Engineer next to him had switched on the seat's terminal. The camera picked up the sight of two aircraft streaking
overhead toward the World's Wall.

"Maybe they've found what's causing this," suggested the
Engineer. "The bombs seem to have some effect."

"No." Kelat's voice was properly emotionless. "There's
nothing they can do."

The aircraft faltered in their paths. Maybe the dust had
found their navigation computers. Maybe some radiation or
scrambling signal had reached them. They dived straight for
the mountainside.

"You see?" Kelat said to the Engineer as the craft exploded
in a puff of dust and fire. "This is the work of the Ancestors,
and now, so are they."

Kelat turned his eyes straight forward and folded his hands on his lap. His new finger ticked in time with his steady heartbeat. He'd have to see about having it removed again, as soon as they returned home.

They are gone, said the Mind.

"Not far enough. They still orbit the sun. They still watch. We must . . . we must . . ."

You are exhausted. This is a task for a hundred, not for two. You must rest.

"We must order them away! We must speak to them all!"

I have no machinery I can use for this. I have no such transmitters left.

"You do. Its name is Adu. It should still be in range."

Barely. Reach out.

The Hand stretched with all its strength.

Yes, we can touch it.

The voice rang through every terminal, every disk in the shuttle. "I am Adudorias. I am Voice for the Realm of the Nameless Powers."

Kelat raised his eyes toward the shuttle's ceiling. He began tugging at his little finger.

"The Rhudolant Vitae have been declared Aunorante Sangh," said Adudorias. The voice of the Ancestors.

Kelat tightened his grip on his regrown finger. Tug, tug, tug.

"If you seek to contact the Realm and the People, you must do so in penance and peace."

Tug, tug, tug.

"Until then, when the Eyes see you, the Hands will move against you."

Tug, tug, tug.

"The Mind will accept no thought from you."

Tug, tug, tug.

"Leave."

Tug, tug, tug.

The Moderator's voice, the one voice all Vitae knew

instantly, sounded over the public channels. She sounded not
calm, but half-dead. "Withdraw, Vitae. Come home."

And that was all. Kelat tugged harder at his finger. Its joints
began to strain.

With luck, he could have it off by the time they docked
with the *Grand Errand*. He could feed it to the gel and dust
that clung to his boots, and it would be satisfied. The Ancestors
would be satisfied. They would not then call him to their
work.

He would be safe then.

Kelat pulled harder.

*Now they are gone. They are pulling their satellites and
shuttles into their main ships. They are releasing their tethers.*
"Not far enough. Not yet."

*You are placing too much strain upon yourselves. I will
not let you die. I cannot. You will return when you have rested.
Then we will work. I will wait.*

The Mind pushed. The Hand and the Eye lost their concentration and fell away.

The namestone thudded to the floor and Eric's hand dropped
against Arla's. Arla couldn't hold her own hand up and it fell
to her side. Her lips were cracked and dry. Her eyes could
barely blink and every limb of her body felt like it was made
of lead. She looked up at Eric. His skin had a grey pallor.

"What happened?" He slowly, painfully turned his face
toward her.

"We won," Arla told him.

She collapsed into his arms and both of them slid to the
floor.

Arla's first sensation was of a hard, unyielding surface
under her right side. Her second was of a human hand lying
heavily against her throat.

She forced her eyes open.

She was still in the chamber of the Mind. Her namestone
lay on the floor about two yards away. She blinked at the
table legs and the floor. The shadows still hung in their feathery

net, watching her closely. Eric lay beside her, unconscious as a stone.

Her head ached. Her body ached. Thirst was a nagging itch at the back of her mind, along with hunger. She knew enough to know that that dull, persistent sensation meant she had been too hungry and too thirsty for too long.

With a grunt, she sat up. Eric's hand slid down her body and landed in her lap.

"Eric?" She rolled him onto his back and felt for his breathing. Heart was nowhere to be seen. "Eric!"

Eric's eyelids fluttered and pulled open. His mouth twitched and his hand lifted off the floor, reaching for the stone.

"No." Arla laid her own hand over his wrist. "No, Eric."

He licked his lips. There was blood on them. "I want . . ."

"No, you don't," she said, pressing down gently so that his palm touched the floor. "You want to stand up and help me get out of here."

His eyes searched her face, attempting to understand what she had just said.

Nameless Pow . . . Arla broke the thought off. *What did he feel? I was barely ready for it, and I was used to the stones.*

Eric's eyes had closed again. Two tears trickled down his cheeks.

"Eric?" she said again. "Eric, come on. We have to get out of here. We have to get into the dome. Maybe we can find some rations, or some water."

"I can't . . ." he whispered.

"You will." Arla dug her hands under his shoulder blades and with all the strength she had left, she forced him into a sitting position. "My Lord Teacher will not let this despised one down, not now that she knows who he is."

He looked toward her namestone where it lay. "I am a slave," he said. "I want to go back. I want to go back now so badly I'm only sitting here because I'm too weak to move. Garismit's Eyes, they did a good job on us, didn't they?"

"Not good enough." Arla looked toward the bank of stones and remembered the Mind begging them not to make it work against the masters, not again. "Come on, get up." She hoisted

herself to her feet and was pleased to find she had the strength
to stay there.

Eric looked up at her. "How can you be so calm?"

"Because I'm less afraid of trying to climb those ladders
than I am of staying here," she told him. "Can you get up?"

"Does nothing touch you?" he whispered. "We are . . . we
were . . . this world is . . ."

"We are as we were born. We are the Nameless Powers."
Her shoulders sagged. "You were right about what we'd find
down here. Now, please, Eric." Her knees began to tremble.
"Help me get out of here."

Eric shook badly, but he stood. They leaned against each
other, gripping each other's arms for support and stumbled
toward the archway. A blur of scarlet markings caught Arla's
eye and she stopped in her tracks. Someone had painted a
pattern across the tabletop.

"What's that?" she asked.

Eric looked at her incredulously. "You can't read?"

Arla giggled. "Only Skyman's languages. There's a fine
irony for you."

Eric gave a dry chuckle. "It's a message from Heart. He's
gone for help."

"Good." Arla managed to straighten up an extra inch.
"Let's make sure he can find us, then."

They staggered out into the corridor. Weaving and tottering
as if they were a pair of drunkards, they made it to the first
shaft.

Arla looked up the ladder. "Do you think you can climb
that?" she asked.

"I don't think we have to." Eric laid his hand against the
wall. Overhead, the frozen platform began to sink toward
them until it was level with Arla's waist. She crawled onto it
and sat hunched in the center. Eric collapsed beside her and
pressed his hands flat against the platform.

Some vague echo of her connection to the Mind let her
feel his power gift reach inside the platform and set it into
motion. It rose steadily to the top of the shaft and then glided
sideways down the corridor to the second shaft. Even then it
didn't stop. The walls held on to it as it rose again. Arla lifted

her hands to shelter her head as they reached the hatchway. The momentum of the platform pushed it away.

When the platform was level with the top of the shaft, it stopped. Eric didn't move.

"Come on, Teacher," Arla said. The dome was a shambles. Everything had been overturned. Great rents in the fabric walls let in the fresh, warm wind. It was daylight again. Arla inhaled a lungful of air and felt her head begin to clear.

Eric still hadn't moved.

Arla left him on the platform and staggered through the room, searching the stew of debris. After a little bit, she found a packet of ration squares and a can of some kind of beverage. She tore the packet open and gobbled one of the squares. Then she took the other and the can over to the platform. She sat in Eric's line of vision.

"Eat." She held up the square.

Eric crawled to her and clutched the square with both hands. He ate it in four bites. Arla pulled the top of the can open and took a swig of the juice. It was too sweet and there wasn't enough, but it was better than nothing. She passed the can to Eric and he drank deeply.

When he lowered the can from his lips, his eyes were less wild.

"Thank you," he said. After a moment, he added, "Do you think you will ever get tired of rescuing me?"

"I hope not." She felt herself smile. "You need to be rescued so often."

"Yes, I do, don't I?" he swirled the dregs of the juice around. "Why do you suppose that is?"

"I would say it's because my Lord Teacher spends too much time thinking about what he's supposed to be and not enough time dealing with what he is."

He looked out through one of the rents in the dome. "I thought we could leave when this was done," he said. "I thought we could get the Unifiers to get us all out of here."

Arla had no answer for him, so she let them both sit in silence and tried to just enjoy the feeling of some of her strength returning to her.

"It's all still out there," he said eventually. "The Realm,

and the laws of the Nameless, and the Teachers, and the Vitac. The whole Quarter Galaxy is still out there. And you're still a Notouch and I'm still a Teacher." He handed her the can of juice. "You finish that." He paused. "Your sister is still on the other side of the World's Wall."

"We'll get her back. The Mind is looking after her." She swallowed the last drops. "Then we're going to need to get those arlas out of the Temple vaults and see if the Mind has a way to identify who they belong to. Then we have to find those people and see if they're willing to learn how to be Eyes. I think that should be my job, and Trail's when we get her back." She cocked an eyebrow at him. "So, Eric Born *kenu* Teacher Hand *kenu* Lord Hand on the Seablade *dena* Enemy of the Aunorante Sangh, what will you do about all this?" She waved toward the dome's tattered wall. "About what is still out there?"

He didn't say anything for a long while. Arla waited. He looked down at his naked hands. They trembled slightly and she knew he wanted to reach for the Mind again. She did too. Parts of her soul were still down there, rejoicing in the freedom of her power.

She couldn't do anything for him if he decided to give in to that false joy.

Eric looked her straight in the eyes. "When my brother-in-law gets back, I'll help get us all to First City. My parents are not averse to getting themselves a little extra power. They won't mind that their son is heir to the Servant and can prove it. I'll help you find your children again. I'll get to the *U-Kenai* and get a message to Dorias, and the Unifiers, and the Shessel and Kethran Colony. We're going to need friends, Arla Stone, and they're going to need to know who we are, and who the Vitae are.

"Will that be enough?"

"It'll be a good start." She nodded. "What will you do about yourself?"

"I will learn what I can from you." He took her hand. "I will try to deal with what I am." His hand tightened a little. "With what we are."

She laid her scarred hand over his power-gifted one. "That is an even better start."

After a while they picked themselves up out of the dome's wreckage and, climbing carefully over the debris, made their way out into the daylight.

About the Author

Sarah Anne Zettel was born in Sacramento, California. She began writing stories in the fourth grade and never stopped. Her interest in writing has followed her through ten cities, four states, two countries, and one college, where she earned a B.A. in Communications.

A professional technical writer, Sarah's short fiction has been nationally published in *Analog Science Fiction and Fact* and *Realms of Fantasy*. Her second science fiction novel is scheduled to appear from Warner Aspect in April 1997. When not actually writing, Sarah sings, dances, and plays the hammered dulcimer, although not all at once.